I0748409

The Thrice-Dead Girl

Laer Carroll

Summary: Alice Willoughby is an immortal shapechanger. She has lived more than 400 years as many people, including a German soldier, a conquering African empress, and a Chinese artist and counselor to the immortal empress of China.

Her body completely destroyed in a fire while rescuing people from death, years later she awakes inside her mother and helps her mother have a safe and easy birth. She is born at the beginning of the 1900s in the Hill Country in the center of Texas.

She joins a pair of barnstormers who are helping America awaken to the promise of aviation. How high can she go? She is determined to find out.

Disclaimer

All people, places, and events are fictional or used fictitiously. They exist in an imaginary alternate reality, and any resemblance to actual people and events is purely coincidental.

Credits

Background photograph was taken by L. E. Carroll while visiting the Texas Hill Country.

The red biplane is a photograph taken from the **needpix.com** website, a library of more than 1.5 million public domain photos and illustrations.

The flying cowgirl is art created by L. E. Carroll using Daz Studio, a 3D digital studio. Studio is free. Hair and clothing were purchased from various vendors. All are available through **daz3d.com.**

Dedication

This book is for my grand-daughters,

Natasha

Staci

It is a kind of fairy tale: a superhero story for grownups but it is also for teenagers.

Especially girls.

Especially you.

Books

by Laer Carroll

Elizabeth Bennet: Shapechanger

The Eons-Lost Orphan

The Orphan in Near-Space

Voyages of the Orphan

The Once-Dead Girl

The Twice-Dead Boy

The Thrice-Dead Girl

The Super Olympian: Bloodhound

The Super Olympian: Mystic Warrior

Sea Monster's Revenge

Shapechanger's Birth

Shapechanger's Progress

Shapechanger's Destiny
(forthcoming)

Chapter 1 - Infant

Her first awareness was of being enclosed all around by something warm. Yet she did not need air. That puzzled her as she drifted back into sleep but, as she felt no distress, it did not bother her.

She was next aware of sound. The beating of a heart nearby was one but there were other sounds, though muffled. These included the creaking of a bed as someone got out of it, the splash of water as they washed their face, snatches of conversation. There were other sounds that she puzzled over until she grew tired and slid into sleep again.

She slept much, awaking again and again, each time gaining more awareness of the world around her. She was in some protecting thing which inhabited a modest house in a green lot in company with other similar houses.

Yet she was still unsure about her situation. What was this thing? It was biological and mobile and did incomprehensible things.

Then one day she understood.

She was a baby yet to be born.

The protective thing was her mother.

How annoying. That she had not recognized something which should have been so obvious.

Her puzzling changed from what was around her mother to her mother. She sent her perceptions all throughout the woman's body till she had a picture of Her, physical data such as height and weight and body shape, organs and bones, a brain and nervous system, hints of the emotions She felt.

Her mother was generally healthy and sturdy but had a few problems: weakness in eyes, veins which were a bit clogged, a liver with a deficiency, a leg which had been badly set after a break and healed crooked. The baby reached out slowly, carefully, carefully, and eased Her toward health as perfect as her genes would allow. Ever so slowly her mother approached that state.

With that came more activity as She left the house for longer and longer trips, once to a grocery store, then to the grocery store again. Accompanying Her was the younger of Her two sons to carry Her purchases, then the older to drive a buggy which could handle heavier purchases.

One day a husband came home from some distant job. This led to him sleeping in Her bed and having sex with Her. Bored with such activity the baby put herself to sleep each time.

The baby...

When she next awoke she turned her curiosity to herself. And was met with a puzzle.

Why was she not a he?

Her memories of her past life were that of a man named Li Wei. He had lived into his eighties before dying in a fire trying to save some people. In China. He had been Chinese.

With the name came the two ideograms which made it up. With that came a cascade of other ideograms and the sounds which they made. They spilled into her mind faster and faster till she flinched into the dark cave of near-sleep.

After a timeless time she eased out of the cave. Returning from the dead had happened to her twice before. She had been a female before Li Wei, a black woman with prodigious physical and mental abilities who'd founded an empire in a country of black people in a hot jungle on the edge of a yellow plain which reached for leagues to snow-capped mountains which proved a limit to her growing empire.

She had before that been a man again. He had been a fabric designer in one of several city states, a great artist and artisan who'd made a fortune with his skill. His life, unlike the two that came after, had been a short one, ended by a fire in his manufactories. He'd died while saving his workers' lives. A theme which Li Wei hoped would not recur in this life.

For a time she explored her three previous lives. The memories came erratically, some calling up other memories, long strings of memories pulling on other long strings.

Weeks passed and she felt her body change as she eased toward birth.

Then it came.

<>

In the middle of the night Sarah Willoughby came fully awake. In the hours before she'd only drowsed, partly woken several times by moderate birth pains. This one was sharper and longer so her past experience told her that it was time to go to the hospital.

"Mom. Mom."

"Yes, dear," came a sleepy reply from Sarah's mother. "Time, is it?"

"Yes."

"I'll wake up Davey." There was the sound of Sarah's mother rolling off the cot that had been brought into the Willoughby family's main bedroom. Then a lamp came on to flood the room with yellow light.

Sarah carefully rolled upright and onto the side of her bed. Out of the side of her eyes she saw the bulky be-robed figure of her mother leaving to awaken Sarah's husband. She gave herself a moment to come perfectly awake, then heaved herself up to begin the by-now familiar process of having a baby.

<>

The small Texas hill-country town of Llano had a small hospital by virtue of it being the seat of Llano County. One doctor was always on site throughout the day and evening, though usually asleep in the evening on a cot. Three nurses were on duty in the night, one a licensed midwife.

The midwife was a black woman, Theresa Blackman. Blacks were rare in the wooded hill country west of Austin, but Theresa was from a long-established family who had been slaves of a rich rancher. She'd gotten her education in Austin but returned to her home town.

They'd welcomed her back. The Blackmans were an institution in Llano. Strangers who insulted any of them might find themselves the butt of the not-always-gentle disapproval of Llano whites. If nobody messed with Texas, NOBODY messed with Llano Texas long-established families. Say what you might about blacks in general, but the Blackmans were OUR blacks.

Theresa at three-something in the morning was fully awake. Not so the two other nurses. They quickly came awake when Theresa nudged them on their cots.

They were outside the emergency entrance as the one horse clopped into the yellow light at the side of the hospital pulling the smoothly sprung light wagon behind it. They quickly though carefully decanted Sarah from the auto.

"'Lo, Terry," said Sarah. "Sorry to wake you."

"Always awake at night, honey. Hush now while we get you inside and prepped."

Sarah had another labor pain near the room she'd be occupying for a day or more. It was sharper and more insistent.

"There'll be one more and then this baby is coming," said Sarah.

"How do you know?" said Theresa. "The last two times you were here a full day."

"If I believed in such nonsense, I'd say the baby told me."

"Well, a mother's instincts are often pretty good. Let's get you into the delivery bay."

The baby, who still thought of herself as Li Wei even though it was a male's name, had indeed told her mother with a series of pulses to the woman's brain that she was ready for her debut. She was now fully awake as she had been for a week, carefully monitoring her mother's health. As the exact time to be born neared she'd initiated a wakeup call to her mother.

Sarah was helped into the birthing bed though she felt strong and full of energy and felt that she could have gotten in easily. She relaxed and let Theresa and the nurses settle her in and arrange the birthing room and shave her pubic area, easy because the hair was stubble from Sarah's at-home weekly shave down there.

A few moments after Sarah relaxed completely from all the fussing, Li Wei triggered one very strong labor pain.

"Oof," said Sarah.

Theresa laid her surgical-gloved hands on Sarah's belly and palpated it expertly.

"Need a little bit of pain med, honey? It's too late for anything strong, but we could ease matters a bit."

"Nope. The pains aren't really painful this time."

Li Wei had made sure of that. She'd changed Sarah's womb and vagina and all the related nerves to insure her mother had a safe and painless birth.

She'd also made her mother sterile. Three healthy kids--and she'd make sure her brothers were perfectly healthy once she was born--were enough family to grow up in.

"Time, honey. It's coming."

IT was. Quickly though not hurriedly the immortal baby made its way into the world. It shed its birth cord, not waiting for it to be snipped, then relaxed as it was cleaned and swaddled and placed next to her mother.

Sarah, also cleaned and her birth bedding that needed it replaced, looked down at the beautiful baby in her arms.

The infant girl looked up. Her mother was beautiful. And so brave and smart. She felt warmth fill her body, love.

"Theresa! Look! Her eyes are focusing!"

"What? That can't be."

She hurried to the bedside from where she'd been tidying up. She looked down. The baby's eyes shifted toward her and focused. It regarded her with great curiosity.

"My God! You're right! I've never heard of such a thing."

"She's going to be a little genius. Just you wait and see."

"Honey, she's already a little genius. What are you going to name here? You and Davey picked names yet?"

"I loved *Alice in Wonderland* and *Alice Through the Looking Glass*. So Alice. Bernice for Davey's mother. And I'm giving her a third name. Theresa."

"Oh, child."

<>

The baby fed and went to sleep, though not before touching her mother and sending a message into her nervous system to go to sleep. Sarah Willoughby did so.

Three hours was enough sleep for baby and mother. They woke up and fed, baby with milk and mother with a hospital breakfast. She complained to Theresa about the amount and blandness of the food. This earned herself an extra pair of eggs and just enough salt and pepper to make them more palatable.

During the sleep time much happened. Davey was convinced to return home with his mother. There they readied the two boys for school and so freed Sarah's sister to leave Sarah's house for her job at the post office. Davey took the boys to school, then retired to the house, taking a day off from work. His mother convinced him to take a nap, then took one herself.

At lunch Davey's stomach woke him for that midday meal. As he quietly tried to make that meal his mother woke and ordered him to sit at the table while she did that task.

Both were impatient to get back to the hospital. They ate quickly and left the house, Davey swallowing a last piece of toast while reaching for the tack to hitch the horse to the carriage that would take them there.

They found an unusual situation at the hospital. Sarah was dressed in day clothes; Baby Alice was swaddled and lying on the bed. Both had fed.

"Honey," Davey said. "What are you doing? Get back in bed."

"Not when I feel so ready to leave. Don't worry, dear. I'm not going to do anything dumb. I'll go to bed as soon as we get home."

Davey looked to his mother for help, but Helen Willoughby was looking at Alice. The infant was smiling widely at his mother.

Helen said, "Look. She's focusing. Not even a day old and she's focusing."

Davey switched his attention to his daughter.

"I see it. But so what?"

Helen approached the bed and leaned down to take Alice into her arms.

"You are a little smarty pants, aren't you, you little darling?"

Alice let out a gurgle which might have been a laugh.

"'SO WHAT?'" Davey's wife said. "I've never seen an infant do that. Or even heard of it."

Davey shrugged and changed the subject. "You promise you'll go to bed as soon as we get home?"

"I do. I'll recover quicker at home."

"Mother," he said. "What do you think?"

Helen turned to her son. "Sarah is no ninny, David. Let's get out of here."

They encountered Theresa as they made to leave the room. She handed a package to Davey.

"Here are some vitamins and minerals for Sarah to take, one of each with every meal. Pace her. Exercise, but very light exercise, will do her good. The doctor examined her at noon and said that she had recovered from childbirth very rapidly. He pretended not to be surprised, but I could tell he was.

"Now, honey, you keep your promise to me not to try to do too much, you hear?"

"Yes, Mummy," Sarah said in a fake little-girl tone. She hugged the black woman, then returned to an adult tone. "I promise. Love you dear. See you in church Sunday--if I'm up to it!" She said quickly to forestall a scold. "Only if I'm up to it!"

On the two-mile ride to home at the edge of town Alice refused to lie on her back in Sarah's arms. She struggled to get upright till her mother gave in and righted her. All the way home she watched the world go by, giving little gurgles from time to time which might be--anything at all.

At home while Davey was taking care of their horse Sarah surrendered Alice to Helen and the two women walked to the master bedroom. Sarah sat heavily on the side of the bed while Helen placed the infant in the long-waiting crib. The baby gurgled at Helen, turned onto her side, and immediately went to sleep.

Helen stepped back and stood for long moments, gazing at the baby.

"What is it?! What's wrong?" said Sarah.

Helen turned to her daughter in law. "Nothing, dear. It's just she turned on her side all by herself. I've never heard of any baby doing that until three or four months."

"Is that bad?" She stood up to let Helen replace the bed sheets with fresh linen.

"It might be if the baby was having problems. But she's not. She takes milk, doesn't cry, is active, alert. It's just that you and Davey did a good job with my newest granddaughter. Now get back in bed."

Helen had finished remaking the bed. Sarah got into it and relaxed with a sigh. Already sleep was taking over but she had enough energy to speak.

"You are so good to me. What did I ever do to deserve you?"

"You made my boy happy and gave him three healthy kids." But Sarah was already asleep.

<>

Li Wei was well satisfied with her new family. That included the grandmother and aunt who helped the husband and wife. They kept her body safe, comfortable, and fed. The two boys were very interested in her at first, then got used to her and so she effectively disappeared from their consciousnesses.

Li Wei found that her body had somehow inherited all the abilities of her immortal shapechanger body though that body had perished years ago and half the world away. Thus she was able to reward them (though they did not know it) with long life and health as perfect as their bodies could manage.

She was able to sit up and so was a fixture at meals, sitting in her high chair and waving a spoon around as if conducting an orchestra. In truth that activity was part of her regimen to exercise her body and so gain strength and dexterity.

Her body, without straining, grew rapidly. At one month she could toddle and by the second month walk. She made it known that she wanted solid food and got it.

By five months she could climb like a monkey and jump like a grasshopper though she kept these abilities secret. She was already gaining more attention from the people of the town than she liked.

By six months she had mastered conversational English and begun thinking of herself as "Alice." She did not speak until two more months, however, in keeping with her decision to keep a low profile.

Chapter 2 - Kiddie

By accident Alice discovered the Speak and Spell Phonics books by which her brothers, both bright lads, had learned to read. She devoured them over a week.

Careful not to get caught, she found other reading material. She rejected the pulp romance novels of her mother and the adventure magazines of her father. Aunt Gloria Willoughby either did not read or never brought anything to Alice's home except tabloids. Grandmother Helen Willoughby did read, quite fat books at that, but only one at a time and it was always in her possession or nearly so.

When Alice searched the boys' room she hit the jackpot. Their books were squirreled away, not so much hidden as neglected. Alice snuck them out of their room one at a time and returned them and read them one at a time.

She got away with it for three months. Then the younger son John caught her.

"That's mine! Stealer! I'm going to tell!"

Li Wei had successfully dealt for well over a decade with the viper's nest of the Chinese Imperial Court. A seven-year old boy was no match for her.

"If you do I'll tell on YOU."

"You don't know anything!"

"I certainly do, young man. Did you think you could keep it a secret from me?"

"You-- You-- Stealer!"

"I'm just borrowing it. When I'm done I'll put it back. Besides you threw it away and forgot it. What are you making a fuss for?"

He grumbled and turned away.

After that Alice made no secret that she was reading the boys' books. John was intimidated. Leonard did not care. In fact, the nine-year old boy considered himself the grownup leader of the three children and the protector of the two younger ones. If little Alice wanted to read books, so be it.

Soon she had read all the dozen books. Her favorites, which she would come back to for a reread every few weeks, were *Huck Finn*, *The Prince and the Pauper*, *Treasure Island*, and *Robin Hood.*

Her least favorite was *Heidi*. Nothing much happened in it and the heroine was a mealy-mouthed goody two-shoes. Alice grudgingly forgave the author because, the immortal understood, she had been forced to write a heroine who was a Good Example for young girls.

Alice was no customer for books about Good Girls. As a Zulu warrior woman in Africa some hundred and fifty years ago she had murdered hundreds directly or indirectly to craft an empire. Then when old and on the verge of losing her grip on the empire she had died by her own hand (or so it had appeared). Then she snuck away in the night a young woman again, leaving her funeral pyre mysteriously empty.

After Alice exhausted the boys' books she made a deal with Aunt Gloria to check out books for Alice from the public library. It was good-sized as the city of Llano, Texas, was good-sized. It was the county seat of Llano County. Straddling the Llano River, the town was only seventy miles to the northwest of Austin, Texas. It was wholly in the Texas Hill Country and the financial center of a large area devoted to farming and ranching.

Gloria had no idea what books were appropriate for an extraordinary little girl. Thus she checked out a wild miscellany: historicals, westerns, mysteries, adventures, biography, self-help, geography, and much more.

The only type of book missing was romances. This amused the immortal. She'd had lovers of all the various sexes, sometime several at the same time. There was nothing about sex and romance she did not know.

In exchange she did chores for Gloria and listened to her chat about the travails of her life, including censored versions of her love life.

Taking pity on her aunt, Alice sent microscopic messengers into the woman which over months gradually turned her mere prettiness into beauty. This, however, was a mixed blessing. She attracted more men, including ones she had no interest in or despised.

One in particular kept after Gloria, threatening her if she did not have sex with him. This annoyed the shapechanger. She lurked near Gloria's house each night until the man approached it. Then she spat a gob of saliva onto the man's face from a tree fifty feet away. Deadly poison infiltrated his nervous system and over a period of days killed him.

At two years Alice was not quite four feet tall and looked like a wiry athletic six-year old. She'd gotten to that appearance slowly enough that her family had become accustomed to her physical and other prodigies. Still, they never referred to her actual age to anyone outside the extended families of Sarah and Davey.

Her parents HAD been concerned when she was six months old and looked like a three-year old. They made a special trip to a specialist in Austin. The doctor, after several tests and an interview with the girl alone in his office, said there was nothing to worry about at the time. The girl was in excellent health, extraordinarily so.

He kept to himself the knowledge that people who aged at an accelerated rate might enter old age in their twenties and die early.

Alice acted like an adult. No temper tantrums or mood swings for her. She was not jealous of her brothers and enacted no drama if her desires were denied. She simply went around the restrictions in some (and sometimes devious) way.

Still, her apparent age was a handicap. She needed an adult accomplice. She studied the individuals in her extended family of some fifteen adults and as many almost-adult cousins. She finally settled on someone close to home: her grandmother Helen Willoughby.

<>

The woman was fifty and busy, one of three librarians in the Llano County Library. Unlike the other adults in the extended family she'd had a higher education, having graduated from a community college. She dated discreetly, a widow satisfied with her unmarried state. She lived three blocks away from her son and daughter-in-law.

Alice gradually spent more time with Helen, doing errands and chatting with the woman. After three months she broached the subject of her maturity.

She did this after Thursday Girls Poker Night for Helen and eight other women at Helen's home. All of them were of an age with Helen and had varied marital experience. One was a widow, one divorced, and the rest married except for one woman who never had married officially. Nevertheless she had three children who were faithfully supported by a father.

Alice was along that night as she often was. Earlier she had helped Helen bake some pies and cookies, then had settled into an easy chair pulled from the living room into the kitchen. Eight women sat at the cleared kitchen table except for the ninth whose religion frowned on gambling. Who nevertheless avidly watched the ongoing game.

Alice idly watched the game as she read her book, getting up occasionally to fetch something from the kitchen or return something to it. Most often it was a wine bottle, the genteel swig for women in public who more often drank beer or whisky at home. Except of course for the abstemious religious woman.

At 11:00 all the guests left, all of them fussing over Alice for a few minutes before leaving. The immortal was "cute as a button" all agreed, with her red hair in pigtails and cute slightly turned-up nose.

Alice helped Helen clean up and wash dishes and glasses and utensil, doing the drying.

Near the end of the process, standing elbow to elbow at the kitchen sink atop a footstool, Alice said, "Grammaw, did you ever wonder at why I'm so grown up and why I'm growing up so fast?"

Helen glanced sideways at Alice. "Once or twice. It's just something you inherited from your parents, is my guess."

"It's because I'm not human. Or not like most humans. For one thing, I've lived before."

"Oh, Alice. Have you been following that Victoria McCann nonsense?"

"The woman is deluded, there's no doubt. But with me it's real."

She took another dish from Helen and worked on it with her towel, letting Helen think.

"You really believe that?"

"Not just believe. I can prove it. Will you listen to me? Keep an open mind?"

Helen finished one last dish, handed it to Alice. "I'll just promise to try. It's not easy."

Alice finished the dish and transferred it to the pantry with all the other dishes.

"Come into the living room."

She turned and walked out of the kitchen, snagging the book she'd been reading on the way.

In the living room she sat on the couch. Her grandmother settled beside her. Alice slewed sideways in her seat, facing more toward Helen. She showed the front of the book to her grandmother. The redbrick cover had black writing on it which read *Der Schatz im Silbersee*.

"Translated it reads *The Treasure of Silver Lake*. But you know that, don't you?"

Germans had long been immigrating to Texas. Just thirty-something miles to the south of Llano was an entire city of mostly German immigrants or their descendents named Fredericksburg. Helen's family had moved from there to Llano when she was a child.

She spoke and read German and had been influential in building up a small section of the library written in German for the small Llano German population.

"I've lived three times before. The first time was about 300 years ago in Germany. Or what would become Germany. At the time it was made up of independent city states, just as Italy was at the time.

"There were a lot of wars, large and small. My father was a printer. He and I were forced to join one group of soldiers. He didn't last long. I thrived. I rose through the ranks to under-sergeant and was finally killed while shepherding my double-squad in a retreat.

"I woke a day or two later on the battlefield. All around me were hundreds of rotting corpses being robbed by locals. One tried to rob me but I stood up and hit him. My fist and arm went all the way through his chest. I'd been reborn very strong, maybe twenty times as much as ordinary people.

"I'd also been reborn a woman. Imagine my shock when I discovered the fact."

Alice smiled at the memory. Helen looked doubtful. She said, "You were a man the first time?"

"Yes, Grammaw. And the third time I was reborn. Now let me prove to you what I claim. I'm going to read this book to you, parts of it. Now remember that German back then was different from place to place, and my version is three centuries old besides."

She lifted the book and read the first page. She spoke with an accent that Helen struggled to understand. But she read smoothly and easily, partly because Alice had practiced reading the page several times before.

"Now I'll read the second page. This time I'll translate to English as I read."

This time she held the book so that her grandmother could read along with her.

When she finished the page she closed the book and set it aside.

"Now do you feel that MAYBE I'm telling you the truth?"

Helen picked up the book and opened it, riffling through its pages, looking at but not reading the text.

"I have to believe that something strange happened to you. Whether I believe what you say is true..."

"I can give you other proofs that I'm not an ordinary human. My strength, for instance. I can lift a wagon and throw it--not that I would, throw it, I mean. I wouldn't want to damage someone's property.

"I can also tell you what each woman's hands were at the game--"

"You don't read minds?!"

"No. I just have a very good memory and I can read people's emotions. NOT minds, just emotions. But that combined with good memory means I can guess the hands nine times out of ten."

She grinned. "You don't want to play poker with me, Grammaw."

Helen's face lightened for the first time since the conversation began, then she sobered again.

"Why are you telling me all this?"

"I want something, of course."

"What?"

"There are some things a grownup can do that a kid can't. Like open a bank account, buy certain items, go into restricted book stacks, more. And sometimes I just want to have a grownup conversation with another grownup."

"You consider yourself a grownup?"

"Grammaw, I'm close to FOUR HUNDRED YEARS OLD. I've fought in wars, been married eleven times, killed hundreds of people, saved the lives and limbs of hundreds more, created and destroyed cities."

Helen Willoughby gazed at her granddaughter. Even Alice's extranormal senses could not read her face and body language.

"You've killed people."

"The world has always been a violent place, especially in olden times. Even right now there are several wars going on. Wars ARE fewer nowadays, but they are also bigger."

Helen was silent for several moments. "Would you, could you, kill people?"

"Not for fun. Nor for profit. But, yeah, to protect you, the rest of the family, this city, this country, I certainly would."

"COULD you?" She gestured at Alice's body.

"Looks are deceiving. I'm very strong and fast. My body is tougher than rubber tires when struck. Pistol bullets would bounce off me. Rifle bullets would penetrate but even if they struck my heart would not do lasting damage. You'd have to shoot my brain for me to be permanently killed. And then I'd be born again, as I was here."

Alice waited to see Helen's response.

"Grammaw, Dad is a big strong man. He could kill any of us, hurt any of us. But you know him. He has a gentle heart. He won't even spank us kids. Instead he just looks hurt when we misbehave and he calls us on it."

She tilted her head, considered. "Works better than a spanking, at least with us kids. Wouldn't with some other kids."

Helen said, "Very well, I'll think about what you've told me. I halfway believe you. You've always been trustworthy. But it will take time to sink in.

"You said in your last life you were a man? Who? What was he like?"

That conversation lasted long into the night.

<>

The first favor Alice asked of her adult friend was access to adult books. It was a favor easy for a librarian to grant. Sometimes Helen brought a requested book home, sometimes Alice checked out the book in Helen's name. If asked about it she said "it's a book I know she's wanted to read." After the first few times the other two librarians no longer asked.

They did not even look at the titles, so accustomed they'd become to checking out the books. If they had, they might have questioned Helen about the choices of "her" books.

Some of them were not that unusual for a mature educated woman: the English translation of Colette's *Claudine at School*, Joseph Conrad's *Lord Jim*, and Theodore Dreiser's *Sister Carrie*.

Others were more likely to be questioned, if anyone was questioning: Sigmund Freud's *The Interpretation of Dreams*, copies of the *Guide Michelin* for several countries, and Booker T. Washington's *Up from Slavery*.

Even more questionable were a few books on philosophy and several heavy textbooks on mathematics, biology, chemistry, and physics.

Alice also devoured books on engineering subjects, especially the electrical ones. This led her to intrude on her father's workshop where he fiddled with clocks and small gasoline engines which powered those new-fangled lawn mowers which only rich people could afford.

At first her intrusions were practical ones: "Mom says it's time for dinner NOW" and "Here's your iced tea, Daddy" and "Here's that wrench you were looking for" and "Can you really put that clock back together?"

So slowly that her father did not realize that he was being manipulated by a master manipulator Alice became a fixture in the big shed he'd converted into a workshop.

Not that Alice stinted on books which were favorites of children. These included *The Wonderful Wizard of Oz*, *The Grey Fairy Book*, and *True Stories of Girl Heroines*.

That last book was one which caused Alice to become a fixture in the lives of her brothers. Up till then she, like all "gur-ruls" to most boys, was an irritant to be ignored and if at all possible forgotten.

Ten-year-old Leonard was a reader, mostly of boy's adventure books. Seven-year-old John was bigger than his age and more interested in athletics, especially local obsession baseball. He WOULD read a book, but only if it was about cowboys.

Leo came across the Girl Heroine book which had been "accidentally" left where he was bound to find it. He read the first page and became hooked. When he asked if there were more such books Alice introduced him to a book on women warriors, both historical and fictional.

Soon the two embarked on games of pirates and African warriors in the tree-shaded stream beds which fed the Llano River and in the nearby forest. Not to be left out, John joined them. He'd been lured in when he'd heard and then read about Annie Oakley and her like on the Western frontier.

There were several such stream beds, some widening out for a few dozen feet to become small ponds before narrowing again.

The near-pond closest to the Willoughby home was frequented by the Willoughby kids and about a dozen others in the same age range.

This was where Alice got a reputation among the kids of Llano.

It was late July of Jane's third year of her fourth life. She was in the large oak tree which had a big branch which extended out over the water. She was about to swing on the rope attached higher out over the water and cannonball into the stream in a competition to see who could make the biggest splash.

A shout brought her attention from the water to the side of the stream below her. Five bigger boys had intruded into "her family's" pond.

"Out all! This is our place now!"

This was uttered by the biggest of the intruder's, a lean muscular blond. Like all of his companions and most of the smaller kids he was wearing cutoff jeans and nothing else, though he did carry a small bag with (probably) a shirt and a few other items.

"It is not! YOU get out!"

That was John. Though the youngest he was the size of all the other of the older boys in the group that he and Leonard traveled in. He was also fearless. He strode out of the shallow streambed water to get in the face of Tyler, whom Alice had seen before and who was the bigger boys' leader.

Alice broke off a nearby limb of the big tree so that one end was sharp. She stripped off the side branchlets by grasping it with one hand and sliding it down to and off the end. At the same time she shapechanged the front end of her sliding hand into a blade-like shape. Almost hard as stone when used this way her hand peeled the bark and all outside it off as well as a knife could. Then she bit off the too-long blunt end of the stick with diamond-hard teeth.

This was a near-automatic action. Most of her attention was on events below.

After an exchange of exhortations Tyler grew impatient and pushed John. He staggered backward and fell onto his bottom. The intruders laughed.

Leonard yelled and launched himself at Tyler. He was intercepted by a Tyler band mate and also pushed. Leonard staggered but did not fall.

John clambered to his feet and helped his brother keep his footing.

Alice leaped. Downward she plunged to land a few feet in front of the bigger boys. Striking the ground she collapsed her body into a deep squat and then flexed back up to her full height.

"Back off, lackwits. Or else we'll find just how deep this goes into your gut."

All five took a step or half-step back.

The entity which had appeared in their midst was a slender girl nearly five feet in height clad only in cutoff jeans like everyone else. It had almost no obvious fat. Muscles in arms and legs stood out, not bulky but stringy but nevertheless obvious. It had washboard abs.

Yet the face was feminine as was the long red hair which hung in ringlets over each of the non-existent breasts.

Most striking was the face and the eyes. It was completely expressionless, totally devoid of human emotion.

One boy turned half away and his head further away so that he did not have to look into what seemed to him to be a demon face. The other four stared at the apparition.

Tyler broke the moment. He sneered.

"You're just a girl. You can't do anything. You won't do anything."

The yard-long spear, up till now butt down and resting on the sandy dirt of the stream bank, rose up and spun in a twirling blur that left its butt under her arm, sharp point forward.

"You want to be the first to find out?"

One of his buddies took hold of Tyler's arm.

"She's crazy, Ty. You see her eyes? Those are crazy eyes. She'll do it. We'll beat her up. But not before she kills one us."

The big boy shrugged off the hand.

"I'll catch you alone, bitch. Then we'll see what's what."

Alice smiled. There no humor in it, only ice. "Yes, we will."

"You won't have that stick then."

The being in front of him let the spear fall to the earth. The hand which had held it struck forward like a snake, open like claws. The arm was so still it might have been the arm of a statue.

"I don't need a stick to crush your throat. Or maybe I'll crush your nuts first."

The arm jerked downward to crotch level. The motion was so fast it was in one place in one instant and the second place in the next.

"Or maybe I'll hook your eyes out."

Both her hands rose to face level so fast there was no motion between. They were fisted except for the index fingers. Those were slightly bent into hooks.

"She's a freak, Ty. Let's get out of here."

"I'll get your brothers, you crazy bitch. Then we'll--"

The demon in the appearance of a girl moved so fast it was a blur. It seemed to just appear inches away from the blond boy.

"Better not," said the being. Its voice held no emotion. The words held no threat.

From inches away the boy could see the eyes of the being. They were glowing bright red.

He shrieked and fled, dropping the rolled up bundle of his shirt containing a meager collection of possessions.

Alice picked it up. Deep in the night she would place it on the doorstep of the house in which he lived.

His four companions turned and ran too, calling out to Tyler to wait.

The boys with the Willoughby kids quickly gathered around Alice, laughing and congratulating her. She ignored them to stand watching the bigger boys as they receded into the forested distance. That took long enough for the praise to falter.

Leonard and John were not part of the happy crowd. As the noise died down Leonard said, "Thanks, Sis. Guys, we're going to be late for dinner. We gotta go home. Come on, John. See you later, Sis."

That broke up the swimming party. Alice followed her brothers.

It was months before her brothers said much to Alice.

She loved them and understood. Their discomfort with her presence would be cured by the passage of time. And an immortal had plenty of that.

Chapter 3 - Machines

By her fourth year Alice had become a near partner with her father in his workshop. She shared his enthusiasm for machines in general and automobiles in particular but was taken by surprise when he brought one home.

Autos had been a commercial reality in Europe for over a decade. Invented on the Continent but most fully developed in the industrial powerhouse of Ireland, they were a late arrival in America. Even so, they flourished on the East Coast in the larger cities and increasingly in the country side.

Texans, never liking to let the snowbirds get ahead of them in ANYTHING, were busily refashioning their larger cities to accommodate autos, especially Houston and San Antonio and to a lesser extent Dallas and its nearby twin city Fort Worth. Austin was slower to adopt them but though smaller was fast catching up.

Alice first heard the auto from her perch in one of several tall trees near home. She was reading a book on airplanes. She hoped to see one in the not-too-distant future. Barnstormers were becoming increasingly active in Texas, mostly in the more populous eastern part.

Her hearing was super acute when she wanted it to be but normally she kept it to merely human levels. So the chuff-chuff of the auto did not alert her until the machine was a quarter mile away.

She looked up and toward central Llano. From this height she could see over the widely separated homes which made up the eastern edge of the city. Behind her was the large apples-and-pecans orchard her family owned, then grassy meadow and finally forest.

The sound was coming closer. Curious Alice put her book into her satchel and swarmed down the tree trunk, eschewing her normal mode of descent: leaping through a space in the branches and plummeting to earth. There were too many possible watching eyes to take the swifter descent.

She went through the back door of the house and through it then out the front door. A few minutes later down the street passing in front of the row of houses a shiny red box turned a corner and came toward her. It slowed to a stop then went silent with a muted bang.

The machine was a truck, a model Alice recognized from the several technical magazines to which Davey had subscriptions. It was a big red box with four black wheels. The front and front sides had glassy windows. And doors.

The nearest door opened and Davey climbed down from the

driver's side of the cab. The bang of the door closing was matched by a bang from the passenger side of the truck. From that side, coming around the front of the machine, came her two brothers. They were shouting and laughing and (as they came nearer her) explaining matters to their sister.

Dad had picked up the truck at the railroad from Austin which dead ended in Llano. He and the sales rep with it had made sure it was operational, had gasoline in it, and then driven by their school. And wasn't it wonderful?!

"Durn right. The most wonderful thing I've seen in a long time. Except how much food you can put away, Kiddo." She ruffled John's red hair, predictably annoying him and amusing Leonard.

Davey came forward and side-hugged her on his way into the house, an arm around her and trailed by his other two kids.

In the kitchen he washed his hands, made his kids do the same, and took stuff out of the pantry and assorted cabinets. Then he orchestrated fixing dinner. On Thursdays Sarah Willoughby worked late at the small department store in downtown Llano a block away from the courthouse.

She and Helen arrived a little after 7:00 and freshened up, then sat down at the kitchen table. They joined hands and blessed the meal, then everyone broke bread, dished up food, poured drinks, and began eating.

"Now," Sarah said, "what's the story behind that monstrosity sitting in front of our house?"

Over the course of the meal the story was revealed. Davey, the younger of the two partners in The Hill Country Financial Management Company, had convinced his partner and the several large ranches that they advised to use a new service that The HCFM Company had started. This was to rent or sell motorized vehicles to them.

The financial company had already brokered a similar deal for motorized and un-motorized farm equipment such as plows and irrigation equipment. The auto service was just a consolidation and expansion of that informal service.

"It's going to take a few months of work to get it up and running. It's already formalized legally and funded by a bank loan. We're looking for three employees to work there. I've an eye on a couple of them and several alternatives if they're not available or interested."

<>

Months later the automotive company was past its birthing pains. It had four employees: a manager with an engineering degree, two mechanics, and a technical assistant and all-around flunky.

It also had an unofficial flunky: Alice. She became this so gradually and discreetly that she was a fixture before anyone noticed she was often around at random hours of the days and evenings.

In those few months she'd made herself indispensable. She almost seemed to be able to read people's minds when they needed something. This included the hired gopher who was the person most likely to object to someone usurping his position.

She owed part of her acceptance to the immortal's esoteric powers. After deciding that the four workers were on the whole good people worthy of the gift she gave each perfect health. This included improvements of their brain chemistry that made them less likely to fall victim to unreasoning anger and depression.

A larger part, however, was Alice's ability to manipulate people, honed by nearly four centuries of life.

The flunky's tolerance also came from the enthusiasm he and she shared for airplanes. Alice had noticed his interest and discreetly let him know she shared it. It wasn't before long that the two of them were having lunch together.

"Why aren't you in school?" he said on the very first time they ventured across the street from the garage to an eatery.

"Because I'm super smart. I could TEACH any subject in school, including high school."

"Oh, Really? Then answer this..." As they ordered and ate their lunch he proceeded to quiz her and she to answer his questions. She deliberately made some mistakes, especially ones about which would have been on an American civics exam.

About mathematics and physics and electricity, however, she let him quickly realize she knew more than he.

The Q&A became part of their next few lunches, each time he trying to bring up a stumper. She let him get away with a few just so he wouldn't become discouraged.

Finally at one lunch he literally threw up his hands and laughed. "OK. You win. You're smarter than me."

"No, I'm not. You know more about life than me. I'm still a kid. Practical stuff, about getting a husband or wife, raising a family--the IMPORTANT stuff--someday I'm going to be asking you for advice."

He thought while he finished a chunk of fish and followed it with iced tea, a very popular drink on the hot days of Texas summer.

"Well, OK. It's a deal. Not that I know a Hell of a lot about that stuff. But you're still smarter than me."

He was correct. Alice had started off her fourth life with a good mind and enhanced it physically the way she had in her previous lives. She already had an enormous store of knowledge, especially from her last life. When Li Wei had died in a fire saving other people he had been one of the Imperial Court's mathematicians, especially expert in esoteric maths such as infinities, multidimensional spaces, and advanced calculus.

As they read about and talked about airplanes they discovered that a few companies sold parts to make model airplanes, most importantly engines. The motor they finally chose was the size and weight of a brick. A model airplane would have to be fairly big to justify such a weight.

The design they came up with had a six-foot wing span and seven-foot long body. For the airplane to be light enough they bought slabs of super-strong graphene, still known sometimes as Miracle Metal though invented almost three decades ago and the name dropped soon afterward.

Alice, who'd become fascinated by the field of semiconductor calculators, programmed a flight path in the controller of a junked refrigerator using the advanced calculator in her father's office late at night. The complex program required an extra 1024-byte memory block. This ate up most of her monthly income as a bicycle delivery boy.

Albert Moseley, her flunky friend, also contributed money. Most of it went to all the tiny parts need to construct the airplane.

At each step along the way Alice, secretly, assembled phantom versions of the airplane in her head and ran tests on the vehicle. This included imagining the airflow over its body. In this way she had an imaginary wind tunnel and test bed. How good her simulations were she could only discover when the airplane flew.

On Thanksgiving she had Albert over for the dinner at her home, with her parents' permission. His family was in Austin, 75 miles away. By the railroad, which dead ended in Llano, it was more than a two hour trip and the train only ran once on Monday, Wednesday, and Friday.

Before dinner Alice and Albert worked on their airplane in her father's workroom, a part that Davey had allocated for their craft. For a time he watched them work, occasionally handing over a tool or part, but soon he left to take over family matters.

At a little after 4:00 the vehicle was as ready to fly as it would ever be. The pair stood back and gazed at their creation.

The cross-shaped machine rested on a long plywood table, its landing gear two long pipes projecting down then curving back to form horizontal two-foot long skids. The body was made of bright white metallic graphene. They had painted the forward edge of the wing over the cockpit lime green. So too the forward edges of both the horizontal part of the tail and the vertical part.

They had used thick bleached-white cord for the cables from the cabin to the control surfaces on the wings and tail. This blended the short exposed lengths into the mostly-white overall color scheme.

It was quite beautiful, they pronounced, turning to each other and solemnly shaking hands. Then they turned toward the door to the workroom to wash up for Thanksgiving dinner.

Albert returned the next morning on his motorcycle as arranged. He accepted with thanks a cup of coffee from Sarah Willoughby and he and Alice went into the workroom. Davey was already there, puttering over a ham radio he had made from a kit. He suspended work to chat and watch them make some tests of the airplane.

These included plugging a crude control console they'd constructed into the plane. They could then activate the vehicle's control surfaces and run them through their range of motion: up down left right, separately and in concert.

Finally they removed the wing from the airplane to let them carry everything out the door of the workroom. Alice carrying the wing, Albert the body, and Davey a big tool kit, they walked through the orchard to the flat green field beyond it. As they did so they were joined by the two boys.

They set the plane's body down, reattached the wing, and plugged a battery and their crude control console into the plane. Alice took out a notebook with a list of startup, preflight test, and operation actions.

She read it and Albert did the actions.

"Plane in place."

The two gazed at the model airplane and nodded.

"Roger plane in place."

"Console plugged in."

Albert placed a hand on the console.

"Roger console plugged in."

It took several careful minutes before they worked their way to the end of the list.

"Motor disengaged."

To do this Albert opened a door over the engine at the front of the airplane, peered in, and flicked a button. This let the engine run without engaging the propeller.

"Roger motor disengaged."

"Starting the engine."

Alice flicked a button on the console. The engine began to turn over from an electric motor. Several actions took place at this: vaporized gasoline spurted into the engine, a spark plug flashed, and the air gas vapor mix exploded. Then automatically the cycle repeated and the engine began to roar.

"ROGER STARTING THE ENGINE."

Alice let the engine run until it was running smoothly and it was warmed up.

"SHUTTING OFF ENGINE."

There was silence, made more profound because the engine racket was gone.

"Roger shutting off engine."

Alice and Albert looked at each other. They took a deep breath and let it out in unison.

Alice looked around. Davey and the boys had retreated from the loud engine noise.

"OK. We're ready to begin. Keep way back."

Turning back to the plane she and Albert went through the process of readying the plane for takeoff. When they were done Alice used their crude console to start the engine again. The propeller at the front of the plane began to turn, slowly, then faster, then faster till it reached its fastest pace.

Wind from the prop blew back along the body of the plane till it ruffled Albert's hair where he was standing at the rear of the plane holding the flat part of the tail control surface.

He looked inquiringly at Alice. She nodded. He released the plane.

It had already been vibrating to the buzz of the motor and Albert's unsteadiness to holding it back. Now the vibration nearly ceased as it crept forward, sliding on its skids on the flat grassy meadow. It picked up speed slowly, then more rapidly slid forward till it was racing over the grass.

A minute, then two passed. And at a precisely calculated moment the plane rocked back on its skids, the engine roared to its greatest speed, and the plane lifted off the grass.

"YEAH!" said Albert. He did a jig as the plane sailed up and away.

Alice found herself grinning as her chest seemed to swell. They had done it! Made a machine that flew!

Suddenly she was assaulted by her brothers. They hugged her from the back on two sides. She staggered, regained her footing, and twisted around to hug them back, her ears assaulted by their yelling.

With her brothers came her father, grinning widely. He brushed away her brothers and reclaimed their place to hug her too.

He loosened his hold and stepped.

"Congratulations, baby. Good job."

Off to the side Albert was looking up after the plane. He was grinning widely.

"Al did it too. Hey, Al." She walked quickly to him. He looked aside at her, then grabbed her in a big hug. She returned it, grinning too.

An unaccustomed sensation of extra sensitivity brought her attention to her breasts. Recently they'd grown into small bumps and her nipples had expanded. A similar feeling of extra sensitivity grew in her crotch. She was edging into puberty.

Quickly she banished the two sources of extra awareness.

"So what happens now?" said her older brother.

"Yeah, what?" echoed John.

A rising buzzing noise brought everyone's head around. The airplane was coming back.

"Now the plane finishes going in a square that ends a little that way." She pointed in the direction of the point where the airplane had lifted off.

"It's supposed to land."

The big device rushed toward them. But it was a little low. When it had made the last of four turns to make a square it was only about ten feet high instead of the fifty feet high it was supposed to maintain.

Having reached its takeoff point the plane nosed down into a shallow dive. It lowered and lowered, then struck the ground and somersaulted, ending on its back and skidding over the green grass.

"Ouch-y!" yelled John and raced to catch up to the plane.

Everyone else followed at a more leisurely rate. Shortly they arrived and stood around looking down at the vehicle.

The motor was still running. It coughed and died. Just at the moment Alice had programmed it to.

The wings had come off when it had struck ground upside down and lay a few feet behind its path across the grass. The wooden propeller had broken off.

"Not bad," said Albert.

"It looks bad to me," said Leonard.

"It LOOKS bad. But the only thing broken is the propeller. We have more. The body, the wings, those are Miracle Metal. Nothing hurts them."

As if to prove him wrong gasoline spilled from the upside down gas tank caught fire with a faint POOF! Everyone danced back and watched as gasoline continued to drip out and burn.

"Well, back to the drawing board," said Alice, grinning.

"You aren't disappointed?" said her father.

"We can repair or replace all the insides. The outsides are of graphene. We just need to wash those and they'll be ready to go. But first I have to figure out why the plane didn't maintain its height."

Chapter 4 - Puberty

Alice's optimism was justified. Within three months Icarus 1, the name they'd given their airplane in a fit of ironic humor, flew again. Despite its unlucky name there were no too-high or too-low flights. This was thanks to an innovation created by Albert: an altimeter fashioned from an expensive barometer which they'd bought.

One successful flight suggested others. Alice programmed more complex paths, first just variations on the square path of the first flight. Then ones which included climbs to and dives from different heights. In the process the two wanna-be aeronauts discovered flaws in the aircraft's design. They fixed them and tried even more complex paths.

Thus far the plane stayed upright during all flights. Alice, remembering how Icarus had leaked gasoline when it crashed and landed upside down, had made sure the gas tanks would not leak at any orientation.

She also decreed that they be tough enough not to easily rupture. Albert protested at this.

"No one will be flying in a model airplane. Why waste time and money on such fuel tanks?"

"Are you content to just work on model airplanes? Don't you wonder sometimes if you can someday work on real airplanes?"

He paused. Thought.

"Hmm. No. I'm just a car mechanic."

"JUST a car mechanic? Do you realize how dumb that is? You're smart, hard working, and NOT just a car mechanic. You're creative and can learn things. You made a fucking altimeter out of a barometer, for God's sake."

"Well, I'll think about it."

Three weeks later Icarus was doing barrel rolls successfully.

On Alice's sixth birthday she got a surprise birthday party from her family and Albert and several acquaintances of her parents and grandparents. The wily immortal was caught completely by surprise. She'd been obsessing too much over her jobs as a bicycle delivery girl and general odd-job helper.

After the party wound down and the Willoughby home prepared for the night Alice walked Helen three blocks home. The air was chill this late in November despite the former heat of Texas Hill Country day.

Texas-smart Helen was wearing a sweater over her regular

clothing. The shapechanger, comfortable naked in subzero Arctic or roasting Sahara climes, was wearing only jeans and sandals and a light sleeveless blouse.

"Honey," said Helen. "Why aren't you wearing a bra?"

"This body does not need such support. You know what I am." In thc two ycars plus since Alice had told her grandmother about her shapechanger nature she'd confided much to the woman.

"Yes. But you do need more covering." She glanced aside and down at Alice's chest. In the dim lights of nearby night-lit houses the immortal's nipples visibly dimpled her blouse. Her body, automatically adjusting to appear normal in the local weather, had reacted to the chill as an average woman's would.

"Oh."

Her nipples softened. But there still was a faint impression of them through the thin material.

"OK. I'll buy a bra or two and start wearing them."

"You need to do more than that. You look more like a grownup now and have to adjust your behavior to appear one."

"Hmm. You're right. I'll do that. Good night."

They'd arrived at Helen's house and turned into the sidewalk leading from the street-side sidewalk to the low stairs in front of the house.

Alice kissed her grandmother's nearest cheek and turned to leave.

"Goodnight, Grammaw."

<>

At six Alice looked sixteen. Changes in her appearance had happened so gradually over the years that the few thousand people in Llano and its surroundings had ceased to wonder at the girl's unnaturally rapid maturing. It was just another mild eccentricity amid all the other eccentricities in the area.

She was tall for a woman, Alice having decided that she liked that height rather than something more ordinary. Her body was child slender, hiding her enormous extranatural strength, but had definite womanly curves. Her face, framed by riotous red hair, still proclaimed her girlish nature. It had beauty which could shock strangers who saw her for the first time.

The locals, however, had grown used to it. Alice was just "that knockout Willoughby girl" whom people sometimes wondered about, especially about when she'd hook up with a Llano boy or, God forbid, some random stranger passing through.

She was one of the local eccentrics for another reason. She didn't go to school. For a couple of years the local authorities had tried to get her to go to one of them but they wrangled about which one: elementary because of her chronological age or middle or high school because of her apparent age?

Helen and Sarah for those two years urged that Alice be given tests to decide where to place her. Head librarian and popular nurse's aide at the local hospital, they had a good deal of influence.

The decision was made when Therese, head nurse at the hospital, weighed in at a meeting of the school board.

"Listen, you lazy boneheads. Give the girl tests and be done with it. You've wasted the county's money for two years arguing about this. Yes, I especially include you, Hester, you ignorant lazy cow. Get this done or the next time any of you come into Emergency for a hangnail you will not like the cure I decide on for you."

None of the local school board was willing to stand up to the stern black woman. They voted right that minute.

Thus for month's Alice took tests. They started with the most basic placement tests, then slowly went up the ladder to college prep.

She aced every one, often zipping through them with a bored but determined air that shamed or angered the test administrators.

One of the admins, curious, added an unnecessary IQ test. He stared, unbelieving, at the results. Alice Willoughby had scored 180+, the PLUS meaning her IQ was so high it could not be measured.

That night at the Llano barbecue place, famous all the way to Austin, sitting at an outside table with BBQ and beer, he confided in his cronies.

"You know that cute little Willoughby girl? The redhead? She scored off the charts in an IQ test. Took half the usual time."

"Yeah, I know the girl. Smarty pants but doesn't rub your nose in it. Respectful of her elders, she is." Sarge being the eldest there and well-liked, everyone nodded their heads.

Mitch, the next eldest, spoke up. "She's a listener, she is. She'll sit for hours letting you tell her your life story."

That was true enough. Alice, despite four centuries of life, was always ready to glean knowledge from the unlikeliest of sources. Being immortal a few hours listening to a mortal was nothing to her.

"I'd do her," said the youngest of the group. He was a hippy decades before there were "hippies" with long hair and long straggly beard and a casual outlook on employment.

Earnest, the test admin, said, "You'd do a lamp post if it would hold still. Which it won't as you're usually too drunk to hold onto it."

They all had a good laugh at that, even the hippy who knew himself too well to disagree.

<>

A high school diploma was assigned to Alice to be given with the regular graduation class, that being the proper way to assign such certificates.

So that spring Alice began to frequent the high school, doing odd jobs. Often that was in the school library since its regular attendant was quite happy to have additional (unpaid!) help.

Often Alice helped girls and boys get the right works to help them write their papers. Boys especially found themselves helpless to find material when Alice was on duty.

That might have angered some girls jealous of the attention and often did. But most cheerleaders, themselves all too often getting unwanted attention, sympathized.

Alice sometimes helped carry things for cheerleaders at practice and bring water to them and otherwise help out. One of them became a friend: Patricia, who had pale skin with long gleaming midnight hair cut in bangs and elegant black eyebrows and large dark eyes.

During a rest period at practice Patricia took a drink of the water from the cup filled by and brought to her by Alice and said, "You've just got to laugh and turn away. Don't give them time to respond to the laugh. Walk away."

"What if they follow you?" said Doris, a blond with a persistent pimple which had vanished one day after a light touch by Alice.

"Frown at them and say 'I'm busy.' Don't use their name; they'll take that as interest."

"What if they grab your arm to keep you still?" said brown-haired Phillida of the unfortunate Shakespearean name.

"Slap them," said Patricia.

"What if they slap back? Or worse?"

"First, always make sure other people are around. Then knee them in the nuts."

"That seems..."

"Hey, girl. We're not Northern snowflakes. We're TEXAS girls."

There ensued a discussion of how to handle persistent boys cut short by the cheerleader coach.

<>

That afternoon Alice "accidentally" bicycled the same way as Phillida on her walk home. In over a mile the immortal discovered much about the girl, cementing a friendship that lasted for years afterward.

Near the girl's home a boy was encountered sitting on a concrete bench at a bus stop.

He was big and blond and on the football team. This gave him a big place in the high-school hierarchy.

He rose and joined the two girls.

"Hey, Phillida. How was your day?"

"OK." She didn't look at him. She hunched shoulders and continued to walk, Alice beside her.

"Hey, don't walk away from me!" He grabbed her nearest arm. Or tried to. An arm interposed itself.

He turned to find Alice very close to him, near nose to nose.

"Back off, boy. She doesn't want company."

He took a step back and glared down at her.

"Go away. This is just between Phil and me."

"Now it's between me and you."

He lifted a fist but thought better of doing anything more. He turned and walked away.

Phillida turned to Alice. "Thank you. Come in with me. I don't want to be alone."

"Sorry, dear. I've got something to do."

"Are you sure. I could really--"

"I'm sure. You're safe for now. And soon you'll always be safe from him."

The girl continued to look at Alice, then said, "OK. Thank you. See you tomorrow."

She turned and walked quickly to her home and entered it.

Alice began to bicycle leisurely in the same direction as the boy. It took ten minutes to catch up to him at a lot with a vacant house on it.

He stopped, turned, and spoke. "You are in real trouble, nosy."

Alice stopped, got off her bicycle and again stood too close to him. She looked up at him, staring at him with eyes which did not blink.

"No, you're in real trouble. You've pissed me off."

He backed up and reached toward her.

Her fist struck so fast an onlooker could not have seen it. Literally rock hard it punched him deep in the gut. Just enough to stun. At full strength it would have gone all the way through him.

He doubled over, went to one knee.

There was a Snick! Close to his eyes appeared the blade of a flick knife.

"You see this, BOY? If I ever hear of you bothering Phillida or anyone else I'll come for you some dark night. And I'll spill your guts. Do you hear me? BOY?"

The words came hard. "I...hear...y..."

A foot pushed his shoulder. He fell over onto his side, holding his gut.

The harpy stood over him for what seemed like forever. Then it was gone.

<>

The boy did not to tell his story. But those around him persisted. The story eventually was pulled out of him.

Most of the boys who heard it either didn't believe him, or didn't care. He was not well liked. Some even secretly rejoiced to hear that Alice had beaten him up.

Six boys decided the girl needed to be taught a lesson. They began to stalk Alice.

The immortal was amused at their attempts. S/he had dueled with assassins much more accomplished than these backcountry rubes. And killed each of her would-be attackers.

A dark joy filled her. She had too long leashed her cruelty.

She began to take shortcuts on the way home. One which she especially liked was through a business section which was abandoned at night.

One night as she bicycled slowly between two warehouses or workshops three boys stepped out in front of her.

She stopped, feet on the concrete. Behind her three more boys stepped out to block any escape.

A near-full moon overhead added some light to the dim nighttime safety lights intended to dissuade thieves.

The middle of the three boys in front of her said, "You've gotten too big for your britches, bitch. We're going to rape you then beat you to death. Slowly."

"Hey," said a boy at his side. "We didn't agree to KILL her."

"She can identify us. She has to die."

"I'm not having anything to do with this." He dropped the pipe he held and walked quickly away. The pipe rang on the concrete. The sound echoed off the nearby warehouse/workshop walls.

"Me neither," said one of the boys behind her. His boots scuffed as he walked quickly away.

The Alice creature was disappointed. There were only four victims left.

She got off her bike, trundled it to the side of a warehouse, laid it carefully down. She shed her clothing, folded it into the carry basket in front of the bike. Then she walked toward the leader of the diminished rape-and-kill group.

In the dim light the boys could see...something...happening.

The creature's skin turned slowly red. It could have changed its skin color instantly. But this would heighten the delicious terror.

Its long curly hair raveled away to nothing. Breasts flattened to hard slabs of flesh. Muscles bulged in its thighs and arms. The chest expanded. Rows of belly muscles bulged to form washboard abs.

The boy beside the hulking leader screamed and raced away. The creature marked him to deal with later. Instead it approached the leader.

That man quailed before the approaching monster. But to turn to run away would expose his back. He shouted and ran forward, raising his baseball bat.

No longer a girl the monster simply let the bat strike it with a meaty Thunk! It punched the man in the gut. He folded over with an audible Whoosh! of breath from his mouth.

Behind the monster the two remaining attackers struck with pipes and fists. It made no attempt to block strikes. It just turned slowly to meet them.

Its eyes shone bright red. One of the men screamed. The other grimly kept hitting out with a baseball bat.

The monster took hold of his neck with a grip of steel and slowly began to punch him. No blow was very hard. But the fists kept coming, coming, as if to tenderize meat.

The other man stopped, turned to run.

The monster dropped the punished man and grabbed the back of the would-be escapee. It began to lightly pound him on his back, paying especial attention to the kidney area, light enough to hurt but not injure the delicate organs under the skin.

As it punished the men the creature felt joy fill its breast.

A short time later it decided this part of its job was done. It put the man she was holding up to sleep with a thought, leaned down to touch the downed man and send him to sleep.

It turned and walked leisurely to its bike, changing its body back to Alice. She dressed and biked away, after the leader's sidekick.

The monster with a girl's appearance caught him in the moonlight in a dusty stretch of packed-earth road, still doggedly jogging away.

"Hey, Joey," she said as she biked close to him. "Watcha doin'?"

"I'm... You... I'm..."

"Doing the sensible thing. Escaping. Stop. I won't hurt you. We have to talk."

He did, leaned over to support his upper body with his hands grasping his thighs just above his knees. His breathing was heavy. His belly hurt.

Alice laid a cool hand on his back and sent a rush of microscopic messengers through the shirt into him. Rapidly the exhaustion and pain receded, then vanished.

"You boys were going to do a terrible wrong. I saved you. You'd never escape it because there were six of you. Eventually someone would talk to the wrong person. Maybe years later. You would be punished. In ways you probably can't imagine, so young are you. Look at me."

Slowly, stinking of fear, he stood upright but with shoulders collapsed in on themselves. With enormous effort he raised his head to look into her eyes.

In the half-moon light but with eyes dark adapted he could see the girl clearly, sight helped by his memories of her in daylight. She looked harmless. But now he knew better.

"I am not human. Nothing you can do will hurt me, not even bullets. Try something like that and I'd catch you. And this time I would not let you live. You would take a long time to die."

The monster with the look of a girl examined him with eyes not hindered by the dark. Good. He believed her.

"Harm, even threaten to harm, any of my family and friends and I will show no mercy. Harm anyone and I will find out, eventually, no matter how well you try to hide it. I have marked you. I have ways to see you and find you no matter where you go. Believe me."

She put forth a hand to his chest. She injected his body with tiny microscopic messengers which though limited could still do much of what she said. She accompanied the injection with a sudden shot of cold like a dagger's stab.

"Ahh!" It was a near scream.

The monster smiled. It liked to hurt those who hurt others. It was one of its greatest joys.

It had done none of that in this life until now. It promised itself that would change.

The boy Joey rubbed his chest and the pain ebbed away.

"Now go home. Tell anyone you like what happened tonight. No one will believe you. But get it off your chest if you want."

She turned away, got on her bike, and sped away.

<>

The three unconscious beaten-up boys were found the next morning when the first workman arrived at the small industrial area where the monster's punishment had taken place.

Furor ensued. The story spread like a flash fire. Everyone talked about it. Except Alice. She simply listened to everyone with wide-eyed fascination.

For two whole weeks it was the top priority for the local sheriff and his deputies. They questioned everyone even remotely connected to the event and the boys.

Their investigation was hampered by the boys' refusal to talk about it except for one: the big boy who'd been the leader. He said they were innocently taking a shortcut (from where to where he would not say) when they were attacked by a red-skinned naked demon.

He didn't say that the demon had come out of a girl. Out of Alice. He gave no reason for the attack.

One of the dozens of people the sheriff and his deputies interviewed was Alice.

<>

Two deputies showed up at the Willoughby household one afternoon just before dinner. The family congregated in the living room and offered straight-backed chairs to the two men while they sat on the couch and two easy chairs.

Dave spoke as the lead deputy settled into one chair. The junior remained standing, hands resting on his equipment belt.

"You say you have some questions about the boys who were beaten up last week?"

"About the incident, yes."

"How can we help you? What in the world makes you think we know anything about that?"

"Your daughter was involved in another incident involving some boys."

"What? What incident?" He swiveled in his seat on the couch to look at Alice who was sitting in one of the easy chairs which bookended the couch. She was sitting on the edge, big eyes wide, the picture of girly innocence.

"A boy was courting one of the high school girls when she intervened and told him she'd beat him up if he didn't leave the girl alone."

"A boy? One who was beaten up last week?"

"No. Someone else."

"Then why talk to Alice?"

"It speaks to a pattern of violence. Violence was central to the incident last week."

"Let me get this straight," said Sarah Willoughby. "You think ALICE beat up three boys?! Three boys who were bigger than her? What did she use? A battering ram? Look at her!"

All eyes turned to Alice. She blinked those big eyes, looked back at the lookers. Sitting in the chair hid her height but not her slender body and girlish face and figure.

"Well..." said the senior deputy.

Behind him the junior deputy shifted his feet. He remembered six years before being confronted by an even less dangerous-looking girl. One whose eyes glowed red.

He suddenly KNEW she was the one who'd done the boys. But he said nothing. A girl turning into a red demon? A girl beating up three healthy boys? He'd be laughed at, maybe even lose his job.

The Alice monster shifted her gaze to his face. Nothing threatening showed on her gloriously beautiful face but the deputy suddenly remembered his idle often-returning idea of moving to Austin and getting a job on their police force.

"Well..." said the senior deputy again. He stood up.

"I know it seems silly. But the boss is checking even the slightest leads. Sorry for wasting your time, folks."

He smiled at Sarah. "My, that dinner smells good, Mrs. Willoughby. I'm sorry to say that Joel and I will probably have to be contented with Burger Barn burgers."

"Why, you're welcome to join us, Mr. Holland. Always room at our table for appreciative members of the police."

"No, no. Thanks much, Ma'am. Have a good day."

He touched the brim of his Stetson and walked away, his junior following him. Davey escorted them out and closed and unusually locked the door behind them.

By the time he returned from this chore Sarah had shooed her kids into the kitchen, followed by Helen who often ate dinner with them.

As everyone was seated fourteen-year-old John (who had recently inexplicably declared he was to be called John-John) spoke.

"I'll bet she did it."

"John!" said his mother.

Seventeen-year-old Leonard looked at him scornfully, said, "Dumbass."

"Well I do."

Davey said, "John-John, Leonard, that's enough. Talk about this is hereafter off limits. Mother, how was your day at the library?"

<>

After dinner the boys retired to their room to do homework. Alice, whose hearing was acute, heard a snatch of conversation as she freshened up in the bathroom.

John: "I still think she did it."

Leonard: "I do too. But you're a dumbass for saying it out loud where the parents can hear it. They don't need to know about her like we do."

"Oh. You're right. Sorry."

"You'll learn, Squirt."

That assumed superiority was silly, Alice thought. "Squirt" suggested a smaller boy, but John was bigger than Leonard.

<>

Alice walked Helen home as usual that night. Well out of earshot of anyone Alice's grandmother said, "Do you know anything about what happened to those boys?"

Alice smiled. "I'm pretty sure you know the answer to that."

"I put it together as soon as the deputy said you'd had a clash with a boy over a girl."

"The boy must have told others about it. So some of them decided to teach me a lesson. I taught them one instead."

"But three against one... I always imagined you were dangerous. But still..."

"Grammaw, you must get over this idea that what you see reflects the truth. Right now I could fight an army and win. Without using any weapons than my bare body. And if I decided to use modern weapons-- Well I wouldn't do it all myself. I'd recruit an army of my own and supply them with weapons and leadership. I've done that before, several times. I'm a historical figure several times over."

"Oh? Which ones?"

At that point they turned into the sidewalk leading to Helen's house. Alice went with her into the house and they talked long into the night.

<>

At school that week some students walked a little wide of Alice, especially the boys. None had a hint that she had anything to do with the attack on the boys in the industrial park by some kook pretending to be a demon. But the story of her confrontation with Phillida's stalker had leaked beyond the small circle of his acquaintances.

The cheerleaders on the other hand quite approved of a girl who would stand up to harassers. At the first break of the cheerleader practice at which Alice worked they clustered around her, asking questions. She fended off the questions and downplayed her role but did not deny it.

Midweek she was approached by Joey, the boy who'd run away when confronted by a red demonlike being.

"Could we talk?"

She stopped on the sidewalk separating the school from the gym. "Sure."

"I wanted to say how sorry I am that I went along with that idiot Raymond. He's not even a student here, just a hanger on who tries to meet girls."

"OK."

"It was really dumb. You made me realize how much I wanted to be liked by the cool guys. So much I forgot being...being...decent to girls."

"OK."

"You ever need anything I can do for you, or get for you, you just let me know."

"I'll do that. See you around."

"See you around."

Hearing about Joey's contact with Alice the two other boys with Raymond and who'd gotten beaten came up to her in the next two days. They separately thanked her for not killing them and made a similar offer of help whenever she wanted it.

From then on when any of the three passed Alice at school they nodded to her stiffly and she nodded back. By the next week their nods were almost proud. Almost friendly. As if she and they were part of a shared endeavor.

Alice had seen this change before in her more than four hundred years of life. Beaten enemies most often hated the winners but sometimes, when they were allowed some honor after losing, the losers came to magnify the power and virtue of the enemy. It reflected back on them, that only a very great force could have defeated them.

This interaction was noticed. The information got around that Alice had had SOMETHING to do with the boy's getting beat up. For a while there was speculation about what, but soon the story grew stale and gossip about something else drew student attention.

Alice was often at the school the rest of spring before graduation on May 1st. She worked at the library as before but did other jobs. A few teachers, discovering her educational precocity, got her to help them. She was especially good at grading multiple choice tests. Three teachers used her regularly for this simple clerical task.

She also visited the high school gym when the girl's basketball team practiced. Using a tactic which often worked she did a small favor, such as returning a basketball accidentally rolling her way, then much later another. Then another, gradually ramping up the frequency of thc favors. Soon she was a regular fixture, informal unpaid assistant to the coach.

Occasionally she gave advice to the girls. Even though she'd never played basketball or studied it her centuries of experience gave her insights into the mechanics of human bodies and actions.

This irritated one of the girls, a tall blond from an upscale family. One day she objected to Alice.

"You don't play basketball. You don't even go to school here. You don't know anything."

Alice was amused. Her mischievous side rose in response.

"I know enough to do this," she said and walked to a nearby rack of basketballs with three balls still in it. She took up each of them and one at a time lofted them backwards over her head. Each throw was done with an idle casual motion. Yet though the basket was nearly half a court away the balls swooshed through its center without striking the hoop.

Then she strolled out of the gym.

<>

High school graduation day arrived on May 1st that year, a hot dry Thursday. At the insistence of Alice's mother and grandmother and with the backing of Therese Alice was allowed to participate, complete with rented cap and gown.

She was called last and introduced as "our able and hard-working all-around assistant." She and the school principal did the usual arms-crossed combined handshake and awarding action. Then she walked off the stage.

The audience of pupils and parents burst into applause, mostly because the ceremony was done but also with more than a dozen yells of Yea Alice! or Finally Alice! Some of the yells were from her brothers who were always willing to be loud at the slightest excuse.

She walked to her family and was enfolded in a group hug, then to receive a handshake from her father along with a half-hug from him.

She was also joined by several cheerleaders including Patricia and Phillida. They shrieked and jumped up and down and Alice found herself doing it too.

Chapter 5 - Grownup

Now seven and looking seventeen Alice slowed her rate of maturation to arrive at the appearance of twenty in the next year. She would then appear to age at the usual rate.

S/he had started over in a new identity more than twice a dozen times. Many times s/he'd done so with property or money inherited from an "ancestor." But many other times s/he'd started with nothing.

Sometimes s/he acquired wealth quickly; there were always bandits or crooks with something of which s/he could lighten them. That was not so easy in these modern times, with so much oversight of wealthy people. Too, Llano did not have many crooks or wealthy people and she didn't want to leave yet.

Till now she'd fallen into jobs pretty much by accident, a bicycle messenger at first, then into odd jobs, prompting her to start a small one-person company called Odd Jobs, Inc. The name had been false; she had not incorporated her company. It had just sounded official.

Now she gave thought to what she wanted to do with herself for the next few years.

First she took stock of her advantages.

She was beautiful and could vary her look to suit situations. This would let her be a prostitute, entertainer, or model. The last was becoming increasingly lucrative as the number of glossy full-color magazines exploded.

She could make people feel better emotionally and physically by touching them. She could also give them near-perfect health, but she reserved that act to people whom she felt deserved it and her standards were very high.

Related to that last ability she could make people well or ill. She could do this by touching them, breathing near them, or spitting on them. The spit could be liquid or jelly-like pellets. Her aim and the distance of the pellet shots were about fifty feet.

She was very tough and very strong, maybe twenty times as strong as ordinary humans. Thus she could leap thirty feet high or a hundred feet long, and drop from two or three hundred feet without harming herself.

Her senses were very acute and she could control how much. This included the ability to read emotions by observing very tiny clues on a person's face and the motions of their bodies. She could not read minds, but knowing their emotions let her guess quite well.

Four centuries of life let her understand people's emotions and thoughts very well. This let her manipulate them with ease, for their good or ill and to their advantage or to her own.

Lastly, her mind was superior to that of anyone she'd ever met and she'd met many brilliant people. Her powers were not only logical and practical, but also creative and esthetic. Her memory was perfect, but only when she wanted it to be. The rest of the time she could shed trivial memories very easily. Doing this, abstracting out the unimportant, let the important ideas emerge more quickly. S/he was responsible for many small and large inventions throughout history.

Having laid out her advantages she relaxed and let her subconscious work on the problem of what she wanted to do with her life now that she was an adult.

<>

Previously Alice had kept a low public profile because of her rapid maturing. Now she wanted to establish herself publicly as someone almost everyone knew. One way to do that was with rodeos.

Most of the performers were men, but there were several events which were women only. Some very tough and athletic women participated in those for cash prizes.

Alice did not participate in any of the women's events. It would be unfair and be bothersome to keep within ordinary human capabilities. But she could and did put on a bull-walking entertainment act.

This involved meeting an angry bull in the arena and waving a red cloth to get its attention. When it charged her she waited till it was nearly nose-to-nose then somersaulted backward and leap high. Passing just barely over its horns she landed on its back straddling its back. As it raced around the ring, she'd stand. Then she rode it wherever it went, every once in a while jumping off and then mounting it again.

To add suspense to her act she pretended occasionally to make a mistake, such as teetering on her feet while on the bull's back. Even rarely falling off.

Another "mistake" was to stumble when she tried to somersault backward, forcing her to jump and roll to the side.

The first year she performed twice during the three-hour event, each time providing a break between hours.

The second year she turned her performance into a comedic event. She landed atop the steer facing backward. Straddling it while it ran facing backward, she acted confused. Until suddenly she realized her mistake and jumped up to face forward, lifting her arms up and wide and beaming with a great big grin.

In the second performance of the event she accidentally lost a boot and had to jump aside. Then she tried unsuccessfully to put it back on as the bull chased her around the arena. Finally losing patience she jumped up and down to pull off the second boot and slam it theatrically to the ground. Then, angrily, she met the bull and this time mounted it to ride around the ring with arms outstretched in victory.

In the third year she added a risqué touch to her act.

Before she'd worn the accepted though slightly scandalous dress of all the other women performers. This was an ankle-length split skirt which was really a pair of pants disguised as a skirt.

In that year she wore pants which were men's pants adapted to a woman's figure. And she wore them tight.

There was no fourth year. She'd established herself as That Rodeo Girl, the Bullrider. That had been her intent.

Rodeo promoters as far as Dallas-Fort Worth offered her money to work for them. She refused.

<>

One area which she found especially interesting was the electrical sciences and the electrical technology derived from them which could be made to accomplish tasks.

Conduits of power to make those devices come alive were growing all throughout the country. To the few power lines which had been built from Austin and spread out from Llano when she had been born had been added dozens, like the branches of some mechanical tree which was shooting out more shoots and limbs every day.

Street lights bloomed on the corners of every block and between. Stores and cafes and homes replaced kerosene and candles with light bulbs and neon tubes. Ice boxes were replaced by refrigerators.

Calculators especially fascinated Alice and her mechanic friend Albert. They'd retired from model airplanes after wringing out all the capabilities of the devices and had not seen a lot of each other since. But they met by accident one day and renewed their friendship. Now at least once a week they had lunch together and rummaged through magazines of thin cheap paper with titles like Popular Science and Popular Mechanics.

They were especially interested one day by advertisements from a new company called Radio Technologies. One of the ads showed a "supercalculator" which could compute complex formulas in record time. It had many practical uses such as speeding up the filling out of income taxes.

Alice convinced her father to replace his mechanical calculator in the office of the company for which he worked and was a junior partner. After hours she worked with his RadioTech SuperCalc Model 3 (there was no Mod 1 or Mod 2) and quickly became an expert.

Thus it was that her Odd Jobs company was given a contract to do the taxes for the several farms and ranches and other businesses that his company serviced. Alice hired two temporary workers to fill out forms from January through April. She also made a deal with an attorney who understood the tax laws to oversee the two temps.

Albert in his spare time studied the calculator technology and became expert in all aspects of using calculators to help businesses. Alice followed his progress and also became expert. More, she understood the scientific background behind the technology. When Albert faltered when solving a problem she could usually solve it or, more often, get him back on track to finding a solution himself.

When he quit his mechanic job and started his electronics business Alice helped him, encouraged him, and loaned him money. Within a year he was able to make a profit and to expand, hiring two other workers.

Odd Jobs expanded, enough so that Alice went through the complications of making it a real corporation. Soon afterward she hired a general manager to run it while she looked for other business opportunities.

By the time she was chronologically ten she looked twenty, owned three small businesses, and owned parts of seven more. None of the process of arriving at this state was difficult for her. She'd been creating and cultivating businesses for three centuries of her four.

<>

In mid-April a buzzing noise caught Alice's attention as she was driving to pick up Albert for their usual Tuesday lunch. She was in her blue sports car, which for the brand she'd bought was really a misnomer hiding its actual make: cheap not sport.

She had the top down (and it would take patient effort to get the top back up for the rare rainy day). She parked by the side of the road and turned off the engine. The cloudless sky of early June shone down so it was fairly easy to determine where it was coming from: the air and from behind her on the main north-south Ford Street which ran through the center of Llano.

Alice got out of her car and faced south, awaiting what she was sure was coming. And minutes later it did: a bright red single-engine high-wing airplane.

It swept over her barely fifty feet up. As it neared her it waggled its wings; the pilot had seen a pretty girl ahead of him. Alice waved back at him then whirled to watch the plane recede toward the center of Llano.

Minutes late she turned left onto east-west Main street and parked head-in at a slant in front of a block of businesses. As she got out of her car she saw Albert crossing the street. As usual he had waited for her in the shade of the trees surrounding the three-story red-brick Llano Courthouse.

"Hey, did you see the airplane?" he said.

"Sure did. Passed right over me and waggled its wings at me. Did you see it?"

"Yes. It blasted by maybe fifty feet up. I ran to the street edge and watched it cross the river to North Llano. It turned left and went west on the freeway. I'll bet it-- Yeah, it's coming back."

Alice turned her face up and north but they could not see the plane. Hidden by the row of buildings near where they stood it must still be very low.

When the sound of the invisible plane receded they went into their destination: Anderson's Wings and Things restaurant. They took one of the tables on the front window side of the big room where they could look out at Main Street and the courthouse across the street.

They ordered their usual: iced tea and pizza, half pepperoni and half tomato so each could have at least one slice of each. Then they caught up on each other's week.

They hadn't gotten far when the airplane buzz returned. This time it was clearly higher in the sky but still low. The buzz increased then decreased; it had returned to their vicinity and turned east.

"What do you bet," Albert said, "that it'll land at Lightfoot's?"

The dozen blocks to the east were covered by houses. Beyond them was a farm about a mile square. It was owned by Adolf Lightfoot, an American Indian of the local tribe whose family had married into a German family, or vice versa. It was irrigated by a stream from the Llano River and by underground water from the river and supplied much of the fresh vegetables for Llano. His father had studied Anglo agriculture and Adolf had followed in his footsteps; he'd gone to an Austin college to learn the most modern farming techniques. Lightfoots (Alice sometimes called them Lightfeet) were minor movers and shakers locally.

"No bet. They've even got that space they're keeping open for some future plan that would work for a landing zone."

They finished their pizza in record time, not hurrying but not dawdling as they usually did. Then without speaking they got into her car and drove to the Lightfoot farm.

There was a fence after the last block of houses whose main purpose was to keep out animals who'd dine on the farm's plants rather than to keep out people. They drove through an open tall gate with a sign above it: LIGHTFOOT AGRICULTURAL.

A quarter mile between rows of green plants brought them near to a big two-story farmhouse. To one side of it was a green field on which sat the red high-wing airplane resting on a tricycle landing gear that tilted it back onto its tail.

On the wide porch of the house were several people sitting in rocking chairs and holding glasses of (surely) iced tea.

As they approached one person stood up. He was in his twenties and bulky and blond. It was Adolf Lightfoot Junior.

"Howdy, Junior," said Albert. "How're things?"

"So-so, Al. Howdy, 'Rider."

Alice and Albert mounted the porch. Albert shook Adolf Junior's hand and Alice gave him a kiss on his cheek. Junior hugged her briefly; Alice was friendly with Hannah Lightfoot.

She said, "How's Hannah? She should be just about done at Austin Uni."

"Graduated early this December. She's already got a job as a vet in Round Rock."

"That's...?"

"North of Austin about ten miles. She interned there last year and they liked her so much they hired her."

"That's good. And annoying. I'd looked forward for her to come back here."

He shrugged. "I think there's a boy involved, too. Come meet our guests."

With that he put a hand on her nearest elbow and guided her to meet two men who were rising from rocking chairs.

"Alice, this is Llewellyn Porter and Louis Delacroix."

Porter shook hands with her and Delacroix raised her hand and air-kissed the back. Then Junior introduced Albert, saying, "Be polite to Al, gentlemen. He can get you gasoline cheap."

Albert said, "Used to. But the person to be nice to is Alice. Her father owns part of an auto company."

Alice said, "I'm sure something could be arranged in exchange for a few flights in your plane. I'll personally pay for the gasoline and wear and tear for my time in the air."

"You?" said Porter.

Albert said, "Alice is a capable business woman who's used to paying her own way."

Porter lifted his brows at that.

Alice knew Albert was pissed at the implied doubt of his words and the insult to Alice. She casually placed a hand on his nearest arm and sent microscopic messengers into him which would calm him.

Insult bothered her not at all. The insulter would be dust several decades from now while she would be alive for centuries. And if by some chance she did get really annoyed she'd kill the insulter the way she'd swat a fly.

"I personally am more interested," she said, "in having you show me your engine and control system."

Delacroix said, "We can arrange that easily enough."

His words showed that English was not his native language even though he spoke it well. Alice spoke to him in French learned by Li Wei when he'd been liaison to the French embassy to the Chinese Imperial Court.

"Would it be more comfortable to speak in this language? If my accent is not too bad?" Her speech was likely a few decades out of date.

She had not thought that her switching languages would have such an impact. Everyone sat back in surprise or shock. She cursed herself for her automatic switching of languages.

The Frenchman was the least surprised. His reaction was that of pleasure. Speaking English might be tiring for him despite his appearance of ease at speaking a language foreign to him.

He said in French, "It would be uncomfortable to discommode those around us. Still, I thank you."

He switched to English. "I'll be happy to show you our, ah, control systems and explain them."

Porter said, "What would that do? A woman cannot possibly gain any benefit from the time you spent with her." He sounded a little pissed.

Albert's calm was flowing away. He said, "That little woman probably knows more about electricity and electronics than most professors."

"Really?"

Alice said, "That's a bit of an exaggeration. But I AM expert enough to program the autopilot of a model airplane to fly complex maneuvers a couple of years ago.

"Monsieur Delacroix, I'll take a rain check on your kind offer. I really must get back to work despite the pleasure of your company and that of Mr. Porter."

She leaned forward to stand up but Porter said, "Please, please, let me apologize for my rudeness. It's just that I have three sisters and each of them professes to be totally lost when technical matters arise."

Albert snorted as Alice sat back.

"Well, that certainly doesn't apply to Alice. She's too modest. To top it off she's expert in mathematics I have barely heard of: two kinds of calculus, whatever they are, differential equations, something called Boolean algebra, and I don't know what all."

"Al, I really don't like to discuss that."

Adolph laughed, "Yes, Lew, you did kind of put your foot in it." He put a hand on Porter's nearest shoulder, revealing to Alice that the two had a long history together. Perhaps in college?

"Alice is our local prodigy. It surprises a lot of strangers when they meet her the first time.

"Now, let's get back to what we were talking about before Al and Alice showed up. I thought it was a lucky chance. But if you haven't pissed Alice off too much, she might just fill your bill for a performer."

He turned to Alice.

"Lew and Louis do stunts for pay. They're also here to publicize their company. The airplane is a model they hope to sell.

"One of the stunts is sort of like your bull riding act. They find a girl athletic enough and willing enough to ride atop the wing and pose while they fly low over a crowd."

Porter put in quickly. "It's not dangerous. She's actually tethered to the wing in ways not obvious to people on the ground. And we practice the acts and keep the aerobatics very mild. Pretty much just a slow flyover."

"Hmm," said Alice. "It sounds like fun. Why don't we talk more about it later? I see you are about to have a lot more people to talk to."

She was looking toward the entrance to the farm. There were three cars coming, and she saw dust behind them which heralded more cars.

Delacroix had taken two cards from a pocket and now handed them to Alice and Albert.

"This phone is in a room that Adolf has been kind enough make ours for the time we are here. We'd like to call you later tonight or sometime tomorrow to discuss matters further."

"I'll be pleased to talk to you both more. Call anytime before midnight. I stay up late."

She and Albert stood, made their pleasantries, and left.

<>

Alice still lived at home. She was after all not quite eleven years old even though she looked twenty. Her parents would be upset if she left. Too, Leonard had left two years ago to attend community college in Austin. That left a big emotional hole in the family. John was seventeen and, though not doing badly in high school, still needed academic help from his brilliant sister. Happily the loss of Leonard in his life had made spending time with Alice less trying than it might have been.

Leonard's absence had a positive benefit for Alice. His vacated room made an excellent office. It had a desk, one of the new "ergonomic" office chairs, three straight back chairs for customers and other visitors, a filing cabinet, a telephone, and a bookshelf full of books and magazines and newspapers which occupied her for a couple of hours every day.

On a table adjoining her desk was an important tool. This was one of the SuperCalc Model 5s, vastly more powerful than the Model 3 on her father's desk at his office. It had a readout screen which could display 25 lines of 80 numbers, punctuation marks, and letters. It showed not only upper case letters but also lower case letters. For input the SuperCalc had an Edison electric typewriter keyboard.

<>

The two aviators called her early the next night and made an appointment to take her up in their airplane the next day, then talk to her about its engine and controls.

When Alice arrived at the Lightfoot farm at 9:00 in the morning she found that a big tent had been erected beside the airplane. She parked her car, got out, and walked into the open front of the shelter.

She found the two men at a table looking down at a big diagram of some sort. It had been unrolled and each corner was weighed down with a brick or a rock. They were wearing grey coveralls and brown boots.

They turned to look at her. Their gazes immediately went to her belt and below. She was wearing the tight woman-cut blue jeans that she'd worn while bull riding at the rodeo. She grinned at their expressions.

"This is no more extreme than those latest New York fashions for 'forward-thinking young ladies.'"

"Ah, yes," said Porter. "Very functional."

"Very attractive," said the Frenchman.

"I'm wearing this because this is what I wear when bull-riding. As Mr. Porter says, very functional. It's also what I'd wear if I agree to ride your machine."

"Your bull-riding?" said Porter. "I must have missed something."

"Oh, Adolf didn't tell you? I have an act that I put on at rodeos. I jump atop a bull and stand atop it while it runs around the arena and tries to buck me off."

Delacroix spoke to his aviation partner. "I remember Mr. Lightfoot telling us about her. You must have been distracted when he did it."

"Oh. Yeah. I just didn't connect that with her. I mean, look how delicate she is."

The Frenchman chuckled. "You mean how beautiful she is. Believe me, my sisters are every bit as lovely and you've met them. They're about as far from fragile as a, a, stone."

Porter wisely changed the subject. He motioned toward the back of the tent where a handful of folding chairs with canvas bottoms surrounded a folding table. They walked back and seated themselves.

"If agreeable, I suggest we give you a briefing about the plane and our company, then take you on a ride, then answer those technical questions you wanted to ask us."

"And then you can brief me on how someone 'rides' your plane. And maybe take me up."

"Ah, yes. Well, Louis and I met when we were at Austin

University."

Porter was taking an engineering program and Delacroix was on a business track. Both were interested in aviation and the Frenchman was a pilot with much experience flying the airplanes owned by his father.

"You're not a pilot?" said Alice.

"Not then but I am now, an adequate one. But Louis not only has the experience he has the talent for it. I might even call him a natural."

As their last year in school progressed they began to think about starting their own company. Like Delacroix's father in France they would buy and sell airplanes and provide servicing for them. They had a fledgling business in Austin.

Their business was making a profit but a modest one. Then they'd gotten the idea of creating an airplane which corrected the deficiencies they saw in the available planes. To spur interest in the model and in their company they hit upon the idea of touring with it and doing the usual acts of other barnstorming pilots.

They'd planned a roughly square route, starting by going north from Austin, then west, south, east, and back to home base. They'd already gone to Round Rock north of Austin and Georgetown a little further north. From there it was natural to go west toward Llano, following the Texas 29 highway and stopping in Burnet halfway to their present location.

"Another reason for going west is because I knew Adolf from AU. He was a senior when I was a sophomore."

"So that's your company. What's so special about the airplane you are flying in?"

In Ireland, where aviation had gotten its start, and in the UK and Europe the plane would not be special. The aviation industry was well developed there with bigger and more sophisticated planes than in the US. But shipping them or the parts to assemble them in the US was still too expensive. Important patents were also expensive. So the US was growing its own industry on the expectation of a big market due to the greater distance between cities in the sprawling nation.

Delacroix said, "This plane is big enough to carry six passengers or a thousand pounds of cargo for 400 miles. That's almost halfway across Texas. It uses automobile gasoline so it can get refueled almost any place with a gas station."

"How high can it fly?"

"It can go up to 5000 feet, close to a mile. Actually it could go twice that height, but it gets hard to breath above a mile. And it's about 20 degrees cooler."

"We've plans," said Porter, "to pressurize and warm our next model. It would have about twice as much fuel capacity and range. But we've got to make this model a success first."

Alice said, "OK. Let's go look at your plane and go up."

Outside the few clouds of the morning had vanished so the day had heated up and sun was bright. Alice barely noticed the change but the two men blinked and opened their coverall fronts a bit wider.

The men walked her around their plane, the Hawk 3, pointing out features. Alice asked about the Hawk 1 and 2.

"The very first one," said Porter, "was a plywood and cloth mockup. Cheap but good for visualizing what was on paper. Number two was flyable but it was made from the cheapest materials and parts we could safely get away with. That included cardboard and heavy cloth and a small automobile engine."

"This one doesn't look cheap at all." She placed a hand on the side of the vehicle. It had the utterly smooth and chill feel of metallic graphene, so-called Miracle Metal.

"Oh, no, it's more expensive than commercial models will be. They won't be of any less quality but the ability to make a batch at a time will bring the price down by at least half. This is our showpiece. Its purpose is to sell itself and our company."

"This is graphene."

"Yes. We contracted with a company that bought the rights to make customized products made out of it. The commercial models will also be made of graphene. And with the same aluminum frame and steel for some parts such as the engine."

Delacroix said, "We designed Hawks to be easy to come apart as well as put together. This lets us replace the engine, as an example, much more easily with an improved version, or a special purpose version. What we designed is not a single airplane but a line of planes. One version might be a passenger plane, another a cargo plane, another for fire fighting or police work or...or whatever a customer wants."

"Very clever. I'm impressed."

"The modularity was Lew's idea."

Porter said, "I thought of it just from an engineering standpoint to make manufacturing more efficient. It was Louis who saw the larger picture, the business picture."

He opened the door in the side of the plane and pulled down a short ladder from inside the vehicle. Putting a hand on the side of the plane he took the three steps up into the plane, then turned around and gestured Alice to come inside.

"Watch your head, and bend over a bit when you get inside."

She saw why inside. The ceiling of the plane was only a little over five feet though the height increased as he led her to the cockpit.

He sat down in one seat and motioned Alice to sit in what she took to be the co-pilot's seat. She looked at the control panel in front of the two seats. There was a common middle panel and two identical panels on each side of it. There were numerous buttons, flip switches, and rotating knobs.

"Looks complicated."

"It is but it's not as bad as it looks at first glance. The controls are grouped together for common functions. These here are all related to fuel controls, for instance."

He gestured at a square containing perhaps a dozen controls.

Behind Porter Louis Delacroix sat in a passenger's seat and pulled a seat belt over his shoulder and clicked it locked closed. Llewellen did the same, telling Alice to imitate him.

He did some mysterious things on his control panel. The engine coughed and came awake. The propeller on the nose of the plane began to turn over, first slowly then faster till it became a blur.

Porter pumped the two foot pedals. Alice felt their matching pair beneath her boots mirror his actions.

"What I'm doing--," he said, raising his voice over the muffled noise of the engine, "--is flexing the various control surfaces to make sure they are moving easily."

He pulled back on a handle.

"Brakes off!"

What he meant became obvious as the plane, no longer locked in place, slowly began to roll forward.

He turned the yoke before him, like a steering wheel with the top cut off, to the left. The airplane turned left and he steered it to a spot on the meadow beside the house. Through the window in front of her, then the window on her right as the plane passed the house, Alice saw an older woman, whom she knew was Adolf's mother, come out onto the porch to watch the plane.

Alice waved at her and the woman waved back. Alice had a

sudden memory of taking gingerbread cookies from a tray offered by her.

(Hester, that was the woman's name. It had been three years since Alice and some more of Hannah's friends had visited this house. The event had been a goodbye party for Hannah.)

The plane picked up speed. The grass of the meadow began to flow backward. Ahead was a rougher patch of green coming toward them: the end of the meadow.

Faster still they rolled. The view tilted up as the plane's tail left the ground. The plane's body was level now.

Then the hissing rumbling sound of the wheels went silent. They were airborne.

Porter kept the plane level for a few minutes, then pulled gently back on the yoke. Alice's yoke mirrored the movement.

The plane--Hawk 3--tilted back and lifted into the sky.

Alice's insides seemed to lift with the plane. She was flying!

The mostly green land fell way below them. Alice could see off to the right the winding Llano River as it wove its way eastward toward Austin. Beside it were the straight lines of Highway 29 and beside it the railroad tracks.

The ground fell further below. She began to notice various houses and gardens and orchards and a line of trees tracing a tiny invisible stream away from the river.

The engine sound had become a distant drone.

"How long to get to Austin?"

Porter said, "About 45 minutes at this speed. It's only about seventy miles."

ONLY 70 miles! Walking that was 24 hours, riding 18.

Suddenly, after four centuries of life, the world shrank in her mind's eye.

The aircraft turned right to go north across the river. It bounced a bit as they crossed.

Behind Alice Delacroix said, "The air is cooler above the river. That causes a slight downdraft and a bounce."

She'd almost forgotten his presence behind the pilot's seat. She turned her head toward him and gave him a smile and a nod before turning back to the sights.

The plane continued turning till it had made a left turn. They were now going west. Ahead on the ground, small in the distance, was North

Llano, the part north of the river.

Rising still, Alice saw up ahead the flat bottom of a low cloud, white and puffy.

They entered it. Suddenly all around was grey fog.

Delacroix said, "It's easy to get lost in clouds. Even lose which way is up and down."

Suddenly the bright world was back.

Porter said, "That's why we avoid them. I always take people into one but at a glancing angle. Even Louis and I can lose orientation."

Alice wouldn't, but then she had extrahuman senses.

The plane was lowering now, the land coming up. North Llano and buildings on both sides of Highway 29 passed under them. Alice caught sight briefly of Hemming's Famous Steak House, a name which it deserved. It was known as far away as Austin.

They crossed the river again in a U-turn which brought them about 200 feet over the court house half hidden in its surrounding trees.

Passing slowly over a dozen blocks of houses brought them back in sight of the Lightfoot property. The land rose up before them. The smooth green of meadow came up, and up. The plane struck ground, bounced up, struck again, stayed down.

The engine roared and the seat belt across her chest was suddenly very tight. The plane was decelerating rapidly with the aid of a propeller which somehow was pushing a wind before it.

Then it was idling over the ground. Its tail dropped down and the plane was tilted back on all three wheels. It turned and came to a stop beside the tent which they'd left a half hour before.

Behind her Louis Delacroix said, "You said you wanted to know about the instruments and controls for Hawk. Still feel that way?"

"More than ever."

"The best place to start is right where you are now. But first let's stretch our legs and get some water."

"OK."

He unbuckled his seat belt and stood up in the aisle beside his seat. He was bent over.

"Watch your head," he said as he began a slow walk toward the back of the plane, holding onto the backs of seats to keep his balance.

Alice reluctantly unbuckled her seat belt and stood up into the aisle. She didn't want to leave the seat which had let her see wonders.

Fifteen minutes later the two men and Alice returned to their previous seats. As he left the plane Porter had opened the windows on each side of the plane, including those of the cockpit. There was just enough of a breeze to air out the insides of the vehicle though it was still warmer inside than outside.

Porter returned to the pilot's seat.

"There are six important instruments. As you can see--" He gestured toward the instrument panel in front of them. "--they are duplicated in front of your seat."

Alice examined the panel in front of her. Each of the instruments had round clock-like faces about twice the size of the face on the clock on the lamp table beside her bed. They were arranged in two rows of three. Porter pointed at the one on the top right.

"That is the most important. It is the altimeter. Helps keep you from getting too close to the ground."

"That's a danger?"

"More than you'd think even for very experienced pilots. All our instincts are based on ground-level life."

He pointed to the middle clock-like instrument. It was two or three inches deep, like a cup embedded in the panel. The "bottom" of the cup had a colored backdrop. The top half was blue, the bottom half brown. A white flat square of cardboad separated the two and went back into the hollow. It had a pivot in its center.

Porter held up his hand, palm down.

"That is the attitude indicator. The white part tilts up or down to show if the plane's nose is tilted up or down."

He waggled his hand to copy the action of the white piece of cardboard as the plane tilted up or down.

"This is the air speed indicator." He pointed to the top left instrument. There were white tick marks on its black background except near the top. Numbers marked off every tenth mark. They ran clockwise from 10 to 100. A white needle pointing straight up would rotate to indicate how fast the plane was moving through the air.

"Those are the speeds we can go?"

"Our top speed is 90 miles an hour. But we avoid anything over 80. The plane begins to shake above it."

"Still, that puts Austin only an hour away. The train takes three hours. A horse would take all day."

She thought a bit and Porter let her take her time, watching her face.

"My world just shrank. If you get your business up and running and sell more Hawks you are going to become very popular."

Delacroix put in, "TRANSPORTATION COMPANIES are going to be very popular. WE hope to be very rich."

Alice laughed and asked about the bottom three instruments. Porter obliged, describing their actions. One showed how fast they were rising or falling, the compass direction they were heading, and how much they were tilting to the left or right.

"And that's it. We plan to add some more instruments such as this fuel gauge in this middle space, such as a clock. But that's for the future."

Delacroix said, "Let's go outside. It's getting too warm in here."

Alice agreed and they left to go up onto the porch. Porter motioned the other two to seats and went into the house to come out several minutes later with a tray with a pitcher of iced tea, three glasses, a sugar bowl, and three long-handled tea spoons. He placed it on a small table and poured and prepared a glass of tea for himself.

Delacroix spoke to Porter as he and Alice got glasses for themselves.

"Alice said that she wants to go up again. This time standing atop Betsy tethered in place."

Porter eyed her but said nothing. Alice stood up and stepped up to the sturdy railing that kept people from falling off the three foot high porch. She put her hands atop it and boosted herself up to stand on the four-inch wide railing.

She faced along the railing which bordered the entire front of the house. She bent far forward and leaped to send her into a somersault. Midair and upside down she twisted catlike so that she landed on her feet facing the opposite direction.

Then she walked a little ways along the narrow top of the railing, arms wide and bowing to the left and right as if to a larger audience than the two men.

She stopped, bent over backward, her upper torso curving inhumanly, and leaped. Once again she somersaulted and somehow twisted to face back the way she'd come.

Then she stepped off to land lightly on the porch and resume her seat.

"That's just a taste of my bull-riding act."

"*Mon Dieu*, I didn't know the human body could twist that way!"

Porter said, "I am very impressed. But nothing like that will be required of you. You will need only to hold your arms wide and bow and wave."

Alice held her opinion to herself for now, but she had decided to eventually arrange to suspend herself below the plane so that she could be more visible than above the wing. And do trapeze acts such as she'd seen in her previous life in China.

They finished their iced tea and rose to go to the tent for a ladder and then to the plane. There Porter and she climbed atop the wing and Delacroix handed up ropes and metal clamps.

There she found two devices bolted to the front of the wing. They were places to insert her boots. Ring bolts in the wing let her be tethered by woven plastique ropes, very compact but also very strong, connected to a wide leather belt around her waist.

The first time she was tied in place the ropes were too restrictive. She had little ability to bow to the audience. She got Porter to give her another couple of inches of slack but he would not OK more.

She practiced holding her arms wide and turning to left and right and bowing.

"OK. I'm ready. Let's get this show on the road."

"Here. Put these on." Porter pulled out of his capacious coverall pockets two items. One was a pair of goggles, the other a leather cap with a chin strap. Alice donned the cap and fastened the chin strap, then put on the goggles and adjusted the strap behind her head.

"Good. Now the first time we're just going to taxi around the landing field, stop, and check to make sure you're OK. Then we're going to taxi along the field almost as fast as if we're going to take off. Then check AGAIN. We want you to be perfectly comfortable up here."

He paused to make sure she understood. She smiled at him.

"Got it!"

He smiled back and retreated down the ladder.

Alice checked the belt holding her in place. If she wanted to she could easily unbuckle it. Not that she was imprisoned even if unbuckling was not easy. With her great strength she could rip it off. Or grow her nails into talons and slice it off.

For the next half hour they put into practice the checks that the aviator had described. Both times she answered his queries with a loud "I'm fine!"

Then Porter climbed the ladder and checked her tethers again and retreated to stand near the tent where he could observe her as the plane flew overhead. He had in one hand a flare gun which he could use to signal the pilot, Delacroix, to cut the test short and land.

Alice had endured the tests with the patience of the long-lived. But now as the plane picked up speed toward liftoff she abandoned her stoicism. She was going to fly!

The not-so-distance edge of the grassy meadow approached faster and faster. Then the rumbling of the aircraft wheels on the meadow ceased. They were airborn!

"Yee hah!" But not loudly. The pilot Delacroix was just below her. She did NOT want her experience to be aborted.

As on her first flight the ground fell away before her. But not far. The plane turned and came back for a pass over the meadow and the house and tent beside the meadow.

The plane lowered to about fifty feet and slowed to about a running pace. Alice raised her arms up and wide and, as she neared the spot below where Porter stood, bowed with a wide gesture as if to remove a Stetson in respect to him or a crowd.

She could see his white teeth as he grinned wide and gave her a soldier's salute.

The plane flashed past him and made a U-turn to come in for a landing.

When it stopped near the house and the men's work tent Porter came running with a ladder to swarm up it and speak to her.

"How was it?"

"Wonderful. Let's do it again. And do it less cautiously."

"OK. But come down. Louis is anxious to hear what you have to say with his own ears."

Alice undid the wide belt and let it fall to the top of airplane's wing, then walked to where Porter was retreating down it. Impatient, she stepped to edge of the wing and dropped off, plopping down to the grass beside the ladder. Delacroix, steadying the ladder for his friend, jerked and stared.

As Porter stepped off the lowest rung Alice spoken to the both of them as she stood upright from the deep squat she'd assumed upon landing--a squat she'd not needed to absorb the jolt from landing.

"Now don't fuss at me. It's about time you two learned that I'm a lot tougher than most people."

Then she led the way to the house to the iced tea that Hester had waiting for the three of them.

As she approached Adolph's and Hannah's mother smilingly spoke to her.

"I see you've started educating the boys how special you are."

"Yes, Mrs. Lightfoot. It will take a while. They've been trained to be overprotective. I swear sometimes I think they're worse than the outright assholes who treat us women like shit."

"Amen to that, little girl."

Alice looked down at the small woman whom she knew would always think Alice was still a "little girl" and smiled anew.

<>

Friday was the first day of the Llano County Fair and Livestock Show which would go on through sundown Sunday. It took place as it had for several years about a mile west of the county courthouse in the center of South Llano. The site was a quarter-mile square of flat grass land with a few randomly placed oak trees. To the north a couple of hundred feet was the eastward flowing Llano River.

The night before Alice ate dinner with her family, which her mother said was "about time"! The immortal had had dinner with the Lightfoots the previous two nights to have more time to talk to the aviators.

Afterwards Alice helped her mother and grandmother clear the table and wash, dry, and put away the dishes and utensils. Then the women joined the men in rocking chairs on the screened-in back porch. A full moon had risen earlier and illuminated the pecans-and-apples orchard.

Alice had talked about the aviators at the table but let the others also talk about their day and about local events. One of which was especially interesting: Leonard would graduate from Austin University in two weeks and return to Llano to take up a job as power-line engineer.

This was partly a repair person's job which might include climbing power-line poles to fix mechanical problems. But the position included the more responsible job of trouble-shooting both point problems and area problems such as balancing power demands in the county. Even more important, he would advise his bosses about how to plan future expansions of lines and networks. It was a responsible position that edged into and could lead to leadership positions.

Davey said, "Boy's got a head on his shoulders. He'll do good."

Sarah said, "He said he might bring that Brinkley girl he's written about to meet us. I've got a feeling they might be more serious than he lets on. There might just be a June wedding in the near future."

John said, "Mom! You're always looking for us to get married! Get off it! Do you see me and Alice mooning over somebody?"

Alice put a hand over her chest and said, as all eyes turned toward her, "Oh, but those two aviators are so dreamy! Lew has those blue eyes! Louis has that Latin romantic manner! I could just eat them up!"

John swatted her nearest shoulder.

"Hah! Pumping their brains is more your style than, ahh..." He got tangled up getting into words with risqué double-entendres and blushed.

Helen was eyeing Alice. "You are getting pretty tight with those boys. Is more going than you've told us?"

Alice shifted in her seat. Best to get the announcements over with that she'd dreaded bringing up.

"I think there are real expansion prospects for their business. I've decided to negotiate buying ten percent of the business in exchange for working on future designs of larger aircraft. And I'm going to ride their airplane Saturday."

There was an explosion of comments at that from everyone but Helen. Alice had to take a half hour to tell them all about the safety aspects of "riding" an airplane and convince them that it was as safe as riding a bull. And that she was going to do it no matter how much they objected.

As usual Alice walked Helen home. The light of the almost-overhead moon made the sidewalk and occasional trees over them bright to Alice's extranatural eyes. A little too bright; she reduced her eyes sensitivity enough till thc scene took on the eldritch appeal of deep twilight.

The two were silent for a few minutes; Alice knew Helen had something on her mind.

"Very clever of you," she finally said, "to put the wing-riding remark after your intent to work on future designs."

Alice sighed. "Yes. I'd have to move to Austin to do that."

Helen did not have to tell the immortal how sad that would make Alice's parents. And Helen.

After a suitable time Alice said, "Have you ever been to Austin?"

"When my husband and I were young. The thing I most remember was how much water there is this far from the ocean. The Colorado River feeds the area and they've built several dams to create lakes.

"Do you like to swim?"

Alice said, "I do. I have an underwater form that lets me stay under for as long as I want."

"You never mentioned this before. You weren't keeping it secret, were you?"

"No. It just never came up."

"Hmm. And it came up just ACCIDENTALLY when you wanted to distract me from the fact that we're going to lose you."

Alice laughed as they turned onto the sidewalk up to Helen's house.

"So, what do you look like when you assume your 'underwater form'?"

"Scary as Hell if you're not me." She went on to explain as they entered Helen's house.

<>

On Friday, the day before the fair fully opened, the aviators moved their plane to the fair and parked it in a centrally located spot, then set up to give people a tour of the insides of the plane and answer questions. While one was doing that the other stood outside it to likewise answer questions. Alice came by midmorning and relieved each of them for an hour. She was as capable as they to answer most questions. Then at noon all three quit for a couple of hours to eat and rest.

Saturday the aviators started up the engine after lunch. Then with an escort of half a dozen sheriffs' deputies shooing people out of the way they drove the airplane to the takeoff point of a flat area which acted as a makeshift runway. Stopping, they placed a ladder on the side of the plane to let Alice and one of the men mount the top of the wing and tether her in place.

Satisfied in the security of her position, Alice donned a spare aviator's cap and the goggles to protect her eyes. Then as her helper climbed to the ground she loosened the cap enough to let her pull her long curly red hair out of its bottom. She wanted to be sure the people on the ground could see that it was a woman atop the plane.

The plane started up, began its roll, and sped up to lift off and tilt back to gain height. Then it turned to fly low over the fairgrounds. That came up quickly and the plane zoomed over it. Alice began waving and bowing to the crowd below. She saw people come alert as the plane approached and then to sight her. Some waved. Some children tried to chase after the plane as it disappeared in the distance.

The plane made a U-turn out over the Llano river and made a second pass, this time over a different part of the fair.

This time Delacroix's speed was slower, so much so that mid-pass Alice felt it edging very close to stalling. This would cause it to crash, not having the height needed to go into a dive to recover the velocity needed for the wings to regain lift. That would kill or injure dozens of people.

The immortal felt a flash of panic, something which s/he had not felt for at least a century. It was not for her sake; her tough body might not even feel stings from a fall from this height. For the people, including children. Many of whom she'd seen or met.

Then her shapechanger body wiped away the distress. AND Alice felt that Delacroix was guiding the plane at just a sliver of speed away from a stall. And continuing to do so through the entirety of the flight. He really was the natural pilot that Porter had said.

Still, she was happy that two passes were all that the aviators had planned. Minutes later Hawk 3 landed and taxied back to the edge of the fair. Where it was met by rapidly arriving crowds.

Impatient to be on the ground Alice unbuckled from the plane, walked to the edge of the plane, and stepped off. She had just stood up from a slight crouch when the plane door opened and Porter let down the short ladder for the people inside to deplane and emplane.

He looked out the door and said, "What are you doing? You could have broken a leg!"

She waited for him to step onto the ground then said, "Not me. I'm tougher than you can imagine."

"Maybe so, but if you turned your ankle you could tear the tendons in it."

"Lew, I can drop from heights several times this--" She waved at the top of the plane. "--and not be hurt. I've been able to do it since I was an infant. To repeat, I am a freak. I'm incredibly tough."

Louis, deplaning at this point, said, "Who's incredibly tough?"

"She says she is. I think she's delusional."

Delacroix looked at her blandly. "So she jumped off the plane? Is that what you're concerned about?"

"Yeah."

"You saw how she got on and off that railing at Adolph's and what she did on top of it. Her body isn't that of an ordinary human. We at least owe it to her to keep an open mind about what she claims. She does not seem the kind to make claims she cannot back up. Now, put a smile on your face. We've got company."

Delacroix set an example by turning to the oncoming fairgoers and smilingly begin to answer questions.

A lot of them were addressed to Alice. In three years as a performer at several rodeos as far away as Austin she'd become well-known and liked. It wasn't unusual for passing strangers on the street to greet her with "Hey, Bullrider!" or "Hey, 'Rider!"

That fact was brought up that night at the Willoughby dinner. The two aviators had been invited to eat dinner and Alice encouraged them to come. She'd been feeling a little guilty about eating dinner two nights in a row at Hester's table. The least she could do was have the men over to the Willoughby's.

"At first," Sarah said, "I was so worried that she'd get hurt, riding those horrible bulls. But I shouldn't have. She's too smart, and too athletic, to get hurt at anything."

"I'll say," said John. "I'll never forget the first time I realized that. It happened when she was only three--"

"John, we don't talk about that," said Alice.

"That sound you hear--" he said, looking at her very directly. "--is me not caring. And me shifting my legs so you can't kick them under the table. If you're going to keep working with these guys they need to know what you're really like."

He turned back to the two men, who were suspended by the interplay with forks or spoons on the way to their mouths.

"At three she looked seven or eight, tall as me. Lenny and me and our friends and Miss Tagalong here were at a swimming hole. Five big boys showed up and told us to get lost. Naturally I stood up to them and told them to get lost."

Alice said, "No one has ever claimed that John was smart."

"That sound is me nobly ignoring comments from the peanut gallery. Anyway, the biggest boy pushed me and I fell down. I was going to get up and smack him in the, ahh, belly, when something smacked down between me and, Junior, that was his name. What kind of name is that?

"It was Alice. She'd dropped thirty, forty feet, out of the tree. She was about to dive in the water. Wham! Then she stood straight, not hurt at all. She got right up in his face. Not saying a thing. Just looked at him nose to nose. He nearly sh-- He nearly fainted and all three of them walked away. Looking back. Scared sh-- really scared.

"I'll say it just this one time, Gents. Don't ever seriously cross my little sister."

With that John forked up a square of steak he'd been cut earlier and began to eat it.

<>

Sunday the aviators and Alice twice did a back-and-back-over pass in the airplane, once mid-morning and once mid-afternoon. Then after the crowds around them dispersed in the afternoon they packed up a few properties in the plane and flew back to the Lightfoot farm.

The men went into the house to freshen up and change clothes. Alice went into the kitchen to chat with Hester as Adolph's mother poured a pitcher full of iced tea and arranged a tray with glasses and sugar and teaspoons.

"You must be happy that Hannah has finished school and gotten a job."

"I am. Just not happy that it takes three hours to visit her in Round Rock. Or her to visit us."

"If the boys have their way some day it will be a half hour ride to Austin."

"Don't you believe it. The ride will be just part of the trip. First you have to get to the airport and buy a ticket and wait for luggage people to load the plane. When you get where you are going you will have to get your luggage then get a taxi or bus to get where you're going."

Alice acknowledged the wisdom of the comment as she escorted Hester with her tray to the porch. Hester was a smart woman. She had managed the complex business of the farm before Adolf had grown enough in years and knowledge to take over. She still was crucial to the success of the business.

She had retired into the house when the two men came out onto the porch, sat, and took up and flavored their drinks.

"Well," said Alice. "Are you satisfied with your trip so far?"

"Pretty much," said Delacroix. "We've made useful contacts,

spread lots of information about the plane and our company. You and your riding added a lot of publicity to the effort. We didn't realize how famous you are."

"I did my act in several rodeos all the way north and south of here as well as here. And they were fairly successful, in part because I'm a woman."

"And because you are very attractive," said the Frenchman. It was not an attempt to curry favor as part of an attempt to get her into bed. She had earlier inoculated the two men with submicroscopic messengers that made her unattractive to them. It was a simple statement of fact.

She nodded and went on.

"I have a proposition for you. I will continue on your trip doing my act until you return to Austin."

Delacroix, the business brain of the two, said cautiously, "An attractive proposal. What payment would you expect?"

"I want to be part of your company. I will pay you for ten percent of your company. In exchange I expect to be part of your technical planning staff."

Porter said, "I remember your friend Albert claimed you were a prodigy at math and science. But I put that down to friendship. My past has not prepared me to think highly of women's brains. Pardon me, but I'd be remiss not to acknowledge that."

Delacroix said, "I on the other hand have been prepared. I personally have met Madame Curie. My father hosted her and her husband when she received the Nobel Prize. Twice. Then there are my sisters."

Porter grinned at him. "Yes. They were a revelation to me. I'm not sure I'll ever live down the way they oh-so-politely listened to me boast about what I was going to do with my engineering degree."

Delacroix grinned back. "And I remember how YOUR sisters acted so charmingly helpless to understand the simplest explanation I made of how an airplane flies."

Alice sensed beneath the jocularity of the two men an edge. Someday she wanted to meet the two men's sisters. They sounded intriguing.

Porter returned his attention to Alice.

"I'm the engineering brains of the company. Louis is the business brains. What you suggest is OK with me, as long as you remember that

I'm the boss engineer. I'll listen to your suggestions but my judgment is final. No hurt feelings or...whatever if I reject them. Also, I want you to be on probation for six months. I can kick you off the team after that, no reason given."

"Reasonable." Alice turned her attention to Delacroix and they began to discuss money.

It was an old dance to the immortal and she had the advantage that no poker face was opaque to her. In the end she drove what she considered a reasonable bargain and one not too bad from the Frenchman's viewpoint.

She finished her iced tea and set her glass back on its tray.

"So. What happens now?"

Porter said, "We wind things up here, get ready to fly to Fredericksburg in the morning where we have a place where we can land, park, and refuel the plane. We also have hotel rooms reserved. If you can't get a room at that hotel Louis and I can share a room and you can have one of ours. You'll drive there? Your car is in good enough shape to travel? If not, we can take you aboard the plane."

"No, I make sure it's in tip-top shape mechanically. As for rooms, that's no problem. After my first year of performing I know plenty of people who will put me up for free."

At that Delacroix told her the cities they planned to visit to the south and then east. Alice knew them all and was known to people in them.

That settled they made plans to meet early in the morning to double-check all details, then leave separately for their first destination.

Alice stood up. She had lots of goodbyes to say and was unhappy about the ordeal of saying them. She and her family would miss each other very much, as would Albert.

Chapter 6 - The Big City

The next morning Alice made a farewell that was tearful all around, even for her father and brother though that showed up as eyes bright with un-spilled tears.

Packed, with her room to be made available to Leonard when he arrived with his lady friend, Alice drove to the Lightfoot farm. There were minor delays there but it was less than an hour before she watched Hawk 3 taxi over the meadow and lift into the skies. She stood on the porch with Hester and Adolf to watch it recede droning away into the distance.

Then she hugged Hester and shook hands with Adolf before she jumped off the porch, entered her car, and drove away.

She drove west and turned left onto Ford street to travel south. She took more time than usual, viewing each landmark which had been part of her world for eleven years, some with heart-touching memories such as the three-story courthouse with its conical belfry and green trees clustered around it.

Then a quarter mile later there was the church where her family went. Not far beyond was a grocery store they frequented.

The houses and small businesses became few and far between. Then they nearly disappeared. The flat landscape opened up before her.

A Stop sign almost a mile outside town marked a junction where one would turn left to drive to the east and south toward Austin.

"Soon," the immortal said to that distant city. "I'll see you soon, Austin."

Then she transferred her foot from the brake to the accelerator and drove south.

<>

The landscape was dusty green on both sides. Low trees were scattered in ones and twos and sixes into the far distances.

Many miles to the left there was a patch of the low slate-blue hills which helped give this area the name The Hill Country.

Occasionally a dusty road to the left or right marked the distant headquarters of some ranch.

Once a road had six mailboxes clustered together. Presumably nearby there were six separate houses also clustered together.

A midsize truck came toward her and passed going north. In its back was a bull. The driver glanced at her and his eyes widened at her fairy-tale beauty then disappeared behind her car.

The road rose a few feet then fell a few feet.

More trees clustered on both sides of the road.

A huge red barn on her left approached and disappeared behind her. It was surrounded by a big sandy parking lot. But no other building was near it.

The land rose more and fell more.

A few miles of highway passed while the shapechanger's ultrasensitive senses smelled a slight increase in humidity. Somewhere invisible to one side or the other there were streams or ponds of water.

A low hill or mound rose to one side, no more than a hundred or two hundred feet high.

A sign announced that she had entered Gillespie County.

A long truck carrying many bales of hay came at her and passed her by.

A dusty road crossed the roadway. No clue to what it connected to in either distance.

The road curved a bit to the right.

Another dusty cross road.

Another.

A farmhouse or ranch house low but large.

More humidity.

Low hills or mounds on each side.

The land flattened.

More humidity.

More houses.

She was nearing Fredericksburg.

Off to the right a cluster of buildings loomed. Behind it was a large ranch house. The shapechanger smelled livestock, chickens, pigs.

There was a filling station. Alice pulled in and a young man came out to fill her gas tank and take her money. He smiled shyly at her. He may never have seen such a beautiful woman, perfect in every feature, with no blemish of any kind, slender but feminine figure covered lightly by a white dress decorated with faint roses, a riot of curly red hair spilling about her bosom, slender legs encased in bootlets not boots or shoes.

She smiled back and said Thank you in a voice that he could have sworn had come from an angel.

She moved the car to a parking spot near other vehicles, a couple of dozen at least, went inside the store which featured not only canned and bottled goods but also fresh vegetables and wearables. She bought a snack just to buy something and to speak to someone. This was a young girl, no more than ten, who stared wide-eyed at the vision before her.

The girl handed Alice her change then her eyes got even wider and she said, "'Rider! You're the 'Rider!"

Alice smiled and said quietly, "Yes I am. Don't tell anyone. I'm on a secret mission."

"Of course!" Then lower: "Really?"

"No, not really. But wouldn't it be fun if it were true?"

"Yes! Definitely!"

Alice wandered into the restaurant part of the rambling structure. Cooking meat tempted her. She sat on one of the round red plastique-covered stools in front of a long chest-high counter.

The thirty-something woman who came up to her recognized her too.

"Hello, 'Rider. Can I get you something?"

"A Pepper-Upper in a glass with ice if you've got it. Then I want..." She consulted a clear plastique-covered one-page menu.

"This half-pounder steak and baked potatoes heavy with sour cream and a little loaf of bread."

"We can slice the bread and slather some butter on it."

"Ma'am, I love you like a sister. Bring it on!"

Mabel (said the name on her shirt front) grinned. "Coming right up, dearie."

Alice finished it off with a second glass of Pepper-Upper.

Her satisfaction was marred ever so slightly by a big overweight man in jeans and red-and-grey checkered shirt wearing the ever-present Stetson almost every Texan wore.

"Hey, little lady. Want some company?"

"No, thanks. Got to get on the road."

"Aw, don't be like that. I can rock your road."

The monster hidden in a girl's form eyed him.

"I've got a knife for company. You bother me a second more and I'm going to cut your belly open like a watermelon."

The words did not come out angry or any other way. Her face was perfectly still, not threatening or angry. Her blue eyes stared unblinkingly into his.

His face reddened then paled. He'd recognized his death standing before him.

"I'm sorry. I only--"

"Ezra," said the waitress who'd scooted into place behind the counter opposite the man. "This is the 'Rider. You're about to get your balls kicked off."

"No," said Alice, still in that flat dead and deadly voice. "I was going to cut his guts out."

The two stared at her for a moment, then Mabel said to Ezra, "Idiot. You should know that the 'Rider isn't any woman to mess with."

Alice said, "Or any woman. Man, if I ever hear you've mistreated a woman I will come find you and do worse than cut you. Believe me."

The last words were freighted with a magic Li Wei had learned a century ago. Ezra believed them utterly. He walked quickly away.

Mabel stared at her.

"You really would have done it."

Alice stared back.

"OK. But... Well."

Mabel made up her mind about something.

"Would you mind leaving right away? Everything is on the house. It was an honor to meet you."

The monster let her face assume its human appearance. She smiled.

"Sure. Thank you. You be safe, now."

It took another fifteen minutes to arrive in downtown Fredericksburg. It was near the same size as Llano but the buildings were subtly different in style and placement. The immortal ascribed that to the fact that the original residents were all immigrants from Germany.

She parked in front of the hotel and went in. The high-ceilinged room was a bit dim after the bright sunlight but not oppressively so. Hidden fans kept it almost cool.

At the reception desk Alice said, "My business partners should be here by now. Llewellen Porter and Louis Delacroix. They're expecting me."

"They're in the dining room, Miss. Oh, hello, 'Rider! Good to see you! Just go on in and a waiter will help you."

The two aviators were sitting opposite each other with the window onto the street beside them. As Alice approached, escorted by a waiter carrying a menu, they stood up. Louis pulled out the chair facing them and the street.

"Glad you made the trip OK," he said.

"Any problems?" said Porter.

"No. Just a boring view. Not that it bothered me. It was kind of relaxing. You get the plane and your rooms squared away?"

"We did. You?"

"Haven't contacted anyone yet. I'll do that after I eat."

"We just finished." The engineer gestured at their nearly empty plates and raised his glass. The waiter was quickly there with a pitcher of iced tea.

"You ready, 'Rider?"

Alice had noticed that a food recently introduced to the area was on the menu.

"I'm going to have this pizza with pepperoni and iced tea."

"Coming right up, 'Rider."

After the waiter left Porter said, "You really are famous."

Delacroix said, "I knew it first. I listened to Adolf when he told us about her while you were... What? Wool gathering?"

Alice interrupted what might have turned into well-practiced good-natured arguing.

"What is the schedule here?"

Before coming on their tour they had lined up a number of meetings and scheduled them to align with fairs or other events. The events usually lasted a long weekend. The one a few days hence was a livestock auction.

"We're settled in," said Porter. "You said you can get a room. How?"

"Just walk around, talk to people, listen to offers, take one."

"That easy?"

"I do have to talk to boring people."

The pizza came. Alice chowed down, enjoying it enormously. How had s/he lived four centuries without the cheesy, flavorful delight?

<>

That afternoon Alice did walk around and listen to people. But what mortals might find boring an immortal did not. With an endless future ahead s/he had learned to live in the moment, find interesting the minutiae of mortals' daily lives. Alice decided finally to take the offer of a back bedroom from on an older couple who should have retired long ago but who remained active and alert working a small farm.

The rest of the week was more of the same: walking, talking. The two men (whom she was beginning to think of as "the boys") talked too, to whom she did not bother to discover. Delacroix presumably talked to business people, Porter to mechanics and other practical people.

When the livestock show and sales event started she talked to owners, buyers, and onlookers about pigs, chickens, bovines, and equines. With centuries of experience she knew a lot about the subject but listened much more than she talked. There were plenty of men and sometimes women who enjoyed talking to the 'Rider, or to the most beautiful woman they'd ever meet who'd also listen to them with an intent air and occasional question that assured them that what they said was fascinating.

On Saturday and Sunday the 'Rider and the aviators made their over-and-back flights. Each time, a hundred or two hundred feet in the air with the wind sending her hair streaming behind her, Alice felt absolutely wonderful. She could see so far! Sense so much with a new sense that she had only learned that she had! It was how far land features were: houses, trees, streams and ponds, roads. How far and what shape were birds and the tops of poles and telephone and power wires.

<>

Monday the "boys" and she were on their way again. This time to the southwest to a town called Kerrville.

For a time Hwy 16 outside Fredericksburg curved and swerved as it avoided the Pedernales River on the left side of the road. Then the way straightened out into pretty much a straight path.

The land was brown now. Traffic in both directions was busier. There were more horses or horse-drawn carriages but also more gasoline-powered vehicles.

For a short distance the road became more twisty as it encountered another section of the Pedernales. Then the road straightened again.

After a half hour the road began to drop and rise further. On the rises Alice could see more miles ahead to the slate-blue of distant forest. She found that her new distance sense had not deserted her. Somehow it knew in feet and miles and compass orientation precisely how far objects were, such as that tree atop a low mound off to her right.

Very useful, the immortal thought sarcastically, if she wanted to direct a howitzer to blast the tree.

She paused at that thought. She HOPED she was done with war. She'd seen and directed too much of it in her long past.

A few then more houses and businesses flowed toward her. A sign off to the right heralded a winery and sure enough a big white barn sat off the road with several vehicles parked in front of it.

Then she was in Kerrville and crossing a major east-west highway.

As before she met the boys in their hotel. And as before she found guest lodging and they did their flyovers while Alice waved and bowed to people on the ground. And as before her new sense told her exactly where she could land howitzer rounds.

Kerrville had been forty minutes southward. Their next destination was New Braunfels to the east. The road started that way then trended more to the southeast.

After an hour Alice came to a junction. Travel on to the southeast would land her in San Antonio, the biggest city in Texas. Travel straight east would land her in New Braunfels. She took that road.

An hour brought her to the city. It was maybe half again the size of Llano and the previous two cities.

It also had a newspaper: the *Neu-Braunfelser Zeitung*, half in German and half in English. Delacroix in the restaurant in their hotel where they met showed Alice a copy folded open to a news story. It had a large black-and-white photo from below that nevertheless showed her atop the airplane. The photo was clear enough to show her long hair streaming out behind her and her by-now-trademark women's jeans.

Reading the copy Alice said, "When did they interview you?"

Delacroix grinned. "They didn't. It just looks as if we talked face-to-face. This is from three letters I wrote them. It's almost verbatim but they did add their own material at the end about you being the rider atop Hawk."

"Proof," said Porter, "how right I was to approve using you."

Delacroix rolled his eyes at the statement but otherwise ignored it.

"One more stop after this one. And it's a step in the right direction. Now we go north. San Marcos here we come!"

<>

Actually the way north was more to the northeast. The land was perfectly flat. It also had more trees. The road had more traffic, which Alice decided must be because the road was the direct path between Austin to the northeast and San Antonio to the southwest. More of the traffic was gasoline-powered vehicles.

San Marcos was bigger still than New Braunfels. The newspaper there had an ad for a rodeo that weekend as well as a copy of the "interview" in the New Braunfels newspaper. Thus Alice was recognized by a lot of local people though she had never gone so far to the east and south when she did her bull-rider act.

Sunday after their rodeo performances the three set off for Austin. Alice had a hand-drawn map and detailed instructions at how to get to the boys' Austin residence.

<>

The last few miles to the residence on the highway was through an area with lots of houses and small buildings. Near the Colorado River Alice left the highway and took a tree-lined side street that led east alongside the river. She could see glimpses of the river to her left through breaks in the trees but the glimpses were few and far between.

Finally she took a right into a residential street. Two blocks took her to the end of the street. There at the end were two two-story houses, white with dark tile or slate roofs. The one to the right was where the boys lived.

Alice slammed her car door, walked up a concrete sidewalk through a green shorn lawn, took three steps up onto a porch that ran all along the front of the house. A door was directly in front of the steps. There was a doorbell in the door frame. She rang it.

A muffled voice inside called out something and moments later the door opened. Inside the doorway stood a slender Black girl.

Temilade, Crown Wearer, the name the immortal had given herself to replace her namby-pamby given name, eyed the girl. She detected several ancestries, including those of two white men who had likely raped an ancestor or paid her for sex.

"Hello," said the girl. "My bosses phoned me to expect you. They are still at the hangars. Come on in."

Alice entered to find a long hall leading further into the house. The girl, who might be thirteen, led her down the hall.

"They told me to show you the place and help you get settled in. This is--" She gestured to her right where an open doorway led into a large room. "--the living room."

She continued down the hall and walked into a second open doorway on the right, then turned toward Alice.

"As you can see this is the dining room. The table seats eight. We can stretch it to twelve if we have lots of guests."

There were chairs at all eight places. On all four walls were framed prints of landscapes. Windows opposite the door showed a green lawn blocked off from the lot further on by a tall green hedge. To the left the wall had an open doorway so wide it took up half the wall. Through it Alice could see a kitchen.

"You can see the kitchen later. Let's go upstairs."

She brushed by Alice and reentered the hallway to proceed to the end where a stairway led up to the second floor.

Upstairs the there was a hallway matching the one downstairs. On each side were four closed doors.

"The right side is the masters' rooms. The furthest is Master Porter's living room and bedroom. This nearest one is Master Delacroix's. The two doors in the middle open into their offices. Here on the left side are four more bedrooms or dens."

The girl walked to the end of the hall, opened the last door on the left, and went in, turning to face Alice as the immortal entered.

"This is your living room, as you can see."

The room contained a comfortable couch against the wall on the right with a lamp table on each end. Two easy chairs sat against the lamp tables turned to make a U-shaped conversation nook. A polished wooden table was in front of the couch and chairs. Magazines lay on the table.

"In there is your bedroom. It has a bathtub and shower stall and all the usual stuff. There's also a closet."

Alice went to the door into the bedroom, opened it, and glanced in but did not go in.

"Those are all the important rooms. You can go into every room and eat and drink anything in the kitchen and pantry, but my mother cooks breakfast, lunch, and dinner and she's really good. If you want something special she can usually cook it. She's studying to be a chef. Master Delacroix is encouraging her and he's been teaching her some French dishes."

"That sounds nice of him."

"Oh, it is! They sometimes spend the evening in the kitchen. He says it's good to get his mind off work, but I think he really likes to cook."

"Why couldn't it be both?"

"Oh! Good idea. Not that her studies matter. Nobody is going to hire Mom to be a chef. Like in a real restaurant."

"Why not?"

"Because she's a nigger. Like me and Dad."

"That might be true. There are some really dumb white people in the world. But if she really loves to cook special foods she shouldn't let anyone discourage her.

"By the way, you may want to not use the word 'nigger.' Some people think it's an insult."

"Oh! I didn't know that."

Bless everyone who'd shielded her from the knowledge. How had they managed it? She was twelve or near it and in most circumstances would have been called that before now.

As the girl took her out into the hallway Alice breathed deeply the girl's scent. The biochemical laboratory inside her shapechanger body "tasted" the microscopic pieces of the girl's body given out by every breath. A minute or so and Alice knew much about her.

She was not incapable of understanding insult. Nor was she given to delusion or excessive optimism. She was just the opposite: very smart and level headed. So she just must have been very lucky to escape emotional hurt.

Alice hoped she'd be around to observe someone call this girl "nigger" with malice. She would be tempted to kill them in any one of several ways, most ways no one would suspect such as a heart attack.

Over the next half hour Alice and Hope, the girl, transferred most of the immortal's property from her car up into her new home. Along the way she learned much.

Hope's family lived in the guest house behind the main house. Her father took care of the grounds and did basic repairs. Her mother cooked for the boys and cleaned their house and laundered their clothing. Both men cleaned up after themselves to some extent so the job wasn't hard. Hope went to a black person's high school. The two men were always ready to help with homework but the girl did not need it often.

Some of the girl's talk was while she was sitting on Alice's bedside while the immortal unfolded and shook out her clothing and hung it in hangers in her closet.

Hope confessed that she sometimes pretended to have problems to get the men's attention but she knew it was wrong but only did it when she was really down about something.

"While I'm here you can call on me if you have problems with homework, especially if it's about math or science. You can also call on me about other problems, like girl problems. The men might be embarrassed or not know the answer."

"Oh, Mom has already told me about girl problems. But maybe I could get a second opinion sometimes, the way you're supposed to do if your doctor gives you advice about serious problems."

The shapechanger heard two car-door slams to one side of the house. A couple of minutes later she heard muted voices as two people came in a side door. Hope stood, said, "That must be Mom and Dad. They went to the store to get more food now that another person will be living in the house. Come meet them?"

"Sure."

Downstairs in the kitchen a tall white man was helping a stout black woman carry in groceries. They turned as their daughter came into the room trailing Alice.

"Mom. Dad. This is Alice. She's just moved in."

Alice nodded to the two adults and said, "Hello."

The man gave a little head bob to Alice, set his bags of groceries on a counter, and said to his wife. "That's my lot."

Then he walked by Alice who held out a hand to shake his. He paused long enough to say, "Pleased to meet you. Got to get other stuff out of the truck." The handshake was just long enough for Alice to read his health and inject microscopic messengers into him to fix a few minor problems.

Hope had taken a remaining sack of groceries from the table in the kitchen and was putting cans and bottles and packages of food into a walk-in pantry behind the kitchen.

"Excuse me Miss," said the black woman as she filled a bin in a big refrigerator with fruits and vegetables. Then she wiped her hands on an apron over her dark blue knee-length dress and took the hand Alice was holding out for a handshake.

Alice read her body and found and began the fix of the usual minor problems and one major problem: a cancer of her liver.

"Hope tells me you are studying to become a chef. I really like my food so I was pleased to hear that."

"Just as a hobby, Mistress."

"Hobby, work, I like it. Could I borrow her for a little bit? I need some more help getting settled in?" The woman was clearly uncomfortable with talking to Alice, and Alice did need a bit of help.

"Sure. Sure. Just don't let her yack you to death, Mistress."

The second use of the term "Mistress" annoyed the shapechanger but she kept her tone pleasant.

"Please, I'm just a guest in this house. I don't own you or employ you, so it makes me uncomfortable to be called Mistress. I'll be asking permission from you to do things, not the other way around. OK?"

"Yes, M-- Yes, Miss."

"Ah, hah! Smart woman! Yes, I'm a Miss. Come on, Hope. Let's get the last stuff out of my car."

Property from Alice's work office in Llano took three trips up to the room which would be her home work office. When it was all there Alice surveyed the room. It contained a desk, bookshelves, a couple of small tables, three chairs, and a few other pieces of furniture.

It was narrower than her bedroom/living room combination but as deep as those two. A window let in some light, quite a bit when the sun was right. She was grateful for the Venetian blinds covering it.

At the end closest to the door she placed a table to hold material which she brought in or would want to take out. Beside the table against a wall she moved a bookshelf with Hope's help. Against the wall with the window they placed the desk. Cater corner to it she placed a second table. On it she put the screen for her SuperCalc 5 and the electric typewriter input device. The calculator went on the floor.

"Wow!" said Hope. "It's big. Bigger than the ones my Masters have in their offices."

"At the factory they and I will probably use something even bigger, but I'll do a lot of work here so I need a big calculator."

"You're very smart, aren't you?"

"All women are smart, if they let themselves be. You, for instance."

"Me?"

"Sure. I hope you don't believe the nonsense that men say about us, that we don't have a head for business, or numbers, or mechanical stuff."

"Well..."

"Do you know why they-- Well, not all men, but a lot-- say that?

It's because they know deep down that history is passing them by."

She plugged in the last cable that she been connecting to different parts of the calculator and plugged the power cord into the house power. She pulled a chair over in front of the typewriter, sat in it, and reached down to flick the On switch on the body of the calculator. Various lights came on in the machinery and the screen flickered as the calculator began to come alive.

She gestured at Hope to pull over another of the chairs and sit in it and turn toward her.

"See, men have gotten by forever because they've got bigger muscles and bones. They can beat up women-- Well, not me. I'm WAY stronger than most men."

"I noticed. You handled that big box of books as if it held nothing."

"See. You're smart. You pay attention to the world around you.

"Anyway, up until about 1800 most power was by muscle, men's or horses' or oxen or whatever. And wind and water power, of course. Then steam power was invented. And gasoline engines.

"At the same time brain power began to be more important. Science helped us better understand the universe. And technology helps to do things, like travel the ocean against the wind, and plan how to build and fly airplanes.

"And women are as smart as men. Smarter even, because men depend on their muscles and women depend on their brains. Women are forced to develop their brains, men to develop their muscles."

The immortal eyed the girl. Her attention was inward as she processed what Alice was saying. She didn't seem doubtful, just busy rearranging her mental world.

She brightened, looked smiling at Alice.

"Marie Curie! Madame Curie! The Frenchwoman. I just remembered. She was just given her SECOND Nobel Prize. They mentioned it at school."

"Right. She won't be the last woman to get that prize and others. It won't happen soon. Big changes like women getting more respect take long times. And men fight against it. So do some women. The pretty ones, mostly. Or from rich families who don't want to give up their easy lives. Easy until babies come along, at any rate."

The girl saddened. "If it happens too slow it won't do me any good."

"I'm afraid so. But meanwhile you can get a LITTLE good from the changes. A little is not NO good."

"And meanwhile I can at least feel good about myself. Even if I don't dare say anything."

"Yes. Be smart about being smart. Pretend to be a helpless CUTE little thing. Let the big strong men do stuff for you."

"Isn't that...cowardly? Cheating?"

"It's smart. Men have been cheating us for thousands of years. About time we used our brains to cheat them back."

Hope giggled. "You are SO radical. Revolutionary. Aren't you afraid the law will arrest you?"

"I don't talk like this to just anybody, silly. And I'm not revolutionary. That gets people killed and lives ruined. I'm an EVOLUTIONARY, contented with tiny victories. I blend in, not stand out to get my head chopped off.

"Now. That's enough corrupting the young. Would you like to learn to use a calculator?"

"Yes!"

Alice turned off the calculator. It had started up successfully so the stresses of the trip had not damaged it.

She stood up and gestured for Hope to take her place in front of the keyboard and screen.

"Let's take this a little bit at a time. Take baby steps. Learn to crawl before you learn to run. You start by turning ON the calculator...."

Alice tutored Hope on using the calculator just long enough so that she could do a few simple tasks on it. Then she cut off the session before the girl could grow bored or confused.

She and Hope had lunch by themselves; her mom and dad ate at different times. Then Alice finished getting her rooms in shape and exploring the house and its outsides.

The front yard was not used for much. Atop the grass on both sides of the walkway to the front door was a decorative white statue. On one side of the house was a garage which was basically a section of concrete big enough to park three vehicles. This would hold those of the two men and Alice. It had a green canvas canopy. Behind the house was a big green lawn. Part of it was shaded by an oak tree. Underneath the tree were three round tables surrounded by a scattering of plastique lawn chairs.

Dinner that evening had a fish base with a nicely savory and complex sauce and steamed veggies. It was served on the extensible table in the dining room next to the kitchen. The two "masters" sat at opposite ends. The cook, Ruth, sat at Delacroix's right hand which put her nearest the kitchen. Her daughter sat beside her and could also fetch and serve from the kitchen.

Joseph, the gardener and handyman, sat across the table from his wife and daughter at Porter's right hand. Alice resisted Hope's suggestion that she sit beside her. Alice didn't like the idea of forming the third on the "woman's side" of the table. Instead she plunked herself down at Joseph's right hand, to his discomfort. The shapechanger did nothing about that right away but would eventually ensure he became at ease with her.

When Ruth set a last item on the table and sat Porter addressed the table.

"I believe everyone has met Alice and knows she'll be here working for Texas Aviation for the next six month's or more. Louis and I are very pleased.

"Alice, the way we work this at dinner is that we have a blessing, then start eating. As we do we tell what happened to us that day that we want to mention. It can be anything, no matter how trivial. We start with the youngest and go up from there."

Everyone joined hands who could, bowed their heads, and Delacroix sat something brief and thankful. Then the meal began.

Shortly Hope said, "Well, I helped Alice get settled in and then she taught me a little bit about using calculators! I think I might someday actually do it! And that's it."

Alice said, "I got here and settled in and chatted with Hope for a while, then met Ruth and Joseph and got acquainted with the insides and outsides."

Porter and Delacroix contributed their resumption of work at their company Texas Aviation and were happy to be home.

Ruth had met Alice and was trying out a new sauce recipe tonight and did everyone like it? Everyone assured her they did, with Alice adding that she hoped Ruth would cook with it again.

Joseph had met Alice and gotten a new grass fertilizer at the store.

Alice fired her first shot at making the man easier with her by saying, "Is that how you made the lawn so green? I noticed yours is greener than that of the neighbors. Not that theirs looks bad, but it's noticeably yellowier."

That got him off onto lawn care but only for a short time. Afterward the immortal sensed that he was moderately more comfortable talking to her.

At meals end Delacroix said, "Well, that's it for me. I'm going to turn in early. Goodnight everyone."

Everyone else mumbled Good Nights or their equivalents and got up from the table as the Frenchman went into the nearby hall. Porter and Joseph disappeared somewhere together. That left those left to clear and clean. Alice joined the women in the activity, though she warned she wouldn't always do it. The three took a lazy time at the duty and had a good talk. During it Alice learned a little more about the Tillotson family, including that they had an older son who had recently graduated from a Black community college and taken a job as an assistant veterinarian.

Alice was quite happy in her new home. She had worked on her rooms that afternoon and a bit after dinner. It now felt just right, her new burrow. She thought of it that way as she tucked the covers around her that night. It was like an animal's leafy burrow, all cozy and safe. She'd had a few nights like that during the first weeks after she'd woken from her first death, a Black woman but incredibly strong and fast and tough.

Sleep came quickly.

The enemy was clustered below advancing on her former village, all peaceably working at their daily lives, women in their homes, men in the fields and barns, children playing.

The land all around was mildly hilly and green. A narrow stream wound through the village. The sky was its usual violet-blue, lazy clouds floating randomly above the land. Shadows of the clouds flowed slowly over the green grass and the trees.

S/he had heard what the enemy did to the villages they raided. Senseless torture and death, a sadistic orgy with the women and children and some men raped till their crotches were bloody ruins. Stupid. Raiders should reap sensibly, leave everyone alive to build up their fortunes anew to be reaped again.

Well. Not this time. Cruel glee coursed through hi/r body. There.

That cloud shadow. The raiders were fully in it. Hi/r distance sense told hi/r its exact location and distance.

S/he tilted from upright to horizontal and fell downward, coursing like an arrow toward the torturers/killers. Wind whistled by hi/r long body with its vestigial wings which had no part of how she flew.

S/he passed the speed of sound. Misty shock waves formed behind hi/r.

Faces turned skyward. Death arrowed toward them. Silent. Sound was following after the dragonet. Shock. Bodies turned to run.

From hi/r outstretched finger tips violet flashes of light winked, winked, winked, each one a dart of faery light. Each one penetrated a raider body, exploding it into brilliant red bonfires.

S/he leveled off, swept over the raiders, and climbed into the sky. Behind hi/r thunder crashed, fanning the roaring spires of fire further. But no one there heard it. They were all dead.

S/he slowed, slowed, till s/he no longer outpaced sound. But s/he did not slow further. S/he had done her job. The village where s/he once had lived in a human body was safe.

<>

Alice sat up in her bed, tilted into a cross-legged sitting position. She gathered the covers around her legs. Blinked sleep from her eyes, her shapechanger body banishing it instantly.

It had not been a dream. It had been a memory, vivid, logical, a complete incident.

But from when? And where? She'd lived four times only, each time a human and her circumstances ordinary even though she was not.

It had been on another planet. In China their astronomers and those of Europeans had known for decades about other planets and other star systems. But the planets were far away and the star systems unimaginably farther away.

She had been a small dragon or something similar, one who had once been the local version of a human.

Alice puzzled over the memory-not-a-dream for a while, then lay back down and went to sleep. Four centuries of life had taught her patience.

<>

The middle-of-the-night memory was only barely dimmed the next morning. This was proof that it was not a dream. Those raveled away with wakefulness.

She ate a breakfast of eggs and bacon and buttered toast and orange juice, saying No to Ruth at her offer of coffee. Her two partners in Texas Aviatin took the coffee but only toast, thanking Ruth automatically. Alice, a few minutes ahead of them, ate quickly and finished when the men did.

"Alice," said Porter. "You want a ride to work? Or would you rather drive your own car?"

Delacroix said, "I advise you to drive yourself. You may want to leave early. Or late."

"I'll drive myself. Thanks."

The men took their own advice and boarded and started their own vehicles. Delacroix's was a gleaming sports car and Porter's a pickup truck. The truck was battered but its motor purred when it woke to life.

Alice followed them out of the housing development then, over the course of five miles, drove east then south then east again. They ended up in an industrial park of a couple dozen buildings of several sizes. Each one had a big sign across its main entrance. The aviators' sign was TEXAS AVIATION. The first word was red, the second sky blue. That color was echoed in a free-standing sign consisting only of two letters: a huge red T superimposed over an equally large blue A.

The two parked in a parking area behind the main building of two and Alice parked beside them.

As she soon discovered, one was the sales and office building. Inside a show room were three aircraft parked on a display floor: a small red biplane, a larger silver four-seater which might have been a rich man's toy, and the largest plane. This was a Hawk 3 washed and polished.

The three walked into the showroom from a side door. They were met by a good-looking Latino dressed in a dark-blue suit with a red-and-blue striped silk tie ovcr a white shirt. His shoes shone a gleaming black.

"Hey, Antonio," said Porter.

"Mr. Porter. Mr. Delacroix. And I'm sure this is the famous Alice Willoughby." He held out his hand to shake. Alice obliged, automatically finding and starting the fix of minor illnesses.

"You must be the famous Antonio...?"

"Rodriguez, Miss Willoughby."

"Pleased."

"Likewise."

Delacroix said, "We've got to handle some paperwork with Alice, Tony. Then you and I can talk if you need to."

Porter said, "Julius around?"

"Just went to the restroom, Mr. Porter. Ah, there he is."

They all looked down a hall to see a portly man in a suit coming into the hallway, presumably from the restroom. The owners did not wait to talk to him however, just waving to him as they ushered Alice into an office.

There they went over the contract that specified the amount Alice would pay for a ten percent interest in Texas Aviation and what she would do for them during her six-month trial period. Alice gave them a check and they all signed the contract. Two copies were made and the original couriered to the appropriate government office.

"The nearness to government agencies in the state capitol," said Porter, "is one of the reasons we decided to start TA here. We get lots faster response time to anything we need from them."

Delacroix said, "Plus we got to know and like Austin really well during our four years at Uni. The atmosphere here, it's completely different from any city we know. More relaxed, more future-forward, more open to difference. 'Stay weird' is the city's motto."

"Plus," the other man said, "you can find more different kinds of music here, more even than in New York which may be the most diverse city in the world with its immigrants from all places."

Porter stood up from his chair.

"Now let's go to where you'll work in the engineering building. Later, Louis."

Alice waved a hand in Goodbye at Delacroix as she followed Porter out of his office. The man absent-mindedly raised a hand in reply. He was already taking up the next piece of paperwork from his inbox.

They left by the side door in which they'd come and walked through the parking lot to an adjacent building. It was huge and barn like. They walked along a long corridor that split the building in half.

A hundred feet down they came to a long expanse of glass which fronted a room. They went through the door into the room. It contained several tables. Most of them were strewn with white-prints of technical plans heavy with diagrams and numbers.

The side farthest from the door was split into two enclosed offices with big glass windows that let the occupants see out into larger office.

"The one on the left is mine. Yours is the one on the right."

He led the way through the tables to her office, opened the door, and went in.

"We've been using this room to store stuff. So our first job is to empty it of stuff you don't need and set it up the way you want. I'll help get you started but when one of our lab assistants or techies comes by I'll grab them and assign them to you to finish the job. Don't ever be shy about commandeering help. You're one of the three owners now and a boss."

It was a half hour before a luckless technician wandered by the office and was seen by Porter. He was beckoned into the room and introduced to Alice.

"Wylie, this is Miss Alice Willoughby. She's part owner now and boss of all engineering after me. Give her whatever help she needs. Alice, you're in luck. Wylie Jenkins is a whiz at calculators. He'll help you get set up when your office is squared away."

"Right, Boss. Glad to meet you, Alice." He held out his hand to shake.

Porter paused half turned away but continued into his office.

The immortal's words were perfectly without emotion.

"Miss Willoughby, Mr. Jenkins. Or Boss. Let's move this bookshelf out and against that wall."

There was a moment of silence then the technician said, "Sure thing, Boss. I'll get this side."

Quick man, Alice thought. Good. She liked quick thinkers.

Finally her office contained only the items she wanted. This included a table cater-cornered to her desk upon which her calculator would go.

She commented on this.

"What's the most powerful desk calc we have available?"

"That would be a Texas Radio model 7."

"Let's go get one."

This involved a trip down the central hall to the other end of the building, nearly 400 feet. There in a big storeroom were several calculators. Alice chose one still in an unopened box and they moved it to a cart. She also chose three memory packs.

"Why get those?" said Jenkins.

"I'm going to increase my memory space."

"We can boost these models only one mem pack. Or so says the literature from AIEE."

"We'd have to double check, but I think the AIEE says that we can boost the Model 7s by one mem pack, not ONLY one mem pack."

"Hmm. You may be right. But if you can gang more together why wouldn't they say so?"

"Professional organizations may make out that they are independent of industry but they aren't. Texas Radio may consider the ability to add multiple mem packs proprietary information."

"But if we guess wrong we could burn up the whole calculator."

"That's why we--or I--am going to instrument everything and measure what happens. That's why I'm taking THIS."

Alice went to a metal shelf and took down a selection of wiring and electrometers.

In the end they--because once Alice had begun testing Jenkins had become interested in the outcome--found that two but not three memory packs could be added to a Model 7 safely.

<>

Much happened in the next month.

The word quickly passed that Alice was to be addressed as "Miss Willoughby" or "Boss." The second gained favor very quickly. Nobody liked her dead-faced look.

"I swear," said one man. "I get the feeling she carries a flick knife and she's about stick to it in me."

That comment quickly turned into the "fact" that she did indeed carry a flick knife. That turned into the "fact" that she HAD stuck it in someone.

She became part of the tech staff and did the same kinds of jobs every other techie did. She did not give orders; she was not a boss. Except in the rare cases when she was. She was quickly acknowledged to be just as expert as anyone else. Her knowledge was encyclopedic.

There was much speculation as to which school she'd learned her trade. It must have been when she was quite young. Even so she was definitely in her twenties. It was just that she was one of those people who looked like a teenager long after she'd ceased to be one.

The truth was that Alice's expertise came from the two to three hours she spent most evenings reading: books, newspapers, magazines, and scientific and technical journals. This was a revelation to Hope after she visited the immortal in her office at home, that grownups did homework. The girl took to doing her own homework in that same office as Alice did. Rarely but sometimes she asked Alice a question, which the shapechanger always answered and rarely but sometimes at length. Ruth soon came to call her daughter "that homework girl" and Alice "that homework woman."

Fearing that she might contribute to distancing Hope from her mother Alice with Hope in tow occasionally did her homework in the kitchen, though never on the nights that Ruth did her chef-study homework with Delacroix.

Joseph, who had become comfortable with Alice, sometimes joked that he was the only one in the estate that did not do homework. A few days later he was presented with a book on grafting and pruning fruit trees.

Not that the people in the house were solemn academics. Austin styled itself The Musical Capitol of the World and the house's occupants often took advantage of the musical bounty available. Porter was a fan of jazz and dragged a reluctant Delacroix along to that music. The Frenchman returned the favor by dragging Porter along to opera.

Alice attached herself to both outings. Hope tried to attach herself to the jazz outings but they were in smoke-filled bars. She failed. She succeeded however with the opera outings.

Those were dress-up affairs so the three aviation partners, with the permission of Hope's parents, bought three sets of clothing for Hope which could be mixed-and-matched to create a dozen or two "looks."

Alice met the veterinarian son one weekend when he visited his parents. He was tall and muscular and good looking with a happy personality. He reminded Temilade of some of her lovers from two centuries ago. She felt juices start to flow in her nether regions and quickly quieted her body's responses. That night she helped her shapechanger's unnatural easing of her responses with natural means.

She also was interviewed by a reporter from the Austin Tribune.

<>

Hill Country Bull Rider Becomes
Austin Country Airplane Rider.

Austin Tribune: Miss Willoughby, you were known for three years as the darling of the Hill Country due to your stint as a bull rider at rodeos. For those of our readers unfamiliar with the term that means what?

Alice Willoughby: I jump atop a bull's back and ride it while it tries to buck me off and scrape me off on the walls around the rodeo arena. I usually stand on its back rather than sit.

AT: That sounds dangerous.

AW: (shrugs, one shoulder) Not really. Bulls have a limited repertoire of escape actions. One quickly grows to anticipate them and counter-act them.

AT: You sound very educated. You are in fact, aren't you? You work at Texas Aviation as a technical consultant. You have also written a few papers on calculator engineering which were published in the AIEE journal. That's a prestigious national organization for electrical engineers.

AW: Only three.

AT: Only three. After working at Texas Aviation for six weeks.

AW: One of those was from before I went to work there. And it was as co-author with Albert Moseley, a friend back in Llano who is very technically knowledgeable.

AT: That paper had to do with programming the flight path of a model airplane that you and Mr. Moseley built. Is that how you became interested in airplanes?

AW: Yes. Al introduced me to airplanes.

AT: So when the Texas Aviation owners came to Llano on their publicity tour you saw your chance to get involved in aviation?

AW: Correct. I hoped that my bull riding skills would get me a job riding the airplane.

AT: Now THAT sounds dangerous.

AW: (Again that charming shoulder shrug) Not really. It's safer than bull riding. I'm actually strapped atop the wing, secure from falling.

AT: Unless the plane falls. That has happened before.

AW: Even then. For me at least. I would have plenty of time to unbuckle and vault off as the plane neared the ground. I might survive if I landed right and on the right surface.

AT: Isn't it true that you've never attended school? That you tested out of high school. How did you manage that?

AW: I admit to being a very smart girl. Also, I read a LOT. Books, magazines, newspapers. I especially like complicated subjects which challenge my mind.

AT: It must be tough for boys to court you, you being so smart and educated.

AW: There's some truth to that. I only like smart boys. I don't care if they are cute and have lots of muscles. Oh, I like those things, but if they just look good they might as well be trees or statues as far as romantic appeal.

AT: Your two business partners ought to fit that bill.

AW: A LOOK (FYI, if you ever get an annoyed look from the Plane Rider you will have to fight an urge to run. Away. Fast.)

AT: I beg pardon. That was inappropriate. If I may ask, what does appeal to you in a boy?

AW: First, that he NOT be a boy. Of any age. He's lived enough, and paid attention enough to living, to gain some wisdom. Not just book learning, LIFE learning. So I tend to like older men. Like you.

AT: (This reporter confesses that he would be less afraid if a hungry lion paid him attention than to get the attention of The Plane Rider.) Ah. Thank you?

AW: I love music, I love dancing. I love Austin because it has lots of both. So a man should know places to go to experience both.

AT: Do you go out a lot?

AW: Now that I'm settled in I plan to.

AT: Thank you.

AW: Thank you. And by your ring I see you are married. Tell your wife she is a lucky woman.

AT: (This reporter would be remiss if he did not amplify on the black-and-white photo that accompanies this story. Miss Willoughby's skin is delicate white with golden freckles, her lips could compete with roses, her hair is the brightest red you've ever seen, a flag that waves when she rides a plane. Her figure is slender but feminine and her face one that Aphrodite might wear. And I'd better stop there before my wife decides to meet me at home with a frying pan in her hand.)

<>

By the end of June the barnstorming tour plus determined selling efforts by Delacroix paid off with a buy by a company that wanted to transport passengers and cargo between Austin and San Antonio. It took three hours minimum by car or truck over a well-traveled but not well-surfaced road which was very uncomfortable to travel. It took an hour by air. The Hawk was comfortable for travelers, one of its selling points. It was easy to fly and quite safe. Porter and his engineers had put in enormous time ensuring that.

On July 4th the Ryan Air inaugural flight took off at 11:00 am from a quarter-mile runway made of tar and sand pointing due east.

The runway was the property of Texas Aviation and was almost two years old. It had been used for those two years by TA, mostly by crop-duster biplanes that TA rented or sold. It had been improved several times.

As part of the publicity for the first commercial flight the week before Delacroix had flown several short out-and-back flights with Alice atop the Hawk. She had worn sky blue woman-cut jeans and a bright red leather jacket over a white turtleneck sweater. Her helmet allowed her long curly red hair to stream in the breeze. Her goggles had blue rims and blue leather straps.

One reporter had dubbed this red-white-and-blue outfit "the patriot's dream" as it wrapped the American flag around "a most delicious female body." The color combination was deliberate: it was also that of Texas Aviation signs: a red T superimposed over a blue A on a background of white.

After the first flight there had been up to a thousand watchers every day. Nearby schools let out for "educational trips" of up to two hours to view the "revolutionary new form of travel." The local police force had been recruited to control the crowds.

After the second flight vendors set up tents and temporary booths, set well back from the runway, to sell food and drink. The police were kept busy ensuring that no alcohol was sold. That did not prevent drinkers from bringing their own drinks.

The flight was preceded by a ceremony at 10:00. The local police chief spoke from a temporary platform to a crowd estimated as 3500. He exhorted the crowd to stay a hundred feet away from the runway, a perimeter marked by a five-hundred foot long ribbon on stakes and watched over by alert deputies. The local state congressman delivered a speech, wisely a short one for the day was hot. The three businessmen who were to be the passengers were introduced, then the two pilots and their business partner Miss Alice Willoughby, also known as The Plane Rider.

Many of the men in the crowd were disappointed in her appearance. Instead of a colorful body-hugging outfit she wore a black silk jacket over a matching A-line dress that ended just below her knees. A dazzling white silk blouse covered her chest. It was closed at the neck by a red-and-blue string tie. Her hair was up in a chignon and diamonds hung sparkling in the sun from her ears.

Every woman in the crowd noted her clothing and demure demeanor. She might look like a hussy in the air but she looked like a lady on the ground. And, given the glitter of her diamonds, she was obviously a rich woman. After all, she owned part of a company that made airplanes. What other sources of wealth might she have? Perhaps an oil-rich family in Houston? Or New York?

She WAS a tad well-off, though it was a modest wealth. She still received income from her businesses and part-businesses back in Llano. She had left them run by good stewards.

Alice and her partners and the businessmen left the stand shortly after they had been introduced and proceeded to the Hawk. They left behind them to talk to the crowd the Ryan Brothers, owners of the new airline. They were local businessmen who owned a chain of grocery stores and the premiere Austin department store, Ryan's.

The plane had been made ready for travel well before by the usual pilot for Ryan Air, George Watson, a former barnstormer and experienced pilot. He would be the actual pilot but the two partners had insisted that Delacroix serve as the copilot. Porter was along as the engineer for the Hawk if it needed it. Alice was along because she wanted to be.

"Hey, George," she said to Watson. "You nervous?"

A compact athletic man of some forty years, he answered her.

"Nope. It's just another plane ride. Maybe number 2000?"

She laid a casual hand on his nearest hand. He was telling the truth. He was also in tiptop health, partly naturally and partly because of the shapechanger.

"I'm not nervous either. Because you're the pilot and because TA has done its job."

Watson finished running through the takeoff checklist read to him by his copilot, Delacroix, at 11:00. Then he advanced the throttle and Hawk 3, on short-term loan to RyanAir, grumbled louder and began to roll out of its hangar toward the runway.

As its silver nose advanced into the sun a roar rose from the crowd.

That roar was soon overborne by the roar of the Hawk's engine. Watson edged the throttle forward more and more. The Hawk turned from an access path onto the runway and pivoted to face due east. It crawled along the tar-and-sand surface then moved at a walking pace, a running pace, a racing pace. Its tail lifted. Its wheels left the surface. It flew. It rotated backward to face into the sky. And raced into it.

Another roar came from the crowd, then clapping, then hooting. Some watched the plane drone away and into history. Many more turned to advance on the waiting vendors.

<>

The Ryan brothers were very good at organizing businesses. It was they who had turned their parents' few grocery stores into a modest grocery chain. They had also copied the famous department stores of the East and Europe to create Ryan's. They were not the first Austinites to do this. But they did it with style and efficiency that caused Ryan's to soon eclipse the other Austin department stores.

They applied their talents to RyanAir and made it not only profitable but fashionable for Austinites to travel to San Antonio by air and return from there. By Thanksgiving they had three Hawks traveling twice a day to and from the huge city to the south.

They partnered with an equally forward-looking family of San Antonio business people to open an air terminal in their city. That family, the Ortegas, bought two Hawks which were stationed in their city. Though they were owned by the Ortegas the partnership was still called RyanAir because by now the name had become synonymous with air travel in the area.

The Ortegas had business interests in Corpus Christi, a small town almost due south with several important ports. They wanted a plane which could travel the 150 or so miles, a five-hour trip over bad roads, in under an hour.

That trip was a little too long for a Hawk. Texas Aviation needed to seriously consider a dream they'd long had of a larger aircraft. The question immediately rose: What to call it?

<>

"Maybe 'Condor'," said Porter. He and his partners were lounging under a tent just outside their showroom. They were eating Mexican meals from one of a line of small restaurants which had sprung up on the road lining the eastern edge of the industrial complex. Not too far away under another tent sat workers at another business in the complex, Carnegie Clothiers.

"No," said Alice. "We need to reserve that for the next size up."

"Definitely," said Delacroix with an overly sober face, "not 'Penguin' or 'Ostrich.'"

Porter favored him with a malevolent look.

"Swan," said Alice, finishing a glass of iced tea and refilling it from a pitcher. "They're beautiful. It would be look good on a billboard. Take a Swan to Jamaica. Or Cuba. Or...Hmm."

"Did you ever deal with a swan up close and personal? They are vicious beasts."

"Like geese," said Delacroix. "I've never been more terrified in my life when a flock of them chased me one summer when I was a teenager."

Porter expressed astonishment that he wasn't still a teen. Delacroix gave him a finger which he quickly turned into a two-finger evil eye gesture when he remembered that there was a lady present.

"Kestrel?" mused Alice. "No, that would work for a military plane, not a civilian one. Albatross? No, too suggestive of bad juju. Raven? Buzzard?"

She began to chuckle, shook her head, picked up the last taco on her paper plate, and crunched into it.

Porter said, "It's so similar to the Hawk. Let's just call it the Hawk II."

Alice nodded. So did Delacroix.

They begin their design with the size of the cargo the Hawk II would carry: nearly twice that of the Hawk I. This was ten passengers with up to a ton of cargo, so a hundred pounds luggage for each passenger and a ton of other materiel. This would include food and drink, equipment to heat or cool the passengers, and air in a pressurized hull.

These last two features were a requirement they'd adopted so that Hawk II could fly up to 10,000 feet: nearly two miles. The decreased air resistance and cooler air at increased heights meant the plane would be faster and the engines more fuel efficient as they could run hotter.

The three designers went the modularity principle further. By removing passenger seats Hawk II could carry correspondingly more cargo. This would satisfy the Ortegas, who mostly wanted to carry cargo from the Corpus Christi ports. Or they could add two more seats by reducing the amount of cargo and the allowable luggage per passenger.

The total range of the new airplane was a thousand miles. This meant that a Hawk II could fly from Houston all the way to El Paso if anyone was willing to pay for it. Or to Florida. Or halfway to New York.

The immortal kept that thought to herself. Her partners did not think as long range as she did.

They also did not think beyond peaceful applications for Hawk II. The shapechanger did. She saw models of the Hawk II being used to transport troops and/or military cargo. She kept those possibilities to herself as well.

With the military aspect in mind she insisted on another capability of Hawk IIs: that they be able to take off and land in short distances. AND on rough runways. She couched these requirements in commercial terms, however. Many of the places in Texas where an airplane could go would not have big nice flat landing zones. At least at first, though those places would surely build such zones when demand for air transportation increased.

As it would, a fact obvious to other industrial thinkers in the US. Already an Eastern company was starting an aviation manufactory in the Dallas / Fort Worth area.

Instead of depressing the two male partners this fact energized them. They were not worried about the competition. It meant that other people than they saw a big future in aviation. They were not clueless lone wolves. And they had a head start and a design which could be upscaled.

Without them knowing it they had another advantage. Alice could hold the complete design in her imagination and "watch" it perform in various ways. This included putting it in a virtual wind tunnel and "watching" how air flowed across its body.

This led her to offer various improvements to the design. Some were dubious but when tested on small prototypes always proved to be effective. After a while they concluded she just had a "natural" "intuition" about aircraft.

So they were not surprised when Alice told them it was time for her to learn to fly airplanes. They were not pleased at the extra effort they would be put to, and the added danger to her, but not surprised.

<>

"OK," said Delacroix at one of their outdoor lunches, today eating sausage sandwiches and potato patties and drinking the ubiquitous iced tea that Delacroix called the National (Southern) Drink. "I'll do it."

"No," said Alice, "I want Porter to teach me."

That worthy paused with his own sandwich halfway to his mouth. "Louis is a better pilot."

"That's just it. He's too good a pilot."

"Wait, what?" The Frenchman looked confused.

"You're a 'natural.' You don't think about what you're doing, you just do it. Like the preflight check list. You hurry through it, never making a mistake, because it's as natural as breathing."

The two men looked at each, shrugged, and began discussing with her when and where the lessons would take place.

<>

On Monday and Wednesday evenings Alice and Porter quit work early but stayed late. He began with theory, often in the technical library that Texas Aviation maintained. There he could point out relevant sections in books and loan books for her to study. Often they retired to the classroom where he could draw on a blackboard.

These theory lessons went quickly. Alice never forgot a fact or idea and quickly understood theoretical explanations.

Next they moved to the hangars where their several planes for rent were housed. They studied the biplanes, called "crates." The name was apropos as they were little more than wood covered with plastique or metallic graphene.

After she had learned the structure of the biplanes the two of them pushed one of the planes out of the hangar, fueled the machine with a small amount of gasoline, donned protective gear and leather helmets and goggles, and climbed in.

The first time they did this Porter had her identify all the instruments and explain their use. Then Porter made sure they went through the startup and preflight checklist very slowly, with her explaining the theory and practice of each item. Finally he had her start up the engine and taxi in circles and squares on the runway.

On the third week at dinner Tuesday night Porter announced when it was his turn to talk about his day he made an announcement.

"Tomorrow evening I'm going to take Alice up and let her handle the controls."

She accepted the round of excited comments but ended them by motioning everyone to calm down.

"We haven't gone up yet. Wait till we survive to congratulate us."

Wednesday evening when Alice and Porter went into the hangar Delacroix joined them.

"I wish Belle had an extra seat so I could join you," he said.

"Everything will be fine. I'm careful, Alice takes her time. We'll be done in no time and safely down again."

Alice was calm and methodical as they went through the preflight and startup checklist. But when Porter took the controls and took the airplane up she felt mounting excitement. It became so strong that she had to use her shapechanger body control to tone it down.

That done she was able to follow along as Porter manipulated the foot pedals, actions which her duplicate foot pedals mirrored beneath her feet. She felt her yoke turn to right or left to send the plane to right or left. Or pull back or push forward the yoke to send the plane up or down.

For half an hour her teacher repeated those routine actions. She memorized them and they quickly became habitual.

Finally he said, "When I take my hands off the yoke you have control. Ready?"

"Ready."

"Remember, keep a light touch. Under-control, not over-control. Belle is like a skittish horse."

"OK."

Alice's hands were barely touching the plane's yoke. Porter lifted his hands straight up and obviously off his yoke.

Alice settled her hands ever so lightly in place.

SHE was suddenly larger. SHE had wings, a body, a tail, and wheels beneath HER chest.

SHE felt wind brushing along HER body. SHE felt HER wings lifting up and the rest of HER pulling down. The two forces cancelled out.

SHE lifted HER right wings, dropped HER left wings. Ever so slightly SHE tilted toward the left. Reacted. Tilted toward the right. Reacted. Came level.

"Good girl! Perfect!"

The composite being felt HER biological body frown slightly. SHE, the composite, was not a girl. SHE was...

A long moment passed.

Then SHE knew. SHE was Belle, a biplane/human thing.

SHE shrugged fully into HER larger self. Inspected HERself. SHE felt...right. All parts, mechanical, biological, right.

SHE looked/felt outside, especially ahead. The horizon stretched far ahead, green-grey forest. SHE knew how far it was. Below were greenish yellow grass/meadow/random trees. A farm grew ahead. SHE knew the exact measures in numbers: declination/forward distance/angle to the side. Perfect for targeting with a bolt of hot plasma.

SHE jerked. Suddenly she was fully back in her biological body.

The immortal took a deep breath and let it slowly out.

She was NOT a dragonet on some distant alien planet.

She glanced to her side. Porter rode, leaned back, eyes slightly shut. He had complete faith in her, or pretended he did.

He saw her head turn, turned his own toward her, grinned, raised the thumb of his nearest hand, looked forward again, almost sleepy seeming.

Alice tightened her hands minutely on her yoke. Slowly that feeling of being larger came back.

SHE turned slightly to HER left, knowing that it was HER feet on the pedals that turned HER rudder to the left that caused the turn, but not feeling HER feet. She just wanted to turn and that happened, just as wanting to walk to the left made her legs and torso act to make THAT happen.

SHE continued the turn, tilted to the left a trifle. Sped up HER engine a trifle to increase HER speed and keep HER from losing altitude.

There. That felt right.

Up ahead was Austin. SHE could see the city but HER biological body wanted to look at the heading indicator on the control panel. Yes. It agreed that SHE was going north.

SHE wanted to ascend. SHE did. SHE wanted to descend. SHE did.

"Looks like you've got it, Alice."

The human words jolted the being. SHE almost separated into HER two parts. An instinct pulled HER back into normalcy.

"There's one thing left to do. The most important skill."

SHE knew what that was. HER biological self had been told. She wanted to grimace but the composite being could not.

"You know what to do. Ready?"

"As I'll ever be." HER voice was far away.

"Here goes."

SHE climbed to a thousand feet, leveled off, surveyed HER

surroundings below. Yes. They were still a few miles from home. They would not give onlookers any thrills.

SHE began to climb again but this time at a greater angle. Then greater. Then greater. Then almost vertically.

SHE felt the lift from HER wings ebb away as SHE tilted more and more. Then--

SHE tilted back toward normal. SHE had almost lost all lift. SHE had almost stalled.

As SHE was supposed to do.

"Sorry, Lew. It's almost painful to go into a stall."

"Yeah. Louis says the same thing. Try again. You almost got it."

SHE tried again. Same result.

"Damn it."

"You don't have to do it today. We can try again."

"No. I must do this. Don't worry. I won't try too hard. I want to end today feeling good, so no forcing things and screwing up the good feeling."

This time as SHE inched up on the stall she jerked--ever so slightly jerked--backward.

Yes. SHE was falling uncontrolled!

SHE sped up her biological self. Time seemed to slow.

First regain a straight descent without spinning. SHE righted HERself so that SHE was diving straight down. The world was expanding below but not spinning and throwing HER biological belly into sickness.

SHE tilted back and the world tilted so that the horizon was ahead and at an angle above HER. SHE tilted more and now the horizon was ahead.

"Good job! You got this."

"One more time. I want to be sure I've got this."

Actually it was two more times. The second time it was so easy that SHE could stall and recover automatically while thinking of something else.

Which might be an attacking aircraft.

Where had that come from?

The being mentally shrugged off the thought.

"Now let's go home."

Chapter 7 - Plane Maker

The next week Alice and Delacroix took Belle up. He checked her out much the same way Porter had done. He was more rigorous, putting her through several more difficult maneuvers than Porter had. This included stall recovery. He had her do that seven times, mostly yelling at her to go into and out of a stall while doing something else.

Back on the ground he said, "You seem to be a natural too."

"I suppose so. Do you ever try to force a stall and find it almost impossible to do?"

"Every time. Now go up and do a go around all on your own."

"Now? While I'm tired? You want to kill me?"

He grinned. "Now when you're tired is the best time to see if you are ready to fly by yourself."

"Slave driver."

The shapechanger was not tired, of course. She went up, did several maneuvers, did two touch-and-goes where she landed for a few seconds then took off again, and three times did a stall-and-recover. Then she landed.

That night at dinner Delacroix and Porter opened a chilled bottle of Champagne in celebration. Hope got a half inch glass of the wine. She frowned, sneezed, and said she was sworn off of sour stuff.

<>

The next few weeks Alice flew more. The Hawk was first with Porter double-checking her, then the Falcon with Delacroix as a co-pilot. This was the sleek silver two-passenger plane in the showroom that was still awaiting some rich man to buy for a toy.

There were actually three of them. Alice flew both Falcon 2 and 3. (Falcon 1 was in the showroom and though flyable it was too much trouble to remove and return it.)

Alice co-opted Falcon 2 as her personal vehicle. She kept it in salablc condition, like Falcon 3, cleaned inside and washed and polished outside. She or a sales person could show a Falcon to a potential customer, one of the owners could take that customer up to show it off, and send it out the door as soon as they got payment.

Several times men came in to "shop" for the Falcon, desirous of having "that Plane Walker girl" show it to them only to be told that she was not currently available (unless they seemed to be serious buyers).

By Thanksgiving it was clear to everyone that the immortal would be kept on as an employee after her six months were up. As a technician, as a designer, and as a salesperson she had become essential. They sold several biplanes because of her and five Hawks.

These were "stretched" Hawks, officially Hawk IIs. There were two versions labeled Hawk II A and Hawk II B (respectively passenger and cargo planes). They were six feet longer, had a more powerful engine, extra fuel capacity, and had bigger wings.

The Hawk II A/B could make routine trips to and from Houston. The distance from Austin was about 150 miles and took an hour by a stretched Hawk. By train it took five to six hours, as the train had intermediate stops. The distance of Houston from San Antonio was about 200 miles and took an hour and a half. By train the San Antone-Houston trip took a full day.

Thanksgiving was a happy affair. The boys had an open house for their employees and their families. A tent was set up in the back yard, tables set up under it, and food arranged on one of the long sides of the tent buffet style. The several kinds of drink included no alcoholic beverages except hard apple cider.

One wife quietly asked her husband why it was "that girl" instead of one of "the men" who would be police.

He shuddered. "Everybody at work knows not to cross her. Her words can take the hide off your bones, she carries a knife and is ready to use it, and she can carry a Belle engine all by herself. Those Hill Country people raise tough cowgirls."

On the way home with well-stuffed kids asleep on quilts in the rear of their truck the wife gave her opinion of that girl.

"I don't know why you men have such a bad picture of Miss Alice. I talked with her for almost an hour. She is the sweetest thing, asking all sorts of questions about our family, and giving me a back rub that took away those knotty shoulder muscles. If I hear you've been making trouble for that little girl I'm going to give you what-all."

"Don't worry, darling. I always treat her right." He kept to himself that he'd rather face an annoyed cougar cat than an annoyed Alice.

<>

A catering crew cleaned up when the Thanksgiving banquet was over. The three Texas Aviation owners sat in lawn chairs under the shade tree and chatted, idly watching cleanup. They agreed it had been a good public relations move. Not only had their workers been pleased but also four of their closest neighbors.

"I swear," said Porter, "that I actually saw that cranky old lady next door smile for the first time ever."

"That's because I was nice to her," said Alice.

"I was nice to her too."

"Yes. But you're only a man."

"What do you mean by that?!"

Delacroix said, "Now you've done it. She's going to lecture to us."

"Oh. Crap. Well, best to get it over with."

The two men assumed a fatuous listening demeanor. Alice kept her smile well hidden.

"It's nothing to be ashamed of. It's just that men have been the protectors and hunters forever. You're outward directed, target oriented. Women have stayed at home with their children and been homemakers. That requires us to be inward directed, to be cooperative, to be diplomats."

Actually Alice had been more than merely nice to their neighbor. She'd injected the woman with two types of microscopic messengers. One set had the short-term effect of taking away the woman's many minor age-related pains. The other had addressed the causes of those pains, beginning slow healing.

"To change the subject, I'm going home for ten days around Christmas. And I'm going by way of a Falcon."

"What?" "You can't." "We need you here."

"No you don't. We're letting most employees take the two Christmas weeks off. And you two will be working short weeks yourselves."

Her partners weren't ready to give up their protests but Alice could tell they were more pro forma than passionate. They were more because they would miss her presence though they'd never admit it.

<>

Alice wrote Hester Lightfoot, manager with her son Adolf of Lightfoot Agriculture, and got permission to land and house a Falcon on their mile-square farm for a week.

She then wrote letters to her family and Albert announcing that she'd arrive on a Monday afternoon at 3:00 of the week of Christmas. That day was a Friday, so her arrival would be on the 21st. She would leave the next Tuesday.

She got back happy replies saying they could not wait.

During the three weeks before she left she finished and tested a number of changes to Falcon 2 and scheduled their addition to Falcons 1 and 3.

It had become clear that the Falcon was unlikely to become a rich man's toy. So Alice had argued that it should be done over as a show plane, able to do acrobatics over an area and unfurl a huge banner advertising a business or an event.

It could also compete in speed races at air shows. It would never win first place against planes built for that specific purpose and no other. But it would usually win 2nd or 3rd places and so advertise for Texas Aviation.

Some modifications made it suitable for police and fire fighting work. These let it loiter very slowly over a spot and so reconnoiter a situation. This also let it be used by the military, both as an observation craft and as transportation of high-ranking officers and an aide or two.

Privately Alice thought it should also be convertible to a ground attack craft to fight ground forces. But she did not mention this to the boys whom she considered to be a bit naïve in the ways of the world.

Mods done and tested, Delacroix once again put Falcon 2 through extensive tests after Alice. Then he OK'd the last of the modifications.

This surprised Alice not at all. She had already tested every mod nearly to destruction. She already was a better pilot than even he or any other human could be. Not only was she a more "natural" pilot than they but she was also unnaturally tough. She could survive situations which would kill anyone else.

Well, except for other shapechangers. She'd met a few in her four centuries of life.

Thus on Monday the 21st of December Alice came to work in a taxi at the regular time but quit at noon. She secured presents and luggage in Falcon 2 and left.

<>

Alice breathed a sigh of relief as Falcon 2 rose into the air. Except for the brief time she'd soloed, when she'd piloted an aircraft she'd had company and had to act like a human. Now she relaxed and became fully a composite being with a biological center and a mechanical skin.

Briefly SHE wondered at how SHE could feel HER mechanical as well as HER biological body. SHE guessed it had something to do with the quantum nature of energy as theorized by the physicists at Trinity College in Dublin, Ireland. Seemingly solid matter was vibrant with energy at the submicroscopic level. Energy which SHE could somehow tap into with HER brain.

Ghostly theoretical models of reality dissolved in HER pleasure at seeing/feeling the dropping away of the land below. Checkerboards of greenery and earth randomly dotted with bushes and tree grew smaller. The flat bottoms of cotton-white clouds came down toward her.

The Alice/airplane creature leveled off at a few hundred feet below the clouds and made a U-turn toward the west. A mile below SHE could see the upward-thrust clutter of city center buildings. Around it was the shawl of grey subcity and green suburbs. The Colorado River wandered through the man-made structures of Austin.

Then the land turned bumpy, none of the bumps rising more than a few hundred feet toward her. Some of the high-rise buildings and houses scattered up onto the sides of the low hills. The square and rectangular lines of city streets turned into curves and U-turns on the sides and tops of the hills.

The creature could feel the land below her. A glance at a landmark yielded a distance and a downward angle and a compass heading. SHE wondered at the reason for this targeting information. Was it really for use of weapons? Or was HER narrow-focused human imagination prejudicing HER thoughts?

SHE abandoned thought and just reveled in the sights and sensations of flying.

HER engine reached temperature equilibrium throughout its body. SHE leaned out the air/fuel mixture it drank. Its efficiency edged upward a few percent.

HER airspeed indicator inched up closer to 200 miles per hour.

The hills west of Austin grew a bit taller. Greenery grew greener, fed by the water of the winding Colorado which soaked into the underground water table.

The hills slumped toward flatness. The farm road which SHE was following westward and a bit northward grew straighter.

A small cluster of buildings flowed toward HER and out of sight behind HER. It was a community of perhaps a hundred and near the halfway point of her trip.

SHE glanced at the clock in the panel between HER pilot's panel and the copilot's panel. SHE was surprised to see that only a quarter hour had passed since taking off. It had seemed longer.

Another quarter hour passed. Then up ahead HER home city flowed toward HER.

There was the familiar Llano River flowing eastward, splitting the city of some 2000 people into a north and a south part. As SHE came closer SHE lowered and slowed.

SHE began to pick out landmarks. The wooden bridge between the two parts which really should be replaced with a metal one. The three-story courthouse on the south side with its conical cap and scarf of trees surrounding it. The Famous Barbecue on the north side.

SHE was tempted to buzz the two parts: slash westward over North Llano, U-turn to slash eastward over South Llano. Then climb vertically pushed upward by the powerful engine of the Falcon, then scream downward till pulling out fifty feet up in a high-gravity structure-straining return to level flight.

But SHE curbed the desire. SHE'd already played with the edge of death the week before, pushing the Falcon to its limits to be sure that no human could come near them except in extreme circumstances.

Instead SHE did her pass over and U-turn at a 1000 feet, lowering to 200 on the last short leg of HER trip.

The Lightfoot farm came up to meet HER. SHE lowered to a few feet up, slowed further, and dropped so lightly to earth that the Falcon barely bounced. SHE reduced propeller spin to an almost visible blurred circle and taxied to a walking pace. Turned, turned some more, till she faced back the way SHE'd come.

SHE cut her engine as the plane halted a couple dozen feet beside the big two-story farm house.

Standing up and walking to the door SHE eased out of communion with HER mechanical part, fluffed her long curly red hair, and opened the oval door outward.

She jumped down to the grass rather than kick down the three-step folding ladder and proceed sedately out. For her mother was just a couple of feet away raising her arms for a hug.

She was quickly joined by her grandmother. Near at hand was her brother who wrapped his arms around her the instant she stepped away from her first hug.

"Damn, Sis, it seems like you've been gone forever!"

Her father squeezed her nearest shoulder and claimed his own hug, only to surrender his to Albert Moseley.

Nor was that the last. Next came Hester Lightfoot and her granddaughter Hannah home from her job in Round Rock north of Austin. She even got a hug from Yvonne, Hannah's shy pretty blond mother.

With Adolf Lightfoot she shared a strong handshake and an

exchange of sentences about how good the other looked.

Alice turned down dinner with her long time friend Hannah and her family that evening but accepted one for the next evening. She refused a ride with her family on the basis that all seats of their sedan was filled and took a ride from Albert, here with his pickup.

Albert's electrical and electronics business was doing well. His personal life, too, he said, but he'd tell her about that the next day when they were supposed to get together alone. For today he just wanted to spend time with her and her family.

At home she settled in quickly into her old room and returned to the living room to visit. A couple of hours of that and her mother and grandmother retired to the kitchen to finish up a dinner they'd begun earlier that day to celebrate her visit. It was elaborate and included some of her favorite foods.

Albert accepted dessert but left after the meal. He had a friend he needed to visit. Alice guessed that was the lady he'd hinted at earlier.

After a long visit afterwards Alice escorted her grandmother home.

"It feels strange," Helen said, "to be doing this again. I'd grown used to hearing you tell of strange people and strange places far away. Then I grew used to NOT hearing you tell me."

"Well, I have a tale to tell of very strange people and a place even further away. But first I haven't heard much from you. How are things at the library?"

It was not an idle question. Over the years she'd spent much time at the library among its small selection of magazines and newspapers and reading the books she'd checked out from it.

When the two were settled in to Helen's modest living room with hot tea Alice recounted her dream of being a dragonet.

"Except it was not a dream. It was a vivid reliving of an actual experience. My memories of it did not fade away the next day the way dreams do. They remain as clear to me as the breakfast I had this morning."

Helen took a sip of her tea, then refreshed it from the pot and added sugar and cream.

"You said the sky was violet."

"Like the sky just after sunrise or just before sunset. Only it was midday. The entire sky was that color.

"Hmm. I just remembered. I caught a glimpse of the sun as I zoomed up out of my dive. It was red and twice the size of our sun. So

I was definitely on a different planet in a different sun system."

Helen shook her head.

"As soon as I get used to the idea that you've lived three times before you spring on me the idea that you've lived more times. Under a different sun. As a nonhuman. Boy, it looks like I'll have to quit kidding Albert about reading those pulp science-fiction magazines."

They chewed over Alice's "dream" for a while more before the immortal hugged her grandmother, kissed her cheek, and left for her bed back at her childhood home.

<>

She stood with two or three dozen other people at the transparent front of the huge flying wing in which she'd ridden from the Greater Moon to the blue planet below. She was looking forward to meeting the nine-hundred-years-old multigenerational family to which she belonged. It had been nearly a century since they'd all congregated. Some of them had come from other stellar systems.

A number spoke silently in her head along with words that said it was time for her to disembark.

She turned to walk alongside the huge window, passing by the other people waiting for their call. She idly noted their variety of clothing, some so skimpy they almost seemed nothing at all, some covering the entire body. She passed by a triple of blue-furred cat-headed centauroids. Near one of the six-limbed creatures was a golden haired dog wearing a collar on which was mounted a button-like radio which would let its owner find it if the dog wandered out of sight.

<>

Alice sat up. She had dreamed again. As before it was a memory-not-a-dream: as clear to her as if it had happened the day before.

She not only remembered the experience, she remembered that the vehicle on which she'd been had been shaped like a wing but had no body, no tail, no landing wheels. It would never touch down. Instead it would fly all the way around the world, dropping off people above their destinations. Literally DROP them off. The people would go the last few miles flying inside a transparent egg-shaped bubble which would vanish an inch or so off the ground.

Further it had traveled not through air but through empty space from her home on an airless moon. It was a spaceplane, not an airplane.

There had been several intelligent creatures which looked like centaurs if the horse part was instead a panther part. Who had an upright body if the human head was instead a catlike head. And strangely it had owned a dog. That looked very like a golden retriever.

The person that she'd been was a human female, one over a hundred years old despite appearing the age of a teenager. She had expected to live thousands of years. It was part of a family made up of several hundred people. Who were getting together to celebrate the birth of three dozen children who would be part of six dozen people who were all married to each other.

That was it. She'd remembered an incident far away in time and space but remembered little about what came before and what would come soon after.

She also remembered something else: a vision of black space dotted with unblinking pinpoints of light which were stars. In the center of which was a twisting ribbon of light bright with all the colors of a rainbow. From her reading she knew what that was: a nebula, a cloud of gas several light years long.

Alice lay flat, turned onto her side, and pulled up the covers. Her world-view had just expanded enormously again. She drifted off to sleep reliving and reliving her recent memory-not-a-dream.

The next morning the memory was still bright in her imagination.

She had little time to revisit it however. Her day was packed with people she was to meet.

She had breakfast with her family who then left for their different jobs. They would not be free from work until Wednesday, the day before Christmas Eve. She left too, riding her old bicycle. She only had to pump up the tires a little bit. Her dad had bought a top of the line one with top of the line tires.

Distances in Llano were not great especially for a being with muscles a couple of dozen times as strong as those of humans. She whizzed along Ford street north to Main street and turned right to visit the Lightfoot farm. Passing under its LIGHTFOOT AGRICULTURE she saw ahead of her the two-story tall farmhouse and her silver Falcon parked alongside it.

She slowed and skidded to a halt near the porch. She jumped off, parked her bike by leaning it against the porch, and bounded up the steps onto the porch.

Before she could open the screen door into the house it was opened by Hannah Lightfoot who stepped outside to hug Alice.

They drew apart to look at each other.

Hannah had become a good friend after the two had graduated from high school. The youngest of three children with two older brothers, blonde like her mother Yvonne, she was a tall pretty girl who was the opposite of shy, unlike her mother.

"Well, stranger," she said, "You look like you've come to work on the farm. Or on your airplane.

"It sounds so strange. To think that someone could actually have personal airplane. And that I know her."

"You want to go up in her? I'm taking your dad up this morning."

"I'd love that. Come on in and see Mom and Grandma."

The kitchen was a natural place for four women to lounge and chat for the next hour. Alice fended off questions about herself, saying there'd be time for that at the dinner she was going to at the Lightfoot home that night. She quizzed the other three, spending extra effort to get Yvonne to talk. This included injecting the woman with microscopic messengers that helped her to again feel safe with the long-time friend of her daughter.

A little after 10:00 Adolf came in from some farm chore, bent down to kiss his wife's cheek, and said Hello to Alice.

"You still are going to take me up?"

"As soon as we top off the tank from your gasoline supply."

"Then let's get to it. You want to come along, Honey?"

His wife said an emphatic No but suggested Hester might like to go. She agreed.

"Good," said Alice. "The more the merrier. We have one more seat available. Hannah?"

"I'm still up for it. Do we need anything special to wear?"

"No. The plane is designed to be arm-sleeve comfortable up to 10,000 feet. That's about two miles."

Despite that assurance the two passengers insisted on changing clothes. The new outfits turned out to be a split skirt for the older woman and woman-cut jeans for the younger.

"You're responsible for these," said Hannah. She turned completely around so that Alice and the others could get a good look at the jeans. "They're all the rage in Austin. I think I even saw your name on one of the labels: 'Plane Rider Style' or some such."

Alice grinned. "The company that puts those out actually got my permission to use the phrase 'Plane Rider.' They pay me a few dollars a month."

It was a few hundred dollars a month and the amount was rising. The jeans company that sold them was adding several colors: not only blue but green, gold, black, purple, and pink (Alice shuddered at the thought of that last hue whenever it occurred to her). There were also blue jeans with sequins.

The same company had changed its jeans jacket line to match the pants line. A few fashion-forward young women were actually wearing the color-coordinated outfits to formal events.

All of which had stimulated newspaper editorials decrying the vulgarization of women's fashions. Thus adding to the fame of "Plane Rider" Alice Willoughby and Texas Aviation.

The advent of inexpensive glossy color paper had also added to the mania. Alice's beauty was already adorning both covers and interiors of several local and New York fashion magazines. One highly fictionalized article in a tabloid titled "Angel or Aphrodite?" supposedly told her life story.

A few minutes later the four boarded the plane. Alice put Adolf in the copilot's seat and began the check list.

Adolf said, "That's quite a list. I'd supposed you just turned a key like on a truck."

"Maybe some day. But there's a lot to do and double-check before you put a few tons in the air. Up there is not a natural environment for people."

Though it seemed to be for some creatures who were also intelligent beings.

Five minutes later the Falcon rolled over the grass of the meadow and lifted into the air.

Over the muffled drone of the engine Alice said, "I'm going to do a low-and-slow circuit of your property. Then we'll spiral up and out. I'll tilt the plane both to the left and right to give both our ladies a better look down."

Ten minutes into the flight the farm owner took out a pencil and jotted some notes on a square of paper from a shirt pocket before stowing them away. Then later, when they were much higher, he did it again.

At 5000 feet Alice leveled off and did her widest circle around Llano at a distance of about a mile. Then she slowly began to descend.

"Is that as high as you can go?"

"No, twice that high is our limit. Same as on the Hawk. It's a good height. The cooler air makes the engine more efficient. The thinner air offers less resistance so you can travel faster. At about 200 miles an hour Austin is 20-30 minutes away."

They were coming a mile away from the farm now and about 500 feet up.

"We're working on a Hawk II, bigger, more powerful engine. Its ceiling will be 20,000 feet, about four miles. It ought to get to San Antone in a half hour, Houston in three-quarters of an hour."

"And Dallas?"

"An hour."

"Damn, I'd better start investing in aviation."

"Good idea, but--hold on a second."

She touched gently down and taxied and turned into the Falcon's preferred resting place. She shut down the engine and returned to her conversation.

"Take extra care investing in aviation. It's a fast-growth industry but that means lots of companies are going to try to cash in on it. This means lots more risky companies are going to get involved."

"Noted. Hey, back there! Think we could eat a little early?!"

The answer came back Yes! Soon everyone sat down at a long lunch where the main topic was the recent flight.

It took a half hour to top off the gasoline tanks of the Falcon. Adolf supervised the effort by two of his hired hands. Meanwhile he and Alice chatted.

"Thanks for the ride, Alice. I got lots more out of it than just interesting sights. Up there I could see some problems--and promises--that I would never have come up with on the ground."

"That explains the note taking."

"Right. It would be nice to do it again."

"I couldn't take time away to do it. But you could hire a crop-duster pilot to take you up. But be damned careful you pick a very careful pilot and plane. Air travel is damned dangerous. It's much more unforgiving than ground travel."

"Hmm. Point taken. I think I could hire some photographer to go up and take photos."

"That would be my advice. See if you can get someone who can take color photos. Take lots of them from different angles. And heights."

Soon the topping off was done. Adolf gave her a brief strong hug totally without sexual interest; Alice had long ago inoculated him against her beauty.

"Later!"

"Later!"

He went off to his more usual farm chores and Alice sat down in the Falcon's doorway, feet dangling to within a few inches off the ground, to wait for Albert Moseley.

She did not have long to wait. A blue pickup soon came onto the farm. It was battered but, as she knew her former mechanic friend well, was surely well-maintained. The purr of its motor as it grew near and parked assured her that her guess was so.

"Hey, Alice!" said Albert as he left his truck and slammed the door closed. He came toward her and hugged her. She returned the hug and checked his health with a probe of his body. All was well.

Another truck-door slam heralded the exit of two women from the other side of the truck. One was Patricia, a girl whom Alice had befriended in high school against a stalker. She was wearing a blue floral-print dress and looked much the same as she had when she'd been a cheerleader in high school. Her eyes were dark and her eyebrows dramatic which well matched her ebon hair cut in her usual page-boy bob.

The other was an older woman. Youthful but with dark hair with grey streaks in it, she was comfortably plump, plain of face, and wore a green dress adorned with gold and russet leaves.

"I want you to meet my friend Julia," Albert said. "And you remember Patricia."

Patricia pushed ahead and she and Alice hugged. As they broke apart Albert's "friend" approached with a hand held out.

The shapechanger shook the hand and sent microscopic messengers into the woman's body to explore it. The information flowing back from the probe revealed a healthy body. The flavor of the information revealed a warmly empathetic and even-tempered person.

"I've heard so much about you, Miss Willoughby. Not just from Albert. I'm happy to finally meet you."

"Any friend of Al's should feel free to call me Alice."

Albert said, "Julia and I met at a birthday party given to me by my family at Famous Barbecue. Her family was doing the same thing. Our parties started at the same time and the two got mixed together.

Everybody got confused until Julia and I decided to combine the two. And we've been together ever since."

Patricia bounced up and down and clapped her hands but then said, "OK, when do we get to..."

She made one flattened hand "fly" straight ahead waggling wildly side to side suggesting an airplane doing acrobatics.

"Right now," said Alice. "But without acrobatics. We'll go around low and slow and tilt to the side just enough to give both sides good looks at the ground below us."

"OH, it won't do acrobatics?"

She looked at the sleek streamlined body of Falcon with its mildly swept back wings. It certainly looked nimble.

Everybody stared at the plane. Julia said, "It looks so pretty. Like it wants to fly and fast."

"It can. It was designed to do acrobatics at air shows and perform in races. But as you'll see the insides are built for comfort. We hope to sell Falcons to generals and company bosses to commute to all the meetings they have to go to.

"Here, now. Use these steps and put your hands on the door jamb to get up and into it."

She demonstrated her advice and stood just inside the door with a hand held out to whoever came up the three-step metal stairs.

This proved to be Julia helped from the ground by Albert, then Patricia who more bounded up than stepped up the abbreviated stairway. Lastly came Albert.

Without prompting he pulled up the stairway and folded it into its well, then closed the door and locked it into place. Alice, already melding into the airplane, felt him do it and do it right. She'd expected no less from the former auto mechanic.

She personally settled Julia into one of the two seats behind the cockpit and prompted the woman to fasten her seat belt. Albert was doing the same for Patricia who waved him off and locked her seat belt with an emphatic clash.

In the cockpit with Albert belted into the copilot's seat she showed him the six round-faced instruments at the top of the several displays and controls in front of each seat.

"These are the essential readouts. They show height, direction, speed, how fast we're climbing or descending, our front-back tilt, and left-right tilt. The gas tank is here--" She pointed out each ending with the gas gauge in the space between the two identical control panels.

She pulled out the checklist for readiness and startup from its slot in her control panel. Prompted, Albert pulled his own copy out from the copilot's control panel till it plopped down at a slant in front of him where he could easily read it.

"We use this to make sure we don't miss a step or do it out of order. Why don't you follow along with me and say 'Check' when I do each of them?"

It took ten minutes before Alice revved the engine a few times and slowly began to pull out to the takeoff point. She rotated to face west and slowly began to roll forward. Shortly they lifted off at the lowest and slowest speed the Falcon could safely handle. She wanted Julia to have the gentlest flight possible.

As in the morning she did a low circle of the town and then repeated it in a few lazy expanding spirals higher. Each tilt to left and right was slow and moderate.

Just below the level of the flat-based cottony clouds she spoke over her shoulder.

"If you've ever wondered what clouds are like you can see now. We're going to dip into one for just a minute, no longer."

She rose into the nearest edge of a cloud and flew through it. She pointed at the instruments in front of Albert.

"You can see why the altitude and altitude indicators are so important. Flying blind like this you can easily get turned around or even way off level."

They abruptly emerged into bright sunlight. Everyone blinked at the sudden change except the shapechanger.

Julia laughed. "It was just like a foggy day!"

"That's right. That's all clouds are. Fog up above us."

Alice began a slow spiral toward the ground and turned into her landing flight path. She lowered slowly, very gently put the plane on the ground, taxied to its resting place, and cut the engine.

Alice followed her passengers out of the plane and closed and locked its door.

"So, Albert, what's next?"

"Next we go to my store. I want to show it off."

Julia said, "While you three do that I've got to get back to my clothing store. Margaret is holding it down right now but I like to have two people at it when we're open."

As they approached his truck Alice said, "I'm going to ride in the back. No way am I going to be packed in like sardines."

Albert said, "I've got my old sleeping bag behind my seat. Let me get it out for you to sit on."

"I'll just stand."

Julia said, "Oh, you shouldn't do that! You might fall and get hurt."

"Kind of you to be concerned. But if I can keep my feet standing atop a bucking bull standing in a pickup bed driving over the road to Albert's shop is trivial."

Albert said, "Don't worry, Honey. She knows what she's talking about and I'll be extra careful with my driving."

The woman still looked troubled but got into the passenger side of the truck and moved toward the middle of the seat. Patricia slid in beside her and slammed the passenger door closed.

Albert kept his word and drove slowly and carefully the mile and a half to his store, Alice serenely standing in his truck bed with only one hand casually placed atop the roof of the vehicle.

Their passage on the city streets was noticed by people on the sidewalks. They got calls of "Hey, Rider" and "Rider! Back in town!" and "Go, Rider!"

Albert had scored a good location for his business. This was a two-story building which was one of a couple dozen businesses on Ford Street which ran north and south by the court house. He had been clued in by her father who was well tuned into business happenings in Llano.

The front of the building had a pair of wide picture windows in the front on each side of the door. Alice entered the door to hear bells ring above her.

"This place looks nice," she said, looking around at a large room with a glass-faced and -topped display counter opposite the entrance from the street. Products in clear plastique hung on the walls to each side. More products were on low tables near the picture windows easily seen from the street. Four shoved-together tables in the center of the floor held four calculators with their screens positioned back to back. A shopper could walk all around the display and see activity on each of the four screens.

"Mostly not my doing. Patricia designed most of this."

The girl said, "Thanks for the plane ride, Alice. I've got some things I need to do in the back. I'll see you at the steak house tonight."

With a wave she exited into a hallway behind the wide display counter.

Julia said, "I'll leave too. I need to relieve Margaret. I thank you too for the plane ride. It was wonderful, how everything looked from up there."

"I'll walk with you. I want to see your store."

"Oh, great!" said Albert. "Once you two get to talking clothes I'll never see Alice again."

Julia stood on tip toes to kiss one of his cheeks.

"Don't worry. I promise I'll shoo her out before long."

He preceded the two women to the door and held it open for them.

Julia's shop was near the end of the block in which the calculator shop stood. Alice thought Albert and Julia must have met eventually but was happy that their shared birthday had led them to meet earlier. The two seemed a good match.

This meant that she had to have a special talk with Julia.

"Can you give your co-worker fifteen or twenty minutes out of the shop?"

"We usually take breaks halfway through the afternoon. Margaret likes to walk around a bit and maybe chat with a friend in one of the other shops."

"Good."

Margaret, a short round brunette, was happy to be relieved at the dress shop but first she had to tell Alice how much she had enjoyed seeing her ride bulls.

"Then when you stood atop that plane...! I was so afraid you'd fall off."

"There was no danger of that. I had a rope attached to a belt around my waist. I couldn't fall."

"I guessed it had to be something like that. But I couldn't see the rope and I wasn't sure."

"It was blue braided plastique fiber. The sight blended in with the blue sky."

"Oh, OK. See you later."

Julia said, "Take your time. Alice and I need to talk about some stuff."

Margaret nodded and almost skipped out the door.

"An enthusiastic girl," said Alice.

"It could be tiring if she wasn't so adorable. And smart. She knows our products and is very good at selling them."

Julia led the way behind the combined counter and display case to a couple of plastique lawn chairs. They sat in them, able to see over the counter if a customer entered the store.

"I think of Albert as another of my brothers, an adopted one. Adopted by me. Now that your family and mine are going to come together you need to know some things about me."

"What makes you think we are going to 'come together'?"

"The pale ring around your ring finger is a clue. But more important is the way you two are together. It's almost as if you are already married."

Julia looked at her left hand.

"I don't see any pale ring."

"I can see things others can't. That is part of what I need to tell you."

"Go ahead. You've got me curious. Are you a Secret Murderer?" *The Secret Murders* was a recent popular murder mystery book.

"I'll begin at the beginning: when I was born. I have a rare medical syndrome. For several years I matured physically about three times as fast as other people. So I looked sixteen on my sixth birthday.

"I matured mentally even faster, so I was maybe early thirties then. Partly because I read a lot, everything, fact, fiction, books, magazines, newspapers. I need less sleep than most people so I read a LOT.

"I could not go to public school because of my rapid aging. So my parents said they'd home school me. Then they and other friends lobbied for the high school to give me all exams required to graduate. It took two years of stubborn lobbying until they agreed. I passed all their tests."

"Patricia told me a little of this, just in passing, not in any detail, just random comments. She also mentioned--just mentioned, no more--that there was some trouble at school."

Alice was not sure just what was going through Julia's mind. All her subtle biological signals said that she was calmly and mildly interested.

"I spent a lot of time in Patricia's senior year in high school working there, helping in the library, grading multiple choice tests, bringing water and towels to the cheerleaders. Patricia mentioned that a boy was bothering her, following her home, stuff like that.

"So I accompanied her one afternoon. He was waiting outside of her house. I told him to go away and never bother her or any girl again. I can be very scary. This is partly because everyone knew me from my bull riding which takes a tough person to do."

"And a skilled person."

Alice shrugged.

"The word got around even though the boy didn't talk about his experience. Some boys, and an older man who hung around with them at school, decided they'd teach me a lesson. They began to secretly stalk me.

"They were very clumsy--"

At that a customer came in and Julia stood up to help them out. Satisfied, the woman left. Julia escorted her to the door and turned a sign hanging just inside the glass door so that its street side read BACK IN FIVE MINUTES. Then she returned to her chair.

"So," the woman said, "you noticed. And...?"

"I started taking short cuts home from school down dark alleys and near places closed at night. One night they waylaid me. When the older man said they were going to kill me two of them left. You sure you want to hear the rest?"

Julia nodded. Her attention was now strongly focused but still very calm.

"The two in front of me attacked. I'm very tough, and as I've said I can be very scary. I ignored the older man when he hit me over my head with a baseball bat and knocked him down. The boy beside him got scared and ran away.

"I let him go and turned toward the two behind me. I knocked them down. Then I beat all three of them very badly, being careful to cause pain but not permanent injury. I enjoyed their screams."

Alice's last statement was intended to provoke SOME emotion from her listener. She succeeded but not in the way she'd expected.

Julia laughed.

"Good. You expected me to be shocked? Honey, I've had my share of hateful attention. I've just glad you were able to dish out some punishment to men like them.

"Plus, what you have said is no surprise. When I knew that Albert was the man for me I looked into his family. My folks and I moved here from Fredericksburg only three years ago, so I didn't know much about anyone here.

"But people here haven't forgotten your history. They just take it for granted. If approached right they are willing to talk about it. And they did.

"I didn't know the details of your fight-- If it can be called that: those boys expected a kitten and got a tiger. They were out of their league long before that night.

"Anyway, thanks for entrusting me with this side of you. I'll have no qualms about having you as a sister. Of sorts."

Alice smiled. "I'll think of you that way. Even if you annoy me. You haven't yet, but it's bound to happen someday.

"Like any sister, if you have need you can call on me for whatever aid or resources I can give."

Her newest "sister" got up, walked to the door, and flipped the sign hanging inside it to show to the world that the shop was OPEN FOR BUSINESS. She came back and spoke.

"Now that we've got that out of the way I have a few items that I think you need for your image."

Alice laughed. "As long as I get a family discount!"

All told Alice spent about forty minutes with Julia and Margaret, returning to Albert's shop with four big shopping bags of clothing and a pair of sleek chic black boots suitable for a formal outing. They would go well with French couturier Coco Chanel's "little black dress" but were suitable for almost any elegant outfit.

Albert was talking to a customer when Alice returned and so only nodded to her. Patricia was also busy, doing something with displays mounted on one of the walls. Alice put her bags away in the back office and returned to the front room to sit in one of the white plastique lawn chairs behind the counter.

Albert sat in another chair when the customer left carrying a hefty box of some equipment.

"Have a good visit with Julia?"

"I did. I think you two will have a good life together."

"I'm sure of it. Ah, did she tell you we are going to get married?"

"She didn't have to. It wasn't long before I realized that was in the cards. So what's the latest in the electronics world? I spend all my time in the aviation world. I don't have time to keep up with electronics too."

"A lot of new stuff from Ireland and the UK, but America is beginning to catch up. I have high hopes we'll eventually surpass

Europe in advances."

Immortals took a long view of events. Alice said, "You will. Your population is bigger and growing bigger all the time. Plus your culture is forward looking and creative, while Europe is still too mired in its past."

Albert was long familiar with Alice's view of the world as if she lived not in it but from high above it, as if a goddess on Mount Olympus. He went on.

"One big advance is 'cooperative' calculation. Tell me, how many calculators does Texas Aviation have?"

"One each for us partners, one in the showroom, several on the factory floor, and one in each engineering office."

"And you share information how? I'm guessing you print out information and take it or send it to the others."

"Right."

"So to get that info into your computers you have to copy it by hand."

"We have started to print stuff out on cards in the form of punches of digital code. Then we can read that with card readers."

"There's a better way. Europe has been converting over to digital, rather than analog, transmission of information over wires for some time."

"I know. How does this relate to cooperative calculation?"

"Simply, you can connect all your calculators together and share information. No recopying."

Alice turned this idea over in her head. Albert let her take her time.

"I see. Too we could send and receive information over telephone lines."

"Yes. With the limitation that you would have to have a box to translate digital info to analog info to send anything. The other end would have to have a reverse translation to digital. At least until America changes over to digital transmission."

Alice thought some more. A customer came in and wanted to talk to Albert rather than Patricia. He stood up and went to the four-calculator display in the middle of the room. A lengthy discussion led to another purchase.

When he sat down he said, "I'm going to start a company to sell products to customers with calculators over the phone lines. The first customers will be people rich enough and smart enough to buy and use calculators. The startup will be slow and a money loser but if I budget the expenses I think I can afford it.

"For people who can't afford a big home calculator they could buy this."

He took a small folding calculator from the display case, opened it to a small typewriter style keyboard, and brought up an image on the screen half of the machine.

They were still chatting when Patricia reminded them that it was time to close shop and get ready for a steak dinner Albert was hosting for Alice that evening.

<>

Hemming's Famous Steak House was in North Llano a few blocks to the west of north-south Ford Street on the major highway 29. The highway went to Mason in the west and much further to Fort Stockton and far El Paso, "The Queen of the West" or so the city said. It went to Burnet in the east and eventually to Georgetown just north of Austin. The "Famous" part of its name was only slightly an exaggeration.

At 7:00 the place was already full and overflowing to the tables placed outside of it cheek-by-jowl with the parking lot which was almost filled by automobiles and a couple of horse-drawn surreys and four horses. It only had a couple of big tables free because Albert had made a reservation and because the Moseley's and the Beckmann's were prominent families in Llano.

Much of the first quarter hour was taken up by Julia introducing Alice to her family: mother, father, four big blond brothers and a slender younger sister equally blond. All had heard of her and the kids were in awe of her. Alice had long become used to her fame but the responses to it still embarrassed her a bit.

Settled down the dozen people ordered. Alice, seated between Beckmann Mama and Beckmann Little Sis, had to answer many questions about life in Austin by the two women. The mother thought life in the big city must include much shady and dangerous activity. The sis thought so too but considered that an attraction.

"Tell you what, Mrs. Beckmann, if you and your family visit me in Austin I'll be sure you only go to the safest parts of the city."

"Aww," said Mila.

Alice grinned at her.

"Don't worry. I'll be sure we go to really neat jumping places. My Mr. Porter is especially fond of jazz and knows plenty of places to hear music and dance."

"I don't hold with dancing," said the mama.

"Now, Mama Beckmann, ministers say that it is an entertainment sanctioned by the Bible in at least four places. Especially in Ecclesiastes you may remember it tells us all the righteous times to weep, laugh, dance, and so on.

"Naturally it must be overseen by respectable people like you and done in a decorous manner. I especially enjoy ballroom dancing. I assure you it is done in Austin in a dignified manner by the most genteel people."

"It sounds boring," said Mila.

"Not at all. One of the reasons I like it is because we women can dress up the very latest in formal women's fashions. Of course the VERY latest is quite expensive. I only own one such dress, which I bought from Julia just this afternoon."

Mollified by the suggestion that respectable and rich people danced Mama Beckmann turned the conversation in another direction: when Alice might find a man and marry.

Nearly an hour into the evening Albert stood up and asked for attention. He was ignored at first until Papa Beckman stood up and demanded it. He was big and loud and his family at least paid attention.

The two celebrating tables quieted quickly. Several nearby tables did too, curious at what was going on.

"Thank you. I will make it short and sweet. My darling Julia has made me the happiest man in the world by consenting to be my wife."

"That's my boy!" said Mr. Moseley. "Cheers for the couple!"

He raised a glass of beer and was quickly joined by the others at the tables. A cheer rose up. It was a loud one, as the nearer tables joined in the toast, then much of the remaining tables, always ready to make noise at any excuse.

Julia rose and smilingly showed off her wedding ring, a golden band with a single medium-sized diamond and several smaller diamonds.

The immortal surprised herself by tearing up to the point of sniffles. Her dear Albert was going to be happy! With a worthy wife!

The party became noisier for a time. By a half hour later, however, it began to break up. Alice stayed till she was the only one left.

On the way to her car she sensed someone watching her. She pretended to be oblivious until she heard a voice call her. It had a tentative sound.

"Miss Alice. Ma'am. Ma'am."

She turned to see a tall man slowly approach her from the direction of the steakhouse. As he neared she recognized Joey, one of the men who'd attacked her years ago. He'd run away when he saw what a near-demonic force she was. She'd caught up with him but spoken to him rather punish him. He'd since become almost a friend.

"Ma'am. I waited until I could say something clear. I just want to thank you again for what you've done for me."

"You are very welcome, Joey. How have you been?"

"You really want to know?"

"I wouldn't have asked if I didn't."

He shifted from one foot to the other.

"Come back to the steak house, Joey. It's quiet enough now to talk."

A half hour before closing on a weeknight there were plenty of tables. They got one near the kitchen. Alice ordered a glass of wine, which the business kept for a few of their fancier customers. Joey ordered a glass of hard cider, one of the least alcoholic drinks available in Llano.

"I don't drink much," he said. "It gets me in trouble."

"Very wise. Now what happened to you in recent years?"

"After graduation I joined the Marines. It suited me. I've always been something of a trouble maker, as you recall."

Alice grinned and saluted him with her wine glass. He smiled slightly in return.

"I figured I really ought to tame that part of myself before I really got into trouble. Like the trouble I was headed for when that asshole tried to hurt you."

"Rape and beat to death you mean."

He grimaced. "Yeah. That.

"So, it suited me. Basic training was Hell, but I was glad of it. It seemed like the punishment I'd escaped when you were merciful with me. I may be the only man ever who ever thought that way."

"It's rare, I'm sure." But embracing suffering, the immortal knew, was not that rare.

"I graduated with honors and got my choice of three assignments. That action in Panama, for instance. I was there. Then in Nigeria."

"Nasty actions that last."

He grimaced. "Yeah. The Marines were good for me. But no way am I going to chance going along with stuff like that. Not that all my duty was like that. Most of it wasn't. But still."

As Li Wei Alice'd had staff who'd been very helpful in getting his work done. It would be nice if she had at least one assistant in this life. He or she did need certain qualifications, among them knowledge of some of her extranatural abilities. She made a decision.

"Are you looking for work?"

"Sort of getting used to being a civilian. I'm staying with my parents, helping out a little bit."

"If you want a full-time job I need an assistant."

"You do? That would be-- I don't want charity."

"You know me well enough, I think, to know I'd not give it."

"Then, sure. What would I need to do, though?"

"You finished high school with good grades, I recall. Can you use calculators?"

He nodded. "They tasked me to provide calc support a couple of times."

"Good. A few ground rules. I will never be your lover."

The revulsion on his face was enough to convince her he'd never want to be one. But then seeing her turn into an all-destroying monster could be a tad hard to forget!

"I may have to kill people some time, but very rarely women and NEVER children. You would have to fight only if we must defend ourselves from attack.

"Violence will be rare in my life. I'll avoid anything that might lead to it. You would mostly be a gopher and a researcher. That's why your calc skills are so important. You will get more of those skills as time goes on. When you quit you'll be a very valuable employee for somcone."

He nodded. "I'll have to find a place in Austin. I can leave--"

"You'll leave with me Tuesday in my plane. There's a garage apartment behind my home in Austin. You'll need to clean it up and make a few repairs--which I'll pay for--when you move in. The rent will be deducted from your pay."

She named a sum. He was happy to hear how generous it was.

"You'll get time off after a certain time, medical benefits, and a subsistence allowance. All the usual benefits, in other words."

Not that he would ever need medical benefits. She'd give him perfect health and if she was around if he was wounded she could fix almost anything short of death.

"Do you have a truck? You'll have to drive it to Austin if--"

"I've been using a friend's motorbike. I could buy it--"

"We can take it on the plane if you really want--"

He was shaking his head. "I'd prefer to get my own in Austin, a good one."

"Only if you want to. I'll assign a company truck to you for work and you can use it after hours.

"So. Sound good?"

"Yes, Ma'am, it does."

"Well, then, you start now by paying for our drinks with this including a generous tip. I'll collect you next Tuesday. Have a merry Christmas, Joey."

She stood up, handed him some money, and walked into the dark.

Alice herself had a merry Christmas. All her family got gifts, several each. Most were modest. Some were humorous. All were tailored to the recipient. She got gifts in return in the same vein.

Helen got her most prized gift on Christmas Eve when she and Alice spent an evening together. It was more stories about what the immortal had done as a man, including the time before his Chinese years when he'd been an Arab.

On Christmas day she visited Albert and Julia who were living together and gave them gifts. They had a few for her as well.

Then at noon Alice delivered a present to her home town. She took the Falcon up and gave an aerobatic air show.

First she flew low over the eastern part of South Llano, then the courthouse, then the western part. By then most of North Llano as well as South Llano was alerted that something was going on in the sky.

She made a U-turn a few miles to the west and began back toward Llano, this time about 500 feet up. She started out with a simple corkscrewing motion rolling over and over while flying in a straight line.

After an eastward pass she reversed and did a westward pass--upside down.

On her next eastward pass she did loops. She began with simple loops then progressed to more elaborate ones such as a double loop with parts of the flight upside down.

The last part of the show began with a vertical climb. The Falcon had been built to safely fly straight up at full power for a half mile, a fuel-hungry maneuver. Alice went up only to a 1000 feet, flying ever more slowly. Till the plane seemed to falter and fall over on its back. It tumbled like a falling leaf, spinning upside down around its center.

Alice released smoke from the wing tips, blue from one wing and red from the other. At first the smoke was a spiraling near-purple as the smoke mixed. Then the plane righted itself in a straight-down dive and the smoke separated into a clearly defined spiral. The idling engine strengthened then roared. The spiral went to two straight lines pointing down. Finally the Falcon leveled off and raced eastward, disappearing into the distance.

On the ground her family, which had driven her to the Lightfoot farm, greeted her with congratulations, her mother saying "I had my heart in my throat at the last."

Alice chuckled. "Even though I told you all several times that I was going to end in a scary finish that was perfectly safe. That I'd done it a dozen times to make it safe."

"Even though," her mother said, chuckling too.

That afternoon the mayor convened a meeting with the town council and decreed Monday an "Airgirl Day" with a fair. Early Sunday the annual fair committee convened and went into high gear planning.

An impromptu fair would be short on exhibits and events but that would be offset by several means. One of those was the contribution "for a small fee" by the Hennessey Spirits Distribution Company. It would give out low-alcohol "free beer" while the supplies lasted. Coincidentally when low-alcohol mixed drinks went on sale.

Meats would be on short supply and so would be sold in various forms of finger food. There would be a goodly supply of several kinds of bread, however. This included bread delivered Monday morning from other towns. These included Burnet to the east, Mason to the west, Cherokee to the north, and Fredericksburg to the south.

At 3:00, an hour after the Airgirl Fair began, the Mayor from an impromptu platform officially declared that it was Airgirl Day and introduced "popular hometown girl" Miss Alice Willoughby. Alice gave a very short Thank You speech and left the stand to shake a lot of hands. After a quarter hour of that she waved to the remaining people in line to see her, gave them all a loud Thank You All, and turned to disappear in the crowd around her

Tuesday morning her family took her to Lightfoot Agricultural and said Goodbye with many hugs from them and Albert and Julia and the Lightfoot women. Adolf Lightfoot shook her hand and said, with a big grin, "See you any time--Airgirl."

On the Falcon Alice showed Joey where to stash his duffle bag and two small suitcases, then led the way to the cockpit. She had him sit in the copilot's seat.

"You'll get a better view up here. Also I want you to watch what I'm doing. Someday you'll be doing this too. Don't strain, just watch. We'll take it easy teaching you to be a pilot. There's no hurry, we'll take baby steps.

"Here's the first." She pulled the Ready and Takeoff Checklist out of its slot in front of him so that it hung at a slant where he could easily read it. "You don't just crank the engine and go like in a truck. Read off each of the items."

"Sure, Boss. Ah, 'Turn to Off all switches.'"

"Turn to Off all switches, done"

Shortly the Falcon rolled to its takeoff starting point, turned toward the downwind direction, and began the roll that would see it lift into the air on its way to Austin.

Chapter 8 - Supersonic

It was just past Valentine's Day that Alice had a memory-not-a-dream unlike other such occasional dreams.

It began as with a previous "dream" with her walking alongside a huge picture window in a flying-wing spaceship. Again she passed the small family, if that what it was, of catlike blue centaur people. She stopped at a line of people three long facing a door. At a silent command that only she heard she stepped to stand in front of the door when her time came.

It slid open and she went in. The door behind her closed. An instant later the floor disappeared and she fell into the air above a sprawling country side.

It was not an uncontrolled fall. She had called up a protective transparent egg shape about her and only then had the spaceship ejected her from it.

She was falling at several hundred miles an hour. Somehow she knew when her speed dropped from supersonic to a slower speed. Her preprogrammed flight took her into a path curving from forward to down.

Below her tall buildings up to a mile high formed a forest made of a form of plastique much harder than that of Earth's. Each building was surrounded by a green park of trees, some with flowering branches of all the colors.

Atop the building she was falling toward was a flat surface with a small park atop it, including a blue-bottomed swimming pool. Her preprogrammed path brought her floating ever so lightly to a stop an inch above one tiled side of the pool.

The force-field egg disappeared and she fell a few inches. She flexed her legs to absorb the impact of the fall, an action as casual as taking a step down to a lower stair step.

The green-skinned woman lying in a lawn chair in front of her, nude but somehow not seeming nude, said--

<>

"Shit."

Alice sat up in her bed. What the fuck had the woman said? In what language?

She lay back and pulled the bed covers up around her neck. The air was chill and, though she could be comfortable naked in the Arctic, she let her body feel what the body of an ordinary person would feel. That way she would without thought act like an ordinary human.

One difference from previous dreams was that in front of her in the darkness of her bedroom she sensed a control...panel? It was somewhat like a calculator keyboard. Even as she thought it the panel dissolved and reformed inside her. The keys of the keyboard became desires she could express: Go right. Go up/down/sideways. Lift off. Form shield. Unform shield. How far is that?

That last was the same desire and resulting action of her now well-practiced distance sense.

She looked up at the light fixture dim in the darkness of--3:13 AM said her internal clock, one she'd had through three lifetimes.

She knew its space/time/universe coordinates instantly.

LIFT OFF. Her body inched upward against her blanket.

Damn! She was flying. STOP. She lay suspended in the air maybe six inches high. DESCEND. Her body eased down to once more lie flat, the weight of gravity slowly reasserting itself to press her lightly against her mattress.

Alice took a deep breath and let it out slowly.

She swung herself so that her feet lay flat on the carpet beside her bed. She stood up.

FORM she desired. An invisible egg shape snapped into place around her. One side pressed against her bed and dimpled inward to keep its outer side outside the bed. She floated a few inches up into the center of the egg shape. Her legs and arms assumed the slightly bent posture of someone jumping off something. The shielding egg shape moved up slowly so that its surface was again an egg shape.

She desired TURN LEFT. Leisurely her body spun on it vertical axis till it faced left. This was the window onto the back yard.

It was big enough to let her pass through. To make that easier if she ever want to do it she'd put a drop or two of light oil on the slide so that the window slid easily and silently open.

Now she banished the bubble around her, landed lightly as her weight returned, dressed for the day, walked to the window, and sat in it, her legs outside and her bottom on the window sill. Then she launched her self into the empty air.

Well away from the window she DESIRED the bubble to surround her and to move upward.

It shot into the night sky, accelerating rapidly. Nearly a mile up it passed the speed of sound. The conical shock wave behind it struck everything below her. The impact circle widened quickly over the surface as the egg flew skyward. A good tenth of the city was jolted awake from a thunder clap out of clear sky.

The thought came to her that she should fly no faster than the speed of sound at any height if she wanted to remain unnoticed.

She did not bother to slow down. The harm if any was already done.

By now she was flying well over 1000 miles per hour and still accelerating: 1500, 2500, 3000, 4000, 6000.

At ten miles high she DESIRED to stop. She did, instantly. With no feeling of change. She just floated, the grey world serene below her, lit by stars and a crescent moon in the west.

Below her she could see the Austin sprawl. Its center, always lit, showed its buildings in a wash of yellow light. From the city center light spread, solid first then interspersed with grey. Here and there points of red, green, gold, and all the other colors lay or blinked where businesses announced their presence. Wider and wider grew the spiderweb of light until it shredded away to the occasional glimmer.

She lifted her eyes toward a line of light angling away to the southwest. It was the road to San Antonio. It grew to dashes of light projected by the headlights of cars and trucks. In the far distance the road to San Antonio brightened again as it neared that city some 80 miles away. It too was a spiderweb of yellow light with a solid center.

She DESIRED to face east. There Houston lay at the very edge of the horizon, its golden light dimmed by distance.

How quickly could she get there? Did she have enough breathable air inside the egg?

Alice drew in a breath, tasting the air.

There was not a hint of staleness. The air was being replenished somehow, though not fast enough to totally wash away the complex sccnts of her bedroom.

She noticed that the air temperature was still in the low 60s, which was much warmer than the air just outside the bubble. It must be at least below freezing, maybe much below, out there.

She was in the same egg-shaped aircraft, or spaceship, that she remembered from her dream-not-a-dream.

The immortal shook her head in wonder.

Beyond the edge of the horizon far beyond Houston was a hint of the twilight before dawn. The day was spinning toward morning at--a little after 5:00 in the morning.

How fast could she go at this height? At a much greater height?

She remembered that at 100,000 feet, almost 20 miles, the air pressure was barely one percent that of sea level. That ought to be high enough to travel really fast!

The bubble was instantly moving thousands of miles per hour straight up. Alice sent it curving eastward, flying toward the dawn.

The dawn raced toward her. Shortly twilight brightened toward daylight and the sun rose. When it was a hands-width above the horizon the immortal slowed to a stop. The coastline was below her and a little eastward.

She recognized that section of coastline from a map. That city on that river not very far from the ocean must be...Jacksonville, Florida. She'd gone a thousand miles in just a few minutes.

New York City was about a thousand miles to the northeast. A thought sent the immortal racing toward the King City.

At a little over four minutes later she instantly came to a stop above it. She'd traveled at about 15,000 miles per hour.

What awesome power she'd inherited from...someone. From what far distance in time and space?

She--the bubble around her--could smash a city by traveling straight down at its maximum speed. This would surely be much more than 15,000 mph. The air pressure it sent ahead of her would pound the surface flat.

She almost regretted recovering this power from some distant ancestor. Almost.

What would Chinese food be like in New York's Chinatown?

She dove to find out.

<>

As Alice walked the early morning streets of Chinatown she let her face morph into that of a Han Chinese, the dominant Chinese ethnic group. Her skin changed to that of most Chinese. She kept her Alice walk and demeanor, not taking that of a woman of mainland China.

She built up an assumed history. She would never volunteer it but it would, like the underwater bulk of an iceberg, shape the above water nature of her character. Alice Wong was a third generation Chinese who'd visited China years ago, the city of Hang-zhou just inland of the Hang-zhou Bay. Alice Wong could easily describing parts of that city if asked. Li Wei had lived there for two decades, a respected academic periodically doing jobs for the Chinese Empress, a shapechanger whom Li knew well.

Some of the jobs had not been public. They had been in partnership with the Dread Reaper, another shapechanger who had assumed a Chinese identity.

The history amused Alice. It had a secret inside a secret inside a secret.

She turned into the Auntie Liang's Szechuan Best Kitchen. It was a middle-sized upscale restaurant filling up already despite the early hour.

A young woman in a long bright blue silk dress decorated with a delicate flower pattern greeted her.

"*Nin hao ba*," said Alice Wong in a Bei-jing dialect with a Chinese east coast accent. She put her hands together in front of her and bowed ever so slightly to the greeter, the sort of casual gesture to formality of an American who was none too respectful of the old ways.

"Good morning, Miss," said the greeter in English. She made no gesture of respect. Let the American feel slighted. She did not care.

"One table, please. By a window if possible."

Alice cast her gaze toward the side, seeing several such tables available.

"I'm afraid we have none available. But we have an excellent one by the kitchen. Much faster delivery."

Alice gave a slight knowing smile. "Of course. I always prefer such a table now that you mention it."

The greeter almost smiled back but she couldn't back down now from her (obviously not subtle enough) insult.

Alice perused the menu given her by the greeter while sipping the hot tea delivered by the waitress who'd served her, another young woman in a long dress, this time made of green silk.

Halfway through her meal, eaten with unconscious skill with chopsticks, an older woman in gold silk came from the kitchen and surveyed the dining room, now full with not only Chinese but also "round eyes" who were mostly older men and women.

She went through the restaurant occasionally speaking to the customers, but only those who seemed not to be in a hurry. She spent more time with the Anglos, most obviously regular customers.

She approached Alice and bowed to her, glancing at the nearby kitchen door.

Alice Wong bowed from her seat, very low, the full angle of formal respect when seated.

In English the woman said, "Is everything acceptable?"

In Mandarin Alice answered, "I am full" which in Chinese was not a statement of fact but meant "I am well-satisfied."

She paused and said with the slightest possible smile on her face and in her voice, "I appreciate the seat by the kitchen. It provides me such fast delivery."

The woman said, "The next time you come you should also try the window seats. On sunny days there is a very good view of the sunrise."

"I will be sure do so."

"May you have a good day and a long life." She bowed the tiniest degree more than the first time, pausing just long enough to let Alice answer her courtesy, and returned to the kitchen.

The immortal took her time finishing, turning down further services, and left a hefty tip. She paused at the greeter station when she left and smiled at the greeter.

"I had a great time. Really." Then in Mandarin she said, "May you have a good day and a long life." And bowed.

In an alley she glanced around to be sure no one could see her then vanished upward.

<>

Alice banished the egg just outside the open window of her room, slipped inside, undressed, and sat on the side of the bed. She felt as if her mind was separated from her body. It was still dozens of miles upward and hundreds of miles eastward, shortly to come down into the early-morning mist that sometimes formed over Austin.

Finally the almost-dizzy feeling ebbed away as the familiar scents and dimly lit contents of her room anchored her thoughts firmly in reality.

It was still half an hour before her usual time to awaken. This gave her time to consider the two connected dreams which made up one continuous memory.

The fact that she's had the exact same ability to fly in the memory and in the here-and-now strongly suggested that the memory was true. And all the parts of it were true.

There had been humans in a society more advanced than that of Earth, more like some of the cities in the pulp science-fiction magazines to which Albert was addicted. That might be what Earth could become in a few more centuries. That was not too difficult an idea for an immortal to entertain. Alice routinely thought of herself living centuries more than her current four hundred.

More difficult to think about was the presence in her dream of six-limbed blue-furred cat-like aliens. Ones who were on easy terms with humans, as Alice recalled that the blue "kitten" with the adult pair had been playing some game with a human boy, tall and thin and with very black skin like the skin of a few other humans in the flying wing aerospace craft.

Assuming the skin color was not cosmetic. Alice remembered the swimming pool atop the building near which she'd landed in her dream. The woman who'd spoken to her from a lawn chair had worn all-over green skin. It had almost certainly been skin not a suit. Alice remembered the genital crease at the woman's crotch and the pebbling of her areolas.

One set of aliens suggested that there might be other aliens, perhaps very different from humans or "cat centaurs."

Some dangerous.

She mentally put aside the possibility that Earth might be invaded by hostile aliens, a common plot device of pulp sci-fi.

So her mental universe had expanded further into the future and further beyond the Earth. It was not the last time when she'd had to adapt to entering larger arenas.

What was more immediate was the question: What the Hell was she to do with her ability to fly?!

For the next few weeks much of her spare time was spent exploring her new capability.

First she used it to get better acquainted with Austin and its surroundings. She appeared in dimmer areas in its downtown late at night then walked into the brighter ones. She also would light atop the taller buildings, walk to their edges, look down, then swoop to land at a selected spot.

She got to the point where she could land at a walking pace, banish the egg an inch above the ground, then step out of it onto the ground into the middle of a walk.

Or in one case in the middle of a run ending a few seconds later when she knocked a man down who was robbing a couple. Assured that he was unconscious (she'd tapped his head almost gently) she swooped back up and away before the confused couple could react.

She chuckled a few times in the next few days when she imagined the story the couple would tell the police! (IF they contacted the police.)

She soon found that her egg would "talk" to her in a limited way. She'd been looking down at the Colorado River as it wound its way through Austin and wondered what would happen if she landed in water. An answer came to her as if it was a memory: she would simply submerge unwet to whatever depth she desired and proceed unimpeded to wherever she wanted to go.

Atop a high mountain top in the Rocky Mountains she "wondered" about a similar situation in the snow below her. The answer was the same: she'd submerge in the snow. Till the egg struck rock at which point the egg would "wonder" if it should go deeper.

Go deeper? Into solid rock?!

Yes.

She found that she could bulldoze through a building in this way, as she did in dry west Texas where a rickety wooden building stood long abandoned. She did not try with a solider structure but it was clear that she could.

She left off exploring her abilities for a few days. That she could become the equivalent of a fired cannon shell was a terrible responsibility.

<>

She returned to flying when someone finally bought a Falcon, a manufacturer of many kinds of furniture, including items not only for homes but also office buildings. The company had started small with beds in the previous century. It had grown big in the last couple of decades till it had factories in all the bigger cities in Texas: Austin, San Antonio, Houston, Dallas and Fort Worth, even El Paso.

They bought the Falcon on two conditions. One was to find a place to house the plane near an airstrip.

Renting one of Texas Aviation's hangars was too expensive, but the location had to be close to the already existing runway near the industrial park where Texas Aviation was located.

Alice thought a flat area north of the industrial park was a good candidate. Was there enough land and was it available for expansion?

So just at sunrise one morning she came to work early and lofted into the air. She over flew the area out to several miles from a mile up to get a good overview. Then she lowered to 500 feet and did a rapid grid search of the area, moving at about 200 miles per hour. She was aided by the very slantwise light just after sunrise; structures, trees, and stone and wire fences (if any) could be easily seen by their shadows.

She "sat" in the weightless hollow of the egg and took notes on a notebook in her lap as she flew. With that info she was able to persuade her partners of the fitness of the Valle Del Rio area (so named because of the fact that the eastward flowing Colorado River looped southward for a short distance nearby).

"I think we and Ryan, and maybe Mrs. Delgado, ought to buy up all this area and begin planning for future expansion of an air park and air port."

"Well," said Porter, "I'm willing to kick in maybe ten percent of the cost. But I'm not sure we should look so far ahead."

Delacroix agreed, though he was willing to go to 15%. That was fine with the immortal. She could now truthfully tell other possible investors in the Del Rio Air Park that it had solid investors.

The Ryan brothers were the next on her recruitment push. The older brother was unwilling to contribute anything but his younger brother disagreed. He thought 20% a reasonable amount. Alice was sure that this was because he'd once had the hots for her until she'd sent micro-messengers into his system to make him immune to her appeal.

There were investors she could pursue but most would be relatively small. She went after the remaining likely biggest investor: Mrs. Irma Delgado.

Alice arrived for an 11:00 AM appointment at the Bremond Block a few blocks north of the Colorado River in downtown Austin. The area was so-called because the dozen houses in the block were owned by various members of the Bremond families. They were prominent in the city's social, merchandising, and banking circlcs.

Large trees with wide-spread branches shaded the streets and lawns. The lawns were uniformly green.

The Delgado house was like several of the others, a two-story structure with half its basement above ground and with a steeply slanted third story containing several rooms with dormer windows. It was made of yellow brick and had a shingled roof colored an unusual dull gold rather than dark grey or brown.

She was met at the front door by the second son of two, late twenties, darkly attractive, with a languid manner. Anthony (born

Antonio) had been educated at Harvard and still affected a trace of northern accent.

"Hi, Tony. You and yours OK?"

"Sure, Alicia. You look stunning as usual. The flying twins good?"

"Yep. You know Joe?"

"Hey, Joseph." The two men shook hands. They dressed alike: slacks, thin long-sleeved shirt for the hot Texas weather, but covered by a jacket in the air-cooled house.

Li Wei appreciated the subtle social signaling of their dress. Joey wore low-heeled work boots but polished as befit an aide to someone important. Anthony wore hand-tailored cowboy boots with a heel and delicate needle work. Joey's pants were light-grey corduroy, Anthony's a soft gold twill. The shirts were both white. Joey's jacket was made of dark blue jean material, Anthony's a thin dark gold linen. He wore a folded gold silk handkerchief in his jacket pocket.

Both men wore their collars open. Joey did so because he was working class though with a clerical job, Anthony because the very upper class did not wear ties. They could say Fuck you to convention.

Alice herself had also dressed to signal her middle upper-class status (well-to-do edging toward rich) and the audience she was to meet: the very upper-class (very rich) Irma Delgado. She wore white sandals with a modest heel and an A-line dress with short puffed sleeves to well below her knees. It was made of white refined cotton decorated with faint pink roses. She wore her curly red hair over one shoulder and covering a breast.

She wore no jewelry of any kind. Such decoration would be excessive. Her perfect alabaster-seeming skin with delicate pink blush and nearly invisible gold freckles had not the slightest blemish. Her face (and figure) could have been sculptured by an artist's imagination of an angel.

Anthony led them to the back of the house where the Delgado matriarch worked out of a large room outfitted as an office. There were a few (but not many) decorative touches in it: portraits on the walls, a free-standing large fern in one corner, a few others.

There were several filing cabinets against the wall nearest the door and book cases on the two walls to each side. They were filled with volumes such as maps, ledgers, histories, dictionaries, reference materials, and a multi-volume encyclopedia.

In short, similar to the office Alice had at Texas Aviation.

It had two desks, a smaller one against a wall, a larger one with its back to a large picture window. From it rose Irma Delgado.

She was short, slender, and had grey hair with strands of silver in it cut short and recently coifed. She wore a long grey dress and slippers. Age sat lightly on her face; she was still a very lovely woman, the sort who might (and had) attracted an older man long past the age when most such men married.

Alonzo Delgado had passed away five years ago. The reins of the company had been taken up by his oldest son and by his mother, both of whom already'd had a big part in running the company. Contrary to popular stories filled with family strife, the two worked together smoothly. He was the face of the company, dealing with the public, government officials, and the boards of other companies. His mother oversaw the day-to-day work. Her languid-appearing second son was (the military would say) her executive officer, anticipating her needs and fixing minor problems so that she could handle major problems.

All this Alice had learned several months ago when Anthony had first visited Texas Aviation and then, later, his mother had visited.

"Alicia! As lovely as ever! I hope your health is as good as your appearance."

Alice returned the woman's embrace, automatically probing the woman's body and finding it in near-perfect health. As it should be, since she'd decided to gift the woman with such health. Her two sons and two daughters had also received a lesser version of that health, contracting the infection from frequent touching by their mother and each other.

"It is, Mrs. Delgado. I would wish you good health, but it's obvious from the bloom in your cheeks that you are in high fettle."

"Fettle! What a useful word. Hello, Joseph. Come sit everyone and let's get down to business. What interesting matters have you brought to us?"

Business had to delay a few minutes till Anthony could deliver refreshments to his mother and her guest, then sit with his own in a chair off to one side of his mother's desk. As he did all this Alice asked how the other Delgado children were getting along and was briefly filled in.

Alice took a sip of hot tea from a china cup, flavored with a few drops of cream and a sugar cube. The others made do with iced tea, the favored drink of Texas--after tequila, beer, and ale, of course.

"Before you ask, your plane order is still on schedule. I'm here to talk about something else: the future."

Irma nodded.

"Europe has shown the way in aviation. America is catching up and will eventually forge ahead. We have more need of long-distance travel with our more spread-out population. And we here in Texas will take the lead away from the East Coast. We have more need than they and we have much the same money and technology as the East does."

She took a sip of her tea, stirred it with her spoon, and took another sip.

No one seemed bored.

"Texas Aviation has had several nibbles about buying aircraft. Two of those were more serious than merely curious. They were investors wanting to start an airline, one for instance to deliver mail and small high-value packages, not passengers.

"The San Antonio airline is doing well. They have ordered two more long-haul aircraft. It seems reasonable that they are looking to start a Houston service.

"There are also some interesting technological advances in the works. One for instance is the move over from automobile gasoline to a type better suited to aircraft.

"Further in the future are even more high-performance engines. Maybe rockets, maybe a type of jet engine that a German inventor has created.

"In short, we need a dedicated airport. Taking off from and landing on a grass and dirt runway is hard on tires and not as safe as we'd like it to be. Rather than three separate runways we need one of concrete or tarmac or something similar. And it needs to be longer for the newer and higher-performance aircraft.

"I've created a plan for the airport, a timeline for building it, and procedures for running it. They are preliminary and need lots of work to turn the three prospectuses into working documents."

She nodded at Joey, sitting beside her. He hefted a briefcase from the floor beside his chair into his lap but did not open it.

The matron made a bring-it-here gesture. Alice's "executive officer" opened the briefcase, took out three blue folders held closed by red ribbon, and rose to place them on the woman's desk before her.

She looked inside each folder, handing them to her own "executive officer" when done with them. She did not hurry but only spent a minute or two on each set of papers inside the folders.

After she'd finished with the last she sat watching Alice thoughtfully, taking occasional sips of her tea.

When Anthony was done with each folder he closed it and set it on the edge of his mother's desk nearest him. Then Mamacita Delgado spoke.

"A lot of work for preliminary documents. Did you do them yourself?"

"Joe was a big help."

The matron (and her son) eyed Joey. He sat impassive. Only Alice could detect his tension at being so regarded.

"Let me summarize my understanding," the matron said. "There are several phases. The first is to buy all the land."

Alice said, "If we can't get it for a reasonable price we consider other locations."

Irma Delgado continued. "The second is to plan for two runways, one for outgoing and one for incoming aircraft. You also want an area for buildings to house aircraft and the service and maintenance equipment and people.

"Third you need to plan the building and the procedures for an 'air-traffic-control system.' What is this and why is this necessary with so few aircraft coming and going?"

Alice said, "Europe has shown that when you have more than one airplane landing or taking off at an airport there is a good chance that eventually two will collide. One such collision early on can shut an airport down permanently.

"The ATC is a tower for good visibility and a two-way radio system. All aircraft using the airport must have a compatible on-board radio. There also needs to be a clear formal language for requests and commands, as the accents can vary widely."

Irma Delgado nodded understanding, saying "Lastly you need to plan the management and maintenance of the airport."

The woman sat back.

"All that is correct," said Alice.

"Who will do all this planning?"

"Joe and I will create a Version One of each. We will hire people to create later versions. A project like this will take time and perhaps a dozen people for about a year."

"A big project. Expensive. Those dozen people will have to be smart and hard-working."

"I have worked up a project plan for the first year. One aspect of the project to keep in mind is that the airport will evolve over the years. It need not spring full-blown as if from the brow of a goddess. The first--"

Anthony said, "Oh, but it did. I think you are quite the model of a goddess."

His mother swatted his nearest leg. "Not that I disagree, naughty boy. But unseemly to say so."

Alice ignored the interruption. "The first generation airport will be fairly modest. Two hard-packed dirt runways. Two or three hangars that are little more than tents. A half-dozen service and maintenance buildings. A dozen management and service people to support the airport. The military in a land war could do this in a few weeks."

Li Wei and Temilade knew this first hand. They had organized such construction projects more than once.

"So are you going to work on this full-time?"

"Joe and I, yes. But shortly we will need to hire a full-time manager. Texas Aviation is our long-term responsibility."

The two Delgados looked at each other.

"You go first," Irma said. Anthony said, "Violet."

Violet and Iris were the names of the two Delgado daughters.

His mother said, "You don't think she's too young?"

"Iris has already committed to her path through life. It has to be Vi."

"She does have that arrogance problem."

Anthony's smile was pure evil.

"This is just the situation to fix that."

His mother laughed and turned to Alice.

"My daughter Violet... You've met her, haven't you? She graduated from Harvard with a business degree a few months ago and has been knocking around the East Coast doing nothing."

"I've met her, just briefly. I think she's just the right person for this. And, Tony--" Alice's smile could also be described as evil. "--just so you know, I'm going to be at her elbow much of the time and giving her my full support. You should remember that many people think that I am more than a little arrogant myself."

Joey was startled into laughter.

<>

Two weeks later Alice and Joey had created a second version of each of the three prospectus documents with much detail, some of it labeled To-Be-Added or To-Be-Detailed.

Alice had secured funding from several small investors and a bank loan. The name "Irma Delgado" carried much weight in Austin.

Violet Delgado arrived in Austin and settled into her childhood home. In tow she brought a tall blonde recent Harvard graduate who could out-languid Anthony. He was from a rich Eastern family and had been spoiled rotten from birth.

He lasted less than a week. He said the wrong thing to her mother and he was instantly booted from the house, literally. Violet and her siblings might insult their mother and even rage at her. Outsiders risked their lives to do the same in their presence.

She showed up at Texas Aviation on the first Monday after her arrival in Austin. She was shown into Alice's office by Joey who acted as Alice's secretary and receptionist for any visitors.

The girl stood and looked at Alice for long moments. Seated, the immortal looked back.

Violet Delgado had a sturdy feminine build and wore cowboy boots, jeans, and jeans jacket over a blue-and-grey checked shirt. She wore a Stetson. None of this was affected; she'd worn this and much like it from birth. The hat was functional; Texas sun could be fierce.

"So. You're my boss now."

Alice leaned back in her chair and tented her hands in front of her belly.

"Nope. You are the boss of you. And you are also, if you take it on, the boss of the airport project. I did not accept a spoiled rich girl to play boss. I accepted one who can do the job and do it well. But, if you want to play spoiled rich girl, go ahead. You can fuck up this job. We can declare bankruptcy and do quite well without this airport."

Her demeanor was not hostile. It was calmly matter-of-fact. Her attitude was genuine; an immortal thought very long-term.

Violet looked at Alice for long moments. Then she sat in one of the three straight-backed chairs in front of the shapechanger's desk and leaned back, moving her hat to her lap.

"So, how do I get started?"

Alice stood and walked around her desk toward the door. She made a come-on gesture with her head. Violet followed her.

Alice's office was in the huge barn-like Research and Maintenance

Building. Different parts of it were set off from others by low partitions which could be moved to reform the different task being performed.

Outside one of the partitions on the concrete surrounding the building a silver Falcon sat on its two big front wheels and small rear wheel.

It was complete except for several panels open which would normally allow work to be done on its insides.

"This is the plane your mother ordered to chauffeur her around the state. It is ready to go, completely tested, including stress tested beyond the usual standards. We really don't want the death of someone as prominent as she to stain Texas Aviation's reputation.

"You are going to learn to fly it, and fly it well. Starting today. We will take her up so you can get a feel for its capabilities. I will not push you in your lessons. We will go as slow as you need to be as thorough as possible. We also do not want your death to stain our reputation."

"I learn fast."

"Good to know. But you will learn RIGHT then BECOME fast. Here. Watch how I close and lock this panel."

The panel indicated was head height to the two women. Alice swung it closed with a quick push at the end to snap it securely into place. There was a built-in key-like lock which added security. It twisted closed and clicked, then was folded flush with the body of the aircraft. Thus the side of the vehicle appeared almost solid. Only the outline of the panel and the recessed key betrayed their existence.

"Lesson one. Just about everything is secured two ways, not one, no matter how secure the one is. Travel in the air is not a natural human function. The skies are deadly. There's a saying that's absolutely true: 'There are old pilot and bold pilots, but there are no old bold pilots.'"

After the first panel-close-and-lock operation Violet did all the other close-and-locks.

When all panels were secured Alice backed off several feet and stood looking at the Falcon. Violet copied her.

"Your mom's plane is a Falcon II. It is longer by a few feet to accommodate two extra passenger seats making up four in all. It also has larger fuel tanks to give it longer range. You can make a trip from here to El Paso and still have a quarter tank of fuel in reserve.

"The wings are slightly larger in all dimensions so that it can lift a full load of passengers and their luggage. The fuselage was studied to be as sure as we can be that it is airtight when the door is closed and locked. It can cruise at 15,000 feet, or almost three miles, which is its operational ceiling. It can go to 20,000 feet or--"

She looked expectantly at Violet.

"Almost four miles," the woman said.

"The Falcon I was designed to include aerobatics as a major task area. The Falcon II has kept that capability. I've wrung it out to find any problems. We did, minor ones. We fixed those and I wrung it out again. The end result is that this is the safest plane flyable right now. Including planes from Ireland and the Brits."

She looked at Violet. The girl tried to hide it but she'd fallen in love with the Falcon.

"Yes."

Alice led the way to walk all around the aircraft, pointing out items to examine such as the tires.

"We always do a walk-around inspection and we don't hurry it. Our lives depend on catching any problems early."

Inside on the way to the cockpit Violet could see that the plane was outfitted for luxury. The walls and ceiling were covered with pale green padding under a cloth exterior. The floor had a similarly covered tough carpet. The seats were padded and shaped for bodies and could be laid back at a 45-degree angle.

The cockpit was more functional, light grey with bright green marks on instruments and knobs to indicate detents.

Alice sat in the pilot's seat and strapped in, having Violet do the same in the copilot's seat.

"That green paint is dosed with radium to glow in the dark. Don't worry. The radiation it gives off is less than what you get outside."

"I know about radium danger. Thank Heaven Madame Curie and her husband arc better now."

Alice went through her usual routine when briefing someone new to airplanes. This included a quick description of the six most important instruments, the use of yokes, and how the foot pedals controlled tilts to the left and right.

Then she had Violet take her through the checklist to get the plane into the air.

Lastly Alice looked out the window, saw a waiting aircraft mechanic looking back at her, made a two-fingered pointing gesture at the runway, and saw him disappear under the aircraft to remove the chocks under its front wheels. When he reappeared he held up the chocks by ropes attached to them with one hand. With his other hand he gave her a salute.

Alice returned the salute and carefully advanced the throttle. The engine grumbled louder and the plane began to move. Alice drove it to the entrance to the runway, craned her head forward to get a better view of the surrounding sky, and pushed the throttle two-thirds of the way forward.

Violet, her hands on the yoke and her feet on the aileron foot pedals, observed everything intently. She felt her body being pushed back against her seat as the Falcon began to move forward, first slowly then gaining speed.

As the plane came light on its wheels and tilted to fly into the sky Violet said conversationally "Yee-hah."

Alice laughed as the ground fell away below them. "Yee-hah indeed."

<>

Joey had found an office near Alice's and cleaned it out with Alice's help the week before. After lunch the three moved Violet's few belongings into it and arranged it to suit Violet.

"Thanks for the help, guys. Alice, you mentioned paperwork for me?"

"Yes. Joey, go get the folder on my desk labeled BOSS." He nodded and left.

Speaking low though no one could hear the woman said, "Are you and he, ahh...?"

"No. He'd rather sleep with a spider than me. And I love him but like a brother. He's free...I think. You're free to date him if he's interested. But I warn you now. If you hurt him I will hurt you, badly."

Violet stared at Alice. The shapechanger had spoken conversationally, as if stating a fact. But her face had been completely expressionless.

Violet felt the invisible hairs on the outside of her arms and legs crawl. A shock went through her body. This woman-shaped thing before her was utterly serious.

She locked her leg muscles to keep from stepping back. She let out a breath which she'd not noticed holding.

Slowly she relaxed. Regained her composure. Settled into a new relationship with the woman before her.

"I won't let you control what I do with Joe. If it leads to heartbreak it will not because I've done anything wrong, or Joe has done anything wrong, but simply because our relationship did not work out."

The creature said, "Good. I can ask for nothing more. I wish you two happiness with all my soul."

The same absolute calm which had so frightened Violet instants before now did the opposite: it convinced her that the Alice creature was being absolutely honest and that Violet was safe.

Within a minute Joey was back with the BOSS folder. Alice had Violet study it and sign various parts of it. When she was done with that task Joey took it from Violet, promising to leave early to give it to the Delgado attorneys for filing. Violet now was the head of the Del Rey Airport project and the likely future manager of the airport when it became operational.

<>

Violet Delgado was smart, educated in business management, and did not feel diminished by admitting ignorance and asking for advice. She settled into her office.

Within a month all the land was the property of the Del Rey Airport. Two runways were plowed and covered with a form of resilient concrete. A week later the surface was fully cured and ready for use.

As the project progressed so did Violet's pilot training under Alice. Occasionally Porter filled in for the shapechanger.

The two women became friendly but the younger woman never forgot that Alice was supremely dangerous. As time went by the fact became comforting rather than scary. Alice could and would protect Violet as willingly and capably as she did everyone else. Just as her own mother would.

<>

Alice's free time had been mostly eaten up by her determination to get an airport built for Austin. With that safely on the way she returned to exploring her egg.

Her trips extended to San Antonio, Houston, and Dallas. Her heights went routinely to 30,000 feet, about six miles. At that height the world's curvature was noticeable, she could see several hundred miles, and the sky edged toward dark blue above her. Most clouds lay snowy white below her, small cotton puffs. Rarely she flew through stringy wisps of cloud which she knew were called cirrus clouds.

It took her ten minutes to get to any of the three cities, which meant she was flying at about a 1000 miles per hour. That made her Falcon at 200 miles per hour a slowpoke!

She got better at "talking" to her egg. She merely needed to want to know something and she then "knew" the answer as if she'd always known it.

Could the egg carry something beside herself and what she wore? Yes, of course. How could she do that? Well, naturally she needed to put her hands on the burden and think of its approximate shape. How much weight could she carry? It was obviously about six tons.

Her little two-seater sports car--which was called a "touring car"--weighed a third of that. As an experiment Alice took it to Llano one Friday and set down on the east-west highway a couple of miles outside town. It took her five minutes all told to go the seventy-something miles which driven would take an hour and a half.

She had a great weekend and left middle of Sunday afternoon to "get home before sundown."

Could the car become invisible? The answer was a memory of a pale blur of color: how the car would look to someone outside it. She flew up beside a bank in downtown Austin which had a black mirrored glass surface.

She looked through the front of the egg at her image on the building side. The building was perfectly clear from inside the egg. But to anyone inside the building looking out of the window (no one was) would see that blur. Examining it Alice could see that a white patch was part of her face and that a red patch was part of her hair. She could pick all the other parts of her clothing, just barely, and only because she knew what the colors meant.

Flying away she thought about her experience and "remembered" what the egg did. It curved light near Alice around it. That did not completely hide her but it did make her image smaller.

The egg also blurred her image and mixed different parts together. White skin became several blotches of white, red hair became several blotches of red. White and red blended in places to become pink. None of the image made anything recognizable. A watcher's gaze might slide right by the blur, then jerk back to find it gone as Alice departed the scene.

Where did the energy come from to power the egg. From "uncurving space," of course. Ah. What? Space had a curve? How did the egg lay hold of emptiness to unbend it? To that Alice had no memory.

Pity.

Where was the egg's engine and controller? Scattered all throughout Alice's body in parts so tiny they'd be invisible outside her body. Each was so tiny it could rest inside each cell of her body, one to a cell. Somehow the trillions of parts connected to make one machine.

Alice soon became knowledgeable about her egg and how it worked and became expert in its use. She went far outside Texas.

She'd long been curious about Hollywood, the movie-making capitol of the world. Alas, it was just a city like any other. The famous Hollywood Boulevard was just an ordinary street with a few extra loonies and teenaged runaways on it. The movie studios were mostly cavernous warehouses full of odds and ends of movie sets and costumes and props like swords and shields and pots and pans. Some warehouses held the occasional furnished room with half its walls gone to let cameras peek in.

In one warehouse was an entire stagecoach.

LA's Chinatown, on the other hand, was not a disappointment. The people on the streets and in shops and restaurants were real in all their sometimes querulous solidity. A female Li Wei had a very good authentic meal and chatted in Mandarin about weather and earthquakes.

The visit to LA woke homesickness in Alice. Three weeks later she dressed herself appropriately and arced up and out of the atmosphere. In empty space she could travel to a peak of 30,000 miles an hour and arc down into Hang-zhou 7000 miles away.

Thirty years had passed yet the city where her body had lived and died had changed little (except for that slum turned modern businesses and shopping areas.)

The immortal changed her face and body and manner to fit in and walked the streets and ate in a restaurant and bought a few keepsakes. Half an afternoon and half an evening later the Chinese woman wearing vaguely European clothing walked down an alley and disappeared.

Chapter 9 - Businesses and Pleasure

Alice's hunger for travel eventually eased. She did consider flying to the Moon but photos through telescopes had revealed that it had a grey and desolate and BORING landscape. She dismissed the idea.

Meanwhile aviation business continued to pick up. The Delgado's Falcon II had made other rich people in Austin interested. Several bit, one bought though a Falcon I. He needed to travel to San Antonio every few weeks, ostensibly on business but rumor had it to visit his mistress. Alice guessed that it was both. He struck her as the type of person to kill two birds with one stone.

The Belle biplane crop duster line also got spruced up. A Belle II could travel further. Outfitted with improved wings and tougher tires the "flying kite" could set down on even shorter runways than the original. Texas ranchers found it useful to keep track of their herds with it. Several sons were trained to fly the Belle IIs, which unfortunately meant that some of them had accidents. That deterred sales little if not at all; stupid or unlucky sons also had accidents with pickup trucks.

One son had the bright idea to bolt a motorcycle to his biplane. He could land on moderately rough terrain and travel further on very rough terrain. He was either smart or lucky; he never killed himself.

It was this innovation that brought Texas Aviation a new potential customer.

<>

In mid-September on a Monday morning the three partners met in the conference room in the Display and Sales building. Louis had set up a meeting with a "government official" at 10:00. He cautioned his partners to be especially polite. This might be the first of more government contracts.

At couple of minutes before the hour the young male secretary shared by the two men knocked on the door, opened it, and ushered in their guest.

The three partners stood up. The man wore a cowboy outfit including Stetson, boots, jeans, a white shirt, vest, and black string tie. This was not unusual in Texas but the vest had a silver star pinned to it and his belt supported a holstered revolver.

Alice heard Porter take a deep breath. Porter was suspicious of police in a mild way. This, Alice was sure, was why Delacroix had only called the potential customer a "government official."

Louis said, "Lieutenant Jameson. Welcome to Texas Aviation. I'd like you to meet my partners. This is Mr. Llewellyn Porter."

"Thank you. Mr. Porter." The Texas Ranger stepped forward and held his hand out to Porter who had come forward from his chair to the right of Delacroix's position at the head of the conference table. The two shook.

Delacroix introduced Alice who'd been sitting to his left. She shook hands with the man, automatically probing him and fixing several minor problems.

The Ranger refused the chair at the head of the table, insisting it was the Frenchman's, and sat to his right. Porter took the chair opposite him and Alice took the chair beside Porter.

The shapechanger approved of the tactical location of the Ranger. He could see the door behind Delacroix and had the other two partners in front of him, also visible.

Delacroix said, "The Lieutenant read the recent news report about the rancher's son who attached a motorcycle to a Belle. He wondered if we might do something like that with two motorcycles."

Porter, the engineer, said, "Of course. It would take an hour or two. I presume this would be so you could pursue criminals out in rough country."

"Yes."

"There are some practical considerations that we--Texas Aviation and your people--would have to address. For instance, the Belle's engine is quite loud. People can hear it from miles away."

Alice said, "One solution would be to use a modified version of the Falcon. But those are expensive aircraft."

"Hmm. And your Hawk is even bigger and more expensive than the Falcon, I'm sure. Well, I knew it was a long shot. I apologize for wasting your time."

He made to stand but Porter, never one to give up on a technical problem easily, said, "Hold on. You just introduced the problem. Give us time to think about it before you give up."

Delacroix said, "He's right. Let us think about it and see if we can come up with something. Meanwhile, as you're here, why don't we discuss other ways Texas Aviation might help you."

"OK. I planned to spend as much time as needed for this visit."

Alice said, "One mistake we're making is to join together the several parts of the problem of finding, approaching, and attacking a target. Another solution is to find the criminals first with one means, then approaching and attacking them by other means.

"For instance, we might locate the target with a high-flying aircraft that the target does not see or hear, or thinks is so high that it has no connection with them. Then we incapacitate them with a non-lethal bomb. Finally we approach them on horseback and arrest them."

As Alice spoke the Ranger's brows had been ever so slightly rising.

Delacroix laughed. "Alice is the more martial of the three of us. She is advocating for each of our aircraft to have military applications."

Alice said, "The military is more likely to be generous, even overly generous, than other customers."

Porter had been frowning as if to remember something. He spoke up.

"In Europe they have designed a small single-pilot aircraft for reconnaissance duty. It can fly high and take photographs of the ground. It can also fly very low and slow to focus on a particular area. Its engine and propeller is very quiet. We could develop something like that."

Alice spoke to him. "We could take a Belle body and delete the low wing to make it easier to look down. The upper wing would have to be bigger."

She closed her eyes, visualized the prospective aircraft, and considered all the modifications to a Belle that would be required.

The others were silent. Her partners knew what she was doing and waited for her to do it and the Ranger was likely taking his lead from them.

After several minutes--remarkably not interrupted by the Ranger--she opened her eyes. "Yes, we can do it. Fairly cheaply. And my quick imagined simulation shows it would be workable."

Porter said, "Thanks, Alice."

He turned to the Ranger. "Alice is our genius aircraft designer. If she says it will work it will. Naturally we test every real aircraft up the wazoo to be sure, but so far she's always been right."

Alice said, "Do you want to go up in a Belle? It would give you an idea of what a--let's call it the Kestrel; they fly low and can hover--would be like."

"Me? Fly? Ahh, sure. Now?"

"My partners will want to spend some time thinking about how we can meet your needs. A quick jaunt in the air would take us up to lunch time. Then over lunch we could revisit this subject."

She turned to Porter and Delacroix. "Sound like a plan?"

The Frenchman said, "If the Lieutenant agrees."

That worthy said, "She's going to fly the plane?"

"Don't worry. She's better than we are." He nodded sideways at Porter.

"In fact, she's better than anyone we know. And we've been knocking about in the aviation world for years."

Alice stood up to put the conference to an end. So did her partners and the Ranger. He shook hands with the two other men and followed Alice out.

In the hall Alice turned left rather than right, the direction which led into the Showroom, just visible from the door of the conference room. The left hall led them to the back of the building and out into a concrete floored plaza, then into the hangar. It was a long building which held three of the biplanes, four Falcons (half Is and half IIs), and the Delgados' Falcon II Special.

Entering the hangar Alice turned to walk along the row of planes to the far end of the building. There a space the size of a large airplane had been turned into a mechanical workspace. A variety of pieces of equipment waited to service an airplane. Against the far wall was a long table with a waist-high top littered with equipment. On the wall hung many types of wrenches, hammers, and other tools.

Three men in grey coveralls stood at a free-standing table, two doing something to a piece of machinery atop it while the third watched.

"*Hola*, Juanito. Which Belle is readiest to go?"

The watcher, a stout Latino, turned to her.

"*Señora*. Betsy. You going up now?"

"*Si*."

The man turned to the two other workers. They'd stopped what they were doing to see if their boss, Alice, needed anything.

The boss mechanic said, "Mo, you're with me." He began to walk away with the man he'd picked to help him. The other man, at a nod from Alice, went back to his task.

Alice said, "Let's gear up." She turned to walk to a large room which was a part of the hangar. Part of it was a break area, a couch and several easy chairs covered with much-creased leather scattered around a low table covered with magazines and newspapers and a potpourri of items. Part of the room included an open air closet. In one side hung flight coveralls. In the other side were bins. One held goggles and another soft leather helmets which would protect heads from chill wind.

Alice directed the Lieutenant to select a coverall, a helmet, and goggles, then go into a restroom to change into them.

"You can take your Stetson and gunbelt on the plane. There's a small cargo area where you can store them. I'll meet you back out here once I've put my gear on."

Her gear was another set of coveralls, goggles, and helmet.

Several minutes later Alice and the Ranger walked to Betsy. Walking by the planes he could see that each had a name painted on their sides. The Belles had red skins and white names: Barbara, Bridget, and Betsy.

Next to one of the aircraft was a platform on wheels with a short stair leading up to the top of the platform. Alice went atop the platform and, turning, motioned for the Ranger to follow.

From atop the platform it was possible to step down into either of two cockpits. The shapechanger waved at them.

"The Belle's can be flown from either cockpit. When used for observation of an area on the ground the observer sits in the back, the pilot in the front where he can better see what's ahead of the airplane, dangers like another airplane, telephone or power poles, or a flight of birds.

"The pilot will take the observer to the observation area and pass by it off to the side. The pilot will tilt the aircraft to make it easier for the observer to see the target area. He can take notes or photograph the target. It takes an expert to keep a camera trained without it being jarred by the vibration of the aircraft. That can be considerable. Not only does the motor add vibration, but updrafts and downdrafts can jog the camera man's arms."

She removed the binocular handset she'd added to her outfit, handed it to the Ranger, and gestured toward the back seat, said, "Get in. Look under the seat. There's a box where you can put your hat and gun belt. Strap in; I'll watch to make sure you are secure. Then put on the cuplike earphones. That let's you and me talk."

She watched as he did as she said, then stepped down into the forward cockpit, belted in, put the communication "cans" over her ears, adjusted the microphone on a wire in front of her, and switched them on.

"Lieutenant Jameson, can you hear me?"

"I can. Clearly. Can you hear me?"

"I can. Now, I'll take us up. Don't bother me until I speak to you again. Then we can take a look at various sights."

"I understand."

"Oh, and these babies lift off the ground really fast, so be prepared when we go wheels up."

Alice waved at the lead mechanic standing nearby and he and his companion took hold of the bottom wing and pushed Betsy out of the hangar and well away from it. All the Belle's engines were the "silent" type but this was a misnomer. They WERE comparatively quiet compared to most engines of their class but still were pretty loud.

She waved her helpers away and they walked quickly away.

"You settled in, Lieutenant?"

"I am. Thanks for asking."

"Here we go."

She pushed the IGNITION button and the self-starter option spurted vaporized gasoline into the five chambers of the radial engine then ignited them. The explosions turned the engine just enough to begin it turning and further explosions turn it more. Slowly then faster the engine turned. The propeller, visible at first, quickly became an almost invisible blur.

Alice listened approvingly to how smoothly the engine had started up and continued to function. The mechanics were very good at their jobs.

She went quickly through the takeoff checklist then let up on the brakes. The Belle slowly began to move, then move faster, then faster still. Its tail lifted off its small rear tire. Alice began to feel her way into the machine.

She did not understand the process but the ability had appeared with her first incarnation. Even such simple machines as wagons and sailboats became part of her when she used them. The more complex the machines the more complete the process. She'd noticed it consciously for the first time when her father taught her how to drive his pickup truck. Airplanes were a step up from them. She became not Alice driving Betsy but Alice+Betsy, a composite creature.

ALICE felt the instant her mechanical part Betsy came light on its wheels. SHE waited a few seconds with HER tail and wing control surfaces turned down to hold Betsy to the runway.

Then the lightness asserted itself strongly. Betsy wanted to fly.

ALICE let HER control surfaces relax to their neutral position. SHE gunned the engine. It quickly wound up to almost to its redline power.

SHE lifted off, leaned back, and fled into the sky like an arrow loosed.

At 500 feet SHE leveled off, slowly so as not to affect the Ranger's stomach, already pushed down and back with HER takeoff. This would let it settle.

To speed up the settling process SHE turned his attention outward. "Jameson, how does the ground look to you from 500 feet? This is the height crop dusters often fly at."

"Feels strange to see everything from above."

"I'm going to make a U-turn and go back the way we came. The left wing will dip as we turn, so be ready for it."

"Roger."

Now where had he gotten that terminology?

SHE had only gone a couple of miles east. They quickly returned to the industrial park. It was to their left, some two dozen large buildings. They had grey, beige, and silver sides and darker roofs.

"It's amazing how much detail I can see through the binoculars. Could you go lower?"

"The engine is too loud for that. In fact I ought to double our height now that residential areas are coming up."

SHE did that. SHE also curved to the right to follow the Colorado River westward toward the downtown area. SHE climbed even higher, to 3000 feet. SHE didn't like to advertise that SHE was flying over the city lest authorities forbid HER to do so.

Beyond the downtown area the first of the western hills rose almost a thousand feet further. SHE turned back after flying for a couple of miles over them. This was enough flying for now.

To give the Ranger some different terrain to look at SHE lowered to 1000 feet and crossed over the southern part of Austin, following a main east-west highway. It passed near St. Edwards College, a medium-sized group of red-topped buildings surrounding a rectangular green. SHE pointed it out and imagined him swinging the binoculars down toward it.

SHE flew south of HER home industrial complex, did a U-turn, and lowered more to slot into HER landing path, tilting a tad to HER left to adjust for the moderate prevailing winds from the south.

SHE touched lightly down, slowed so that HER tail wheel came down to bounce a couple of times, and taxied to HER home hangar. There SHE turned back toward the east and cut HER engines.

As always it was a bit disconcerting to return fully to HER biological part. She shook her head, disconnected the cans, and stood up.

By then her ground crew had shown up, chocked the wheels, and pushed the pilots' disembarking platform to the side of Betsy. Alice stepped onto it and turned to assist Lieutenant Jameson to exit his cockpit. She let him climb down the ladder first, then followed him.

At the bottom he was walking in small circles, lifting his legs a bit high and once shaking them.

He turned to her, grinned, and spoke.

"It takes a minute to adjust to being Earthbound again. For me anyway. What about you?"

"It takes a few minutes. You ready for lunch?"

"I am. Thanks for the ride. I'll never forget it."

Alice turned toward her ground crew, thanked them, and escorted Jameson to the robing room.

<>

Lunch was at a TexMex truck. The Lieutenant ordered liberally. He dosed his food with hot red pepper sauce.

Porter said, "Careful with that. It's pretty fiery."

"I grew up in El Paso right across from Ciudad Juárez. We kids of both races mingled freely. There were no border restrictions then and the races didn't matter. Who was good at kickball was what mattered and which girls were friendly and which weren't.

"I was semi-adopted by my good friend Felipe's mom and stuffed when I ate at their home. That's where I learned to love hot sauce. I ate there often as my mom worked two jobs and got home late. That was good in one way. I learned to cook and feed my brothers and sisters and learned to be a grownup. So I missed the usual teen rebellion against adults. I WAS an adult."

Alice said, "Does your family still live there?"

"Dad got a sales job that paid pretty good. His company moved here to Austin so we moved here too. He's still going strong. Mom could only find one job for a while. That was good thing. She learned to make do with one job which led to her being promoted to manager. Not much of a pay raise, but enough.

"Enough about me. What's the story with you two and aviation?"

That conversation took them through them meeting each other in college and meeting Alice while barnstorming.

At the end of the lunch the four began to put their paper and plastique dinnerware onto trays to take to trash. As they stood Porter said, "If you've got the time you should have Alice show you her Ideas Wall."

"What's that?"

"It's where she's pinned up drawings of possible future aircraft. I guarantee you'll find it interesting."

Delacroix nodded as he led the line to the nearest trash can.

Thus it was that the two male partners headed away from the picnic area toward the Display and Sales building. Alice and the Ranger headed toward the Engineering and Manufacturing building.

Porter was the head of the offices in the building and Alice worked for him officially. However she was a partner and genius with math and machines, so she had her own sub-department labeled Research and Development within the E&M department. She could call on any of the technical and clerical employees for any help that did not interfere with the rest of the department.

She led the Ranger to a large long office. Stepping inside the doorway anyone could look through a long picture window and see the hangars and runways outside.

Just inside the doorway to the left was a hat stand and coat rack and low table atop which letters and newspapers and magazines lay in random array. Far to the right was Alice's desk facing toward the doorway.

Between her desk and the doorway and opposite the picture window were three corkboards mounted on stands placed ends together. They were placed backs against the wall.

Jameson followed Alice inside the room and turned with her to look at the corkboards. On the three were mounted many sketches large and small and colored paintings also large and small.

Alice pointed at the corkboards.

"This first one is the Now board of current projects. The second and third boards are for Near-Future and Far-Future projects."

Jameson stepped closer to inspect the Now board. He recognized different portrayals of the Belle, Falcon, and Hawk aircraft. Each had its own section on the board.

The black-and-white drawings mostly were diagrams showing the vehicles from top, side, and front with information such as dimensions nearby. Other information included maximum ceiling, ranges with different fuel loads, numbers of passengers, and weights of cargoes.

The color paintings were nearly photographic in appearance. Often they showed three-quarter views from below with blue sky above or from above with green and brown land below.

What impressed him most was the artistic quality of every image. Even the near-blueprint black-and-white drawings had an economy of line and placement of text and numbers that was perfectly balanced in their frames. The paintings to his uninformed judgment could have been hung in an art gallery without anyone protesting their inclusion.

He said as much. Alice was not surprised. He was not the first who'd said as much. S/he reverted to Li Wei whenever s/he created the portrayals. In China he'd been recognized for the last two decades of his life as an artist of national merit. When s/he had visited Hang-Zhou in her egg thirty years after hi/r death s/he had found the museum dedicated to him was still open and well-visited.

Jameson spoke, half to himself. "Now what do we have here?"

He had moved to the second corkboard. He was looking at a Belle with only a high wing. There were other differences from the vehicle he'd earlier flown in, he felt, but he could not put his finger on them.

"The idea of a reconnaissance version of the Belle did not come to us this morning. This is one possibility. And this is what we call a close-air-support model."

The second version of the Belle was equipped with machine guns on both sides of the engine. Below the body was what the Ranger recognized as bombs.

"What you cannot see is that the cockpits are surrounded below by a 'bathtub' of metallic graphene. This is to protect the Belle from enemy gunfire. You also cannot see the several hardenings and backups of critical subsystems."

He gazed at the angelic beauty before him. The idea of an Angel of Death suddenly came to him. He might be looking at one for real.

"The CAS Belle I deem not practical. Here is a Falcon set up for close air support." The Angel had moved a little further along and was pointing at a painting of the Falcon. It was subtly different, perhaps a bit longer? The wings wider and...fatter?

"This last--" she said, "--looks like a Hawk I or II but it's about twice the size in every dimension. We call it the Hawk III publicly, but we think of it as the Eagle. If it ever goes into production that's what we'd call it. It would be able travel to either coast in one flight from here with a full load of either passengers or cargo."

"Do you think it will? Sell, I mean?"

"I have no doubt that it or something like it will. Air travel is already big business in Europe. It's expanding rapidly here in the US. Faster on the more populous East Coast, of course, but I suspect Texas and other South Coast states will begin to catch up."

The immortal was certain in hi/r beliefs. S/he had seen emerging historical trends before and this one had all the marks of inevitability.

"So this last board is your Far Future one. What do we have here?"

The third corkboard bore no black-and-white drawings. It was all realistic color.

"Much of this is speculation with little basis in current technology. It will have to wait on further extensions of various technologies, most importantly of engines."

"Then why speculate?"

Alice examined the Ranger's face. It was curious, not skeptical.

"Speculation prepares us so that when a technological advance comes along we are ready to quickly take advantage of it.

"And advances WILL come along. The arc of technological history is trending upward, accelerating even.

"There are two changes in all technology. Bigger, and smaller.

"Airplanes will get bigger. Ships will get bigger. Buildings will climb higher. Power lines will get longer, more communities will become electrified.

"At the same times batteries will get smaller. Transmissions for automobiles will get smaller, more compact, enabling smaller sleeker vehicles. The calculation engines of calculators will grow smaller, more powerful. The memory units will also shrink. Soon we'll be able to put an encyclopedia in one of them.

"But I'd best stop there lest I bore you."

He turned from her to examine one large wide diorama-like painting so convincing he could almost believe that it was a photograph. It showed a huge aircraft on a grassy field. Part of its rear end was folded down into a ramp to the surface. Out of it a truck was being driven down the ramp while a squad of soldiers with rifles guarded its exit. On the truck bed was a stand supporting a very heavy machine gun, its snout pointing forward over the truck's cab.

Below and above the painting smaller paintings showed the scene from different viewpoints.

He walked a few feet closer to Alice's desk and examined another diorama painting. This showed an aircraft with a long pointed nose and swept-back wings and tail. It was traveling at a slant down toward a railroad on which traveled a train. From under its wings a lance of fire trailed a long rocket with tiny vanes at its back. Far ahead of it red fire and smoke from an earlier rocket bloomed to shatter a truck.

He looked at her.

"I thought I was bloody minded, a soldier, a hired killer some would say. But you scare the... You scare me."

"Europe is building tanks for a land war that, God willing, will never happen. Ships have cannon that can fire over a mile. Submarines have torpedoes which can sink a ship. Yet this scares you."

He made a wry face acknowledging the irony then moved on to several other fantastic aircraft.

Then at the very far end he came upon an aerial scene which caught his gaze. A cowboy floated in midair looking down at a herd. He was standing atop a flat plate with four poles mounted on it. They surrounded him up to waist level and kept him from falling off the plate. Surrounding all this was an egg-shaped bubble visible only by faint rainbow iridescence at its edges.

"So. The ultimate trend to miniaturization."

She nodded.

"Well, with this kind of willingness to look for unusual solutions I suppose the Rangers are in good hands when we come to you for aviation assistance."

"'Unusual solutions' doesn't sound like a compliment."

He began to walk back toward the door. Alice walked beside him.

"Not an insult. Just a statement of fact. THIS--" He stopped at the first corkboard and waved his hand at the drawings. "All this shows you can do practical precision work. I'm going to recommend we pursue further study of your suggested reconnaissance aircraft. Something like your Kestrel but with improvements."

"Texas Aviation looks forward to working with you, Lieutenant Jameson." She shook his hand, reading his sincerity, and wished him a good day.

<>

Along with her work at Texas Aviation Alice was also involved in "lifestyle" commerce. Austin being the state capitol and centrally located it supported several newspapers and magazines.

One was Lifestyles Magazine. It was part of a chain headquartered in New York. Every large city had a version with a section which ran stories and ads of local interest as well as stories and ads with a wider reach. Alice was interviewed for the local section about her preferences in clothing and cosmetics and other products for daily use. Accompanying the interview were several color photos of her on the glossy paper stock of the magazine. For this she was paid a substantial sum.

Some of the photos were of her wearing party clothing at parties. Some were of her wearing daily clothing in her office and in the hangar. The second photos had captions such as "Alice is chic even when running a big department."

That was not the only interview she granted. Several newspapers and other magazines approached her and she accepted a few requests.

She was also featured in ads for the "forward thinking" product lines which bore her name on clothing and cosmetics. All of the products she'd inspected to be sure she could honestly endorse them.

She also endorsed "other products." Her partners were most highly and loudly amused at the Alice Toilet Bowl Cleaner.

Wearing some of her fashion finery Alice attended parties put on by supposedly glamorous people having fun. In reality the much-photographed parties were shows put on to bolster those people's media images. Too, much deal-making went on behind the scenes, or discussion leading to deal-making.

Violet also had to attend those parties for the same reason. She was a Delgado heiress and a business woman who had an image to maintain. Often she and Alice went together. As time went on they became friends, occasionally leaving parties together and having a sleepover with long wine-fueled conversations. Victoria was a kind person with a snarky sense of humor. She was sometimes very lonely. A rich girl's suitors usually had mercenary motives. Also they were often of the same class, a small all-too-well-known pool of mates.

Porter and Delacroix sometimes attended these parties, also for publicity and deal-making purposes. Alice noticed that Victoria and

Louis spent more and more time with each other, speaking French. Victoria had studied it in college and spent a year in Paris as an exchange student.

Less often the Delgado matriarch attended the "glamorous" parties. Alice and she usually chatted for an hour or more. The shapechanger enjoyed the older woman's company--older by appearance but a spring chicken to an immortal. She often resisted efforts by younger people to pull her away from Irma.

The woman usually pushed Alice to go on and have fun.

"I'll just languish here bereft of your company." That was a joke; the woman had developed a matchmaker's interest in seeing Alice attached to a man.

"Yes, it's such a burden, being rich," Alice said as she laughingly let herself be pulled away to dance at a party.

Mrs. Delgado put the back of a hand against her forehead in faux ennui then used the hand to urge Alice toward the dance floor.

That one time she went willingly. The orchestra was playing an Argentine tango, the real version not the European butchery perpetrated by the British. Her partner, a blond god of a man, was one of a tiny group who were enthusiasts of the genuine Argentine dance and music.

Victoria joined her with Delacroix. As France had become besotted with the authentic version in recent years he had perforce learned the dance though he was not enthusiastic about it.

<>

One day in the first week in December Alice arrived at the Delgado residence for a business meeting with Irma Delgado. The company wanted to buy another Falcon. Irma had flown in the one they owned often enough to have developed a list of improvements she wanted adopted in the second aircraft.

Violet was home that day, an unusual event at 10:00 in the morning. She said that Irma was indisposed and so not available.

That was unusual. The immortal had given the woman perfect health.

"Is she hurt? Did she have an accident?"

"No. she's just... She just wants to stay in this morning. She doesn't feel like doing business right now."

That was unlikely. The Delgado matriarch loved to do business.

"Did someone else have an accident?"

"Alice! Just go!"

The girl's eyes were reddened. She'd been crying.

The shapechanger was suddenly a killing machine. She recognized the signs.

She pulled Victoria out of the house's foyer into the living room, ignoring the girl's protests and feeble efforts. She made her sit on the couch and sat beside her, turned to look directly at her.

"I love your mother-- Look at me! I love your mother. I will do almost anything to protect her. No matter how illegal. I will KILL any asshole who hurts her. WHAT HAS HAPPENED?"

Victoria began weeping and haltingly told the story. The night before Irma Delgado had been kidnapped just outside her home as she was returning home. Her driver had been beaten up and was in the hospital, going to it only after he'd relayed a message to Victoria and the Delgado servants.

"They want five million dollars this afternoon or they'll kill her. They're going to phone soon to tell us where and how to get it to them. So you'll have to leave, let us do this. Oh, and don't you dare going to the police. They say they're watching the house and if they see police they'll kill her!"

"Don't worry. The police are out. But I'm not going anywhere. I know how to handle this."

"You can't interfere! You..."

Victoria's voice trailed off. Because her friend Alice was changing. Her hair was turning blond, straightening, assuming the same style that Victoria wore. Her face was changing, looking more like that of a sister...then more like Victoria...then identical to the image Victoria saw in her mirror.

The girl whispered, "What are you?"

"I am your friend and your mother's friend. I am a creature out of fable who is going to bring your mother safely home."

Victoria stared. Was that what she looked like? Prettier. With eyes not reddened by crying. With... her beauty mark was on the wrong side. Except... Yes, she mostly saw herself in mirrors. The beauty mark WAS on the right side.

"I am very old, dearest Victoria. I know how to handle this to keep your mother safe. When they call I will answer the phone as you. You'll notice that I sound just like you now.

"I will tell them we have a million dollars now. But the bank won't release the rest till tomorrow. To prove our good faith I will take the million dollars now, wherever they want--

"You do have the money?"

Victoria said, "Yes. All of it."

"They can't know that. So, they will get a million dollars NOW. They will also get me--that is, you--as assurance that we are acting in good faith."

"Will it work? What if you get hurt? What if--"

"I can't be hurt by a cannon, by landslides, certainly not by any weapon mere mortals have.

"Now, look at the situation from the kidnapper's viewpoint. The only person who has arrived, if they ARE watching as this house as they said they are, is the family friend Alice. She has not left. No police have arrived. You in your car-- Your car is here?"

Victoria nodded Yes.

"The daughter leaves the house in her car carrying a satchel. She goes to the collection point, followed by watchers who make sure no one else is following. She sits on a park bench, maybe, with a satchel with her. They drive up, in a van probably, tell her to get in, and drive away. No one follows them.

"They count the money, maybe in the van, maybe in their hideout. It's a million dollars. They are rich! They throw you in the room where your mother is.

"Then things go very badly. You should almost feel sorry for them, Vicky. Because I am terrible when I'm angry."

The Victoria monster put up a hand where Victoria could see it. The skin was turning red, the fingernails becoming claws.

For the first time Victoria felt hope. More, she felt a vicious satisfaction. She knew the monster was real, she knew that it was Alice, her trusted friend, and she knew Mom would soon be home safe.

Matters went mostly as the monster predicted. Not-Victoria told the kidnapper on the phone its story, the kidnapper railed at not getting all the money, Victoria wept and repeated that she would go with the money to prove she was telling the truth about getting the rest of the money the next day, the kidnapper calmed and told Victoria where to go.

A mile away from the money pickup location a battered white van pulled up next to Victoria, a gunman inside the opened back door pointed a gun at the girl and told her to get in.

The girl did so, saying, "Oh, thank you, thank you, thank you! Here's the money. Thank you!"

The foolish girl did not realize what it meant that the kidnapping crew was not wearing masks: that they were going to kill the girl and her mother.

The van wove its way through city streets toward one of the slum areas in South Austin. It parked next to a rundown house of several such houses with a For Sale sign posted in the overgrown front yard.

Inside the house the four kidnappers pushed Victoria down into a broken-down easy chair in the living room then eagerly sat on a nearby couch and spilled the satchel's contents onto a coffee table sitting in front of the couch. The leader, a stout man with red hair shot with grey, counted the banded bundles of ten-dollar bills.

"It's all there," said Red. "We did it. Lock her in with her mother."

A tall bald man looked at Victoria. She recoiled back into her chair even further.

"She's a real looker boss. Let's have some fun with her."

"Tomorrow, when we're ready to leave. Not now. You two, go keep watch. We can't let up. These rich-bitch types can hire people to look for them. We don't want to risk being surprised so close to getting rich."

Grumbling the tall man and a fat companion stood and walked out of the living room. The third, a very broad white man, came over to the girl.

"Get up. You get to see your mother now."

The girl rose, shrinking from the touch of the meaty hand which grabbed her upper arm, to no avail. He dragged her with him on wobbly legs into a hallway. Down it, past a dilapidated kitchen, past an empty storeroom or pantry they went, ending in a closed door secured with a padlock. The lock was not fully engaged so all Red had to do was lift it out of its slot, open the door, and push Alice into a bedroom. She stumbled to a stop as the door closed behind her.

Irma Delgado was standing up from lying on a broken-down bed clad only by a mattress. She rushed to hug Victoria/Alice.

"Oh, baby! They got you too!"

"No, Irma. They got me."

Alice was relaxing into her natural self including her voice. Irma leaned out of her hug, took a step back so she could see the woman before her.

It took a few minutes to change fully back into her Alice appearance. Irma watched the process with fascination.

"Alice? Is it really you?"

"Yes, dear. Except you got one thing wrong. They don't have me. I've got them. And they're going to be real sorry real soon."

"What do you mean? What are you going to do? Are the police outside? Is Victoria all right?"

"Yes, she's all right. Are you? Did they do anything to you?"

"Not so far, but there's a tall man who says he's going to rape me."

"I see you have a few bruises and scratches. Give me your hands and I'll fix them."

"They're nothing. Oh, all right. Here. Oh!"

Alice sent microscopic messengers inside the woman's body. Distributed throughout her by blood, they gave orders to every cell in her body to heal themselves. Which they did, the ones closest to her body's surfaces.

"The hurts went away. How did you do that?"

"I injected you with medicine. It will take a day or so to repair minor injuries like yours. But I preceded it with a pain killer."

"What are you? Are you Alice? Or just look like her?"

"I'm really Alice, Irma. I just am more than the girl you see. Now, I'll tell you more later. Are you ready to go home?"

"Yes. But... There are five of them. They have guns. Sorry but you are just a girl."

Alice grinned. Irma flinched back. She'd never seen teeth open that way, as if they were ready to tear into flesh.

"Irma, a tiger next to me is a kitten. And those men are mice. Now, follow me but stay well back. Bullets can't hurt me if they get a chance to fire their guns, but they can hurt you. Ready?"

"Yes. Yes I am."

"Don't look too closely at what I do. There may be lots of blood. Here we go."

She walked further into the room, turned, faced the door, and began running. Her legs blurred. She leaped high, rotating in the air so that she tilted to the horizontal. Her legs contracted then expanded so that the double kicks against the door added to the momentum of her leap. The noise of her heels slamming into the door was loud. Even louder was the bang as the door tore loose from its hinges and lock to crash onto the floor ten feet along the hallway.

Following close behind came the monster with Alice's appearance. It ran faster than the fastest of the great cats as it sped down the hallway and then turned into the living room. Irma following cautiously behind heard shouts and crashes and screams and a pistol firing then abruptly not firing followed by other screams.

She peered around the doorway into the living room to find three bodies on the floor and Alice crouched over the furthest. The woman looked at the nearer bodies and jerked her gaze away from them. One man's head was smashed into mush, the second had an arm completely torn off and still gushing blood. As her eyes flinched away she could see the blood's flow pulse once then cease.

The Alice creature lifted its head, turned it to the side, and dashed out of the room past Irma. It vanished down the hall and through the open doorway to what Irma knew was the kitchen. There were shots and screams and the sound of a body meatily slamming into a wall or floor.

From another side of the house a door slammed. Out of the kitchen popped the Alice creature as if shot from a gun. It froze in a listening attitude, then it vanished like a bubble bursting and the distant door slammed again.

Moments later the door slammed a third time. Irma heard, "Mrs. Delgado. The last one is getting away. I'm going to let him go."

Alice came into the hall and walked toward Irma. When she came close Alice said, "I'm going to let him get away so that he will pass the word that it's a bad idea to mess with the Delgados."

"The word could get to the police. Maybe we should call them to get ahead of any accusations that we..." She gestured vaguely at the living room.

"There's no need to involve the police. We'll return to your house and act as if nothing happened. I don't want to try explaining what happened to the authorities."

Irma saw the wisdom of that. No one who had not seen--or half-seen--the Alice creature in action would believe it. They would see the massacre scene as some elaborately staged hoax covering multiple murders.

"I'll get your money, Irma. No need to go into the living room yourself to get it."

"No. These kidnappers were going to rape and murder me and my daughter, probably in some horribly painful manner. I want to see them."

Alice nodded and stood aside as Irma Delgado walked past her into the living room.

She stood just inside the door for long moments surveying the death scene. She walked over to one of the bodies. It was Red.

"This is the man who planned everything. I'm glad he's dead. I'm really REALLY glad he's dead. I only wish it hadn't happened so quickly."

The shapechanger came from behind her and began to place the wrapped stacks of money back into the satchel they had come in. Every once in a while she slid a hand over a stack and the blood on it disappeared. When everything was packed she zipped shut the satchel and slung the strap over one shoulder.

"We ready to go?"

At the front door Alice stepped outside and looked around.

"No one's watching. Come on."

The kidnappers van was still in the driveway of the house. Alice held the passenger door for Irma, threw the satchel through the van's side door into it, and got into the driver's seat. She pressed a hand against the key slot and the engine coughed and started. They drove away.

As they wound out of the streets holding the abandoned houses the Delgado matriarch said, "So. What are you, Alice? Some magical creature that modern sophisticates no longer believe in?"

Alice glanced at her briefly.

"No. I'm a human like any other but from a planet from very very far away. I'm here gathering information about cultures and languages and artifacts. In a sense I'm an anthropologist studying you though not just for pure knowledge. Eventually my people will contact you and we want to be sure we do so diplomatically, not unnecessarily step on anyone's toes."

This was one of the many themes of the science-fiction stories that Albert loved. It made sense to Alice unlike many of the plots of those stories.

"So not magical."

"No, unless you consider technology magical. I do, in the sense that it's awesome that such miraculous processes come from real flesh-and-blood fallible creatures. But, no, everything about me and what I can do is natural not supernatural."

Irma thought about this for a little while, speaking when they turned right at a cross street on the corner of which was a gas station.

"So I and Victoria and my sons are just grass-skirted natives to you, study subjects?"

"No. You're my friends. I like you, like your company, appreciate you. Though I suspect I'd better avoid you for a while to let you adjust to my differences."

At the house Alice drove into the driveway and parked in front of the door to the mansion. She got out of the van, retrieved the satchel of money from the van, and followed Irma into the house. She set it on the floor of the hallway as Victoria rushed down it to embrace her mother. She waited till the two broke apart.

"I have to leave to dispose of the van. I'll be back to check on things. Tell Vickie everything, Irma. Tell Mrs. Andersen everything too. I trust her not to blab about me."

Victoria said, "If you get rid of the van how are you going to get back here? I should follow you in one of our cars."

"I have a way. You and your mother, and Mrs. Andersen, have to relax, take a pill, take a bath, whatever. See you later."

Leaving had to wait on a hard hug from Victoria and her thanks. Then she got in the van and drove away.

She turned onto a cross street and called up her egg. It surrounded her and the van. She flew upward, brushing aside some of the branches and leaves which spread out over much of the street in the tree-shrouded neighborhood. Rising further she accelerated quickly upward.

Arcing toward the south she rose to some hundred miles out over the Gulf of Mexico. Pausing there she opened the door of the van and pushed herself out of the van. When she was completely clear of the van she retracted the part of the no-longer-egg-shaped shield. The van, back under the influence of gravity, drifted downward, slowly, then faster and faster tumbling end over end. It would come apart as it fell through thicker and thicker atmosphere.

Alice, relaxing in the weightlessness of her egg, enjoyed the blue globe below her covered by dots of white clouds and wispy crescents of cloud fronts. Far to the west, just on the horizon, a more substantial crescent heralded the possible arrival late tonight of a band of showers.

Briefly her mind replayed the deaths she'd dealt. It was too bad she'd not had time to stretch out their pain to make up for all the pain they'd caused.

It had not taken much time to get rid of the van. She glanced downward at the thought, just in time to see the distant fire of its debris burning up.

She could not keep relaxing up here. The three women in the Delgado household needed her to answer some of their questions and spend time in talk coming to terms with the dangers now past.

She tilted her egg and fled downward.

Chapter 10 - Revolution

Within a year Mrs. Delgado was essentially recovered from her ordeal. There were still occasions when she woke from nightmares. Sometimes Alice slept over when she and Victoria stayed out late partying and dancing. She was there when one nightmare woke the older woman and rushed to her bedroom to keep her company. At that time she injected the woman with messengers to help the woman's body fight emotional trauma. They helped a good deal.

Aviation business continued to pick up.

<>

Near the one-year anniversary of the kidnapping a small army of Mexican revolutionaries crossed from Mexico into Laredo, a small city about 150 miles south of San Antonio. They captured the city and robbed everyone and the banks to finance their part in the long-standing Mexican Revolution. No one was killed though a few policemen were hurt.

Two weeks later a smaller group of self-styled revolutionaries captured Piedras Negras just across the border from Eagle Pass. They made no distinction between Mexicans and Texans and stole from both. More people were hurt this time; all the Mexican police were killed and their counterparts in Texas. They also stole a couple of dozen young women to be "revolutionary wives" meaning military prostitutes.

American soldiers were dispatched to protect the border. They garrisoned several border "cities" (really villages). The bandits/revolutionaries merely avoided those cities or in one case massed enough men to destroy the detachment despite heavy casualties.

Three companies of twenty Texas Rangers each were added to further protect the border. One bandito group avoided the forces against them by traveling forty miles inside Texas and attacking a town called New London. They killed all the men then raped all the younger women, some as young as twelve, and strangled, beat, and stabbed them to death. They then killed the other women and all the children including three infants.

<>

Alice learned of the atrocity the morning after when Lieutenant Jameson hurried into her office at Texas Aviation.

"How soon could the recon Belle be ready to go into operation?"

She spun her office chair away from her desk to look at him.

"A week."

"Can you hurry that?"

"Three days with overtime."

"What about the close-air-support Falcon?"

"Tomorrow. It's ready now but I would have to run a complete inspection-and-correction course. Then fill it with gas, oil, and supplies. Why the hurry?"

He collapsed into an office chair and told her about the New London massacre, looking down at hands strangling each other. His voice broke when he finished with the infant deaths.

As he spoke the immortal began to change. When he quit talking and looked up he saw a woman standing whose skin on face and body was blood red. Her eyes looked like coals of fire.

Yet he could see that the monster was also Alice.

His voice was almost calm as he spoke.

"What's happening?"

The being said nothing. Then: "This is me when I am really really really pissed. I will kill many men over this. I will burn them, butcher them, send them screaming for their mothers."

The emotionless matter-of-fact voice gave his body an electric shock. The hairs on his outer arms and outer legs seemed to crawl. An urge to pee assaulted his penis.

Yet at the same time his heart leaped and tears flooded his eyes. This was exactly what he felt.

The deadly being stood perfectly still, like a statue. It did not blink. It did not breathe.

Then it took a deep breath and collapsed back into the angelically beautiful Alice. Its red skin color was washed away by pinkness and then paleness.

She collapsed back into her seat.

"I'm glad only you were here to see that."

The calm rationality of her voice sent a wave of calm through him, easing a body racked with surging waves of rage and grief that had filled him since he'd heard the latest news from the Mexican Border war front.

He sat in one of the three easy chairs in front of her desk and crossed one leg over another. The ordinary actions helped him speak almost conversationally.

"What are you, Alice?"

"Human. From very far away."

The fiction which she had employed successfully during the Delgado incident served her equally well with Jameson: she was a sort-of anthropological researcher from an advanced civilization. She recited the story briefly, then turned the subject.

"My answer is still the same though the details are different. The CAS Falcon will be ready in the morning. I will leave in it then for the front. Will you come with me?"

"You can't go without me." Then, remembering the death angel he'd just seen, he quickly added: "You need me to clear the way for you to operate there."

"I'll fill the free space with extra ammunition and fuel and some other items such as changes of clothing and such. We can't be assured of hotel space, so may have to camp out under the Falcon. Bring whatever you need for a two-week stay. Then if necessary I'll fly back here to replenish any expenditures."

"Can you take two more people?"

"Yes. Who would they be?"

"My boss and his aide need to get to the front. I could get more resources if we take them."

"Good."

She said, "I've got stuff to do. See you at 8:00."

Then she was writing rapidly in a notebook, ignoring him. He left just as abruptly.

<>

The next morning the immortal did not have to wait for the three Rangers to arrive. They were dropped off by a pickup truck. They wore the rough cowboy outfit that was the Ranger's unofficial uniform and wore various weapons and ammo belts. Each also carried two large suitcases.

Jameson introduced his captain who expressed gratitude for the aid donated by Texas Aviation. Looking at her slender form her said, "No weapons?"

She was clad in black woman-style jeans, black sleek boots with a thin but tough sole, a black long-sleeved shirt that fitted well but not tightly, and a black vest. Her red hair was "dyed" black and adjusted by her shapechanger body to fit in a tight black cap which seemed to have been trimmed to such sleekness.

"My personal weapons are in the plane. I'll put them on at our destination.

"But my main weapons are these."

She reached up to caress the nearest of two .50 caliber machine guns mounted on the nose of the aircraft just aft of the cockpit.

She beckoned him and his aide to the nearest wing. She pointed.

"Under the wing are mounted four 50-pound bombs. I can lay them into a yard-round circle from 100 feet up. And these--" She pointed at the sharp snouts of several long rockets little fatter than broom sticks.

"--these can take out a truck or a railroad car from 1000 feet."

The aide was a boyish-looking Ranger whom Alice could tell was a tough and experienced soldier despite his appearance. He spoke.

"Where did you get this ordnance? It's hardly the stuff a civilian outfit has laying around."

"I developed it myself for just such an emergency. These are all the items we have on hand, being development test items. However Texas Aviation has the plans and procedures for making more if the Army, or the Rangers, decides they need them.

"Now let's get aboard. Captain, you come up front with me. I'm sure you have more questions. Jameson, you and Clark, please store all possessions in the cargo hold. Please try to balance items to the left and right equally."

In the plane Alice strapped into the pilot's seat and oversaw the captain doing the same in the copilot's seat. She looked out her side window to see the head of the ground crew waiting for her. She pointed at the hangar doors with two fingers of a hand. He nodded then saluted her. She returned the salute, a sharp crisp motion, then spoke to the captain.

"I'll be quite busy till we get safely into the air. So please hold any speech until then."

"Yes, sir."

"No need for that, sir."

"You are the captain of a military aircraft now. There's every need of respect for the chain of command."

Alice nodded and began the preflight list. It was abbreviated as this was a military vehicle but was still strictly adhered to.

Soon the loaded Falcon trundled out of the hangar and toward the take off apron onto the outbound runway. It had been lengthened and toughened during the previous year.

Alice leaned forward and scanned the skies above. Until the control tower became operational each pilot had to stay alert for collision potential.

As she did all this she was slowly merging with the Falcon. The merger was more complete than with previous machines. This model had more of the electrical nervous system than any aircraft made in American and maybe even Europe.

Ready for take off ALICE lumbered down the runway, went light on HER wheels, and lifted into the sky.

SHE breathed deeply of the cool fresh air entering HER several intakes and scanned the volume ahead of and around HER with HER mysterious distance senses.

Well airborne SHE curved toward the south, climbing still. At 1000 feet SHE was traveling almost southwest.

SHE spoke over the microphone mounted on the headset holding the two cans containing earphones.

"Well, happy campers, we are safely at cruising altitude. Everybody report your condition, low ranks upward."

"Private Clark well and present, Sir."

"Lieutenant Jameson well and present, SIR."

"Commander Acton well and present, Sir."

Good, SHE thought. The captain had enough knowledge of naval tradition to adopt their traditions aboard vessels. Anyone with a captain's rank was called "commander" to separate themselves from the only person who was officially the captain of the vehicle. In a crisis only that official was called and called themselves Captain.

"We are well on our way to Laredo. We'll stop at San Antonio to top off our tanks, though we could make it all the way and use only a third of a tank. It will take us 40 minutes to get to San Antone and twice that to get to Laredo. So settle in to enjoy our in-flight entertainment."

Clark said, *"The only in-flight entertainment I see is what looks like the side of a cereal box."*

"Those are the safety instructions. You are encouraged to read them."

"Gee, thanks. I am so relieved. Uh, maybe not so much. It talks about what to do when ditching at sea."

For the remainder of the first leg of the flight Alice talked with Captain Upton, answering questions about herself and Texas Aviation mostly.

It took a full hour and a half to get to Laredo. Alice had Upton relinquish his seat to Jameson in order for him, Alice said, to brief her on their activities in and around that border town.

Part of their speech was indeed review. The twenty-strong Ranger company they'd join was stationed in Laredo. A second was in Eagle Pass to the north across from the Mexican town Piedras Negras. A third was in McAllen to the south 60 miles in from the coast.

The Ranger companies would be under the orders of Captain Upton. They would coordinate with but not be under the command of an Army company headquartered in Laredo. Army companies typically had between 100 and 200 men; he thought the border expedition was some 150.

Alice said, "That's a piss-poor number. They need ten times that many to be close to effective."

"Chalk it up to our Washington bosses being so pinch penny."

"I tell you now that I will not acknowledge any authority but my own. I and my plane are volunteers on loan to the Army and the Rangers. I will coordinate with them but not take orders."

"They could draft you."

He was trying to be helpful, Alice could see. She fell back on her space-alien story.

"Fat lot of good that would do them. I'm part of an empire of hundreds of star systems advanced far beyond this planet. You think anything your people could do will do more than inconvenience me?"

"Just be diplomatic, OK? Don't bring up your volunteer status unless it's absolutely necessary."

"Of course. I am always diplomatic."

He chuckled. She joined in.

<>

What with their downtime at San Antonio they arrived at Laredo at close to 11:30. Thirty miles out ALICE spoke to HER passengers in the rear.

"In ten minutes we'll pass over Laredo. I will loop around and tilt the plane a few times to one side or the other so the two of you can get better views as we lower to land. Lieutenant Jameson tells me that the Army and the Rangers have set up camp a few miles north of the downtown area. They also have a tarred dirt runway for aircraft. We'll set down there."

Captain Upton said, *"Thank you, Captain."*

The buildings of Laredo could be seen on the horizon a few minutes out. So also could be seen the Rio Grande off to the right flowing toward the southeast. Near Laredo it turned straight south, then jogged east a few miles before turning south again.

SHE had dropped to 500 feet by the time SHE passed over the military area that was HER destination. HER engine was loud enough that people below could hear HER. SHE perceived many of them coming out to watch HER recede southward, still lowering.

SHE crossed the eastward jog of the river and so was flying over Mexico's Nuevo Laredo. The Mexican city below looked pretty much like the American city.

SHE climbed a bit as SHE made a U-turn, tilting HER left wing down. SHE leveled then tilted HER right wing down, then leveled again.

SHE passed over the Rio Grande at 100 feet. It was about 150 feet wide and shallow with very green grassy banks. People, mostly younger men and boys, could be seen wading in the water close to shore. The mild waves of the water were clearly visible.

SHE waggled HER wings twice more to give HER passengers good looks at the city from above. People below, thinking the waggles were for them, waved upward at HER.

The black runway showed up a little off to one side. SHE lined up on it and came gently down to the surface without a bump. SHE dropped all flaps and ailerons. SHE also reversed the pitch of HER propellers to slow HER motion, revving the engine furiously. SHE slowed so fast that everyone inside HER was thrown forward against their seat belts.

At a sedate five miles an hour SHE taxied toward a makeshift hangar made of canvas. SHE stopped, set HER brakes, and killed HER engine.

Dropping back fully into HER biological part was jarring. Alice sat back into her seat and took and let out a deep breath.

"Well, we're here," said Jameson. "You look a little tired. I'll arrange to offload everything, so relax a few minutes before you exit."

She thanked him and did as he suggested. Then she stood, went back to the rear, removed her other clothing and gear from a bin, and began to put them on.

The light was bright as Alice came down the short stairs of the

Falcon. She stood still on the concrete to adjust to the brightness and look around.

There was a low whistle as the ground crew and her passengers caught sight of her. She was something to behold.

In addition to her black outfit her thick vest was also black. It had a dozen sewn-in sheathes holding small flat throwing knives whose grey handles were still just thick enough to be used as daggers. More throwing knives were held in sheathes in something like cowboy's chaps but much slimmer.

High on her waist were two holsters holding automatic pistols, butts facing forward. In front of and behind the holsters were four holders of magazines for the pistols. Two round pockets on the gun belt held, though no one there knew it, silencers for the pistols.

Over one shoulder was a strap from which an automatic carbine hung barrel down. Around her waist was a girdle made of magazine pockets holding magazines for the carbine.

At her waist tilted forward projected the grey hilts of two long daggers. Also on the gun belt was slung a hard black helmet.

Only a few watchers dwelt on her equipment. Most were struck by the woolly black cap of her nearly bald head. Even more so they were jolted by her skin. It was the light grey of someone hours or days dead.

Someone whispered *"Una niña muerta!"* Others whispered *"La niña muerta."*

By nightfall the word was all throughout both cities. All the girls murdered by the Mexican intruders had returned from the dead. And they thirsted for revenge.

By the next day all along the Mexican border and the land beyond that message traveled. By the next week all of northern Mexico knew.

The Dead Girls brought back from the beyond had inhabited this one Texas girl who flew in airplanes. And who walked with impunity atop them. And they swarmed in the body of the sleek blue airplane which mounted machine guns on its nose. They filled the bombs and rockets under its wings.

The African warrior empress Temilade did not know the specifics of this flood of mythic stories. But s/he knew it was happening. S/he had used hi/r enemies superstitions against them time and again. As had Li Wei in his early years as a dread reaper of Chinese souls.

The Anglos of Texas knew nothing of this. Their reaction was exemplified by Captain Upton's comment: "Great outfit, Miss

Willoughby. A bit circus-ish, don't you think?"

Alice smiled and said, "Oh, to be sure. But a girl likes to make a fashion statement, don't you know?" Then she conferred with the ground crew for the Falcon and the three other aircraft in the makeshift hangar.

Jameson accepted the outfit though he was puzzled by it. He was certain, however, that it had a purpose. Alice's hatred of terror makers held no place for frivolity.

Clark merely looked thoughtful. He didn't know this Alice Willoughby but he was sure she was the smartest person he had ever met. She had the beauty of a goddess but he knew his Greek and Latin mythology. Goddesses toyed with and tortured mortals. The thought of bedding Alice shriveled his balls.

A staff car took Alice and the three Rangers to meet Colonel Smith-Jones, the leader of the Army task force. He occupied a floor of the top hotel in Laredo with his staff. He met the newcomers to his theater and shook their hands. He eyed Alice's outfit but more from curiosity than anything else. He had long ago gotten used to the eccentricities of boffins, including or especially females of that persuasion.

"So glad to have your addition to our forces here. We're small and stretched. I don't know what Washington was thinking sending such a small force."

"Perhaps," said Alice, "they recognized the powerful mind they set to command the force."

"Ah, young lady. You tease an old campaigner with your flattery. It's pleasant to hear but not for a second do I believe it.

"Now, Captain Upton, let's go over how we can combine our forces to better advantage."

The Colonel and his staff chatted with the Ranger contingent for almost an hour, solidifying responsibilities and operational details. Then they turned to Alice who had been carefully listening. She privately approved their planning but was not optimistic about the success of the task force. The border was too long and there was too much territory to cover.

"What can I add? Two elements.

"First, the outfit I wear, I suspect you already know, is no whim. The Mexican culture entertains many superstitions. Included in it is the idea that the dead retain a close connection to everyday life. They celebrate, for instance, the Day of the Dead each year. Which they stretch into pretty much a Week of the Dead.

"Lieutenant Jameson grew up in El Paso where he was almost as much a Mexican growing up as an American. He would be an asset to your intelligence people when they try to anticipate the reactions of the native populace."

The Ranger nodded his head but said nothing.

"Just by walking around looking like one of the girls murdered by the so-called revolutionaries I attack their morale. Naturally they will counter-attack, maybe even tonight. I plan to sleep under my airplane and this will be added incentive to attack me and it.

"When they do I will be ready. What you see is the least of the weapons I have prepared for them."

"We can help fight the insurgents. No need to go it alone."

"There is every need. Most simply, I will not need to differentiate friend from foe. Too, I am more than adequate to repel an attack. I will not catalog my resources but they are formidable."

"We can't do nothing."

"Unless you promise to stay out of my way I will take my marbles and go home. You can try to force me to your will. If you do, you will find I am a dangerous foe."

"You dare to threaten me?" He did not seem incensed by the idea despite his words. Boffins, after all.

"Merely pointing out consequences. You CAN help, however. Station your forces well away, far enough and well enough concealed so that the attackers are not warned off. When you hear the firing cease then move in to mop up."

The Colonel looked around at his aides and the Rangers. Then he lifted an eyebrow.

"As you wish. My career is already well-fooked, pardon the language, so I might as well add one more impossible task to this task force."

"Thank you. Now for the second element that I can add to the task force.

"Use of airplanes as a military asset has been explored in Europe. Some of the outlines have emerged. There are two prongs--well, three, if you count aerial combat which is not relevant here.

"One is reconnaissance. It is not an easy task in this theater because it is so vast. The human eye is not up to the task though we must try. Future technological advances such as the use of cameras and calculators will tackle that problem.

"Meanwhile we can use tactics to aid recon missions. As an example we will do missions in the hour or two past sunrise or before sunset. Shadows will paint themselves on the ground under those conditions practically painting arrows at our targets.

"Another prong is ground attack. The airplane I brought was specially designed for this. It has two .50 caliber machine guns fed by a chain. I slowed its rate of fire way down so that firing passes on targets are more likely to suffer at least one hit per pass.

"It also hangs bombs and rockets under its wings. I've tested them and they can be very effective with a pilot like me, a 'natural' in pilot slang. Future versions will have mechanical aids so that an ordinarily competent pilot can be just as effective.

"Well, sirs, that's it. What this volunteer can bring to your job."

"I'm overwhelmed, Miss Willoughby. Or should I say 'Dead Girl'? For the first time I have some tiny hope that I and my career may survive the impossible task I've been set."

<>

Starting the afternoon of her arrival she flew a recon mission over the areas suggested by the Army's intelligence crew. She was accompanied by Jameson in the copilot's seat and by an Army intel staffer in one of the back seats. The staffer wielded a bulky camera with a long lens.

She quit for the day in the late afternoon and had her plane refueled and otherwise made ready for the next day. Then she ate in the Army chow hall among the lower officers and enlisted men. She left the skull-like helmet and carbine and waist belt locked in her plane but kept the rest of her weapons with her.

A woman as beautiful as she even with her corpse-grey skin attracted attention. Her display of weapons and willingness to work led most to respect her. She made friends by asking people about themselves and listening well.

Not all of the attention was polite. The loudest comments about little girls playing dress-up came to a head four days later.

It happened after sundown when the makeshift mess hall was transformed into a club house with tables set up for card games and chats. A bar magically appeared with beer for sale but nothing stronger. That was supplied discreetly by various attendees. Officers and enlisted mixed freely, something strictly forbidden in larger more established military venues.

Alice was playing a game of darts with a half-dozen soldiers. She had agreed to play with one or the other eye covered as she inevitably won without the bandanna. Three or four other non-players always looked on, offering advice and good-natured insults.

That evening some of the insults grew less good natured. They were made by four soldiers that included one big man with a big black beard.

The immortal was not bothered by the insults and ignored them. Not so her companion players. They replied in more and more heated words. A fight seemed to be brewing so Alice stepped between the two factions.

She looked at her defenders.

"Back down, boys. I appreciate the support, but you insult me by acting as if I can't fight my own battles."

She turned on the four men with the loud mouths. "You. Back off. We've got enough fight on our plates without doing the enemy's job by fighting among ourselves."

The biggest loud mouth stepped forward. "And if we don't?"

"Then I'll make you."

"With what? These piddly little knives?"

He reached to take hold of one of the throwing knives on her vest. She blocked his hand with one of hers.

"Don't touch my weapons."

"I'll touch your CUNT if I want to, dress-up bitch."

He reached down toward her crotch.

The dead girl stepped close. Her punch to his belly was invisibly fast. It sounded like a watermelon being thumped. He bent over. Alice narrowly got out of the way as he vomited on the floor.

One of the men's companions rushed toward her, a beer bottle held high by its neck. She leaned back and snapped a kick into his crotch. He gasped loudly and fell to the floor.

The other two men paused after a step forward. The dead girl was standing relaxed, looking steadily at them. Her blue eyes were perfectly expressionless. Her hands were held up in front of her, palms together almost as if praying.

Or ready to pluck a couple of knives from her vest.

They backed up, their own hands held up in front of them. But in a

"See no weapons" gesture.

"What's happening here?" came from behind the crowd of onlookers. A senior officer pushed people aside to look over the scene.

"Nothing much, Sir," said Alice. "Just a couple of men who are having trouble holding their liquor."

Her eyes speared the two accomplices.

"Their friends here were just going to help them. Right?"

The two men were happy to have a job to do which got them out of the sight of an officer. Each hurried to help their two acquaintances to stand and wobble off toward the restroom.

A junior officer who had been one of the dart players said, "The two men were being a bit loud. Obviously couldn't hold their drinks. One puked, the other tried to help him but tripped over his own feet."

The officer spoken to looked around at the crowd. He had an idea just what had happened but the problem seemed to have been handled.

His gaze fell on a sergeant in the crowd.

"Get this mess cleaned up." He pushed his way back through the crowd as the sergeant's voice answered him.

"Well, shit," said one of the dart throwers who was one of the two men picked by the sergeant for cleanup. "Just as I was about to throw the winning throw."

His statement was met with derision.

Never after did anyone have anything negative to say about the little dress-up girl. At least not in her hearing.

<>

The recon mission's only successes were to tell the task force where the enemy groups were not. This info was useful in building a detailed map of northeastern Mexico and southwestern Texas. But it did not find enemies.

More successful was Alice's forays in her egg just at sunrise. She found two small groups. In her afternoon flight she often "wandered" after covering the assigned areas. In two cases she overflew the small groups and "accidentally discovered" them. They were caught.

The long-awaited attack on Alice and her aircraft came a couple of days later.

Each night well after dark Alice dropped a few dried leaves and wads of newspapers in a circle a few dozen feet from her aircraft. Then she went to bed under the plane inside her egg safe even from natural disasters.

Near 3:00 am a dozen "revolutionaries" cut a passage through a chain link fence protecting the Army camp, then carefully closed after them the bent-open makeshift door in the fence. There were random fence checks by soldiers in military pickups.

They proceeded stealthily to the dimly lit area of the hangars. The crunch of one man's boots when it crushed a leaf was very quiet. But it was enough for the shapechanger's ultra-sensitive hearing. She came instantly awake.

Her ultra-sensitive eyes were not needed to detect the intruders. Her esoteric location sense did it for her.

The dead girl rose in her egg till she floated five feet up, her legs and arms stick straight to counteract their usual flexed stance when she was weightless. She still did not perfectly look as if she was standing in a gravitational field but the strangeness added to her supernatural appearance.

She triggered the egg's darkness-fighting lights, turned inward not outward. She was lit all over, brightly to the dark-adapted eyes of the killers.

A dozen weapons barked, again and again. The only change in the floating image was for it to slowly spin so that its face rotated to gaze at the shooters. Its eyes glowed like red embers.

Weapons clicked to empty. There were clashing sounds as men desperately tried to reload. Too late.

The lights on the dead girl winked out. The apparition plummeted to stand upright on the concrete. Its pistols were in its hands. It began firing.

Men screamed and fell, or bent over holding wounded arms and sides. Half died. Half remained alive to be questioned. Five dropped their weapons and ran away. Two got thirty feet away before the front of their heads exploded outward. Three more ran frantically, zig-zagging to avoid the shots that struck the concrete under them.

Quiet descended broken by moaning and weeping men. The dead girl stepped among them and leaned down to touch the ones left alive. Their pain eased, bullet holes stopped bleeding, began to heal.

From the darkness came Army soldiers, bent over, weapons ready. When the now-peaceful scene became clear in the dim light they relaxed minutely. They could see the dead girl, unharmed, ministering to the fallen.

The lieutenant leading the squad came up to the shapechanger. He said, "Looks like you've got everything under control, Miss Willoughby."

"Yes. I'm done here. Please take over. The wounded men should go to the hospital and be treated and hospitalized under guard. Your bosses will want to question them."

"Yes, sir. Ah, yes ma'am."

Alice climbed into her plane and shut the door behind her. She lay down in the aisle, pulled her egg around her and closely conformed to her body, and fell instantly asleep.

The immortal awoke just before dawn, stood, and opened the airplane's door. She looked out to see a peaceful scene, the lights which lit the area at night pale against the blooming brightness soon to come to the sky. The air was cool, the scene quiet except for the distant sounds coming from the mess hall where cooks and servers were readying breakfast. Below her the concrete held only faint stains where blood had been imperfectly cleaned up.

No one was around. She stepped off into emptiness, formed her egg around her, and plummeted into the sky.

At breakfast in the mess hall of her usual scrambled eggs, bacon, buttered toast, and fruit juice her usual coterie of soldiers joined her at a round table that was had become "their" table.

One of them said, "Heard you had a bit of excitement, Alice."

"Yeah. The shit-heads finally attacked me. Dumb asses. They couldn't figure out I'd be ready for them?"

"You left some alive, I heard," said another.

"About half. Enough for questioning, enough dead to get the message across: Leave me the fuck alone."

At 9:00 Alice got a summons to headquarters. She got into the pickup truck beside the messenger and rode into the middle of Laredo to the hotel where Army HQ was sited.

She was ushered into the usual conference room and nodded at the Colonel sitting at the head of the table. He nodded back and motioned her to sit. The place left open for her was beside Jameson who sat beside Captain Acton. Beside him was his aide Private Clark and one other Ranger. With all the Army staff there were two dozen people at the table.

Colonel Smith-Jones said, "As everyone has heard, I expect, the so-called revolutionaries attacked Miss Willoughby with the expected results. Expected by her but, frankly, not by me. Congratulations."

"Thank you, Sir."

"About half of them survived the attempt. All are wounded but with superficial wounds. Was that deliberate?"

"Yes, Sir. I figured six would be enough to cross-check their answers. Expending the others would get the message across that I am hard to kill. Or maybe impossible to kill if I am truly already dead."

Smith-Jones called on his intelligence chief, an older man with some Mexican blood from two or three generations back. He said, "We'll be interrogating all the partisans today starting at 1:00. All will have been treated and hospitalized, treated well, and fed breakfast and lunch. As usual we will not brutalize them in any way, which they surely expect."

At that he looked at another staff member who looked defiantly back.

Jameson said, "I consider that good policy. Mexicans, from what I know of them, are used to privation and highly resistant to pain. Also, treating them well will disconcert them as they expect the opposite.

"I have a suggestion. When you do interrogate them have Miss Willoughby in the room. She should stand in a corner and just look at the prisoner. If no one interacts with her he will be unsure she is really there in the flesh. No matter what she does, I repeat, everyone should ignore her as if she isn't there."

The intel chief nodded.

The Army commander then changed the subject to other procedural matters.

<>

The first interrogation at 1:00 was in a bare room with a table between the two Army men and the prisoner. He was seemingly the youngest and so, maybe, most likely to talk. Any facts he let slip or volunteered could then be used on the next prisoners to be questioned.

When he was brought into the room Alice was in a corner of the room on the side opposite of the table where he was told to sit. There she could look him in the face but from the side. He could also see her.

The questioners were calm and matter of fact. One did most of the talking, speaking in Spanish which Alice mostly understood, having picked up some in the last few years. The other took apparently detailed notes. They asked his name. He gave one which Alice could tell was fake. The questioners likely guessed that too but acted as if they believed him.

The next questions were innocuous, such as How old are you? Where were you born? Where did you grow up? What was your childhood home like? All were questions they'd answered so many times in their lives that their answers were automatic. It would take an effort of will and a good imagination to come up with lies, much less plausible lies.

All the while Alice stood perfectly still, almost unblinking, and stared at the insurgent. He tried to ignore her but his eyes kept twitching in her direction.

One twitch turned into a longer look before he jerked his gaze back to the men in front of him. The questioner slammed a hand down on the table.

"What is so fascinating about a wall? You idiot!"

The man pointed a trembling finger at Alice. "Her."

The questioner turned his upper body and looked at Alice who kept her eyes pointed at the revolutionary/bandit. Then he slowly turned back and exchanged a glance with his companion.

In English he said, "Is he crazy? Or just pretending to be?"

Alice noted that the insurgent understood English though perhaps only at a basic level. She had no doubt that the questioners knew or guessed this.

"I vote for crazy. Let's get rid of him and go on to the next. I want to leave early."

"I feel kind of sorry for him. He's only a kid. You know what they'll do to him if we let him go now."

The man's fate eventually was to be stood with his companions before a firing squad but for now it was just to go back to a cell and decent treatment. But he could not know that.

The main interrogator turned back to the man and asked another of this long list of questions.

This time the insurgent was more cooperative though not by much. This was partly reluctance but more because he knew so little about the most important info such as who were the higher-ups in the insurgent movement and what their plans were.

<>

It took two days to interrogate the other insurgents. During that time Alice continued to help by standing in a corner and staring at the guilty. Except for one time, when one man refused to talk at all. Then Alice drifted in her egg to a few feet height, still staring. That was effective to get him speaking. Once started it was hard to get him to stop.

<>

Freed of her interrogator duty Alice went back to afternoon recon flights and very-early-morning flights. Neither turned up any camps or other evidence of insurgent/bandit activity.

Until one Saturday afternoon a week later.

The Army had requested that Alice fly circles around Laredo, each one further than the last. Half of that area was in Mexico, triggering protests from the Mexican government. That area was in the control of the rebels' territory and the source of much of the intrusions into the US. The US government officials included that fact in their reply to the first protest. They didn't bother to reply to the second.

The latest circle included a swath of the US 90 many miles north of Laredo and as many miles east of Eagle Pass and its sister city across the Rio Grande, Piedras Negras.

The area was fairly though not perfectly flat and dry. However the Nueces River flowed from the north through the area. It was joined occasionally from the west and east by streams. It itself was little more than a stream being only about a 100 feet wide and shallow. Still, all along it grass and low trees made a mile to two-mile wide strip of green. The underground water cisterns extended even further.

The area ALICE crossed over at 1000 feet included several small villages and farms. This was part of why the rebels had invaded it and set up a camp.

ALICE detected it with HER esoteric senses from miles away but said nothing. This would allow Jameson to officially discover it and gain credit for his work.

"Shit!" he said, looking down through his binoculars. *"They're about to execute some prisoners!"*

ALICE said, "Hold on! I'm about to go belly up!"

SHE made an abrupt left turn, HER wing dipping low. Then lower still till SHE rolled onto HER back. The wings that before pulled HER up now pulled HER down.

SHE put HER nose down and went into a dive. SHE revved HER engine to the red line and sped downward. The air whistled loudly past

HER body and around HER wings. HER engine screamed.

The people below jerked their heads up at the sounds. The sky-blue plane was invisible at first then suddenly seemed to blink into existence diving straight down.

Then suddenly it leveled off, flipped right side up, and came racing at little over tree top level toward the dirt plaza where the watchers stood.

"La muerta! La muerta! Viene! Viene!"

Machine guns chattered and blazed as the sky dragon rushed toward them. Twin puffs of dust stitched lines in the dirt toward those on the ground. They scattered to both sides, running, leaping, falling. The slower erupted into rag dolls and blood flew dozens of feet.

It flashed overhead and raced away. A mile away it reared back and flipped over on its back and twisted to right itself. It was coming back!

The rebel soldiers scattered, some racing into the surrounding area, some diving behind a pair of wagons parked on one side of the plaza, some crouching behind a few large barrels. Most ran toward the three large tents despite the fact that canvas would be no barrier to bullets.

In fact Alice was lowering toward a flat area to one side of the impromptu village. The Falcon just might be able to take off from it.

The aircraft rolled to a halt with low bushes harshly scraping its belly.

Alice killed the engine, leaped out of her seat, pressed keys into Jameson's nearest hand.

"Lock the door! Follow but carefully!"

Then she was gone, seeming to Jameson as if she flew.

He rushed to the door. To see that she did indeed fly. Like a cannon shot from a shell Alice vanished in the direction of the village.

Quickly but carefully, as commanded, Jameson followed the pilot toward the village where there surely was much screaming. Without hearing them he knew what the rebels were screaming: *"Lady Death! Lady Death! She's coming! She's coming!"*

The Dead Girl flashed into the middle of the plaza and stopped instantly ten feet up. Her metabolism was sped up so that the world seemed to slow down.

A glance showed a dozen men tied to poles ready to be shot. Two leaned forward against the ropes which bound them.

An instant later she was beside them. The dead one was still warm, only seconds or minutes dead, perhaps from a-- Yes, her probe revealed, dead from a heart attack.

She put her wrist against his nearest wrist. Big veins and arteries in the wrist opened up, mated with arteries and veins in the shapechanger's wrist. For half a minute the blood of the immortal flowed into the body of the mortal, blood from him flowed into her. Then the flow ceased as the two bodies detached from each other.

A fold shaped itself out of her egg's shield and narrowed to a razor's edge. It sliced the ropes binding the dead man to his pole. They parted and Alice gently laid him on the ground. She put a hand to his chest and jolted his heart with an electric pulse. He coughed and began to breathe.

She leaped up and sliced the ropes of the other unconscious man, laid him to the ground, freed a third man. She said to him, "Find knives! Free the others."

"They'll come back!"

A shot came from the largest tent. Alice flashed into the air and to a position above it. An instant later she plunged through the top.

Ten feet up she saw a man with a pistol in his hand changing his aim from one woman lying on the floor of the tent toward a second woman cringing from a shot.

The egg slammed into him and sent him and it to explode through the side of the tent.

Moments later the Dead Girl plummeted back through the tent top. She halted and looked around.

Ten or so men stood to one side, weapons discarded on the floor, hands up.

Alice looked at the dozen or more women standing near another side of the tent. The no-longer-cringing woman stood up and dusted the seat of her dress. Alice quickly knelt to heal the woman who'd been shot, then stood again and said to the women, "Does anyone know how to handle a gun?"

Most of the women raised their hands. Alice was not surprised. This was Texas, after all.

"Get their weapons. Guard them. Don't kill anyone unless you have to. But if you have to, don't hesitate."

"Don't worry, dear," said the oldest-appearing of the women. "We're downright HOPING they'll give us an excuse."

The faces of most of the men showed Alice that they were sure of the truth of the woman's words.

Seconds later the human meteor punched through the canvas into the second largest tent. At the sight of the grey-faced black-suited apparition one man threw up his rifle to aim at her. The weapon never rose far; the man beside him blew his brains out with a pistol. Then the man slowly crouched and put his pistol on the floor, his other arm raised high as he stared at her face.

Alice glanced around as all the men followed suit. Several women were off to one side, several shielding children with their bodies.

"Who can handle guns? Good. Get those--" She pointed at the weapons on the floor. "--and guard the men. Don't kill anyone unless you have to but don't hesitate if you must."

She waited till her orders were safely carried out then burst through the roof headed for the third and last big tent.

Fifteen minutes later Alice was administering to the dozen men who had been slated for execution. They'd hung and stood overnight and were suffering from exposure to the chill cold air of the night and the sunburn of the day.

A gun fired in the direction of the Falcon. Instants later Alice was fifty feet above a man crouched over a body. It was the Texas Ranger.

"Hoy, below! Coming down!"

Jameson looked sideways and up at her and stood as she drifted down to stand before him.

She looked at the man on the ground. "Some idiot trying to outdraw a Texas Ranger?"

"Nah. We both had our guns out. He wasn't expecting anyone. I was, having been warned by a certain someone to be careful. He tried to shoot it out despite me having the drop on him."

She shook her head at human stupidity. "Stay alert. He's not the only one who got away from me. Join me as quickly as you can. I've got work to do. Later."

She drew her egg around her and rocketed away toward the camp.

<>

By nightfall the camp was secured. Male prisoners freed, made healthy, and issued weapons guarded some seventy prisoners who were penned in the area fenced in with barbed wire where they themselves had been imprisoned. Some women carried weapons too. They felt, as one woman had said, "I'm never going to be without a gun again."

Messengers had been sent to the three closest villages that

everyone had been freed and was safe. Already an armed party had arrived from the nearest bearing supplies as well as weapons.

Food had been prepared and was being eaten. Every half hour Alice lofted into the air to fly a circuit around the camp. She did not need the star light and the crescent moon to detect any enemy creeping back toward the camp.

Well after dark Alice told Jameson that she was going to radio for help using one of the hand-held shortwave radios in the plane.

"You don't want to show up in Laredo as a flyer."

It wasn't a question. He already understood that Alice was going to go back to being a pretend Dead Girl instead of an actual Death Girl who flew and was invincible. He'd asked why the stories of the villagers and the prisoners wouldn't reveal that. He halfway agreed with her answer.

"Unless the people in Laredo actually see me fly they're not going to believe what some hysterical villagers and cowed Mexican prisoners tell them to justify being outfought by one Texas Ranger and one egghead pilot who dresses funny.

"Besides, in a week those people's memories will fade and they'll begin to remember ordinary explanations rather than the fantastic events they experienced."

<>

Two months went by without any contact with the enemy within the areas to the east of the Rio Grand. Even reports of bandits operating inside Mexico were scarce and the bands were small and poorly led.

This was partly because of the several Mexican armies in the Nuevo Leon state southwest across from the US. They had gobbled the bandits up or enlisted them in their rebellion against the old Mexican government.

The capitol of Nuevo Leon in Monterrey had been captured and the old government army had been defeated. The city and its revolutionary army under Pancho Villa were busy firming up their possession of it and its surroundings, especially the farms and ranches which fed them.

At least it had been. Recently Villa had been assassinated by his lieutenant who had taken his place.

Then one bandit group organized in the border town of Ciudad Acuña crossed the Rio Grand to capture Del Rio, Texas.

As soon as the small US Army outpost was attacked it hunkered down and called for help from the Army outpost in the border town of Eagle Pass 50 miles to the southeast. They responded by mobilizing a strike force and sending it up the road toward Eagle Pass.

The call for help reached Laredo also. Within fifteen minutes Alice had the Falcon in the air with Jameson as her spotter and copilot.

Eagle Pass was 150 miles away. The Falcon cruised at 170 miles an hour at 10,000 feet so it would take about an hour to get there.

When well aloft Alice said, "Do you feel comfortable flying the rest of the way? And landing if you need to?"

"Getting there, fine. Landing, not so much."

"You shouldn't have to land but I have more confidence in you than you do. So I'm going to go on ahead."

"How? Oh, of course.

"Shit. If you get me killed Miss Dead Girl, you know I'm going to haunt you forever."

"Your company would be welcome. Later."

She unstrapped from her seat, got up, ran down the aisle to the door. She opened it, having to press hard against it to squeeze through it. As she fell away the door slammed shut and latched closed.

She called up her egg and shot away.

Jameson could see the figure of Alice standing in the air for instants before she shot forward and disappeared. Seconds later he heard the distant crash as she accelerated far past the speed of sound.

A few minutes late the egg passed over the fort at 10,000 feet. It was decelerating rapidly but was still moving at supersonic speeds. It trailed a spreading cone of highly compressed air. As the lower part of the cone hit the ground those below heard a loud WHAM!

The rebels, some fifty strong, were arrayed all around the small military fort of the US Army. They ceased firing at it and turned toward the explosive sound.

When nothing happened they returned to their siege. Until someone shouted and pointed.

From the direction of Mexico, the southwest, came a black figure standing on nothing. It expanded from a tiny stick figure to a human-sized figure, its grey face like a bare skull.

WHISH! It fled by at fifty feet up, leaving a hurricane of wind behind. Men stumbled, some fell, weapons clattered on stone and hard-packed earth.

A hundred yards away it reversed its course and came back. Its course this time was at an angle that took it around the back of the fort where it wreaked the same upsets on the insurgents.

Those in the front heard firing. Hope turned to fear as the black figure whipped around the edge of the fort and came back to the front.

It halted directly in front of the besiegers clustered behind barriers to counter fire from the fort. It stood on nothing just looking at them. Some alert or foolish men began firing at it.

To no avail. Bullets deadly to anything living had no effect. They simply vanished or were devoured, perhaps.

"Stop shooting! You can't kill the dead!" cried one man.

He laid his rifle on the ground and stood erect with his arms over his head.

The black figure was sinking toward the ground. At ten feet up it stopped.

There was nothing under its black-booted feet.

It stood oddly. But no one expected the dead to be ordinary.

With it still and close those looking on could see fine detail: a hard close-fitting black helmet covered its skull. The helmet and black vest and shirt and pants framed its face, the contrast with the light grey of a dead person making the face seem more like that of a skull.

It pistols were black in their black holsters. The hilts of its knives peeking around from its back were black. The only thing not black were the eyes. They were barely visible at this distance but even so it could be seen that they were blue as the sky.

Even years later those who'd seen those eyes swore that they were windows onto some place else, some place with a sky as blue as those of Earth but very far away.

Rifles and shotguns sagged in the hands of their wielders.

The dead girl spun on its vertical axis, not turning, just slowly rotating, almost like a ceramic doll on a turntable.

It flew forward, rising as it went, to stand on nothing a few feet out from the façade of the fort. From behind the top of that barrier a head came forward. It was the second in command of the fort's commander.

The two conferred for some time. Then the dead girl returned to its previous position.

"They are willing to take your surrender but promise no harm will come to you from them. They are angry because you wounded three of them, one seriously. But you have not killed anyone so they will only jail you.

"However, they cannot know what penalties a civil authority might impose. I suggest you stand down but keep your weapons until another me shows up to help you treat with those authorities."

"Another you? What does that mean?"

But there was no answer. The dead girl had vanished into the sky. It left behind it a distant explosion from far above.

<>

It was a struggle to get back aboard the Falcon even when it slowed to a hundred miles an hour. Finally Alice popped through the door. It slammed shut behind her.

A bit battered even for a tough-as-tire-rubber shapechanger Alice walked forward. She sat in her pilot's seat but only donned her seat belt. She kept her hands off her controlling yoke.

"How's it been?"

"I've been reviewing how to land a thousand times over. Don't you ever leave me like that, DEAD GIRL."

"I promise. Unless I need to."

"Fucking Dead Girl," Jameson muttered as he turned his attention back to piloting the Falcon to Del Rio.

The news that there were at least two and likely more Dead Girls was electrifying both in the US and Mexico. The excitement lasted for a week. Then it just became business as usual. OF COURSE there were hundreds of Dead Girls. What idiots had ever thought otherwise?!

The second Dead Girl spent two days going between the rebel forces and the civil authorities before almost negotiating a surrender. Then her efforts were taken over by the head of the Army force who, naturally, took credit for the successful resolution of the conflict.

Jameson was annoyed but Alice was not. The sooner her actions in the Mexican-American Border Conflict (a capitalization adopted by the newspapers) were forgotten the better. She wanted to go home!

The week before Christmas she did so.

Chapter 11 - Electricity

Alice spent most of the Christmas holiday with her family in Llano. As she had before she flew her car inside her egg to a spot near Llano then drove the last few miles. Publicly an hour and a half drive privately took ten minutes.

Her mother fretted over her short black hair. Alice comforted her by showing that her hair's roots were coming in its usual bright red. Her two brothers, home for part of the holidays, instead thought it cool that their sister had adopted a Dead Girl look and scared the shit out of Mexicans. Her father just said, "Good job, Al. Hope you never have to do something like that again."

Alice spent a few hours during her holiday with each of several friends in Llano. In addition to keeping in touch with childhood friends this let her double check that their perfect health did remain perfect. These included Albert and his wife and Therese. The black nurse was still going strong at the Llano hospital, newly added to, refurbished, and its customer base expanded.

She spent more of her time with her grandmother. With the only person who knew of her immortality she could reveal her deepest concerns.

"In four centuries of life I've seen atrocities. To be honest, three or four times I've committed or caused atrocities. I thought I was inured. Apparently we immortals, or I, start over each new life newly sensitized. It broke my heart to hear of and witness what was done to so many innocent folk during this fucking 'Border Conflict.'"

She wept and was held and comforted by her grandmother.

By Valentine's Day Alice's again-red short hair was a few inches in length, enough that Irma Delgado firmly declared that she MUST get her hair-do redone by the fashionable and capable hair dresser she and all her girls went to. A protesting Alice eventually gave in.

Afterwards, looking at her image in a mirror from several angles, she admitted that she was glad she'd gone along with Irma--though only privately. Publicly she was still grumpy about her surrender.

Her use of the Falcon had convinced the Army to buy two to evaluate by their own people, one as a reconnaissance platform and one as a close-air-support weapon. Alice refused to be involved in either effort, assigning a bright energetic Texas Aviation engineer to advise the Army researchers.

She was more interested in reviving work on the Eagle codenamed the Hawk III. It would be roughly twice the size of the Hawk Is and IIs, have half again their ceiling and speed, and have easier to use pilot and navigation systems. It would also have two engines on a unitary wing since a single wing was stronger than two separate wings.

The electrical technology behind the pilot and nav systems was very much influenced by calculator tech. They would essentially be special-purpose calculators which used the new flat-screen multipurpose-display technology developed by an Irish/UK company.

Texas Aviation hired three calculator engineers to support the companies foray into aviation electronics. Each had a degree in calc tech, a relatively new engineering discipline separate from the huge field of electrical generation and distribution engineering.

At Easter holiday in Llano she and Albert spent more than one evening chatting about new advances in electrical and calculator technologies.

He said one evening, "I honestly don't know which advance will be the most influential."

"I certainly can't. I think it's partly that some of them dovetail and influence others. Like digital phone lines. This lets digital databases be easily accessed from the next county. Or even the next state. Or country. Did you know that Canada has a completely digital phone system?"

He nodded, took a deep drink of his ale. Alice imitated him with her iced Pepper Upper. He spoke.

"Or the new high-resolution full-color flat screen tech coming out of fucking Ireland/UK. It lets us see color photos stored in digital databases."

His wife looked up from her curled-up position on the same couch. She was reading a book on baby care.

"Don't say 'fuck.' The baby might hear." She patted her belly.

"I'm fucking sorry, baby. I'll never say 'fuck' again. Or 'fucking.' Or..." He kissed her forehead.

Alice reminded herself yet again to be on hand when Julia had her baby to double check that she would have an easy and safe birth.

<>

July 4th holiday in Austin was a big deal. It was patriotic and even hard states-rights Texans were patriotic, often loudly so.

Alice like many other prominent people was drafted to participate in the celebrations. She wasn't all that rich, though she was widely acknowledged to be moving on up, but she had actually fought against the Mexicans.

Her contributions were three aerobatic flyovers of the downtown area, her wing tips trailing one line of red smoke and a second line of blue smoke. This was especially spectacular when she flew in a corkscrew path, the two lines twining about each other.

She capped her two days of aerobatics with her well-known Death Dive maneuver at the end of her third day. She climbed to a mile height, corkscrewing as she did so. Higher. Higher. Slower. Slower.

Then she failed to gain height. Her plane fell, tail first. It fell over on its back. It spun in two directions at once, tumbling like a leaf. Its nose dropped more toward the ground. Her engine roared, its propeller fighting to bite into the air, to regain control. Closer the helpless plane fell toward the Colorado River.

Watchers assured others that this all part of the show. They'd seen it before. The pilot was perfectly safe. But many of them seemed uncertain of the truth of what they said.

The corkscrewing action slowed. The plane assumed a flat dive toward the water. It seemed to be in control again. But it was fast approaching the surface. Would it turn its dive into a safe flat path?

It seemed not to. Till it was a mere hundred feet up. It tilted toward level--too slowly? It was still coming closer to the water even as it twisted toward survival.

At the last minute it snapped fully level and its engine roared and screamed toward redline power. And raced over the surface of the water, low enough to leave a frothing wake behind it as it disappeared toward the east.

<>

The week after Thanksgiving one of the three calculator engineering hires came to Alice with a plan to replace all the company's calculators. Alice had assigned this task to him and given him all the time he wanted to development the plan. He'd done a complete job of specifying the items, schedules, and costs of the job.

Alice and the other partners approved the plan. Thus for the next several weeks all the parts of the network were replaced in a schedule which would have the least impact on daily work. By February it was done.

The increased nimbleness of the company was felt as "paperwork" done on one calculator could be immediately available on any other. Alerts of a possible customer could be more quickly followed up on by the Display and Sales Department. Purchases and bills could more quickly be acted upon.

Another calculator engineer completed his work on the "glass cockpit" alternative to the old purely mechanical cockpit. Though this split between the two types was more a convention than fact. His design integrated the two in a way that let pilots use the purely mechanical part if the electronic part died.

Displays of and talks about the glass cockpit done by Alice at air shows were well attended, though this was the result of as much her beauty as anything else. Her year-ago participation in the Mexican-American Border Conflict also helped. A few orders by a couple of aircraft manufacturers came in, one from one of the three other Texas aircraft makers.

<>

A second July 4th came around. Alice participated but the aerobatics were mild. This was because they were a group effort put on by her, Delacroix, and a young but very capable Army pilot who'd participated in testing the two Falcons for the Army.

That weekend was a long one that let the Texas Aviation people have Sunday off. The huge technology building had almost no one in it, just Alice and a forty-something Latina.

Alice respected the woman. She'd been a cleaning lady but studied to do better. For the last year she'd been a general technology assistant, doing "paperwork" on calculators and lending an extra hand in laboratories. In her off time she still was studying.

Selena came knocking on Alice's door jamb just after noon. The shapechanger was finishing up her brown-bag lunch as she gestured the older woman into her office.

The Latina said, "Director--"

"Alice. Sit."

"Yes, Ma'am. I have been studying electrical theory. The book shows me circuit diagrams and I'm invited to build and test them. Mr. Oglesby said I could use our equipment as long as I was careful and did not damage anything and to return them to their storage bins or closets."

"I remember. He told me about it and I approved, naturally."

Texas Aviation was like a lot of technology and engineering

companies in that employees were invited to study for more advanced jobs and certifications. Texas Aviation would pay half of any tuition as long as the courses were in specialties which would help Texas Aviation in some way. Alice, who'd volunteered to oversee the employee education program, interpreted very loosely what course subjects were beneficial.

"I noticed something peculiar in one of my latest circuit board setups. Could you come over and look? I know it's your lunch hour, so if you don't want--"

"I do want. Anything to get out of doing what I've been doing all day: paperwork. I'm drowning in paperwork. Never become a boss if you hate paperwork, Selena."

Alice was rising as she said the last, crumpling up her empty brown bag and dropping it into her waste basket.

A room near the electrical and hardware supply room had wire-mesh walls. It was small and had a couple of tables on opposite sides of the room, to the left and right side of the room's door.

On one of the tables were a number of circuit pegboards. Circuit components could be attached by pegs on the board and wires run to other components. In this way experiments could be quickly set up, run, and broken back down into their parts.

Three of the experiments were fairly small. One was long and took up all the space on the longest edge of the table.

An open book sat on a chair near the table. Alice picked it up, slid a bookmark into its spine to keep the Latina's place, and opened it to the first page of the Introduction.

"This book on Basic Electricity by famed Electroscientist B. P. Steinberg is Everyone's guide to the Fascinating and Powerful field of ELECTRICITY. It comes with a Basic Experimentation kit. Several Advanced Experimentation kits are also available."

She looked around to see a long flat box leaning against a wall nearby. Printed on its side was an illustration that showed a pegboard with its surface peopled by an assortment of electrical parts.

She examined the experiments set up on the table. The three small ones were likely copied directly from the book. They all had a battery at one end and an instrument at the opposite end, a cheap version of a voltameter. In the middle were cheap versions of resisters, capacitors, diodes, wire coils, tiny light bulbs, and so on connected by lengths of wires. All must have come in the box.

There was only one professional voltameter. It had been connected to the big fourth experiment.

This one was constructed on a base of three pegboards placed end-to-end. It held a seemingly random collection of components heavy on electrical coils both with air cores and metal cores.

"When I left midweek to get ready to take my family to the celebrations the next day I was tired, so I just put this last one together pretty much at random. Then this morning I shifted stuff around to make more sense but I stopped when I noticed this."

She stepped close to one end and put her hand near the last of several inline air-core coil electromagnets. With the other she closed a knife switch. The needle on the voltameter swung abruptly to a value. But that was not the focus of the woman's attention.

"Come here and put your hand where mine is."

Alice replaced the Latina's position and held her hand near where her hand had been.

There was steady flow of air coming out of the coil and flowing over her hand.

She felt her egg instantly form around her to protect her. It was pulled close in to just outside of her skin.

Slowly the cyborg Alice+Egg relaxed and began to expand outside HER skin to other machines to pull into the gestalt ALICE creature.

There were many. SHE rejected most of them. Narrowed HER attention to the hodge-podge active experiment on the table. Flowed into it. Let it become part of HER.

The biological being standing nearby said, "Ma'am? Ma'am? Are you all right?"

ALICE said, "Yes, thank you. Let me think, dear Selena."

The female being said, "Yes'm." She was frowning. ALICE cyborg knew SHE was not good at showing natural-appearing emotion. SHE really must practice that skill. But for now...

HER attention delicately washed over different parts of HER experimental setup. SHE saw/felt/scented the electrical energy flowing from the battery through the rest of HERself. It went through THIS and THAT part, bypassed THESE and THOSE, twisted and coiled and roiled into another space/time/universe and out again, and caught air in this space/time/universe and pushed it beyond the last air-core magnetic coil.

The goddess ALICE memorized that path and dropped out of HER gestalt fully into her biological part.

She turned to the Latina.

"Congratulations, Mrs. Gomez! You have just made a great discovery!"

"I have?" The Latina was confused and a bit distressed.

"Yes you have! Now let's get a better idea of what. Do you have more of these pegboards?"

"Yes. There are a dozen. They are very thin."

"Good. Let's clear off that table and move it closer to this one. We're going to duplicate your setup and work with it, not disturb your original one."

Together they set up the second table close to the first leaving a path between them. This let the two women look back and forth between the experiment on the first table to duplicate it on the second table.

At last the job was done. Alice stood next to the output end of the second experiment and put her hand near it. She nodded at Selena.

The woman closed the on-off knife switch.

"Yay!" said Alice. "It works!"

"It does? Let me see."

Alice moved to let the Latina put her hand up near the output coil. Her expression brightened.

"It does!"

Alice rubbed her hands together. "Now let's see just what parts are needed and what not. Turn the setup off, take out a part, and connect the broken parts back together."

For over an hour they slowly deconstructed the air-blowing machine. Most times removing a part did not affect the machine. Occasionally it did. That part was obviously necessary.

They quickly grew impatient with using a hand placed near the machine's output to check whether it functioned or not. They constructed a framework of wood near it and draped a long swath of toilet paper over it. This provided a quick visual display of air flowing from the machine.

Alice was guided by her knowledge of what path was crucial to success. She used this to speed up the search for that path.

Finally the search was ended. The machine on the second table was much smaller, using thirteen magnetic coils, two resisters, and one diode. And one battery.

"Now," said Alice. "Let's see if we can duplicate THIS one."

A third setup on a rickety folding card table proved that they could.

"OK, Selena. Now we do paperwork. Now you get to experience the ABSOLUTE JOY of being a boss!"

They retired to Alice's office. She had Selena sit beside and a little behind her to see what the shapechanger was doing.

"You probably know that Texas Aviation has a procedure for requesting a patent. Both on its behalf and of any employee who wants to use it. You don't have to take our help. You can use your own."

"What would I know about all this? I'll use your help."

"It costs. We insist on owning part of your patent. Either 10% or 20%."

"That little? Ahh, yes. Let's do it."

"OK. Here is the form, the first page anyway."

Alice turned on the big calculator on her desk and brought up an electronic form. On it she entered information such as the inventor's name, address, and title.

Selena Gomez turned out to be an incomplete name. The full one was Selena Sofia Graciela Gomez-Ryan.

"My mother was Irish three generations back. That's why my hair is red, like yours."

On a second page Alice said, "Now this is important. I'll explain it to you and you must decide what the answer is.

"You did all this work on your own time. After hours, right?"

The Mexican-American nodded.

"You used your own materials, not any of ours."

"We used your table. And your room."

"And our power to the room's lights. So that gives us 10%. But as all parts and time was yours, we don't get 20%."

There was more of the same, such as the identification of the parts, enough to fill out the second page.

One the third page Alice said, "Now here is the tricky part. We--you--need to be specific enough so the machine can be clearly understood. But general enough so that someone can't change an insignificant part and declare it as a different invention.

"Luckily the lawyer who helped us build this form gave us several examples we can duplicate and tailor to our need."

That took up much of an hour. From then the rest of the process was lengthy but easy.

"That's it. Now let's print this out."

Alice changed the thin draft-paper stock in her office's printer to heavier official-business stock paper. Then she printed out four copies.

"This is your copy. Take it home and store it with all your legal documents such as your birth certificate.

"THIS is your office copy, in case you need to refer to it while at work.

"THIS is my copy, as backup for your copies.

"And THIS is the copy that goes out to the Patent and Trademarks Office. I want you to put it personally in the mail box outside the office complex. Let's go do that now so it will go out first thing in the morning."

Alice handed Selena a big manila yellow paper envelope and a roll of stamps suitable for mailing the manila envelope. The woman printed the address of the P&M Office on the front of the envelope and her home address, sealed the envelope, and put the proper postage on it.

Then they went back to the experiment room. There Selena got her purse, Alice put a sign on the room of the door declaring WORK IN PROGRESS DO NOT DISTURB, and had Selena lock the door using her Technology Building key. Then she escorted the woman outside the building to witness her put the patent-request envelope in the US Post Office mail box.

She put out a hand to shake. Selena took and they shook.

"Congratulations, Mrs. Gomez. You now have a place in the Twentieth Century history books."

"Me?"

"Yes, you. Your invention will be used to make all sorts of products. It will take time. Such things always do."

"I couldn't have done it without you."

"Nonsense. You are smart and stubborn woman. You would have gotten around to this moment. I just sped it up."

Impulsively Selena hugged her and hurried off.

Alice was in no hurry to return to work. She looked around the empty parking lot. She was alone.

She looked to the west. The setting sun was just above the horizon. The western sky was washed in glowing amber.

She lifted her head to the darkening sky overhead. Moments later Austin was rocked by thunder from high above.

<>

Much happened in the next year, and the next.

<>

Women were given the right to vote in the United States of America. Alice and her friends took advantage of it. She did it in Austin in the company of Irma Delgado and her youngest daughter Victoria and eldest son Arthur.

At the entrance to the polling place a man coming out spat in Victoria's face. She slapped him so hard he stumbled and fell. She stood over him ready to fight if he stood up. He crawled away before standing and leaving.

Alice stood back but ready to wreak havoc on him and any friends who counter-attacked but neither he nor anyone else did anything except slink off. One young man chanted, "Go Blondie! Blondie for Governor! Go Blondie...!" Several other men took up the chant as the Delgado party entered the polling place.

Alice hurried ahead of her friends, voted before them, then went outside to see if the spitting man came back with friends or a gun or both. He did not. Luckily for him.

Political writers in newspapers predicted that the newly enlarged voters would infuse American politics with progressive ideas. There was such a movement, but more often women voted much as men did.

In Europe several nationalistic movements urged their countries toward war. However the several most influential men in the movements died from heart attacks or auto crashes or other natural causes. Except for one man walking across a street toward a brothel. His head was sliced completely off as if from a blade infinitely sharp.

The countries teetered backward toward peace.

In the winter a deadly strain of flu appeared which came to be called the New York flu. Alice learned of it while reading a Los Angeles newspaper. LA was one of a dozen cities that she visited via newspaper at random intervals for at least several minutes each week. She did this at breakfast at home to help start her day. It gave her a feel of what was happening in the whole country in politics, the economy, business, entertainment, and other interesting areas.

The headline which caught her eye was DEADLY NEW YORK FLU ARRIVES IN LA?

Both Temilade and Li Wei had lived through an epidemic at least once. Her fabulous shapechanger body protected her from all illnesses. She also gave that immunity to those she cared about. But she could not protect everyone. So she and they were vastly inconvenienced by all the disruption around them, not least the heartbreak of seeing good people die or go broke or both.

At least she could not protect many the first time. During the second time she'd figured out how to create a counter-illness. It infected everyone and ate whatever particular invisible monster made people ill.

Maybe it was time to do that yet again.

She checked the time. Could she get her long-time executive assistant on the phone? He would be just about to go to work.

"Hello?"

"Hi, Muriel. Has Joey left for work?"

"Joey! Joey! It's your boss!"

"Be right there!"

"He's coming, Alice. Is everything OK?"

"Yes. I've just got to go out of town suddenly."

"Good... Here he is."

"What's up?"

She told him she'd be out of town for a few days and that he was to handle routine matters. He should also substitute for her at meetings when he felt he was able. If he didn't feel he could he should ask one of the other partners to do so.

She finished her meal, planning her next few moves, and spoke up loud enough to be heard in the kitchen adjoining the dining room.

"Mrs. Tillotson?"

The housekeeper and cook came to stand in the doorway separating the two rooms.

"You heard I've got to go away for a week? Good. It might be two. Carry on as usual, please."

"You want me to fix you something?"

"No, I'm good. Thanks."

Upstairs she packed a few items in a small suitcase including a couple of changes of clothing and toiletries. That done she changed to informal everyday clothes suitable for New York City. This included a heavy jacket as it was late spring and chilly in the northeast right now.

Shortly she called her egg about her and arced into the sky.

<>

Fifteen minutes later she was over the eastern seaboard above New York State. It and part of the Atlantic was under a heavy cloud cover. The clouds were brilliant white from above but turned rapidly grey as Alice slanted down out of the sky and through the clouds. A steady drizzle coated the egg but only the top. That left the bottom clear. Through it she could see the city.

She located Columbia University in northwest Manhattan, near the long north-south Central Park. Dropping lower still she located the main library and landed atop it in front of a door into a small room that covered a stairway.

She shrank her egg to within an inch or so outside her body, clothing, and suitcase and opened the door. As expected it was not locked from the outside. Inside she banished her egg, stowed the suitcase against a wall. In the dim light of what was in a sense the attic of the building it was unlikely to be noticed if anyone came up this high in the building, a highly unlikely event. No one would go out onto the roof on a rainy day.

The time was a little past 7:00 am. Even so the large newspaper and magazine section on the first floor had a couple dozen customers seated at the reading tables. A few of them were females even though Columbia was an all-male school. The women were probably from Barnard College, an all-female institution across a street on the west side of Columbia.

Alice with her youthful experience could well be one of those women. No one did more than glance at her as she began to look through the New York newspapers for stories on the "New York flu."

None of the larger newspapers had anything that she could easily find. Two of the smaller ones did. The story in the Worker's World was DAY 13 OF THE COVERUP. Christian Weekly's story was AMERICAN MISSIONARIES FIGHT THE NIGERIAN FLU about the flu's devastating progress in that country.

After an hour Alice decided that the city's authorities were downplaying the disease. They must certainly fear the impact on tourism which would usually pick up in the spring. Perhaps they thought any flu would fail as the weather warmed up.

Where would she most likely come in contact with the disease? Hospitals, of course. She racked the newspapers she'd been perusing and found a city directory and made note of the nearest three.

The closest was only a few blocks away. Alice rose quickly up the stairway which had brought her down to the first floor, retrieved her suitcase, and arced up and quickly down to the top of the hospital. Again she found a place to hide her suitcase. She left her coat with it and set off to find a disguise.

The first stage was easy. She aged her face to appear fifty and her hair to grey. She willed her long curly hair to assume a bun at the back of her head and adopted a habit of moving slowly. Walking with an uncertain step she found a closet containing hospital gowns and stole and donned one.

It wasn't long before she found a sanitary recycling bin for gowns, stole one from it, folded it into a tight ball, and retired to a bathroom. Sitting in a stall she closed her eyes and ran her hands slowly over much of its surface.

The immortal had long ago come to esoterically know the causes of diseases, especially bacteria and the much-smaller viruses. She sorted through nine of the first and seven of the second. The number did not surprise her. Hospitals were after all where sick people went or were sent.

She discovered two different strains of flu. One was more prevalent than the other. She focused on it, coming to know its biochemical structure well. It was very virulent, one of the worst she'd come across since this esoteric ability came to her while she was a black woman in Africa.

Slowly, over the period of an hour, she built up a twin of the deadlier strain of flu but with a twist: it was totally innocuous. It would propagate as the original did, by coughs, sneezes, touch, and so on. When it encountered its original the twin flu would eat it, then split into two innocuous copies.

That done she let grow in the back of her throat an organ which would manufacture and release her counter-virus to be exhaled through her nose and mouth.

Three hours after entering Mount Sinai she exited it. Now she needed to get herself a hotel room and set about spreading her manufactured disease.

She spent a week in New York. Then she proceeded along the American coast, spending a few days in each of the largest coastal cities. These were the entry points into the US of the "New York" flu which had had a European origin.

That done, she sent a telegram to her partners in Austin. It said, "Sorry to bail out on you. I've overworked myself almost into illness. I badly need a vacation. Am taking it now. I'll see you in a month."

She had not lied too much. She HAD needed a vacation, she now realized. Next stop, France. Then the rest of Europe. Then, maybe, the Middle East? Africa? India? China?

Why not Australia and South America?

<>

In the year after Selena's patent application was mailed Selena got back a multi-page document reporting approval of her "Induced Magnetism Method and Several Possible Devices Using the Method." She immediately brought it to Alice.

She greeted Selena's news with enthusiasm. They went to lunch early, the Latina's treat, at a nearby steak house which was a favorite of the workers in the industrial complex and surrounding suburbs.

After ordering food and while sipping iced tea Selena spoke.

"Now I've got this, what?"

"Now you get an intellectual properties lawyer, one that specializes in mechanical and electrical inventions. He will help you make sure any company which wants to use your patent to make and sell products and services pays you what they agree to. He can also sue anyone who tries to use your patent without your permission. He can also help you negotiate deals.

"A good one costs a lot, but they're worth every cent."

"I don't have a lot of money saved." The woman looked distressed but tightened her jaw.

"I'll loan all you need to get you started. With no interest and the only time limit when you first start getting your income."

Selena looked at Alice very carefully.

"That seems too good to be true."

"It does sound like it. You're wise to be suspicious. But consider what you know about me. You've been with us, what, going on four years, five? You've heard all the gossip about me. You know me pretty well even though we're not friends. I suspect you know you can trust me.

"Logic is also on my side, and yours. You know that I believe this invention is going to be very profitable, and you know why. It's going to revolutionize aviation and lots of other industries as well. Through Texas Aviation I own a third of ten percent of the profits from your invention. That might sound small, but compared to what's coming it's huge.

"Anyway, you know enough about me to know I don't care a lot about money. I care about designing and building airplanes. And this is going to make those lots of fun."

"You make such good arguments. I want to believe you, but..."

"There's no hurry. Think about matters. Talk to people. Find an attorney who'll work an hour or two for free on the possibility that you'll hire them. You're a smart, cautious woman. You will make the right decisions."

"OK. Let's just suppose that I take your loan offer. How do we find a patent lawyer?

"The company has worked with several. Right now we use Barton and Barton, a father and niece firm who are very experienced and good. You might also like the Scanlon firm. It's just one person but he's been around a long time."

"So suppose we go visit one of them. What do we say?"

"This calls for more iced tea."

Alice looked around and waved to the waiter. They settled in to talk. It had gotten easier to hear each other as most of the lunch-time crowd had thinned out by now.

<>

Three days later Selena had taken Alice's suggestion to think and consult friends and colleagues. She took Alice's loan offer, asking and getting an informal written agreement from Alice. Then she sat down at her drawing board at home and drafted two sets of drawings of suggested inventions. Alice reviewed both and pronounced them good.

She asked Alice to come with her to Barton and Barton to back her up.

They arrived at the firm in downtown Austin at 10:00 in the morning. It was in an old bank building on Shoreline Drive on the northern edge of the Colorado River. They were ushered into a small conference room with an oval table which would seat eight people. On one of the two longer sides of the room was a large picture window overlooking the river.

Two people on that side of the room stood up from chairs nearest the entrance to the room. They came forward to shake hands and gesture to the side of the table opposite the window. Alice took a seat there but Selena took the seat at the end of the table.

Alice smiled to herself. She sat to the woman's right. This put her facing the picture window. This put her face in light and the lawyer's faces in dimness. This would have slightly bothered an ordinary person and put them at a disadvantage, but bothered her not at all. Selena had cannily chosen the best seat, with Alice to her right and the attorneys to her left.

Joseph Barton said to Alice, "So glad to meet with you, Miss Willoughby. What do you bring us?"

He was a small slightly portly man with receding blond hair. His niece was tall and slender and had plenty of straight blond hair. She was more stern-looking than pretty but had made herself attractive.

"Talk to my friend and colleague Mrs. Selena Gomez-Ryan. She's the inventor. I'm here because Texas Aviation has an interest in the technological method for which Mrs. Gomez has the patent. We consider what she has come up with the technological breakthrough of the century."

The attorney's attention slid easily to the Latina as did that of the niece. Their concentration could have disconcerted someone unsure of themselves. Selena instead opened a brown folder and glanced down at its contents. Then she looked up again.

"Two years ago I was in my lab at Texas Aviation working on some experiments. I noticed an interesting phenomenon and went to Alice's office to get her to observe it."

Alice said, "I was intrigued and went with her to her lab."

Selena said, "The experiment was to demonstrate an idea I had. It didn't. But what it did was to act as if there was a small invisible fan inside a coil of wire. You could feel the jet of air coming out of the coil if you put your hand near one end of the coil."

Alice said, "You could also feel the air flowing into the coil if you put your hand near that end."

The older attorney said, "So you created a new kind of fan."

"What she created was also a new kind of aircraft engine, one that does not use propellers to create a jet of air that pushes an aircraft through the air. It uses electromagnets to create that jet.

"This has several advantages. Spinning propellers make noise even if the engine has a muffler like those on automobiles. The propellors are highly stressed and can shatter. There are also limits to how fast and strong the jet of air can be, and thus limits on how fast an aircraft can be."

Selena said, "The heart of this kind of engine is a device that can induce magnetism in non-magnetic material like air. This is the technology that I patented.

"It has many more applications. It can turn rocks, dirt, and pavement magnetic. This would let us build automobiles which don't ride on wheels, but ride on magnetic fields. So floating trucks don't need roads, at least not paved ones."

The two attorneys had been alert before. They went hyper-alert now. They leaned forward. Their eyes seemed to try to look inside the head of Selena Gomez.

The niece, Olivia Barton, looked at Alicia.

"Is this true? It sounds too good to be true."

"Yes. I've been in Mrs. Gomez's lab. I've seen her experimental setup work. I duplicated it myself to be sure this was not some kind of fluke. Then I built a more compact version to be sure I understood how to do it.

"It's real. And we want to build these engines. The floating car, I leave that to someone else. Airplanes are a big enough market for us at Texas Aviation."

Selena said, "These two applications only scratch the surface of how induced-magnetism technology can be used. It could be the foundation of conveyers and pipes, for instance. Because it can pull and push on gravel, coal, water, kerosene, finished products. Any thing at all."

"People?" said Ralph Barton.

"Well... I suppose. But I'll leave anything like that to medical doctors and scientists."

Alice said, "I cautiously put my hand near the induced magnetism effect. I felt nothing except an almost ghostly pull. But I quickly jerked my hand back. I curse myself for how stupid I'd been. Still, my GUESS--"

She paused. "My GUESS is that this effect is fairly harmless to living organisms. But, as Selena says, that will be up to medical scientists to decide."

It was more than a guess. Her ability to sense her own biology and those of others down to below the cellular level told her just how living tissue was affected. There was nothing like the nuclear radiation which had almost killed the Curies.

But flesh could be manipulated by machines using induced

magnetism. This could be used to harm or help in a variety of ways.

The elder Barton said, "We should caution buyers of rights to this technology that they should take precautions in its use. We do this with other dangerous technology. We have shields to keep people away from boilers, spinning machinery, and so on, for instance."

Olivia said, "That puts the burden of remaining safe on the people who use your technology, not you."

The conference continued up to lunch time. The Bartons invited Selena and Alice to lunch. During it the attorneys, seemingly casually, interrogated the Latina about herself and her situation. Selena, wise in the ways of the world and of its people, would have known what they were doing even if Alice had not warned her to expect it. She used the lunch to return the favor.

Alice sat back, amused, to watch.

Lunch over, the four retired to the attorneys' offices to draw up contracts. Selena Gomez was on her way to becoming a millionaire.

<>

Alice continued to advise Selena, sometimes accepting dinner invitations the woman extended. She came to know the divorced woman's three sons and two daughters. All were smart and ambitious.

The youngest daughter, still in high school, warned her mother during one of those dinners.

"You know that dad is going to come sniffing around when he hears you might come into money. Don't fall for his 'I am reformed' bullshit."

Selena's next to oldest son, reaching for a platter of potatoes, spoke to Alice.

"Dad is a sleaze. We love him, but we know him. Margarita is right."

Margarita wasn't finished. "And Aunt Isabella. That snooty bitch who has always put you down. Don't you believe her when she comes simpering around and saying 'How lucky you have been while I have had such bad luck lately.' Don't give her a cent!"

Selena smiled, looked at Alice. "See what wise children I have, Alicia."

"I do indeed. Takes after their mother, surely."

<>

It was more than a year before one of the companies to whom Selena had sold rights turned out a product. It was a fan. Portable, cheap, using so little electricity that its rechargeable battery had to be topped off only once a month, it quickly became a popular item.

Next came a floating forklift, one modified from a popular standard model used by a lot of warehouses.

A British motorcycle company put floater "feet" on its tricycle model instead of wheels and paired its engine with a generator to provide power for the feet. The two rear feet were angled backward as well as down to push as well as lift the "TriFoot" floater.

A motorcycle competition company banned it from its races. This galvanized some fans to form a TriFoot Association and sponsor a Rough Rider cross-country race.

<>

Alice and her engineers were doing a lot of puzzling too. They designed the Hawk III / Eagle and tested it, finding lots of problems small and large, which was the purpose of testing. No matter how well-designed, every design was imperfect.

The success of the testing, though only Alice knew it, owed much to the fact that Alice could merge with a machine to form a cyborg who could examine HERself minutely.

The first production Eagle came out of the assembly barn the week before Texas Independence Day in March. This was a deadline many had worked overtime to meet. Alice and Delacroix took it up for its final test flight of several and finally jointly pronounced all its rough edges smoothed over.

They announced its availability for sale and (Austin city giving them permission) conducted a once-and-back flyover of downtown Austin. It trailed red and blue smoke from each wingtip and was accompanied on each side by Falcons.

March 2nd was a Monday that year. Independence Day being a state holiday all sorts of activities were planned especially those with a patriotic theme. A number of businesses held open houses. This including several in the Del Rio Industrial Park, including Texas Aviation.

There the interior of the two incomplete Eagles were open for people to view, their cockpits blocked off by transparent plastique. The production model flew several times filled with VIPs. The last couple of flights the VIPs weren't too terribly important.

<>

The Eagle project done, Alice and three of her top engineers turned to work on the design and testing of induced-magnetism jet engines. Progress was slow; it always was on new technology. It was over a year before they produced a workable reliable model, a seemingly miraculously short period. Again the brevity was because of cyborg ALICE.

Power was supplied by a gasoline engine paired with an electrical generator. Even though fuel was still burned to fly a plane, only a little over half the amount was needed. Fuel was expensive so this alone made jet engines desirable.

Jet engines also were quieter because the gasoline engines were smaller and there were no whirring propellers. They were simpler too, having no moving parts except those in the gasoline engines. Aircraft designers wistfully looked forward to a far future when superbatteries eliminated gasoline engines entirely.

<>

Jet engine research and testing done, Alice thought next about what aircraft to put it into.

The easiest would be the Eagle as it had two engines mounted on its wing. They could be swapped with other engines. But Alice decided not to. Too much would have to be reengineered; too much manufacturing facilities would have to be changed.

She concluded that in the long run it would be more efficient to create a new aircraft specifically designed around jet engines.

What to call the new airplane? Alice was tired of using names of predatory birds. She thought a bit, consulted a book on bird watching, and decided on a name that was not only a bird but descriptive. The new aircraft could easily pass 300 miles per hour, maybe come close to 400. She chose Swift.

If the aircraft were to be a practical airliner it needed to carry enough passengers to be economical. She decided on ten, divided into two rows of five people each. Each seat should be large enough for the largest likely passenger. Its aisle should let such a person walk without bumping the seats and walk fully upright.

It should have an in-flight lavatory and a small kitchenette for handling prepackaged food.

She wanted a cockpit sized for plus-sized people and a cargo space large enough for ten passengers, two pilots, and a steward.

Thus she came up with a size halfway between a Hawk and an Eagle: eight feet wide, 60 feet long, and a wing span about that wide.

She decided on a low wing for several reasons. Also mildly swept-back wings to help streamline the aircraft. The tail would be the tried and true single upright fin and flat horizontal stabilizers, also mildly swept back.

Engines. Where should they go? Under the wing would work but that would require the wing be extra strong. Alice decided on the waist. Attached not melded into the body. This would make it easier to swap out the engines than a melded-body approach.

While designing the housing for the jet engines Alice played with several improvements to the engine. The very first engine had two air magnetism inducers, the first to pull air into the engine and the second to push air out. One of her engineers had the idea to have four in a pull-push-pull-push configuration. When that worked out they then extended the engine again by adding another paired pull-push inducers. Then another. That last addition proved to be too much and they cut back to three pairs.

Alice now saw an opportunity for another innovation. Each of the three pairs could be pivoted downward. Thus instead of sending the jet backward it could be sent downward, thus letting the aircraft take off and land straight up and down.

Adding complexity always means adding problems. Alice with a little help from her friends solved them.

One problem was not so easy to solve. Blasts of air hitting the ground sent up dust and debris flying everywhere, or on rainy days water.

One solution to this was just not to take off from or land vertically onto anything but clean surfaces.

Another was to add floater landing gear to the bottom of the craft. More complexity, more problems. Engineers LIKED problems. They meant more work, more fun.

Managers did not. But Alice was the manager in charge.

Finally the design was completed. On that weekend Alice came to work, brought up the design on her powerful calculator, closed her eyes, and merged with the machine. Inside its virtual space SHE SENSED the Swift. SHE merged with it.

As SHE explored HERself the calculator's flat-screen display began to bring up window after window, some with text, some with numbers, some with images, some with all. They cascaded onto and off screen at an increasingly furious pace.

An hour was enough to generate several dozen needed improvements. ALICE sent a copy of them to HER printer and descended back fully into HER biological part.

She got a snack and a drink while the several pages slid out of her printer. Then she sat back in her chair and began to read. Satisfied with them, she made up work orders on her calculator and emailed them to their several destinations.

Then she left the office. There was a new band of tango players at one of her favorite dance venues. She needed some fun.

<>

AUSTIN SENTINEL

Always Alert For You!

Hometown Hero Accepts Award

by Jackson Steadman

It was Alice Willoughby's birthday and she was to receive an award in her hometown of Llano some ways to the west of Austin. She was to be pronounced a Hometown Hero.

To get home from Austin she was going in style, in the Texas Aviation's latest aircraft, the Swift. This reporter was one of several invited to join her.

"Hurry up and wait" is not exclusive to the military. PR departments practice it too but more stylishly. I was on my second glass of Champagne when the word went out: She's coming!

We Members of the Press abandoned our air-conditioned comfort for the concrete out back of Texas Aviation's front office building. I, of course, did not abandon my Champagne glass. Indeed, I topped it off.

Alice (PhD Emeritus Willoughby courtesy of Austin University, where she never went, mind you) had taken the Swift up for a "check" flight earlier. Whose purpose, of course, your sophisticated and jaded Servant knew, was just to let her make An Entrance.

It was successful, enough at least to unjade your Servant. The Swift was nowhere to be seen as we peered up past the mid-morning sun. Then it was, seeming to jump into place a half mile above and beyond us from some eldritch place.

The first sight of that creature of the sky makes the hairs on my arms crawl. Its wings sweep back very like the wings of those creatures of the air for which it is named, as does its tail. Its sleek body is broken at its waist by two long "cans" which house the jet engines which drive the Swift through the skies at unheard-of speeds.

The aircraft spirals down and then settles gently toward Earth a hundred feet from us, eschewing the lengthy setdown and takeoff of older aircraft. Dust begins to swirl underneath it then settles as it travels the last few feet downward. The Swift is outfitted with a "floater" undercarriage which takes over support from its jet engines near the ground.

Then the Swift settles onto its tricycle landing gear as the floater undercarriage powers down in turn. The Swift rolls sedately to the edge of the red carpet being unrolled toward it. When it stops the two Texas Aviation ground crew in red coveralls in charge of the carpet twitch it nearer and fade to the sides.

Moments later a door in the side of the Swift opens, folding out and down to present us with a stairway which not quite touches the red carpet. A figure appears in the doorway dressed in full cowgirl gear including white Stetson (and surely cowboy boots though they can't be seen from this angle).

That is Alice Willoughby, Bull Rider, Plane Rider, part owner of Texas Aviation, pilot, Dead Girl, tango dancer, and now Hometown Hero. She is slender but feminine, has a face which Aphrodite might envy, has long curly red hair, and freckles (a fact Your Servant later witnesses close up).

She waves her cowboy hat and yells "Y'all come in now! Let's get this show on the road!"

Then she disappears inside.

(Part 2 continued in the Style and Entertainment section)

<>

An Austin newspaper reporter wasn't the only one to get goose bumps upon seeing the Swift approach and land. Dozens even hundreds of people did so when it appeared in the skies over Llano, arriving quickly from Austin in the east. They were part of the crowd near the Llano courthouse gathered to see her receive the award of Hometown Hero.

The three-story courthouse-with-cupola was surrounded by trees and a parking lot on all sides. The eastern side lot was blocked off. The empty space was just large enough for the aircraft to land in when it slowed and lowered toward the lot.

The hum of its gasoline engine was quiet enough to be unheard until it was a couple of hundred feet up, drifting straight down, its wings spread, its sides white except for a large light-blue circle just forward of the wings. Inside it was a white cowboy hat. Under the circle red script read ***Texas Girl***. This elicited laughter and pointing.

At fifty feet, almost motionless in its descent, the hum was loud and was accompanied by the hiss of air being furiously expelled from the cans on the airplane's waist. Dust began to fly up from the surface of the parking lot. This forced the waiting crowd away from it, holding their hats and skirts and covering their eyes.

Then both hum and hiss cut off. The Swift hung five feet up on its floater field. The quiet was broken by a higher pitched hum as three sets of wheels folded down on stilts to lock in place. The airplane lowered another couple of feet till the wheels touched the concrete. Then the plane settled its full weight onto them and rocked gently as the floater field cut off too.

Moments later the nearly invisible outline of an oval door in the side of the plane darkened as it folded down to reveal that its inner surface was a stairway. It locked in place at a moderate angle. For a moment a figure was visible, a man in a grey-green coverall.

The crowd waited ready to applaud their girl-made-good but was disappointed. Out and down the stairs came a crowd: eight men and two women dressed in the kind of semiformal clothing that marked them as city people. They moved off to one side and turned to look up at the doorway.

Standing in it was a girl in a cowgirl outfit of various shades of blue wearing brown cowboy boots and a white Stetson hat.

"Howdy, y'all!"

A great cheer went up. She waved and began to descend the stair.

Out of the crowd came two big men: her brothers. They reached up and took one of their sister's elbows each and swung her down the last couple of steps.

On the ground she pulled each man by their necks down to give each a kiss on a cheek.

Unnoticed the man in grey-green coveralls seen earlier walked down the stairs onto the concrete, turned, pushed something on the door/stair. It folded up and locked into place. The side of the plane was smooth again.

He stood, arms folded, while his boss disappeared into the crowd. Then, as the area cleared, he went to the belly of the plane just forward of the cans, opened a hatch, took out two big suitcases, closed the hatch, and began to follow his boss into the crowd.

It took some dozen minutes for Alice to make her way to the temporary dais set up at the edge of the parking lot, a place blocking the sidewalk to lead up to the stairs and door into the courthouse. Her brothers blocked most of the people who wanted to shake her hand or touch her, but could not block the many loud greetings showered on her.

Finally she mounted the steps up to the floor of the dais and walked toward a podium. Waiting there, flanked by several others, was the Mayor of Llano. He greeted Alice and shook her hand, then faded to the side to let the other half-dozen people do the same. The two women and four men were the town council.

Eventually the council was seated in a row of chairs at the rear of the dais, their backs to the court house. The mayor remained standing, an arm around Alice's shoulders.

He waited for the shouting and cheering to diminish then raised his free hand to wave at the crowd and call for quiet. It came fairly quickly. The late morning coolness was diminishing rapidly under the hot Texas sun. Everybody was dressed for the weather but even Texans didn't spend much time washed in sunlight if they could help it.

When he could be heard he spoke.

"Y'all know our little girl, Alice, daughter of our fine citizens Davey and Sarah Willoughby. There they are down in the front. Hi, folks."

"Hi, Mom and Dad. Hi, Grammaw."

"I'll make it short and sweet."

He turned to Alice and gave a short speech extolling her qualities and accomplishments then finished up by saying, "...and for these reasons and many more, We, the mayor and town council, of the great city of Llano, Texas, do hereby present you with this award."

With that he brought up a plaque he'd taken from somewhere. He raised it high and showed it to the crowd in front of him, then to each side. Lastly he held it out to Alice with one hand and presented his other hand for shaking.

Mindful of the ceremony Alice shook his hand and held it, turning to smile at the crowd and the photographers who rushed forward from the edge of the crowd to take lots of fast photos.

Then each of the council members had to file by and shake her hand and murmur something.

That done Alice stepped close to the podium and lay the plaque atop it. She waited for the crowd's cheering to die down.

"Thank y'all for that kind welcome. I can't put into words how good that makes me feel for my home town to recognize what I've done.

"I feel good because I deserve it. I've helped build an industry that employs and will employ more people. I've made a fair amount of money and that's nice. I've--"

"Fought Mexicans!" "Yeah!" "Right!"

"I did indeed. I killed Mexicans. Shot them dead. But they were criminals trying to hurt others. Most Mexicans are just people trying to get along like anyone else. Several work for me. More are friends. So if any of y'all just hate on all Mexicans you and me are going to go round and round. And you better believe this Texas girl is gonna make you hurt."

There was a moment of silence. Suddenly the little woman on the stage didn't look so little anymore. And some of the younger audience members had heard the stories about what happened to a group of men who'd "gone round and round" with this girl one night in a deserted industrial complex.

"So yeah I've made a name for myself bull riding, plane riding, helping design clothes that fit women better.

"But when I think 'heroes' I don't think ME. I think of my mom and grandmom and dad and even those annoying brothers of mine. I think of Nurse Therese in the hospital, the ladies in the library, the teachers in the school. I think of the people I see right now right in front of me. People who work hard to make a living and provide for their families. And sometimes go out of their way to help their fellow men and women.

"I'm holding--" She held the plaque high. "--one plaque. But it belongs to all of us."

She put the plaque back down on the podium and began to clap. Her brothers and then the rest of her family and the crowd began to clap. Several people shouted and whistled and stomped their feet. The clapping infected everyone.

When the crowd was quieting down Alice looked and found her aide Joey near the front of the crowd. She nodded to him and he stepped forward to reach up to her with a brown leather folder in one hand. Alice went to the stage edge, bent down, and took the folder back to the podium. She opened it and looked down at its contents.

The noise decreased suddenly. People peered curiously.

Alice looked up.

"One of the nice things about making money is that you can give some of it away. Oh, not all of it. The pesky IRS wants a good chunk of it.

"Here's a check--" She held up one. "--for the library. I spent many happy hours in it and at home reading books from it. I'll hand it over later today at the library."

She put it back in the folder and took out and held up another.

"This check goes to the high school. I was home schooled as some of you know because I had a medical condition, since cleared up I'm happy to say. But the school was kind enough to give me all the tests I needed to graduate high school. That meant a lot to me in later life."

She held up a third check with one hand, then a fourth with the other hand.

"Here is enough to put over the top the fund drive to add a wing to the hospital just down the road that y'all have going on.

"And here is enough to add another wing devoted to women's health and obstetrics. I was born at the hospital 25 years ago to this day, so I have an especial fondness for the OB people of Llano.

"Now, what say we all go for a nice, co-o-ld iced tea?!"

There was hearty agreement, though with a goodly amount of enthusiasm for beer.

Chapter 12 - Visitors

Alice visited a good many people in Llano in the next several days. Near the top of the list were her old friend Albert Moseley and his wife Julia. They were expecting a baby in a few months. The immortal made a few changes to the woman's body to ensure the birth would be easy and safe.

The most frequent topic of discussion was the rapidly growing Information Web. Albert had read a lot about the significance of it.

"There's this scientist Norgard from one of the Scandinavian countries, Sweden or the like. He says it's the next stage of evolution which he calls the infosphere.

"The first was based in the physical sciences: physics and chemistry and geology. He calls that the geosphere. The second stage is based on the biological sciences. He calls that the biosphere. The third is based on the human sciences: psychology, sociology, anthropology, politics, economics. That's the psychosphere or mind sphere or noosphere.

"The fourth and last is the mechosphere or infosphere. It's based on cybernetics and library science. The idea is that books and other information will migrate to the memories of calculators all over the world until all knowledge is online."

"All recorded knowledge. What about fairy tales? Fiction? Can those be counted as knowledge? All those sci-fi stories in your magazines? Most of them untrue?"

That began a lively argument, with Alice arguing more out of amusement than to any real point. Albert replied in the same spirit.

<>

Back in Austin Texas Aviation began to turn the Swift from a prototype into a production vehicle. Every component was examined and redesigned, most in minor yet important ways to make it sturdier, more failure free, more efficient, and (if possible) cheaper. The windows were made into ovals as the square shape made them more prone to blowout at higher altitudes. The engines were made more powerful and more efficient.

The interior, bare bones and utilitarian as befit a prototype, were redesigned. Three versions were created. One was for cargo-carrying only, one for passenger carrying only with a small luggage compartment, and one (at Alice's insistence) for carrying stretchers and medical treatment in flight. They were designated the C, P, and M types: Cargo, Passenger, and Medical Evacuation.

Alice, initially in charge of the overall production redesign, soon turned the project over to another manager. She had a new project that consumed her.

The USA being backward had an important benefit: it could skip Europe's several stages of technical evolution in many fields. It could go directly into the most modern stage in any field without having to undo then redo the current installations.

In communications this meant that most telecommunication systems could go directly to digital means. Happily old telephone wiring did not have to change. However new telephone wiring could be the new higher-speed digital-friendly wiring. Automatic telephone switchboards could replace manual switchboards without firing anyone; most of the operators could be retrained to sell and service the new switchboards being manufactured, sold, and installed.

Those people were sorely needed as there were a lot of the new wiring and switchboards being installed. Telephone service was rapidly expanding into the more remote areas of Texas and the other states. Local service companies were bought and consolidated into larger companies. Several multi-state companies came into existence, including would-be national companies such as American Telephone and Telegraph: AT&T.

A related area that interested Alice was information storage technology. It had gone through several phases of development and again the US and Texas benefited from skipping those early phases. Most medium-to-large sized companies now had at least one large-capacity storage calculator that all other calculators in the company could use to store and retrieve information. Texas Aviation in fact had two, one for the Sales and Advertising building and one for the Research and Manufacturing building. That second master calculator had to be expanded several times as Texas Aviation manufacturing doubled and then redoubled its number of buildings dedicated to turning out more and more planes. By now the manufacturing buildings stretched 400 yards.

Smaller companies had to make do by renting space on someone other company's calculator. This had the drawback that those smaller companies had to use the telephone lines to put information into and get info out of those "server" calculators.

But there was a happy side effect to the existence of these phone-accessible servers. Small "personal" calculators were becoming cheaper and more powerful. And they too could talk to those servers. People could thus do all sorts of things, some practical, some simply entertaining. This included playing games, some with other people who might be far away. Calculator games rapidly turned into a big business.

What happened because of this, Alice later decided, was because of all the telephones and calculators near her day and night.

<>

The Sunday after Thanksgiving she left in the late afternoon from Llano to return to Austin. As usual she drove a mile or two on the road then called her egg around her and arced upward.

She paused when she was so high that the curvature of the Earth was obvious and she could see all of Texas and the further states below. Far eastward the oncoming edge of night was visible. Within it were the golden glows of nighttime cities coming alight. To the southeast she could see the crinkly olive-colored land around Houston and Galveston and beyond the blue of the Gulf of Mexico.

She watched for a time as the world turned toward night. Then she plunged like a meteor toward Earth, aiming for Texas Aviation. She had some paperwork she wanted done before Monday morning.

She alighted in a road between two buildings in a shopping center a couple of miles away and drove away. In her office she turned on her calculator. This was when she noticed a sound.

It was very quiet, noticed only because it came on the instant she flipped the calculator's On button. She strained to hear it. It was a buzz.

No, it was more a complex sound, something like an orchestra playing very very quietly.

As soon as she thought that it dropped in volume to not-quite-silence, then came back as a buzz whose volume rose and fell in a pattern that suggested meaning but not one she could tease out. It was like a crowd of people talking in many foreign languages.

The sound disappeared. Alice sat for several minutes waiting, then gave up and began working on the paperwork which she wanted to have done the next morning.

<>

When she turned on her calculator again the sound she'd heard the night before came back. This time she knew more; her subconscious had been its usual busy self while she slept. It had delivered an answer in several parts.

Her egg, which she always had thought went away when she

turned it off, had only sunken to just below her skin. There it remained ready to shield her from the rigors of flight. It also shielded her from more ground-bound rigors, up to and including bombs.

That function struck her as an embarrassment of riches. Already her shapechanger nature protected her from wounding by bullets, knives, and other weapons, her skin turning rubber tough when struck. It could repair in seconds most injuries she did suffer. And if she was killed she could return to life, even if her body was completely destroyed.

Now she was as invincible as a god.

She thought about that for a while. Then she shrugged. She'd long known she was immortal. This just added another kind of protection.

Another part of the mystery of the noise, her under-mind had revealed, was that her egg did more than protect. It also could heighten that distance sense she had.

Or had she always had the egg and the distance sense was part of the egg, the first hint of her egg's existence?

She abandoned that question for another part of her answer: the egg could talk to electrical machines. Such as telephones, telegraphs, the wires that carried power and information, the tiny and complex and subtle minds in calculators and telephone switchboards.

This meant--

Alice closed her eyes and listened.

That buzz...hum...mutter...strange orchestral music rose from near-silence to conversational level. Then it faded.

In its place were images. Before her closed eyes the telephone and calculator on her desk became entrances to a mountain cave system. The telephone's was a mouse's door compared to the calculator's castle gate. Alice flew as if blown on a wind into the giant cavity.

All about her in a starless night were luminous globes like Chinese paper lanterns. They were all colors. Linking them were the tiniest of crystalline lines. Along the lines dots and strands of golden lights traveled very fast both ways.

Each of the globes were calculators, the realization came to her. The nearest was hers.

At that she rushed toward it and through the luminous wall closest to her.

Then she was in a huge building. It was filled with a three-dimensional framework of...girders. They ran right and left, up and down, near and far. On them were hung/stuck boxes. Inside them were bricks...or packages...or tinier boxes.

Inside some bins were motionless/unchanging things: information, data. Inside some others were moving things: calculator programs doing work. They reminded her of squirrels busy sorting nuts and sending them sliding along wires between the bins.

The programs did simple and complex things. Over THERE was a simple one, a clock counting click click click, each click a second. At each click a second hand advanced around the face of a far-off clock shown on the upper right hand corner of the calculator screen. Alice could see the screen, a tall wall as far off as a football field scoreboard.

A more complex program awaited email message to arrive through a pipe. It slotted the messages into categories of urgency: emergency, urgent, important, and so on. The first was red, the second orange, the third merely yellow, and all the cooler colors of the rainbow.

A glance showed that all the messages were cool. Then one jumped into the message queue which was yellow.

Wonder what that one is?

Alice opened her eyes.

On the calculator screen was opened a window into the calculator's mail program. A yellow star beside one line of a list of messages was surely the heading for the IMPORTANT message she'd just noticed when she was...inside...her calculator.

She opened the message though the title of the message made its contents clear: remember that at 10:00 she and her partners in Texas Aviation had a meeting.

She closed her eyes and dove back into her calculator.

For a time she explored her machine. Then she flowed into the telephone line. It led her to another: the master Sales and Advertising computer in the building next door. From it she flew into the several calculators that it served. This included those of her partners and the several sales people and clerical staff.

She quickly exited those calculators. It would be wrong to snoop.

She felt no qualms about snooping in the several dozen or so calculators outside of Texas Aviation, though she did so only briefly. They were all in the industrial complex where Texas Aviation was sited.

From the complex she fled further into Austin, then into other Texas cities. Finally she dipped her toes into New York City.

She opened her eyes and sat for long moments.

She was dizzy with the vistas opening up before her. Perhaps a little drunk.

It was clear that this ability was enormously powerful. She could snoop on all sorts of calculators whose owners wanted to keep much information secret. That presented all sorts of ethical problems.

She in her several lives had transgressed more times than she liked to remember. Alice made several rules for herself.

Most times she would only visit only the sites which were public, such as the several newspaper sites and Congress's national archive. Criminal enterprises, what few she might encounter, were fair game. Business rivals were hands off unless they ventured into criminal activities.

There. That was a good start. A glance at the clock on her calculator screen reminded her that is about time for her 10:00 meeting.

<>

In the Sales and Advertising building Alice got a cup of coffee for herself in the refreshments room and seasoned it to taste. She was the first in the main conference room but was soon joined by her partners. They made small talk as they settled in to work.

Louis Delacroix sat at the head of the table for this meeting as he had accepted most responsibility for negotiating a new job for Texas Aviation. He had with him three fat bound volumes of legal contract. He handed one of them to Llewellyn Porter and another to Alice.

This version of the contract was the third go-around of the legal firm they used to weed out clauses they did not like. Each of the partners paged through it, commenting briefly at several points.

By the half hour they'd finished and closed the contract. They looked at each other.

"So," said Delacroix, "do we all agree this version is acceptable?"

Porter nodded. Alice followed suit.

Delacroix opened his copy to its first page and signed on the line above his name. Porter and then Alice took the copy from him and added their signatures. He then closed the copy and moved it to one side, sighing in relief.

"So where are we on the design?"

Porter, who was head of all engineering at Texas Aviation, said, "Alice and I have made a draft version. Here it is. Take a look at it when you have time."

He slid a manila folder across the table to Delacroix. The Frenchman opened it, glanced at the several pages of diagram-heavy contents. Then closed it.

"Looks good. Do you think we can actually make a truck fly?"

Alice laughed. "No. But we can make a Dodge pickup float."

That was the job they had before them: to design and build a prototype of a Dodge pickup truck which could carry up to a half ton of cargo and float a foot above the road. This way the truck could travel over bad roads, debris-strewn roads, and off the road entirely.

"And what about a two-ton truck?"

Alice said, "That's going to be trickier. We will have to use more than two pairs of engines."

Each "engine" consisted of a permanent magnet bolted to the structure it supported and a can near it which projected a beam of something (which no scientist could yet explain) onto the ground. The ground became temporarily magnetic and (if it was the same polarity as the magnet) repulsed the magnet and the vehicle it was bolted to.

This "floater" engine had almost no moving parts and ran cool making it one of the least likely parts in a vehicle to malfunction. Alice had already put floater engines on the bottom of the Swift so anticipated few problem doing so with trucks.

"OK," said Delacroix. "We're done. Let's get close out this meeting. Anyone up for an early lunch?"

<>

Alice was the leader of the pickup truck floater project. She began by finding a used Dodge pickup in good condition. She found her ability to "fly" within the telephone networks handy. Companies were increasingly putting their advertising on the Net (as people were starting to call it) as well as newspapers. She soon had a truck in the space set up for the truck floater project.

She had mechanics put it into perfect condition, had a pair of Swift floater engines put on its bottom, and put a massive electric battery in the trucks flat bed. Connected to the four floater engines she had a working prototype zooming around the concrete behind Texas Aviation within a month.

She sent a message to the Dodge office in Detroit which had commissioned the project.

"I'm happy to report that a Dodge floater truck is now operational. Enclosed please find several photographs of it operating. This is of course only the first step in creating a commercially viable vehicle. This test vehicle has two separate sources of power, for instance. We at Texas Aviation would like to replace them with a single engine. There are other steps that need to be implemented. Enclosed please find a rough schedule of those steps. A detailed and more accurate schedule will follow."

She signed the message A. H. WILLOUGHBY, HEAD, RESEARCH DEPARTMENT, TEXAS AVIATION. No need to bother anyone at Dodge by letting them know a woman was overseeing their project.

<>

By the week after Easter the prototype was done. A delegation from Detroit visited Texas Aviation to see what they had bought.

They arrived at 4pm by private plane at the industrial complex where Texas Aviation was located. Four airlines operated out of the airport with two runways to the east, one for outgoing and one for incoming aircraft. Traffic control was managed by a company which had sprung up, the Austin Airport Corporation.

The weather was fortunate, still cool despite it being April. The incoming aircraft flashed reflected sunlight once as it turned from a mostly southerly direction to a westerly one while still too far away to be more than a dot.

As it lowered and made contact with the runway Alice's 3x binocular vision revealed it to be an all-metal high-wing Ford Trimotor. Nearer still it taxied near the airport reception and embarkment area and turned so that its right side was facing the building. Shortly the three engines shut down.

A minute later an oval door just behind the wing opened. By that time airport personnel had wheeled a low stairway to the door. One of the men in bright yellow overalls reached up to help the first person to exit the plane. This was a twenty-something young man in a gold three-piece suit. Following him, helped by another young man, was a young woman wearing bell-bottomed white pants and a white sweater over a lilac blouse.

The three partners moved forward to greet the arrivals. Delacroix took the lead in extending his hand to the young man. They shook.

"Welcome to Texas. I'm Louis Delacroix."

"Horace John Dodge, Jr., sir. This is my sister Delphine."

The young woman had the sleek short-haired look of flappers

Alice had seen in women's magazines. Her outfit was obviously fashionable by its fit and fine materials but also was of the modern "comfy" style. The Mister Dodge by contrast was all conservative three-piece corporate style although with a bright blue pocket kerchief in his light gold suit.

Porter stepped forward to shake the newcomer's hands. "Twice and thrice welcome, Mr. and Miss Dodge. I'm Llewellyn Porter, head of engineering, and this is our third partner, Alice Willoughby. She's the head of the research department."

The young man turned Alice's hand palm down and bent to give the back of her hand a European air kiss. Delphine shook Alice's hand with raised eyebrows and slight smile.

"So this is the august A. H. Willoughby, he of the stuffy technical progress reports."

Delacroix ushered the two Dodges and his partners toward the reception area as other passengers exited the plane, gathering luggage from the yellow-overalled airport personnel who had opened a door to the Trimotor's cargo bin.

Inside the cool airport reception area Delacroix said, "I thought we'd send your luggage on ahead to your rooms in one of Austin's finest hotels. You specified nine in your party, I believe. Meanwhile we can take a few minutes to take a peek at the object of your visit."

"Sounds like an excellent plan," said Mr. Dodge. He turned and called. A moment later an older man in a dark suit was at his elbow.

"Jerome, would you see about getting everyone and our luggage to our hotel in the city? Mr. Delacroix, this is our executive assistant Jerome Hussler without whom we at Dodge would be totally lost."

Hussler shook the three partner's hands without any raised eyebrows to find that one was a female. As he did so he said, "Total nonsense, of course. But I do try to lend a hand now and then. I'll see to it, Horace, Delphine."

Delacroix led the way out the front of the airport to a golf-cart-like electrical runabout which took them four big buildings southward to the Sales and Advertising building. Its front contained high picture windows which let the westering sun into the showroom.

Inside Alice quickly feathered the Venetian blinds to reduce the glare of the sun to manageable light cooled by the blue-tinged semiconductor plates overhead. Then she turned to see how the Dodges took in the pickup truck prototype floating a foot above the floor of the mostly empty room.

They were looking on in silent awe.

The overall shape was of a pickup truck: a snout holding the engine, a blocky cab for two or three riders, and a flat bed. But the overall impression, she'd tried to give, was of a futuristic machine.

The snout had a slightly rounded front, the front window in the cab tilted back a bit and rounded smoothly into the top, and sideboards on the flat bed rose up to meld into the cab. There were none of the abrupt angles of most motor vehicles. The color was a glistening royal blue except for the shiny silver wheel caps.

"My God," said Mr. Dodge.

Miss Dodge smiled. "We'll never sell such a work of art to practical men. But, oh, I think some impractical women might be interested!"

Delacroix smoothly went into seller mode.

"We thought that a futuristic but PRACTICAL vehicle should have an image that emphasized its futuristic nature. But if the look is not the one desired, we made it customizable so that your customers could request a look fitting their business. That took little of our time. We threw this look in for free."

"It will float?"

Porter said, "As you see. We spent much of our time making sure it can do that and in a safe and sturdy way. You would really have to work to roll this vehicle, though I'm sure some fool will eventually manage that feat. That is why we incorporated stabilizer arms underneath and roll bars in the cab. In the very rare event it does roll the cab will not be crushed."

Alice said, "Understanding that you might not want to advertise that feature the bars are camouflaged as part of the decor."

Delphine moved forward and opened the nearest door, the driver side. She peered in and ran a hand over one of the camouflaged roll bars.

She nodded. "Johnny, they are right about that. If I hadn't been told of this feature I wouldn't know about it."

"How fast can it go?" her brother said. "And more importantly, how fast can it stop?"

Porter said, "On its wheels, in regular drive mode, 30-35 miles per hour on the usual roads which, as you know, are none too straight and smooth. In what we call 'floater' mode rather than the 'utility' mode it can reach 100 miles an hour. And brake as quickly. This is why we have seat belts which we call 'comfort' belts."

Delphine laughed, a clear joyous sound. "Oh, you Texans with your smooth tongues!"

Horace Dodge said, "It can really reach 100 miles an hour?"

Porter said, "Under special circumstances only. Airport runways, beaches at the waterline where incoming surf soaks and firms the sand. Across flat plains with little vegetation.

"Not that vegetation is a barrier to the induced magnetism. Dirt, sand, brick, wood, even water, can become temporarily magnetized. Water is a problem. It can conceal holes which interrupt one's smooth flow across the plain."

Alice said, "To some extent a rough or indented surface is not a problem. Your truck will float an average of two feet higher when traveling over rough terrain than when it is on its wheels. The problem comes when traveling over abrupt high drops. But then that's true if that happens while one is driving on wheels."

She did not mention that floating vehicles handled landing after a drop much better than wheeled vehicles would. They still had a two-foot magnetic cushion upon landing and could even bounce into the air afterward.

"Well," said the young woman, "I most certainly want to know more. But I need some down time now after that trip."

"Long?" said Alice.

"We traveled all day with layovers for refueling, once in St. Louis where we had lunch, and once in Dallas. We could walk around to stretch our legs, but there still were those hours of sitting."

Porter said, "That sounds like my cue. We have four cabs here ready to take you and your people to your hotel. You can get settled in and rest, then get ready for the dinner and welcoming party afterward."

With that he ushered them out of the display area into their transportation. He joined them to ease them through any problems that they might have at the hotel.

<>

The dinner and party was at 7:30 at the Delgado mansion. It was only a few blocks from the downtown hotel where the Detroit party was staying. Irma Delgado was one of the city's pillars of Austin upper-class social life and wanted to meet the Detroit visitors. She had invited a dozen or so people who might help make the visitors welcome.

Alice arrived a bit early as she usually did. The butler let her in and told her to go on into the huge dining room. Alice had been there before and needed no direction.

As always she enjoyed the room. The ceiling was high and white and held four chandeliers to help light the room. More discreet lamps added to the illumination. The walls were paneled in light-colored wood and were decorated with nature paintings. The table was a long oval which could seat thirty. It was covered in white table cloths and was decorated with silver and crystal and porcelain dining ware. Every few feet in the middle of the table were vases holding red flowers surrounded by green leaves.

Irma Delgado was talking to a black-and-white clothed serving woman. The woman nodded to her employer and walked away. Irma turned to greet Alice. They exchanged hugs and air kisses. Irma complimented Alice on her dress.

The immortal had fluffed her long curly red hair to its fullest body and length and flexed it to lie over one shoulder. Her ankle-length dress was green velvet and her low-heeled half boots bright red. Her jewelry was all emeralds on gold: a necklace of one large green stone in between her breasts and long dangling earrings. She wore no rings on her fingers.

This was unlike her hostess who had three on each hand, all holding rubies which matched her dark red silk dress. Her ebon hair was as long and luxuriant as Alice's but was sleekly straight. With her dramatic eyes and eyebrows on unlined golden skin she could have been any thirtyish matron. Her apparent youth was owed not only to her health-care regimen but to Alice's secretly administered microscopic messengers which gave her perfect health.

"What are our Detroit guests like?" Irma wanted to know.

"Young. Energetic. Smart. Willing to please. The young man is rather conservative in manner and thought. His sister is forward thinking and quietly confident. I think she was a party girl when she was younger.

"Speaking of party girls: where is Victoria?"

"In the kitchen annoying our chef. Oh, here is Grant."

The tall second-oldest brother, manager of the Houston branch of the family business, wore a black tuxedo with a black bow tie. He came near and leaned down to kiss Alice's cheek. Being a smart man it was only an air kiss.

"Ah, Alice, as lovely as always. Killed any Mexicans lately?"

The shapechanger had gone out with Grant for most of a year some years back and they remained friends.

"The only Mexican I want to kill is standing right in front of me. How is Serena doing?"

Grant's other sister lived in Houston with her husband. She was a shy girl intimidated by Alice when they first met. The immortal had spent the time needed to bring the woman out of her shell. Nowadays she considered Alice almost as a friendly aunt.

"Busy redecorating the nursery. I think this is the third time she's changed the color palette. I'm not sure."

Serena was a couple of month's pregnant.

"And here is Victoria," Irma said. "I do hope you've not upset the chef. Again."

"Of course not. Hello, Alice."

Victoria advanced to exchange air kisses with Alice. She was a small woman with short wavy blond hair dressed in blue to just below her knees. She wore blue high heels.

A few minutes later the guests who lived in Austin began to arrive and the three Delgados went to greet them and encourage them to get drinks. Shortly after that the Detroit guests arrived shepherded by Delacroix. Drinks lubricating the social ambience the two groups began to mingle. Both sets were mostly in their thirties and forties and curious about the other.

At 8:00 it was announced that dinner was served. Irma settled Horace Dodge, Jr., on her right at the head of the table and Delphine on her left. Alice sat beside Delphine with Victoria to her left, Grant sat beside Horace. Delacroix and Porter joined the other end of the table. There they set to making themselves agreeable to the Detroit mechanics and clerical stuff who had accompanied the Dodge siblings.

After everyone had put in their food and drink requests Victoria said, "What are some of the things you two do in Detroit? Any special activities?"

Horace said, "We have a large river that runs through the city and it lets into the Great Lakes. I'm partial to sailing. Delphine is keen on roiling the water with power boats."

"I'm a sailor too. Perhaps we could get together after your business is done for a sailing party, all of us."

Horace said, "I'd like that. I'm afraid we have to leave on Thursday, however."

"Really?" said Delphine. "I thought I might stay on over the weekend. I thought I might prevail on the Aviation people to educate me about what else the company does."

Alice said, "We'd be happy to spend some time showing off. Tell you what, you stay as long as you like and I'll personally fly you back to Detroit when you're done. I'll take one of the Swifts and in Detroit you can set up meetings so I can show it off. Texas Aviation is trying to widen its customer base."

Horace looked about at the other people at the table.

"Is that quite safe? Flying? All by yourself?"

"Oh, I'd hire one of the airline pilots to act as a copilot. We would relieve each other so that neither gets tired."

He still looked doubtful.

Grant said, "If you're concerned about a girl flying an airplane, feel at ease. Alice is widely acknowledged to be the best pilot flying."

Alice said, "I wouldn't say that, but I am competent, have several kinds of licenses, and so on."

Grant grinned, "Of course, she wouldn't SAY it, being a modest lass. But everyone knows it."

The conversation turned to Austin nightlife. Victoria was happy to praise Austin's music and dance scene. Alice boosted the Argentine tango dance scene.

"This is the elegant Parisian style, mind you. The French seek to stay true to the authentic Argentine style, not that stick-up-your-butt English parody you see in the movies."

By dessert time the two Delgado siblings and the two Detroit siblings had become close and made luncheon dates between them, Delphine with Grant and Victoria with Horace.

The other Austin and Detroit groups also got on well. They mingled freely after dinner in the Delgado ballroom. It was capable of handling a couple of hundred people but for this smaller group a partition had been unfolded that downsized the room to comfortably fit the crowd of several dozen now in it.

At one point Horace said to Grant, "How about we get some fresh air?"

"Quite. I'll rescue a bottle of wine, shall I? How does this brand suit you?"

"I am partial to white. I'm sure whatever you Delgados favor will suit very well."

The patio of the mansion had a pool and picnic tables. The pool had underwater lights which gave the nearest part of the patio a watery ambience. A few other guests had preceded the two scions in pursuit of coolness and quiet but spaced themselves well apart from each other.

Grant pulled a couple of wooden lawn chairs a bit further from the pool and the two sat in them, legs up and out. He topped off Horace's glass then his own and sat back with a sigh.

"Tired?"

"I'm here for a week from Houston and am spending a lot of time in meet-and-greets. So I've done a fair amount of walking and standing up today."

"My problem is just the opposite. The plane ride from The City was most of a day just sitting, though we did have refueling stops in St. Louis, where we had lunch, and in Dallas."

"When you get back to Detroit and Alice arrives there in that plane of hers, the Swift, do what you can to promote the airlines there to buy a few. The thing cruises at 400 miles an hour and needs no refueling for a cross-continent trip. I think that's right."

Horace whistled. "That advanced?"

"It is indeed. Get her to tell you more. Better yet, get her to show you her steps-to-the-future corkboard. It's in her office. It shows us going all around the world in rockets."

"I'll do that. Ahh. I hope I don't intrude but...do you and Alice, ahh, have an understanding?"

"Not at all, old chap. I get asked that often. No. I will say this. We in my family consider her part of the family. We're extremely protective of her."

"Meaning you'll kick my ass if I offer her insult."

"Well it would mean that, but she could kick your ass herself, probably better than I could."

"So she's something of a spitfire?"

"No. In fact she's slow to anger, slower than me, and I'm slow myself. The thing is..."

He settled himself, freshened his glass with wine, and did the same for Horace.

"Alice is what we in Texas call 'A Texas Girl.' It has connotations not obvious. Imagine someone like a flapper combined with a féministe." He pronounced the last word the French way: fay-ma-neest.

"Add to that a touch of frontier woman who knows how to shoot and is willing to do it. That's what we mean by Texas Girl."

He sipped and let Horace digest what he'd said.

"So. It's seeping in. I think I get it."

"There's more. We have a couple of sayings here: 'Don't mess with Texas.' And 'Don't mess with Texas girls.' But with Alice a goodly number would add a third saying: 'And sure as Hell don't mess with a Dead Girl.'"

"Now you lost me."

Grant recrossed his legs.

"You may have heard that sometimes back we had some troubles with Mexican revolutionaries and bandits crossing the border into Texas."

"Yes. It was in all the papers."

"It could have gone on a lot longer. It's still going on in Mexico. Part of the peace on our side was that we, the US, mounted a military protective force and stationed it on the border.

"One part of that force was aerial. Texas asked Texas Aviation to send a military plane down there and recruit pilots to fly it. It turned out that Alice interpreted that in her own unique way."

He lubricated his voice. He was now getting to the part that he liked.

"Alice hung some bombs and rockets under the wings and made arrangements to have replacements sent for any expended ones. She stuck a big-ass machine gun under its nose. And went down there as the one-and-only pilot."

"She saw action?!" The Detroiter sounded disbelieving. Or maybe disapproving.

"Several times. She killed more Mexicans than all the other military forces together."

Grant let that sink in for several minutes.

Horace said, more to himself than to his companion, "She seems so...gentle."

"She's like a momma cat. Oh so nice so pretty. But threaten her kittens and the claws come out and she goes for your face."

"Hmm. Yeah. My mom is like that."

Grant refreshed his glass, forgetting to offer to do the same for his guest. He was getting to the part he REALLY liked.

"But that is not all. The Mexicans quit coming over the border because of what else Alice did. She dressed all in black, including her gloves and boots. She dyed her hair black and all of her skin you could see she dyed corpse grey and circled her eyes with black. She stuck a shotgun on some kind of scabbard on her back, strapped two automatic pistols to her thighs, and a big-ass knife the length of a sword onto her belt.

"The first time the military authorities saw her they told her to go away. You can't tell one of the richest women in Texas go away. She ignored them.

"Some men that first evening laughed at her. One made free with her person. She knocked him halfway across the room then pulled that big knife and just stood there, looking at the louts. I wasn't at the incident but I've seen that look. Perfectly calm. Perfectly relaxed. But you just know she can explode in an instant."

"This is so hard to believe."

"After the first time rockets and bombs came out of clear blue sky, or out of the sky-blue plane she flew, she quit being a laughing matter. The Mexicans started calling her The Dead Girl. Then ONE of the dead girls. You see, some of the 'revolutionaries' were just bandits. And they killed whole families, including infants. Alice seemed just like one of those victims come back for revenge. And if there was ONE, there could be more."

"So she scared the superstitious bandits and the real revolutionaries away from the border."

"After a few months. But, Horace, there's also a mystery here. At least once while Alice was flying her plane, with a Texas Ranger beside her, another Dead Girl showed up. She didn't need a plane to fly. Nor did she need guns to kill people.

"You may think this was lies and mistakes but THIS dead girl was seen by over a thousand people. It flew over a city leaving thunder behind it and was clear to see. It doubled back and flew around a military barracks under siege by bandits. The wind of its passage scattered the barricades the bandits were hiding behind, exposing them to counter-fire. They surrendered, the ones who survived anyway. And never again do bad guys cross that part of the Mexican border."

Grant could see the face of his Detroit counterpart in the watery swimming pool light. He didn't believe Grant's story. But he didn't disbelieve it either.

Finally Horace drained his wine glass and stood.

"We need to get up early tomorrow. I thank you and your mother for your hospitality. We'll have to have lunch soon."

Grant rose and shook the hand proffered him. After the Detroiter left he sat again. He had half a bottle of wine to finish and thoughts to revisit.

<>

The next morning the Detroit visitors arrived in cabs at Texas Aviation at 9:00. In the hour before Texas Aviation had worked to set up a review area in one of the several hangars for Texas Aviation planes. It included a big coffee urn and pots of cream and sugar on a table against a wall.

The three Texas Aviation partners seated their visitors in a circle of a dozen chairs. Delacroix began the discussion.

"Before we view our products in detail I want to say that we are proud of what we've done for Dodge. But as nothing is perfect we are sure there are changes that you, the experts in automotive technology, will want to make in our two vehicles. They are the fancy one you saw yesterday, and a second variation."

He waved over his shoulder at two pickup trucks sitting in the glare of the lights from high above them. One was the blue truck. The other was a black one.

"The one you saw yesterday combines, as you requested, a vehicle that would operate as a conventional truck but could also act as a floater to get over bad sections of road and get over unpaved ground when needed.

"We accomplished that as taking a standard Dodge pickup, making sure it was in tip top condition, and adding on floater technology. That consists of a second engine which generates electricity and stores it, and two pairs of floater engines just inboard of the two pairs of wheels.

"This hybrid approach has several disadvantages but gets you a working model right away to evaluate. You can take it home with you and use your own engineers, who know automobiles better than we can hope to, to create a merged product."

The visitors took that in and gazed at the blue truck they'd seen the day before.

Horace Dodge said, "We'd anticipated that you'd create something closer to a product that we could just duplicate and sell."

"We imagined so, but the more we reviewed the contract that our two companies came up with the more we realized that we could not do that. We are aircraft engineers, not automotive engineers. Dodge is acknowledged to having among the most expert and forward-thinking automotive engineers in the US, and maybe the world. We could not hope to equal that expertise.

"So we created the hybrid vehicle we showed you. Then we went ahead and created a second one. This is a pure floater vehicle. As much as possible the driver operates it as if it were the truck they are familiar with. But it has no wheels. Instead it sits on skids when sitting still and floats just above them when flying. Let's go on over and look at it."

The dozen people stood, some finishing their coffee and setting their coffee cups on the seat they'd vacated. Some quickly detoured to refresh their cups.

The black vehicle was like every other Dodge pickup, many of which Alice had seen in and around Austin. With the difference being that instead of sitting on wheels when operating it had skids like those underneath sleighs. Tucked up just inside the skids were four wheels the size of saucers. They had been swung down to protrude half their width to below each skid. This was how they were arranged now.

Delacroix continued as the Detroit visitors clustered on the near side of the truck/sleigh vehicle.

"In this configuration we could push this truck into and out of a garage. Production versions would have motorized wheels. For a prototype we didn't bother with this extra design task.

"Miss Dodge, would you take the driver's seat? I'll take the passenger's seat. All of you surround the cab so you can see what we do inside."

The other two partners hung back so as not to block any Detroiter's view of the inside of the cab as Delphine and Delacroix entered the black pickup.

"Press the Start button please." The Frenchman pointed. "Yes, that's it."

The gasoline engine in the hood of the truck purred to life within the electric generator. It was not very loud.

"Now notice the indicators on dashboard." He pointed some more.

"See the Charge gauge. Notice how it shows a 97% charge of the battery? And now is climbing toward a 100%. A driver should always check that, even if only very quickly.

"Ah! Good. See the green light coming on beside the Gauge. That gives you a second indication that the charge is up to working level.

"Now punch that button. That turns on the floater engines. They lift us up to a quarter of a foot. See! You are now flying!"

The pickup lurched slightly as it rose off the floor of the hangar, then it floated serenely in the air.

Horace stepped back. His companions did so too.

"As I understand it the floor beneath the floater engine is now magnetized," he said. "And we are standing on that floor. Is there any danger that our feet will be touched by the beam that induces magnetism in the floor? If so, would that harm us?"

"The answers are No and No. The beam is highly directional and does not spread. Only a narrow strip of the concrete is magnetized and it is directly under the truck and a little to the inside. Even if the inducer beam touched human flesh it would only cause it to be magnetic. Numerous tests using animals alive and dead have shown this to be safe. You might feel a tingle but nothing more."

Alice knew this was not quite true. Faint to medium-strength inducer beams mildly improved blood flow for reasons not yet understood but strong beams reduced it. However the strength of beams diminished rapidly with distance. At nine feet it was almost zero. It was not about to be usable as a science-fiction death ray.

Delacroix mentioned the drastic drop-off and said, "Four feet is about the highest height a practical floater system can reach so adults would have to lie down to be run over by a floater. Yours is set to fly at a quarter foot normally. That is what the blue button you just pushed is set for. The green button above raises your vehicle to a half-foot, the yellow to one foot, and the red to two feet.

"Now you'll notice, Miss Dodge, that there are two foot pedals. They are located the same place as the brake and accelerator pedals normally are. You want to drive around a little? OK. So press LIGHTLY down on the accelerator foot pedal. Yes, like that."

For the next several minutes Delphine drove in circles and figure eights in the hangar. Then Horace took over, asking to be let out of the hangar. Delacroix motioned to Porter who pushed a button which set the big double doors to slowly slide left and right.

When there was enough space he drove out onto the driveway which connected to the two aircraft runways. Everyone followed and watched him play with the truck. He stayed close to the hangar and tried the truck at all four heights that it was set to reach. Finally he returned it to the hangar.

He set the brakes on the truck. This lowered the vehicle onto the saucer-sized wheels and locked them. Slamming the truck door shut he said, "I'll wait for our people to pass on the two prototypes for sure, but right now it looks like Texas Aviation has done its job. Is it OK if my people run some tests?"

"Not only OK, but expected. Why don't we leave it to them for a few hours, up to quitting time? Also, Porter would like to distribute all the documentation on the two trucks to your people. Alice says that's as important as the actual machines when you get around to designing your own floating vehicles."

The two Texas Aviation male partners led Horace Dodge and his technical people to a conference room to talk further. Meanwhile Delphine approached Alice.

"Horace said something about a corkboard you had which sounded very interesting. Would you show it to me?"

"Sure. Let's just let the men do their thing. Come this way."

She set off walking south past the fronts of the several hangars. Delphine joined her.

<>

Inside Alice's office Delphine looked around at it. It was as big as the Detroiter expected the head of a research office would be. It had several large bookshelves filled with books, bound reports, and magazines and newspapers. There were several tables upon which rested various parts and plans and more reports. One corner was set up as a small conference room for up to a half-dozen people.

One entire wall was windows which revealed the runways and the line of aircraft hangars. The opposite wall was taken up with several free-standing cork boards placed end to end. Pinned to them were pieces of paper. Some were newspaper or magazine articles, some were photos, some paintings or sketches.

The board nearest the door Delphine thought of as The Past. It showed biplanes and a few single-wing airplanes and a few weird experimental planes that might never have flown, or did so disastrously.

The next board was contemporary. Among them was a Ford Trimotor. She also recognized from her reading the Texas Aviation planes they sold. There were others, some from Europe.

The third board showed several views of the Swift which Delphine knew from the reports she and Horace had studied about Texas Aviation. It was recognizable by the cans on its waist that contained the induced-magnetism jet engines. Other planes also had jet engines. She spotted two that must be military as they sported bombs and rockets underneath them or the wings. She could also see the snouts of machine guns protruding from several.

"Horace said you flew one of these and actually shot at Mexicans invading Texas."

Alice was at her elbow.

"I did more than shoot AT them. I killed several hundred."

Delphine peered at the woman beside her. She looked like a teenager, a very beautiful one, one who was gentle and kind. It was hard to square that with the grim realities the woman admitted to.

"I've always thought women should be superior to men. Kind and nurturing, cooperative not competitive."

"That's the nature men assign us. I know women's real nature. Much of it is the same as men including the ability to commit horrible acts. We've just had to do more circumspectly, working through men because men have bigger muscles and bones."

"So you are a féministe?"

"I care not what others label me. I am me. I follow no party line."

"We can have babies. Eventually we must or the human race will die out. We need husbands to support us and protect us while we're pregnant."

"There's no reason for every woman to have a baby now that medical care is good enough that few of us or our children die in childbirth or soon afterward. Some of us can choose not to have children. Or choose other women to support and protect us."

"Are you a Lesbian, then? Some of my friends pretend to be because they think it's fashionable."

Alice laughed. "No, I like men. Some are friends. Some are lovers. Some are both."

"Contraception is expensive and hard to come by. It doesn't always work. I'm afraid to let myself do what I want. So that's one difference from men. We have to be very careful."

"Quite true. Let's defer serious discussions for dinner time, shall we?"

Delphine was happy to. This discussion was getting too personal for her comfort.

She moved to the fourth corkboard. This one had futuristic illustrations, some from science-fiction covers.

"Do you think some of this will come true?"

"I have no doubt. Partly because I can see the sweep of history from past to the future more than most. Partly because I'm already working on the future."

Alice glanced at Delphine to see if she was interested in pursuing the subject.

"The future of travel is rockets. Until the induced-magnetism discovery I thought rockets were too weak for practical use. Even the most reactive chemicals have too little energy to be widely useful. Rocket-propelled vehicles had to use so much fuel that it took a million pounds to put a pound in orbit. You do know that what goes up must come down? Unless it goes so fast that it can stay up?"

"I know that. I don't know the math, or care to. But I know that."

The strange woman nodded.

"I believe I can design an engine using induced-magnetism with rockets that is much more efficient than conventional rockets. I've got to do a lot of research before I'm sure."

Alice brooded on the board or something far beyond it.

Delphine said, "What's this?"

THIS was a painting of an alien creature that could have come off a science fiction magazine cover. It showed three six-limbed creatures like blue centaurs but with cat genes instead of horse genes. They looked like a mother and father with a kittenish child looking up at them mischievously. The painting was so naturalistic and detailed it was hard to believe it was not a photograph.

"This is beautiful! Who did it?" There was such grace of shapes and subtle use of color that it must be painted some great artist she had not yet heard of despite her obsession with modern art.

"I did. It came to me in a dream."

Delphine stared at Alice. Both Delphine's intuition and years of art education told her that the artist was a true virtuoso. Could it really be this mid-twenties...girl?

It must be. She could not imagine Alice lying about this.

She turned back to the painting. After a moment she smiled.

"They sure don't look like the ravening monsters of science-fiction!"

Alice nodded. "I'm sure there are such creatures out there. But there are bound to be ones who are as peaceful as the monsters are warlike. Though I suspect the peaceful ones embrace weapons as much as or more so than the predators."

Alice was sure of it. She'd been having more dreams ever since that first one she'd had years ago. All were fragmentary, but all were too realistic and detailed not to be true.

"Enough of my corkboard. Let me show you a project I'm working on. We have a contract with an English motorcycle firm. They sell a three-wheeled version. They want to replace the wheels with floater skids."

Texas Aviation had built four prototypes. Alice loaned one to Delphine and mounted a second, then after a short practice period the two women set off along one of the airport runways. The Detroiter was annoyed that the vehicles had limiters on their engines which kept their top speed to thirty miles an hour. But after driving in company with Alice a mile down and back on one of the two airport runways with the wind in her a hair she forgave the prodigy.

Chapter 13 - Wider World

The Dodge people left on schedule minus Delphine. She wanted to spend more time exploring what Texas Aviation could do for Dodge.

She spent time with Alice chatting about Texas Aviation's near term plans for new aircraft models, with Delacroix about sales and marketing, and with Porter about engineering in general. In the evenings she spent time with Alice and Victoria exploring Austin night life.

On Saturday morning Alice picked her up at the Delgados where she'd been staying since her brother and the other Detroit people had left on the chartered Ford Trimoter.

After stowing her luggage in the Swift Alice told her that if she really wanted to become a pilot she'd show the woman from the ground up--literally. Delphine said that she had meant what she said a few days ago. If Amelia Earhart could become a pilot so could she.

Alice was dressed in comfortable everyday clothing which included woman-cut blue jeans and cowboy boots.

Delphine said, "Shouldn't you be dressed in something special? Coveralls? Or like that leather jacket Amelia Earhart wears?"

"No. The Swift is completely pressurized and heated inside. It has to be. Its ceiling is 20,000 feet. That's almost four miles. The air is thin and freezing cold up there."

It was at little after 10:00 in the morning and late spring. Austin was already getting hot, so Delphine had dressed in an informal walking around outfit similar to the one she'd worn on the Trimotor: white pants and so on but minus the white jacket she'd worn on arrival.

Nevertheless she shivered.

Alice said, "The first thing you do as a pilot is file a flight plan. The skies are filling up enough that we need air traffic control to keep us separated. You might think the skies are so empty collisions would be rare. But it's not empty close to airports. There are only so many paths we can take.

"The next thing we do is do is a walkaround. Once we're in the air our lives depend on the aircraft being in near-perfect condition. There are a lot of things to go wrong and it takes only one or two bolts to come apart to start a plane's destruction. The air is moving very fast along it and all it needs is a little opening to start pulling it apart."

Alice eyed the woman beside her. The danger of flying was starting to seep into Delphine's head. However she was holding up well: neither ignoring danger nor panicking.

"There are several critical parts we give especial attention to, though we must look at everything. Landing gear is crucial. We use the floater system but have tires as back up. Look at these. Notice they show signs of wear but minor ones."

Alice pointed as she began to walk around the Swift. She took her time, even more so than usual so that Delphine could soak up details.

"A little bit of wear, as on this tire--" She pointed again. "--is good. It means the part has been stressed and survived. It may even be sturdier, as the flexing of the tires can soften the tire just enough to make it more flexible."

It took them a half hour to walk all around the aircraft. The last item on Alice's list was to open and close the cargo door and make sure it was latched securely.

Inside she walked them from the passenger cabin from back to front, starting with an inspection of the tiny galley and two restrooms.

"This may seem trivial, but snacks on long flights can keep your energy up and provide breaks in the monotony. That helps keep your alertness up. Also, you do not want to have a tummy upset without any place to go. Don't snicker. It can happen to the best of us!" Alice smiled at Delphine.

They were testing the passenger seats to make sure they were firmly attached to the floor by pushing and pulling on the seat backs when the backup pilot stuck his head in the door.

"Hi, Captain. Sorry to be late."

"No problem, Al. We're in no hurry to leave. This is Delphine Dodge. She thinks she wants to learn to fly. Delphine, this is Albert Camden. He's one of the best. We're in safe hands when he's got the command."

"Good to meet you, Miss. Listen to the boss. She's the best there is. Cap, I'm going to do my walkaround." He left as abruptly as he'd arrived.

"Why is he doing a walkaround when you already did? If he really thinks you're 'the best'?"

"You always do your own walkaround. The more double-checks of other people's work the better."

"He's kind of old. Our pilots both looked younger."

"The air industry is still young so most of our pilots are still young. That isn't a problem with your pilots. They are very competent. I've met one and I recognized the signs that showed that the second one knows his business.

"Al's age is a good sign, actually. There's a saying about pilots. 'There are old pilots, and there are bold pilots. There are no old bold pilots.'"

"Are you trying to scare me, Alice?"

"No, dear. Just reminding you of the realities. You seem to be bearing up under the strain."

"You're testing me!"

"You got it, sister."

They reached the cockpit, sat in the pilot and copilot seats, and buckled in.

Alice showed Delphine how to pull out of their slots the takeoff checklists. They were attached to metal backs so that they hung down just above their seat level. Alice pushed hers back into its slot.

"You're acting as the copilot, so you run down the checklist and make sure I do each action item and in the right order. Unlike a car or truck you can't just hop in a plane, turn the key, and go."

They were halfway through the list when the backup pilot came into the cockpit, sat in the navigator's seat behind the copilots's seat, buckled up and donned the "cans" which held the earphone's connected to the intercom system, and spoke into the microphone positioned just to the side of his mouth.

"We're A-OK, Captain."

"Thanks, Mr. Camden. Next item on the list, Miss Dodge?"

<>

The checklist finished, Alice told the tower she was proceeding as planned, pushed the button which raised the Swift to its three-foot floater height, and pushed the throttles for the two engines gently forward.

Delphine, sitting with her hands resting lightly on the yoke and her feet on the foot pedals, felt the plane around her almost as if were part of her. As if she WAS this powerful giant machine.

Her body was pressed back in her seat, making her feel even more melded with the Swift. She also felt when her wings lifted her above her floater field and she zoomed into the sky.

The runway, needed for more primitive wheeled aircraft, stretched brown and grey for over a mile ahead of her. It fell away below her. So did the green and brown grasslands on each side of her. The land, divided into squares and curves by roads and fences, faded ever so slightly. The horizon faded much more.

The sky above darkened slightly toward a deeper blue.

Alice's voice, coming through her "cans" now, startled her.

"We are coming around to just 15 degrees less than directly north. This will lead us to Detroit. See this indicator here? That's the heading."

One slender finger pointed at one of six round pieces of glass on the dash board like the coverings of clock faces. Behind it a dial swung to point at white tick marks, every fifth one marking one of several going clockwise. However instead of 1 through 12 the numbers ran from 10, 20, and 30 up to 350.

At the same time the yoke under her hands twisted leftward and the pedals beneath her feet moved. One dropped her left foot and the other raised her right foot. Alice did not have to explain, for Delphine could almost literally feel her left wing tilting downward and her right wing lifting upward. The horizon up ahead followed suit.

The world below swung as the plane turned to not quite north.

The yoke and the pedals moved again, this time in the opposite directions and the plane leveled off.

The yoke pushed back at Delphine's hands. She could feel the plane tilting slightly upward.

"We're going to 20,000 feet and will stay there till we approach St. Louis. The thinner air will resist our movement less and let us use less fuel for the same result."

Ahead and above Delphine could see wisps of cloud. They rushed toward her and disappeared as the Swift plunged through them.

As the plane flew on and on Alice continued to explain what was happening and what the indicators told. She was silent for long stretches of time as Delphine puzzled over what she was being told and slowly incorporated the knowledge into her view of the world.

She did so well that as they approached St. Louis Alice let her lower the plane and guide it into a quarter circle toward the east-west runway that traffic control assigned to them. Then Alice took back control and landed the Swift.

On the ground Alice let Albert Camden deal with refueling. As she and Delphine walked into the reception terminal Alice said, "We don't really need to refuel. The Swift can fly to Detroit and back on full tanks, or to either coast. But I always like to top off our tanks whenever the opportunity arises."

It was early for lunch but Delphine decided that Alice felt about food as she felt about fuel: ever ready to top it off. After ordering her food Alice ordered a takeout meal for the copilot: a sandwich and an apple and a glass bottle of Pepper Upper. It would be delivered to their table in a brown paper bag near the end of the hour-long meal.

The two talked about Delphine's parents and about Detroit and the auto business. Delphine was very knowledgeable about that last.

"Both Horace Jr. and I are determined not to be idle rich kids. We're going to make our own mark on the world. Not that we're dumb enough to ignore the advantages of having access to money."

She'd gotten a business and management degree but also taken courses in engineering and automotive engineering. This was unusual for a girl but having a rich family was one of those advantages that she used ruthlessly to get her way. She was sure she wanted to continue in engineering but for the last three years had been working as a drafter in the Dodge Motors design department.

"Whatever field I eventually work in, being able to make clear and detailed drawings will be useful."

"Think you might want to work in aviation?"

"That's become more appealing since I've gotten a taste of flying a plane. But I had a little sailboat when I was a kid. That got me interested in ships. Detroit has access to the Great Lakes and there's a lot of commerce. That's my focus for now. I wanted to come to Texas because of your Swift jet and its induced magnetism air jet. Am I right to think that an underwater version would work?"

Alice nodded. "It would."

"That's good. You see, propellers have a problem called cavitation which are cavities in water, bubbles. The shock of them forming and collapsing can damage the propellers. There are also efficiency problems caused by cavitation."

"Don't forget that jets also use less fuel than propellers to get the same result."

From technical topics they moved to what nightlife and other recreational activities were available in Detroit. It included a big Black musical scene featuring swing dancing. A lot of younger white people were fans and visited Black clubs, though cautiously. There was a lot of racism in the city.

"I hate that," Delphine said. "We have Black servants and Horace Jr. and I had Black nannies who were as much as our mothers as Mama was. Our Black gardeners were always polite to us, I mean more than just the necessary amounts. They are PEOPLE, God damn it!"

The woman sat frowning for a couple of minutes and Alice let her.

"Sorry. I get carried away on the subject sometimes."

"No need to apologize. I feel the same way about racism. In Texas it's especially bad for Mexicans. I do what I can to fight it. If I hear some yahoo mouth off about them I often get up in their faces about it."

"I don't have the courage to do that with strange men. Aren't you afraid that one of your cowboys will resort to violence with you?"

"No. For one thing I have very fast reflexes and have no compunction about kneeing them in the groin and poking their eyes out. For another, I have a reputation in Texas."

She went on to a brief description of her days as a bull rider and plane rider and an even briefer description of her participation in the Mexican border conflict.

That description and the discussion it elicited took them up to the time to resume their flight to Detroit.

<>

An hour later they could see Lake Erie on the horizon. Closer still the lake expanded to their right. On the lake's western shore was Toledo, Ohio, sand-colored central spires of the city center and the greener areas around the city.

North from the lake they could see the river which cut through the center of Detroit, which showed in the distance as an even bigger set of sand-colored spires and surrounding green suburbs.

Alice called air traffic control and was assigned a landing pattern. As they followed it they saw off to both sides other aircraft. There were several airlines working to serve the several large cities of the northeast US. There was Chicago to the west, Indianapolis and Cincinnati and Columbus to the south, Pittsburgh to the southeast, and Buffalo and Toronto to the east. Further east were the east-coast cities of Washington, DC, Philadelphia, and New York City.

On the ground Alice taxied to the hangar where the Swift would be housed during her stay in Detroit. Upon settling in place she said goodbye to Albert, who'd come along only to satisfy her need for a copilot and to do some family business. She then proceeded to supervise the offloading of the two women's luggage and to talk to ground people about topping off the Swift's fuel tanks.

Meanwhile Delphine was on the phone to her family, arranging for transportation and chatting. There would be a wait of a half hour and she grew bored waiting while Alice was busy.

She was joined by Alice in a messy lounge in the hangar, where she'd used the telephone, while she was reading a day-old newspaper.

"Sorry about that," Alice said. "Your arrangements all made?"

"Oh, no need to be sorry.

"I noticed a lot of onlookers doing nothing. Was that due to you?" Alice in her informal cowboyish clothing was not a sight anyone in Detroit had ever seen even if she was not so utterly beautiful.

"Some. But this is the first time anyone up here has seen a floater aircraft or one with jet propulsion. It might as well be a spacecraft from Mars to people here."

Delphine stood up to walk closer to the long windows that looked out into the huge hangar. She had grown use to the appearance of the Swift over the past few days. Now she saw with fresh eyes its sleek white body and swept-back propellorless wings and streamlined tail with fresh eyes.

"Yes. It does look like something from a dozen years from now. It could even be one of H. G. Wells time machines."

Alice's attention was diverted by the sight of two men coming in a far door who might be chauffeurs. One was an elderly Black man in a black uniform including a black cap. He was accompanied by a younger white man similarly attired.

"That's them!" said Delphine.

The woman grabbed up her purse and walked quickly out of the room, then broke into a run which ended in her hugging the older man.

As Alice came up to them she was gabbing excitedly with him and the younger white man, both of whom were grinning at her and occasionally squeezing an answer or a comment into her conversational floodtide.

"Alice! This is Carleton and Richard! I've known them all my life."

Alice held out a hand and shook the hands of each, routinely probing them and launching fixes of several minor health problems. She also read their startlement and wariness to be so treated by a white woman.

"It's good to meet you, sirs. I take it you're here to help us get to Delphine's home."

"Yes, ma'am it is." They looked around.

"The luggage is over here. I had them place it on an airport cart."

Just outside the hangar was parked a large old automobile with seating for six passengers on two bench seats and two more in a driver's cab with a window between the driver's and the passengers' compartments. The servants rolled the cart up to a large luggage area in back and placed the luggage from the cart into it. When they finished the younger man did as Alice had told them: roll the cart back into the hangar and leave it anywhere just inside the door.

The older man got into the driver's seat and started the vehicle. It made a discreet purr after coughing once.

Alice said, "Well-cared for engine."

Delphine spoke a bit loudly, directing her words toward the open window separating the passenger and driver's compartments. "Alice is an engineer, Carleton. You saw that white plane inside? She designed it."

"She did?!" The news was enough to startle the discreet older man into a comment.

"Indeed. And, Alice--" She half-turned on her seat toward the immortal.

"The reason this car runs so well is Richard. He is the mechanic who sees to all our cars and trucks out at Rose Terrace."

"That's the name of your home?"

"Yes."

The day still had a couple of hours before sunset so Alice was able to see the city as they drove through it on a street called Jefferson Ave. This afforded them a good view of the Detroit River a few blocks off to their right.

Further on the street diverged slightly from the river as it entered a tree-shaded suburb which Alice later discovered was called Grosse Point. A mile further they came in sight of the water again, but by then the river had widened out to become the Lake St. Clair.

Rose Terrace was a mansion on the lake two stories tall and massive with many windows. They parked on the street in front of the building.

The two attendants were already out of the car and already unloading it when Delphine exited the car to stand looking at the house. Alice came to stand beside her.

Delphine had tears in her eyes. Alice pulled her into her side, squeezed, and let her go.

"Home, eh. Nothing like it," said the immortal. She'd had hundreds of homes over four centuries. She knew the hold they could have over one's heart.

"Yes," Delphine said, then began to follow the servants up the walkway toward the front door.

Tall massive front doors swung open and two other servants, both women in sandy-colored uniforms, came out to take the luggage from the men. The men turned back to bring in the remainder of the luggage.

A dignified older man in a uniform, a butler or some such, suffered a hug from Delphine. He said, "The Master and the Mistress are in the little parlor off the terrace, Miss. The young master is with them."

"Thank you, Oldham. How is your health?"

"Quite well, Miss. As is that of my missus."

"I'm so glad."

She turned toward Alice.

"This is my very good friend, Alice Willoughby, Oldham. Alice, this Mr. Oldham. He has had as much to making me a worthy person as anyone."

Alice shook the man's hand, proffered only when she stuck her hand out toward him.

"A pleasure, Mr. Oldham."

"Likewise, Miss Alice. I am called Oldham, if you please. It is the convention."

He turned to indicate that the two women were to follow him through the house.

The path they followed encompassed three hallways. On the way the immortal saw entrances into several reception rooms, a formal dining room, a library, and a music room which could also serve as a ballroom.

The little parlor on the lake side of the mansion was not so little. It had a high ceiling and tall windows looking out over the lake. On each side of the windows were red velvet drapes which could be drawn over the windows. The walls were all light brown wood covered in many places by paintings. There were several chairs upholstered in dark red velvet against one wall. Near them a couch similarly upholstered sat against the wall which faced toward the windows. On each side of the couch were two matching easy chairs. On a wall to the side a fire burned in a large fireplace.

From the couch rose a couple in their late fifties or early sixties. Horace Dodge was well-cushioned but not quite stout with close cut blond hair which might once have been red. He wore a smoking jacket over his clothing though there was no hint of smoke in the room. Anna Dodge had short curly blondish hair and was slender with a hint of fragility. She wore an evening dress of cream white and a pearl necklace and gold bracelets.

"Miss Delphine," announced Oldham. "And Miss Alice Willoughby."

Horace Dodge said, "Arrange for dinner, please, Oldham. Delphine, girl, come here."

His daughter came quickly near and gave him a long hug then a longer hug to her mother. The woman finally put her at arm's length and looked at her.

"And have you been eating properly far off on the frontier?"

"Mama, you know that Texas is a civilized place. Behave. You will shame my friend. Daddy, Mama, this is my friend Alice Willoughby."

Alice, who had been shaking hands with Horace Jr., turned toward the parents.

"A pleasure, Sir, Madam. Delphine, considering how I'm dressed I would certainly forgive your parents for thinking a barbarian had just been introduced into their civilized presence."

"You would be partly right," said Horace Jr. to his parents. "Alice is one of a new breed of American girls, one part frontier girl and one part modern girl. She is the brilliant engineer and business woman I've been telling you about."

"You are very welcome," said Horace Dodge. Anna Dodge said, "You certainly are. Come sit beside me, Alice."

The woman moved to make room on the couch for Alice, who sat to her right. Horace seated Delphine beside Alice, then sat beside his daughter.

He spoke to Delphine and Alice. "Did you have a good trip from Texas?"

Delphine answered him. "We did indeed, Papa, Mama. We came in this fantastic new airplane, the Swift. It is well named as it travels at 400 miles per hour. Alice flew it and taught me much about how to pilot an aircraft."

Horace Jr. said, "Oh, no. I can just see her abandoning her poor sailboat for a pet airplane. No doubt one of these dapper red biplanes that the barnstormers used to fly."

His sister said, "Silly! Don't listen to him, Mama, Papa. I'm more interested in adapting the jet engine that Alice invented to working underwater."

Horace Dodge perked up at that. He was a talented and hard-working engineer whose fortune had come from those qualities. But he said, "Junior and I want to hear more about that later, but tell us a bit of the people and places you visited in Texas."

His son, standing near the easy chair nearest Alice, held up his glass of red wine and lifted his brows. Alice nodded. Minutes later he returned from a side table and handed Alice a glass of red wine. She nodded and mouthed a silent Thank You to him.

Delphine had launched into a description of Irma and Victoria Delgado and was beginning to talk about the music and night life of Austin when the butler announced that dinner was served. Delphine said that she and Alice needed to freshen up and got permission to meet the others in the dining room in a half hour.

Alice had been given a room on the second floor adjoining Delphine's regular room. Most of her luggage had been emptied into a wardrobe and dresser drawers and into the *en suite* bathroom. That room was large and white with mirrors above a white porcelain sink embedded in a white countertop.

She quickly freshened up, then fluffed her curly hair and straightened it and put it up into a bun. She did so without touching it as it was alive all along its length rather than like ordinary human hair. Then she dressed in a short-sleeved blue dress with a square-cut bosom and an A-line skirt to just below her knees, a new not-quite-modest fashion. On her feet she put matching blue shoes with a one-inch heel.

When Delphine knocked on the connecting doorway Alice opened it and entered the girl's room. Delphine had dressed in a similar outfit of summer yellow but kept her hair down.

"Do I pass muster?" said Alice.

Delphine eyed her and approved. They left to join the others at dinner.

The dining room was as ornate as one might expect, one of several smaller ones. Under a chandelier in its center was a table able to seat six. Delphine went to sit by Horace's right where he sat at the head of the table. Anna Dodge sat at the other head and requested Alice sit to her left opposite Horace Jr. That put Alice next to Delphine who continued her description of Austin night life.

Both Horace Sr. and Anna were interested in the music their daughter described. Horace told Alice that he played the organ and did so frequently to distract himself when he was uselessly obsessing about some technical problem. He'd met Anna through music, while she was making a living teaching the piano. Together they were actively involved in Detroit's music scene, supporting it and sometimes giving grants to deserving musical causes.

After dinner everyone retired to another parlor for a long rambling conversation well-supplied with drink though no one drank a lot. An hour till midnight the party broke up.

Sunday morning after breakfast Alice dressed to attend church with the family. She had planned for this by including a long grey silk dress with a matching long overcoat. It was open to reveal a high scoop-necked collar. A grey silk belt cinched the flowing garment to her narrow waist which served to emphasize her wide hips, a look at odds to the now-passé straight-bodied flapper look still favored by many.

Dressing complete Alice looked into the bathroom mirror and sculpted the look of her face with her shapechanger powers. She added darkness around her eyes and dyed her eyelashes and red eyebrows black. Her lips she turned the palest pink. She shortened her hair and curled it into a flattened helmet.

Satisfied, she knocked on Delphine's door and entered upon receiving permission.

"How do I look? Am I modest enough for church?"

The girl examined her, had her spin in place, and pronounced her fit for company.

"Except for one detail. Here, let's try on this."

THIS was a narrow-brimmed grey hat. Both decided this made a too-monochrome look. A few colored hats were declared too colorful. A black hat seemed to work best.

Delphine, clad in a palest yellow outfit with a matching sunny hat, led the way downstairs. There Horace and Anna Dodge dressed in their Sunday finery looked on approvingly, pronounced them two fine-looking girls. Horace Jr. suggested they looked like a butterfly and a moth, hastily adding that moths were very decorative insects when Delphine scowled at him. To make up for his comment he offered both his arms to act as escort for the two ladies.

The party of five were driven to a large Presbyterian church a few blocks away by the two men who had chauffeured Alice and Delphine the day before. After the service the family and the immortal exchanged their church clothes for informal clothes, then had an early lunch on the terrace of the mansion. The somewhat chilly weather of the morning had moderated and become sunny.

This was likely part of the reason why the lake was decorated by well over a dozen sailboats. There were also two power boats which seemed to be racing each other back and forth further out.

As the party ate Anna Dodge, with occasional interjections by Horace Sr., filled Delphine in on the activities of their cousins by the elder of the two brothers, John Dodge. From various clues Alice deduced that they were several teenagers going to private schools in a northern suburb of Detroit.

After that topic was exhausted Alice said to the older man, "Sir, as I have one of the foremost authorities on automobiles at hand I'd be remiss not to ask: What you see for the automotive industry in the near future?"

Anna said, "Dear, please do not bend our ear for too long on this subject."

Her husband placed a hand on her nearest arm and patted it.

"Don't worry, my dear."

He turned his attention back to Alice.

"In a word: more. More variety, more price variations, more advances. More and better roads.

"The economy is booming and more people can afford automobiles. We expect a larger amount of cheaper automobiles for the masses. This will require more road building, more secondary businesses such as roadside cafés and shops, more gas stations. That will give a shot in the arm for the petroleum industry. Since Texas is a major oil producer, I see your state booming as well.

"This brings us to your floater technology. It eliminates the need for many major road improvements. Floater trucks can brave the rough terrain where oil wells may be found. Once found, the roads can be made which are little more than packed earth. Or so John and I read the documents you gave to Junior."

"Substantially correct. But if a road is to be well traveled it should be hardened better than just packed earth. Floater fields don't tear up roads as bad as tires as the weight of the vehicle is distributed over a larger surface. But there still is some stressing of the surface."

"But rough terrain is still much easier traveled so exploratory vehicles may travel to many more locations, including very rough terrain?"

"That is correct."

"With more demand for automotive travel we shall see more advances in automotive technology. People will want faster travel. I was impressed at the model you built with tilted front windows and smoother corners. I expect to see more streamlined cars able to travel at 50, 60, 70 miles an hour, first in racing cars, then in commercial vehicles."

He turned back to his wife. "And that is that! Satisfied?"

"Yes, thank you, dear."

He smiled mischievously. "Don't be so hasty to thank me. Because I am now--" He turned back to Alice. "--going to ask Alice what she sees in aviation advances in the near future."

Horace Jr. laughed. "Got you there, Mom."

Alice smiled at Anna.

"Don't worry, Madam. I'm going to suggest that we all retire this afternoon to board my airplane and have a short jaunt somewhere. As we fly I will answer your husband's questions while you view everything from the air."

"Oh, I don't know. I'd rather stay on the ground."

"It's great fun, Mama," said Junior.

Delphine said, "It is. But I had my fill of flying going to Texas and returning, Mama. You and I will stay on the ground and let the boys have their toys."

<>

Thus it was that in the early afternoon Alice changed her skirt and slippers for soft woman-cut blue jeans and comfortable old cowboy boots. Horace Sr. and Anna looked askance at the outfit and Horace Jr. laughed.

"Ta-da, behold the Texas Girl I told you about. All the younger women in Texas dress like this, believe it or not."

Alice said, "Don't believe it, dear host and hostess. I wear this because I need more freedom of movement when I pilot an airplane."

It took half an hour for the chauffeur to drive Alice and the men to the hangar where the Swift was stored. On the way she spoke to the question of the future of aviation.

"What you described in automotive progress, Mr. Dodge, is being paralleled by aviation. The thriving economy and improvement in technology means more air travel, which fuels more demand for ancillary services such as ground workers and ticket takers. Also the rental of autos by travelers upon arriving at a destination.

"The floater technology and air jet technology will be a big part of the advances of aircraft. Incidentally, I did not invent the induced magnetism technology that underlies each. Someone else did that. But I did use the technology to design floater 'wheels' and air jets.

"Floater technology will enable aircraft to take off from and land on rough or even nonexistent surfaces instead of the expensive concrete runways of up to a mile long. This will speed up spreading air travel to smaller cities or even private landing fields.

"Jet engines use less fuel and are much simpler than propeller-driven aircraft and so less expensive. They can also potentially go much further and faster. The 400 miles per hour Swifts are only the first of these faster aircraft. I confidently expect for future planes to travel at 600 to 800 miles per hour."

Dodge said, "Let me anticipate your next point. Routine trans-oceanic travel."

Alice smiled. "Exactly."

Shortly afterward they arrived at the Swift's hangar. There they were met by Albert Camden. Alice apologized to him for interrupting his family visit.

"No need for that. You just saved me from being driven crazy by my family. Dad wants to know why I'm not making more money. Mom wants to know when I'm getting married."

"Good." She then introduced him to the Dodges and began her walkaround of the aircraft. Dodge father and son followed her, examining the airplane with great interest. She gave the older Dodge much the same talk she'd given Junior a few days ago and Delphine yesterday: airplanes had to run perfectly and checking them carefully before takeoff was vital.

Inside she put Dodge Sr. in the copilot's seat while Albert sat in a passenger's seat to read a book.

"What is Mr. Camden's function, if I may ask?" said Dodge Sr.

"Regulation. All two-engine aircraft must have two pilots. I break that rule and I could lose my license."

"I am surprised they let you get one in the first place."

Junior spoke up. He was sitting in one of the two crew seats behind Alice and his father.

"Alice is something of a celebrity in Texas. They wouldn't dare. Especially since she is part owner of one of Austin's biggest businesses."

"Oh. Yes. That business about being a wing walker."

"Also she lent an aircraft to the Army when they were fighting that Mexican border matter."

Alice changed the subject to the preflight checklist and enlisted the older man in the process of checking off each item on it.

Checklist done Alice called Air Traffic Control, identifying herself and her plane.

"I am ready for takeoff. Is my previously filed flight plan still current and approved?"

"This is the Texas girl, right? Sure is, Honey Bun."

"You get fresh with me, Sonny, and I'll come up there and kick your butt."

"Just a friendly welcome to Detroit, Texas girl. Be advised that you are clear to takeoff from now to fifteen minutes. Then we'll have to reschedule."

"Thank for your friendly welcome, Air Traffic Control. Y'all have a good day now." She said that last with an extra heavy drawl.

There was laughter over the radio.

Alice lifted the Swift on its floater field to its four-foot height and gently advanced the throttle. The airplane slid away from its hangar and began traveling the hundred feet to the entrance to the runway assigned to her. She began melding her mind with the machine. SHE rotated to a direct line down the runway, gathered HER power fully under HER control, announced that she was beginning her roll, and began to speed down the runway. Shortly SHE felt when HER wings fully supported HER weight, tilted back, and raced into the sky.

Confident all was in order SHE dropped back into HER biological body.

"How are you doing, Mr. Dodge? Like what you see?"

He was bent forward a bit against the tilt of the plane watching the land fall away below.

He turned to her.

"Quite all right. Is it usual for the traffic people to insult you?"

"That was just friendly banter, Sir. I give as good as I get. Usually there's not much of it. The guys in the tower are pretty busy people."

Junior said, "As far as I can tell, Dad, the aviation community is pretty small and everybody knows everyone else. They at least know the female pilots like Amelia Earhart and Alice and the other three or four. Plus this plane and its sisters are famous. Everyone knows they are the future of aviation."

Alice's egg senses were instinctively probing the air space further and further out and up, cataloguing all possible collision threats. This included even flyers as small as a few flocks of birds, now rapidly falling below. It also included a few meteoroids infalling from space.

This let her pay attention to more interior concerns, including dialing a number on the Swift's radiotelephone connection to the telephone system below.

"Hello, Delphine. This is Alice. Are you and your mother on the terrace? Yes, it is me."

"No, we're in the kitchen."

"Get her and go out on the terrace and look out over the lake."

While Alice waited for Delphine and her mother to walk outside she explained the situation to Horace Dodge.

"One of the services our Swift's provide is connection to the national telephone net. It works best close to cities, especially the larger ones. I'm talking to Delphine and Anna. Just a minute."

"OK, we're outside. What are we looking for?"

"A little white sliver or dot. That's us in the airplane."

She punched buttons that added the earphones worn by the two men to the radiotelephone channel.

There were several seconds of silence then a shriek from Delphine.

"We see you! We see you!"

"Horace, is that you?"

The elder Dodge looked at Alice who nodded and pointed a finger at the walnut-sized microphone suspended on a slender arm near his mouth.

"Yes, dear. I believe it is. We're out over the lake now. The view is amazing. I must be able to see a hundred miles all around."

From 5000 feet the horizon was about 85 miles away but 100 miles was close enough that Alice saw no need to correct him.

The Dodge family talked about what they could see. Shortly those on the ground could not see the air plane. It was cruising at a low 320 miles an hour and after ten minutes the signal began to break up.

"Dear," said the old man loudly, "we better end the call. I can barely hear you!"

"Us too...bye...call when...."

"That was amazing, Miss Willoughby. How much does it cost?"

"Quite a lot but we absorb the expense. The prices will drop as there's more demand.

"Now, where would you like to go? A large city within a couple of hundred miles would be best but we can land anyplace with a fairly flat surface."

After considering several possibilities the men decided on Chicago almost directly to the west. Alice made a great looping left turn that took them out over Lake Erie and Toledo on its westernmost shore. She also climbed to 10,000 feet, nearly two miles height.

The two men watched the sprawling city pass below them. It was quickly left behind as Alice increased the Swift's pace to its normal cruising speed of 390 miles per hour.

The father and son made a game out of identifying landmarks on the highway that Alice paralleled on the trip.

When the southern shore of Lake Michigan heaved over the horizon thirty minutes later the Swift's radiotelephone became able to pick up signals.

"Hey, Al! Could you contact Chicago Midway and arrange for a day of hangar space?"

Camden was sitting in the navigator's station behind Alice and next to Junior.

"Sure thing, Boss. What max price do you want to spend?"

Horace Sr. said, "Don't worry about that. I'm paying."

"You got it, Mr. Dodge. If that's all right with you, Alice?"

"Certainly."

Chicago was more than twice the size of Detroit and so had that much more air traffic. Air Traffic Control did not waste time with friendly chitchat. Alice was quickly given a spiraling downward path which went twice around before it lowered to one of three runways.

Inside the hangar Alice revolved to face out of the hangar double doors before settling to the concrete. She left Albert to arrange topping off of the plane's tanks and to baby sit the plane. He was well supplied with books and told her he'd be fine. If he wasn't in the airport's waiting room when they returned he'd be in the airport restaurant.

"So what shall we do?" said Alice.

The older Dodge said, "Go to Marshall's to buy our ladies a trinket or two."

Horace Jr. liked the idea, so the trio hired a cab and traveled to downtown Chicago. On a street within sight of the lake was the multistory building which housed Marshall Fields. It was a fabled building even in Texas and Alice was wide eyed despite her centuries of life and exposure to fantastic buildings.

The interior of the building was hollow to three stories of height. Escalators, the first she'd ever seen, zigzagged up on two opposite sides of the hollow. One escalator was for up traffic, the other was for down traffic.

They took the Up escalators to the third floor, then an elevator to the seventh floor. This was the level for the most expensive purchases. These included gems and furs and designer dresses.

Alice stopped at one display of clothing. It showed a photo of her wearing woman-cut jeans like the ones she wore. She was dressed in a blue silk shirt as well as the pants and was leaning against a bar with a Champagne glass in hand.

She said, "I didn't want to pose for the company which made those and refused to model for them. The photographer kept upping the price. At $10,000 for a session I got tired of saying No and said Yes. The photographer instantly whipped out a contract and had me sign it before I could change my mind.

"I regretted it by the second hour of posing and changing clothing and posing again. The lights were hot and they kept moving them to get better or at least different light. Still, I bought my family all of their Christmas presents with the money that year."

"So," said Junior to his father, "You see what I mean about Alice being a multitalented woman?"

The older man nodded and led the way to the gem counter.

There were three sellers in the store: an older man in a tuxedo and two young women, both svelte and lovely and fashionably dressed. The instant the Dodges entered they all perked up. The men were obviously not newcomers to the establishment.

The two men separated, the elder to get something for his wife, the younger something for his sister. The man and one woman went to

Horace, Sr. The other woman went to Junior.

"Good afternoon, Mr. Dodge," said the dark haired beauty who approached Junior. "What can we do for you? Do you perhaps wish something for your companion?"

"Oh, no. We want something for my sister." He turned toward Alice.

"What do you think Delphine might like? I confess I really don't pay that much attention to fashion."

"I've noticed that she likes sunny colors. Perhaps something in gold? Or yellow gems?"

Of course Marshall Fields had "just the thing" and for the next quarter hour the saleslady brought out necklaces and bracelets and pendants for a lady's ears. Naturally they started with the more expensive items and worked their way down.

Finally Junior and Alice selected a matching set of bracelets, pendants, and a necklace upon which was suspended a single gem. All metals were gold or golden. The gems were each a garnet called topazolite. They had a brilliant cut which made up for their modest sizes.

The selection made, the saleswoman disappeared into the back to box and wrap their selection. They ambled over to see what Senior had picked.

He had bought two items and two boxes were being handed to him as the duo arrived. One had red wrapping and one had green wrapping.

"Couldn't make up your mind, eh, Dad?"

"I can't deny it. What say we have dinner before we head back? Is there a problem flying at night, Miss Willoughby?"

"None at all. We have no need to hurry back."

"Better call Mom, Dad. Let her know we'll be a bit late."

His father asked for and received a phone from the jeweler. He was happy to help.

The waterfront was only two blocks away and Horace Sr. had a favorite restaurant on the water. They were taken to a window table with an excellent eastward view of the lake. As the shadows of buildings thrown by the sunset stretched further into the water the sky darkened toward the darkest of blues and finally into star-studded night. As night came on so did lights from buildings on each side of the restaurant and on the wharf and boats moored on the lake.

Further out in the lake three massive ships steamed to their left, the north, carrying freight. One smaller but still impressive ship was a passenger vessel with dozens of windows shining golden.

Conversation rambled over politics and business and the arts. The Dodges were all supporters of both music and the visual arts.

"I confess," said Dodge Sr., "some of our support is to gain the approval of the older families. Both John and I are upstarts compared to most of the upper crust here. We are straight talking and honest and not practiced in talking the way the sophisticates do."

Junior laughed. "Especially Uncle John. He can be downright crude, Alice. Personally I love him for it, but the ones he sometimes sets his tongue to most certainly don't."

"I would not be surprised if I liked him," said Alice. "You see me on my best behavior but I find I have a talent for ripping the hide off people with my tongue and indulge it all too often."

In actuality the immortal's last comment was untrue. She was always in control and used her verbal skills to flay people when she judged that the best way to get what she wanted. At other times she was expert at subtle verbal rewards.

She took a sip of her wine and caressed the sights with her gaze. She sighed.

"It's so lovely. Perhaps I'll paint it. In fact... Yes, I shall. Four paintings, one for each of you."

Junior straightened from his slight slouch.

"You mean it?"

"Yes. When I get back home. I'll make a project out of it before my memory fades."

It wouldn't fade. When she wanted her memory was photographically perfect--which could be a negative since photo-perfect paintings could lack creativity.

"Delphine tells me, and even I can see it, that Alice is as great a painter as anyone who has ever lived. Father, you cannot understand until you see Alice's painting."

"That's...quite a compliment, son."

"Just wait. You'll see."

It was unlikely that some art historian or another shapechanger might recognize her painting style, but Alice resolved to change her style enough so that it would differ from that of Li Wei.

They stayed at their table till they had dessert. Then they left for the airport to return to Detroit.

<>

Back home Anna Dodge scolded her husband and son for staying out so late, which amused Delphine greatly. The presents from Marshall Fields soothed Anna and pleased Delphine. The mother received rubies which apparently were among her favorite gems. When Delphine was told that Alice'd had a big part of deciding just what gifts she received she squealed and hugged the immortal. This led Junior to complain about not getting any credit. His sister then gifted him with a hug.

Alice looked on with a grin. Then with confusion when Dodge Sr. pressed a box into her hands: the green-wrapped box that he had bought. It contained bracelets, pendants, and a necklace similar to what Delphine had received. The gems, however, were all emeralds. It turned out that Junior had been in on his father's plot and had suggested that green was a good color for Alice.

She thanked them and exited the room for the nearest room with a mirror. Delphine joined her and the two took turns helping the other don the presents.

Back in the parlor from which they'd come they showed off their gifts. They were joined by Anna Dodge who had put on her own presents.

After the little fashion show everyone retired to a cozy parlor while the two Dodge men recounted the trip to Chicago.

Chapter 14 - Detroit

The next several days were busy for Alice.

She began Monday with three hours of consultation with the Dodge engineers and technicians about details of floater technology. She contributed little important information. She and her engineers had committed a lot of information about that technology to the documentation which was given to Dodge. The company's staff was very capable and had absorbed the theory and practice quite well.

She did, however, clear up a few misunderstandings of the documentation and discover limitations of it. She made notes of those problems and would roll the information back into the documents for correction of and future use of the documents on other floater projects.

More important was that she provided a face for Texas Aviation and helped the Dodge people feel more of a connection to her and to the company. This would be valuable in the future. Alice anticipated that Texas Aviation would have more dealings with Dodge.

After lunch she organized a visit on the Swift of several managers and engineers to several nearby cities. Big companies like Dodge used many subcontractors for auto body parts such as ball bearings and oil filters and rear-view mirrors. Not all of those were in or around Detroit.

The furthest subcontractors were in Indianapolis, Cincinnati, and Columbus a hundred or so miles to the south of Detroit. She flew nearly a dozen Dodge employees to those three cities for free and left them there to return by train when their business was done.

At each airport she had the Swift's fuel topped off. This was unneeded as each trip used only a few percent of its tanks. Her purpose was to lounge around and chat for an hour or two. The futuristic appearance of the Swift drew a dozen or two of aviation professionals.

It also drew others who were interested only in her. One overly entitled man laid a hand on her bottom. He had less than a second to enjoy his endeavor before his errant hand was captured and hauled down and around which forced him hunched over one of his knees. An attempt to move away from the posture caused so much pain that that it brought a squeak out of him.

"You are lucky I'm in a good mood. Else I'd break your wrist and stomp on your crotch."

The several nearby men laughed. None of them believed her. The recipient of her ire did. Her voice was ordinary and without emphasis but the dizzying and instant action had him unsure what was up and what was down.

Albert Camden had been standing so that he'd seen what had happened. He didn't believe her threat, but he'd known her for years and he was pretty sure the idiot would have suffered SOMETHING very painful if she wasn't in a good mood.

<>

The rest of the week was similarly spent in talking to people, sometimes flying them to nearby cities and once to New York City not quite 500 miles away. The most important of the personages was the New York passenger, Edsel Ford, the sole son of Henry Ford. He was the head of the Ford Aircraft Division and keenly interested in the induced magnetism technology.

That Saturday night the Dodge's held a going away party for Alice. After dinner with nearly a hundred people Delphine and her mother put on a piano duet. Tendons in one of Anna's hands had been nearly severed when she was young so she used only her good hand during the duet.

She would in the weeks to come regain use of her damaged hand as a result of Alice's secret gift of near-perfect health.

The next day Alice was driven to the airport where she and Albert Camden returned to Austin.

<>

Several weeks later Edsel Ford contacted Delacroix and, after much negotiation, secured a contract for a version of the Swift.

This angered Horace Dodge Sr. He made a heated phone call to Alice, calling her a backstabber. He was convinced Ford would apply floater tech to their ground vehicles. Alice listened then when he wound down she replied.

"I anticipated that eventuality. So I ensured that the contract with the Ford Company explicitly states that the technology can only be used for aerial vehicles.

"Maybe they can get out of it. I'm sure they can hire some very good attorneys. However, I suspect that if they want to use it in their cars it will be less costly to go through you.

"After all, you have two working prototypes and very skilled engineers who are already well on the way to creating a commercial version of the hover truck. Your people also have begun to plan for further floater vehicles, including a hover tank for military use. With the border expansion ambitions of Napoleon IV they may well be needed in a year of two."

Dodge was an excellent and experienced engineer well practiced in bringing a product from design and manufacturing to market. He knew the truth of what she said. After he'd secured a promise from her to help his engineers if they needed it Dodge hung up, going so far as to invite her to come stay with him and his family "some time soon."

<>

That time was not to be any time that year, but some time in the next when Alice took on another job for the Dodge company.

That job was one that Delphine had thought up. She had secured the promise of money to create a practical induced-magnetism jet which operated under water. She also wanted to explore the possibility of making a floater version of a boat.

Alice agreed to take on the job but a good deal had to be done before Alice would be free to pursue the aquatic project. Most importantly was design work on the SuperSwift. This follow-on craft was to be able to carry 32 passengers rather than the Swift's 12 and have a correspondingly greater cargo volume. It would be wide enough to seat four abreast and allow all but the tallest passengers to walk upright as far back as the two toilets.

By Thanksgiving the design was complete. Alice and the engineers under her had stored all the specifications inside calculator data servers, several of them in widely separated parts of Texas Aviation to guard against loss of the valuable information.

Alice worked that Thanksgiving Sunday, all alone and so undisturbed at the factory. She entered the network of forty design calculators and became the superbeing ALICE made up of Alice+the network+the data servers. Operating at over a dozen times the speed of an ordinary human brain SHE spent all that morning "living" inside the SuperSwift. SHE had to take several breaks to let HER biological part rest and eat and take toilet breaks.

For a subjective week SHE "lived in" and operated the SuperSwift. SHE made dozens of suggested improvements, all the way from minor ones such as seat comfort and convenience, to operating the kitchenette and two toilets, to making the pilot controls easier to operate.

Most importantly, the superbeing crashed or near-crashed the plane in several ways. To prevent them or allow them to "crash safely" SHE invented several technical improvements and safety procedures. Then she spent most of the afternoon printing out all the design changes.

The next two weeks Alice spent making sure that all the improvements were understood and adopted by the designers under her.

Then she called her executive officer into her office.

"Joey, I'll be leaving some time in the next several months to spend a year, maybe more, in Detroit. That leaves me with a problem. This office has the SuperSwift to build, test, and put into production. I need someone to take over for me."

Joey had long ago felt free to express his opinions.

"The two best candidates are Majors and Voltek. I..."

"Right. But a better one is you. I'm appointing you--"

A panicked look washed over his face. He had a good poker face but a shapechanger could read tiny symptoms of face and body that most people could not.

"I can't--"

"Don't worry. Nothing will change except your title and the distance between us. You will continue to do what you've been doing, handle the details I can't because I have to spend time on bigger issues. I'll just be a phone call away, and you know you can talk to me any time day or night."

He calmed.

"Joey, it's been years since you last asked me how to do any of the things I've asked you to do. You always come up a way to do them. You often know what to do before I do. You can do this.

"Did you think I was going to drag you to Detroit? Drag Margie away from the home the two of you have made here? When she's several months away from having your first child?

"Beside, think of what you can do with the extra money from being Assistant Manager of Engineering. You can save some of it for the future of your kid, and future kids."

By now her long-time assistant had begun to think of the new opportunities which his promotion would open up to him.

Likely he wasn't thinking as far ahead as the immortal was. S/he guessed that in a year he'd be able to accept being promoted yet again to full Manager of Engineering and begin to forge his own path in Texas Aviation without needing the crutch of having Alice to lean upon when he encountered difficult problems and decisions.

<>

Thus it was that in the week after Easter Alice packed everything she owned into two sets of boxes. One would be sent by rail to Detroit and one went into her car. She said her last goodbyes to the caretakers of the house which she shared with her Texas Aviation partners and set off driving north out of Austin.

Well away from any watchers she drew her egg out of her body and around her and her car, then went invisible and arced upward and toward the northeast in a straight line toward Detroit.

By the time she passed over Dallas and Fort Worth a little off to her left she was already well above most of the atmosphere. The Earth was covered in blue and lightly plastered in the white dots and clots of clouds, while far to the west a crescent swath of clouds marked a cold front which was bringing a spring rain to the country. The sky above was black edging toward blue at the horizon.

At many thousands of miles per hour she passed over Arkansas and Illinois, dropping down into St. Louis for an early lunch at an restaurant known for its barbecue steak for the last two or three decades. In the unlikely event that anyone in Detroit asked about her supposed three-day drive she could convincingly describe her visit to St. Louis.

After a leisurely meal she distanced herself from the city then flew upward again. Within ten minutes she was fifty miles above Lake Erie to the south of Detroit. From that height she could see all of the Great Lakes to the north.

Dropping down into the atmosphere she passed over Toledo, Ohio, to land under a grey sky on the highway which stretched along Lake Erie toward Detroit. It took her some forty minutes to drive through Detroit to reach the suburb of Grosse Pointe where the Dodge's lived. On both sides the land was covered with snow except in the city center. She bypassed the core of the city but could not avoid all traffic, when traffic slowed drastically.

She'd been away from the Dodge's mansion for almost a year yet it seemed to her as she pulled into the driveway that she'd never been away. Someone in the house must have been near the front of the house and alert because the front door opened just as Alice exited her car and closed the door.

It was butler Charles Oldham who looked out at Alice, a middle-aged half-white half-black man. He half-turned and said something to someone inside then walked to meet Alice.

"Welcome, Miss Willoughby. We've been expecting you. We have your room ready for you."

"Thank you, Oldham. I would appreciate it if everyone would call me Alice, as I asked the last time I was here."

"Of course, Miss Alice. May I help you with your luggage?"

"Thank you."

The two took several pieces of Alice's luggage and boxes out of her car and were walking toward the house when a half dozen servants and Delphine met them halfway. Alice had to set her suitcases down to hug Delphine.

"Oh, I'm so glad you're here safe. Was the drive very dreadful?"

"Just the opposite. I took my time and enjoyed seeing the country."

"Mother is eager to see you. But let's get you inside out of the chill and settled in first."

With several servants helping all Alice's possessions were soon in her room. With Delphine's help everything was put away in the closet and the dressers and the *en suite* bathroom. The latter had a bathtub as well as shower long enough to take a long soak and a long countertop for cosmetics and toiletries. All was in gleaming cream.

The last items were Alice's clothing and shoes. Delphine watched seated on the bed as Alice smoothed and fluffed her clothes and hung them on hangars in the closet.

"That's all?" the woman said as Alice emptied the last box of clothing.

"This is everything I anticipate needing in the next few days. The rest of my belongings are coming by train."

"You have some nice things. But, really, we have to do some shopping for you!"

Alice smiled. "I don't mind wearing the same items more than once, rich girl."

"But we have so many parties and galas to go to! And clubs, and concerts. You have to put on a good show."

"All I HAVE to do is do a good job of engineering for you. I'm not here to burnish your social life." Despite her words' severity she was smiling.

Delphine pouted but jumped up from Alice's bed and grabbed Alice's nearest hand.

"Come on! I'm sure Mother is wondering what's keeping us."

Anna Dodge was in the music room on the second floor. It was small and cozy and held two pianos side by side. There was another music room, Alice recalled, which held a large organ which Horace Dodge played for hours at a time when the mood caught him.

Delphine's mother was seated at one of the pianos playing a version of "Für Elise" by Beethoven. Alice stopped and put a hand on Delphine's nearest arm to stop and silence her. Anna was working on a section of the music which required both hands and rapid fingering.

The immortal routinely gave people s/he liked or wanted to use health as close to perfect as their bodies could manage. The gift was given only after careful thought, not from caprice.

But it was an almost automatic process: she touched them briefly and injected them with a virus. For the rest of their lives it made their genes reset as much as possible to their body's state to when it was born. This did not affect aging but it ensured that they never got sick. And that any damage and scars would slowly go away.

After that touch she might never see them again. Or if she did their robust health was simply a given to her. She didn't think much if anything about it.

But now, seeing a woman she liked a lot who'd lost something precious to the woman, the ability to use all of herself to make music, brought tears to her eyes.

Delphine glanced at Alice but obeyed the shapechanger's unvoiced command. The two stood listening for a minute.

Then when the passage was done and a new one begun Delphine roused to walk over to her mother. Alice followed.

"Mom, Alice is here."

The woman stopped playing and slewed around on the piano bench to look up at her daughter. Catching sight of Alice she hurriedly stood to stand before her with her two hands out toward Alice's hands. Alice joined hands and the two stood looking at each other.

"You look well, Alice dear. Not too weary after your drive. Is that an illusion?"

"Not at all. As I told Delphine I enjoyed the trip."

They retired to one of the parlors for tea and conversation. An hour later they were joined by Horace Dodge and Horace Jr. It wasn't long afterward that dinner was announced. After dinner they retired to the parlor once again to continue catching up on what had happening in the time since Alice had left Detroit.

At 11:00 Horace Dodge glanced at the clock in the room.

"Eleven o'clock already! I need to get up early tomorrow. We'd better quit bending Alice's ear about ourselves."

Alice stood up with him.

"I want to get up early too. But before we break up I want to repeat what I said earlier. I don't suffer boring conversations. If I don't shut you up in some way you can be sure I WANT to hear what you say."

<>

The next morning, a Monday, Alice woke at sunrise and made her usual toilette. Since she would be working in an industrial environment, she dressed accordingly. This was in woman-cut blue jeans and a gold-and-white checked flannel shirt and sturdy brown work boots. Over it she threw on a blue-jean jacket.

Quietly she exited the house, reflexively avoiding the various servants already bringing the house awake for the day. Outside she walked down to the mansion's dock on the other side of a wide green lawn. It was made up of a pier reaching two hundred feet into Lake St. Clair.

On opposite sides at the furthest end of the pier floated a sail boat and a motor boat. They were named Delphine I and Delphine II. A boat house provided housing for sails and other supplies for the two boats. It was on the shore but extended fifty feet into the water and was open at the water end.

She examined everything briefly but soon returned to the house for breakfast by the Polish cook, a longtime employee with whom Alice had become friendly the first time she'd been in Detroit. She was joined partway into it by the Dodge family.

Just after 8:00 Alice and Delphine left for the Detroit main plant in Alice's car. The day was chill and grey but, Delphine said, would become sunny by noon.

Following Delphine's instructions Alice drove in a zigzag route toward the west and a bit to the north, their destination a small city called Hamtramck.

Delphine said, "It used to be mostly farmland just to the west of Detroit but the city has nibbled away at it until it's completely enclosed by Detroit."

When they arrived Delphine had Alice drive completely around the factory. It occupied a rectangle about a half mile wide by a mile long. Most of the two dozen or more buildings were several stories and were faced with a checker board of windows. At one end there was a very tall smokestack and at the other end a quartet of closely spaced smokestacks, all of the issuing thin streams of grey smoke.

"Dad and Uncle John began working on factory floors. The buildings were always dirty and too cold or too hot, so they determined that that they would do better when they started their own work spaces. Things aren't perfect but at least there are heaters in winters and lots of fans in the summer."

Delphine had Alice park her car in Delphine's personal slot in front of the main entrance to the factory. She'd long ago had paperwork done so that Alice had total access to the factory at all times, so the two had only a short visit at the security department to introduce her physically to everyone on the day shift.

Leaving the security office Delphine said, "There is a complete 24-hour security presence. There's also a fire department and a medical facility working around the clock. Hamtramck is too small for us to depend on the city to serve us. Last count I heard we have over 42,000 people working here."

The next stop was the "Welfare" department. It did things such as help new workers find lodging, sign up for city and state programs, and take short courses or even academic classes. There Alice was again introduced to several people. As a contractor the shapechanger was not qualified to use it but Delphine was proud of the fact that "The Dads" wanted their workers to be well cared for.

"Part of it is self-interest, I'm sure. With the UAW trying to enlist all auto workers happy workers are less likely to join them. I imagine they all will eventually, but this department is one of the ways we'll delay that day."

Their last stop was called the Play Pen. It was a large area with all sorts of machines and equipment.

"This is for workers to fix or invent stuff after hours. You'll be here in the daytime so you'll have it pretty much to yourself. But you can get help from the shop steward. He comes on at noon and works till 10:00. You can order anything you want and ask for anything to be done. Unless it's really big or expensive you'll get it without asking permission."

"That is extraordinary confidence you are placing in me," said Alice.

Delphine regarded her with amusement.

"You are an extraordinary person, dear Alice. And we know you already."

They spent a couple of hours looking at the facilities and discussing what Alice would do first. Then Delphine said, "OK. Uncle John wants to meet you. We'll be having lunch with him fairly soon. It's a bit of a walk to the company cafeteria."

As they walked, stopping frequently for Alice to watch some activities, the woman explained that John Dodge, the older of the two brothers at sixty-something, usually ate in the executive dining room. On Mondays, however, he ate at the main cafeteria of three.

"That keeps the cook and serving staff on their toes. It also lets the workers see him and see him eat the same food they do."

"A smart man, your uncle. And your dad."

"Yes they are! But I do have to warn you. Uncle John is pretty outspoken. Please try not to be offended by anything he says."

Alice grinned at her.

"Don't worry, Cookie. I won't be offended. But I have to warn YOU. I give as good as I get."

When they finally arrived Alice saw that the cafeteria was huge with a high ceiling of glass that let in the sunny light of late morning that Delphine had promised.

There were several lines serving hot and cold food. The women separated each to fill a plastique tray of food and drink, then paid at separate cashier's stations. Then Delphine led Alice to her uncle's usual dining area. This was in one of several open-faced alcoves along the side of the two long walls.

John Dodge was seated at a large round table. At it were several men and two women, all dressed formally. John Dodge was not. He was a big man dressed like most of his workers in dark pants and a white open-collar shirt with the cuffs rolled up.

As the two women approached he shooed away all the executives and stood to greet Delphine with a kiss on a cheek and a handshake for the immortal.

He stood holding her hand for a moment and looking her up and down. He released her hand and beckoned for her to sit at his right as he himself sat down.

"You are a well-looking woman, at any rate."

As she sat Alice said, "I'm sorry I can't say the same about you. You really need to cut down on your diet. You have put on too much weight."

This was true, though his weight would go down slowly in the next few months as the virus the immortal had just infected him with worked its magic.

Delphine looked horrified as she settled on her uncle's left. Dodge, however, barked in laughter.

"You don't pull any punches."

He turned to his granddaughter.

"Did you put her up to this?"

"No!"

He turned back to Alice.

"Are you always this frank?"

"Yes. Especially to pompous assholes. I'm happy to see that you are not one of them."

"You could get into trouble expressing yourself so freely."

"From what I've heard you speak from experience."

His grin was wry. "I do indeed. I've tried to moderate my speech. Haven't I, June Bug?"

Delphine replied. "It's true. I'm proud of you, uncle."

Dodge was well into his meal and the women began on theirs, discussing a variety of topics. One topic was Alice's intentions for marriage.

"That is none of your business but I'll answer it anyway. No, I'm not interested in Junior as a husband. Nor anyone as a husband in the near future. I have too much I want to do."

"Don't you want babies?"

"I can't have babies, according to my doctor. Someday I'll adopt. There are plenty of kids who need a family."

Dodge was clearly unhappy with her answer but dropped the subject to talk about what he saw as the future.

"Now that the banks have begun moderating their insane push to take on unwise loans I see an increasingly healthy economy. And that means more desire for automobiles."

The immortal agreed with the mogul about how banks had been unwise in how they treated loans. So much so that she had spent the last few years secretly discouraging the policy. She would drop down out of the sky into the homes of selected bank presidents at three in the morning. She'd warn them to moderate their actions or else suffer from a second visit from her. Only occasionally had she had to carry out her threat.

She thought other immortals had been doing the same in Europe and elsewhere. Even someone as powerful as she could not alone shift the course of all nations by such actions.

"Which means," she said. "More improvements of streets and roads and businesses which support travel: gas stations, roadside restaurants, auto parts stores."

Delphine pointed out that floater "tires" meant decreased spending on actual tires. It would also mean less spending on highway and street improvements as autos would increasingly be able to travel on plain earth.

Dodge said, "True. But I expect the increased business in other areas of transportation will offset that."

Alice said that what was true of ground travel would be true of air travel. Dodge asked her what advancements she thought could be expected. Alice was a bit surprised. Dodge was fairly old and seemed to be fairly conventional. She hadn't expected that he'd be open to the opinions of a "mere" woman.

"We can extrapolate from trends that are already obvious. We'll travel faster, further, higher, more cheaply. Our--Texas Aviation's--Swift and SuperSwift can already travel between the east and west coasts with one tank of fuel. Such travel will become routine. Transoceanic travel will become routine. Even across the Pacific.

"This means that American manufacturers will be faced with competition from China and other Asian countries. Their labor costs are lower and can undercut our prices."

"Much to think about," said Dodge. He wiped his mouth with a napkin and stood up. Delphine followed suit and so did Alice.

The man shook Alice's hand a second time, kissed his niece's cheek, and left.

<>

Delphine took Alice back to the Play Pen by a different route. They stopped for a time at the paint application part of the auto assembly line. It covered several floors and over a dozen different actions.

Alice noticed that in several places women worked. She mentioned that to Delphine.

"They're used for the more delicate operations such as painting pinstripes and assembling dashboards and wiring in tight spaces. I pushed Dad and Uncle John to improve their working conditions, such as separate bathrooms.

"Some of the men took advantage of the women. When I found out about that I got so mad I stormed down here and knocked a man down and got him fired. When I calmed down I set up a complaint service so I or our welfare people hear if something is happening. Every once in a while I do a surprise visit to the welfare office so they don't slack off or try to discourage women coming to them."

When the two of them arrived at the Play Pen the shop steward was there doing some paperwork. Delphine introduced Alice to him, a Pole named Oskar Mazur. He was a short stout man with a mustache who was losing the hair on his forehead. Though he was unsmiling he impressed Alice as having subdued but happy energy.

"Oskar here has been with us since he left school. He's worked in all sorts of jobs so he knows where to go to get just about anything.

"Well, that's it for me. I'll leave you here and get a ride to the next thing on my to-do list. I'll see you tonight at dinner. Don't be late."

After she'd left Alice turned to Mazur.

"I need a door or a door-sized piece of wood."

The man made a phone call and a door showed up. It was a bit smudged and all metal parts had been removed from it.

Meanwhile Alice with Mazur's further help had collected a number of items. One was a powered drill that would make a half-inch hole in wood. With Mazur she laid the door on two tables with the top hanging off. In the top left and right she drilled a hole all the way through. Then she did the same to the bottom left and right.

She and the steward propped the door against the brick wall a few feet from the front door to the room. With him holding it against the wall she drilled a guide hole in the wall behind each of four holes in the wood. Then she screwed four half-inch screw bolts into the wall to hold the door to the wall.

Next she drew an outline in black paint of a man about six feet tall. She also added a fist-sized heart shape on "his" left breast.

Then she walked to about twenty feet from the door. On the way she picked up a half dozen marble-sized ball bearings from a table where she'd placed them. Stopping she said, "Watch me. Me not the door."

She turned casually, transferred one of the ball bearings to her throwing hand, drew her arm back, and threw the ball bearing at the man shape very hard. Then she repeated the action with the rest of the ball bearings, so rapidly that the sound was like that of a six-shooter firing.

The man's gaze was drawn to the door bolted to the wall near the open doorway. The six ball bearings were half sunk in the wood. Two had penetrated the lines suggesting eyes, two were sunk in the "shoulder joints" of the masculine outline, and the remaining two in the middle of each "thigh."

"This is a reminder of what can happen to anyone who lays hands on me without my permission. And this."

She took a couple of steps to a nearby table and picked up a big somewhat rusted flat-head screwdriver. Seemingly casually she threw it at the painted outline.

It made one complete turn and plunged deep into the "heart" of the figure.

She'd used enough of her enormous strength to send the point of the screwdriver deep into the brick wall. It would take strong men two hands to withdraw the screwdriver.

"Pass the word. Now, the next thing I need is a glass-sided fish tank. A big one. At least two feet high, three wide, and five long. Placed here."

She walked to the roughly ten-foot square corner of the room allotted to her work. HERE was in the middle of the area. Around the center were several tables, a couple of chairs, and a wooden desk. Empty shelves stood against one wall deep enough to hold small machine parts and books.

Mazur had followed her to her area. Standing in the middle he glanced around and said, "Should be no problem. I'll make sure the sides are really tough. We'll have to fill it with buckets from the restroom over there. Anything else?"

"Not right now. Thank you. Now I've got to do a bunch of paperwork. Talk to you later."

He left and she sat down at the desk to make several lists and draw up several diagrams.

<>

Word of her presence at the Dodge main plant spread fast. A lot of men and a few women showed up at the Play Pen during the next few days for all sorts of reasons. The reaction of the men to the figure on the wall was muted. The reaction of the women was usually a smile.

The first order of business for Alice was to build a magnetic induction projector. This was not difficult. The technology was simple, consisting of some coils of wire of a particular configuration, some semiconductor circuitry, and a power source. She mounted the box containing it on a framework that positioned it above the water in her "aquarium."

She focused the inductor on a circle of water a foot wide. Nothing happened, of course. Then she placed a round saucer-sized electromagnet a foot above the focus of the induction ray and powered it on to produce a very weak magnet.

The water dimpled, forming a bowl-like depression in the water when the magnet was the same polarity as the water. Or it humped, when the magnet had the opposite polarity.

She then began to run tests and collect data on the effects of the inducer on the water at different power levels of the inducer and the magnet and different distances between the water and the magnet.

This continued for a month.

Mazur, who had closely watched her efforts at first, soon became bored. Alice, a lovely and mysterious sight at first, became a fixture. Occasionally she asked for and got help from him but for the most part she kept busy and to herself.

At least that was the case when she was working. She took breaks at mid-morning and mid-afternoon and for lunch. The breaks were short but her lunches were long. She soon acquired a big round table where anyone could sit and readily talk to her. She was not standoffish. Just the opposite. She liked to listen and encouraged others to talk.

Some of the men and a couple of the women tried to flirt with her. She just smiled at the efforts but otherwise ignored them. Most of those who tried soon gave up. A few did not.

A favorite ploy of the persistent was to walk with her back to her work area. Few of those who went inside the Play Pen remained persistent long.

One man who did not take the hint dared to put his arm around her waist halfway back to her work. In the next instant he was bent far over with that one arm pointing straight up and in a hold that put painful pressure on his elbow.

In his ear he heard, "Just a few more ounces and you'd have a broken elbow. Do you understand? Nod, or grunt, if you believe me."

All he could manage against the pain was a grunt. She let him up, smiled at him, and pushed him back the way they'd come. She stood watching him for a few moments, then turned back toward work.

At his break that afternoon one of his friends, who'd seen the byplay, teased him about it. The others sitting at the break area just outside the building in which they worked laughed and consoled him. He perked up shortly.

"At least I got to touch her. And smell her. She smells like roses."

"Roses have thorns," said the betraying friend bringing on another round of laughter.

A large woman named Zofia, who was like a sister or a mother to most at the table, spoke up.

"You're lucky she did not do worse. Like kill you."

The rest of the dozen or so workers looked at her. They knew there'd be more.

"If any of you lackwits ever read a newspaper you'd know to be REAL polite to that woman."

"But KILL me?"

"She could do it and get away with it. For one thing, she's rich. She owns a third of an entire airplane company. And she's friends with the Dodges. Rich people stick together and can get away with anything.

"And she's a killer. You know about that Mexican Border war a couple of years ago? No, I thought not. You lot don't read the papers.

"Our military wanted to use an airplane to fly over the border and spot Mexicans coming into the US. She took one of her airplanes, mounted machine guns on it, and hung bombs and rockets under its wings.

"Then she painted her face grey, dyed her hair black, put on black clothes, and flew the plane down there to help out. The Mexicans took one look at her and called her the Dead Girl.

"The nabobs tried to get her to go away but you don't tell a rich woman what to do. She killed more Mexicans with that plane than the rest of the Army combined. She even landed the plane one time and got in the thick of fighting. She shot at least a dozen men. And you think she wouldn't hesitate to shoot your sorry butt, Filip?"

The story was too good not to repeat. Naturally it gained some dubious details. When it finally got back to her she discovered that she carried concealed two two-shot Derringers and a dozen flat throwing knives and picked her teeth with a dagger.

She laughed when asked about it at lunch.

"Well, it's certainly a good story. But why would I carry weapons when they're all around us?"

She held up a spoon and everyone at the large round table laughed.

"A spoon?" scoffed one of the other eaters.

"You want me to scoop out one of your eyeballs, Filip?" She angled the steel spoon at his face.

"No!" He laughed but he quickly sat back in his chair. You couldn't always tell whether she was serious or joking but better to be safe than sorry.

<>

By the time autumn came Alice had finished her research and turned to making a water jet. The first model was a round plastique pipe four inches wide and a foot long. The walls of the pipe were a little over an inch thick and so the engine had a bore just under two inches wide. It circulated the water in The Aquarium quite well.

Watching a test run one day Mazur said, "You know, you could use that as a water pump and not just as a boat engine."

"Hmm. You know, you're right. I'll have to put that in the patent application."

She did so, stating that it was a "general mover of fluids including but not limited to water, oil, and coal slurry." It went into the Dodge Intellectual Property office, was massaged into a more general and legalistic form, and sent off to Washington.

A week later she loaded onto a truck the engine in its bulky cradle-like framework with its battery power supply and controls and had it driven to the mansion that Delphine called home. Just after lunch she had the underwater part lowered into the swimming pool and, just before dinner, gave a demonstration of it.

It was met with cheers from the family and Champagne.

Alice accepted the accolades and said, "The essential work on the water jet is done. To make it practical I need to turn it over to your engineers to make it easier to use and more compact and reliable and rust and corrosion resistant. Your engineers are better able to do that than I am."

"You mean," said Delphine, "that you've done the interesting parts and are ready to have someone else do the boring parts." She said it with a smile however.

"You got it. Now I'm ready to turn to your second task."

"What is that?" said Anna Dodge.

Delphine said, "I wanted to know if Alice could build a floater engine that would work over water as well as earth."

Alice said, "My research suggests Yes but it will take some work. There will also be limits. A normal floater engine pushes down on dirt and water. That's OK with dirt because it is solid and unmoving. But water won't stay still. I've several ideas how to proceed, but this job won't be as easy as your first job."

<>

Alice launched into more research. She wanted to answer such questions as how deep below the surface of water the induction beam could magnetize the water and how wide the circle of magnetized water could be made.

Thanksgiving neared and Alice said temporary Goodbye to the Dodges and set off in her car for the supposed three-day trip home. As soon as she got into a street out of sight of anyone she went invisible and lofted into the air.

As Detroit fell away under her she felt her heart seeming to lift inside her. She'd missed being airborne in her invisible bubble of force, mistress of all she surveyed.

The experience had not gotten old, of seeing the planet turning rounder then round, the sky turning black and strewn with stars, the feeling of limitless freedom. Out of joy she accelerated to many thousands of miles per hour, then many more.

The Earth shrank to the size of a blue marble and the Moon grew large, a grey pockmarked world. She swung around it, noticing as she flew over the far side that always faced away from Earth that the view subtly changed. She puzzled over why for a few minutes but forgot it as she swung back around toward Earth.

She came down over the Pacific just off the coast of China. It was night time and the ocean was dark but the coast was limned by golden light. She sought out Beijing, lowered to a mile above the familiar sights. Like all cities nowadays the city never slept. The streets of the enormous center were lines of golden light, the tops of buildings darker if not dark, forming a vast checkerboard for the most part.

She skimmed the grounds of the Imperial Palace and wondered. Was the immortal Empress, a shapechanger like herself, sleeping or awake pondering the complex responsibilities of overseeing the affairs of an empire?

The Empress was welcome to her job. Alice had never wanted to be a ruler, even when she as Temilade had created and governed an ancient empire in Africa. She had taken the job because she had thought her people needed it done and done well.

Enough. Her family was awaiting her back in Llano.

The immortal launched upward, passing the speed of sound far above and leaving a faint clap of thunder far below.

<>

Alice came arcing back toward Earth facing down so that she saw the Earth ahead of her over the hood of her car. There were three weather systems over the US as revealed by white clouds. One was over the west coast, one covering all of the eastern US, and a smaller one over Texas.

She set down on the road from Austin to Llano, shrugged off her invisibility and egg-shaped force field, and started her car. It was mid-afternoon of the Wednesday before Thanksgiving. The sky above was clear but hazy. There had been showers recently and the air smelled of the greenery on both sides of the road.

She was greeted with hugs at her old home by her mother and younger brother. Her older was with his wife and child but would join them the next day. His wife was cooking something to bring. Her father and grandmother were both at work but would soon arrive.

The dinner was long and complicated by Alice's nephew of nearly one. He was energetic and dropped food items and utensils from his high chair at the table. Then after dinner he toddled busily here and there, occasionally dropping to his knees. He tired early and Alice helped her step-sister to put him to bed in his carryall.

Alice, soothing a stray strand of hair back into place, said, "Is he sleeping all the way through the night?"

"Since many months ago. Wakes in the middle of the night and wants to pee, but otherwise he's no trouble."

The immortal looked at Charice. She was a hefty but healthy blond beauty with wide-set eyes.

"You and Lenny have done a good job with him. I'm happy to see that he's very healthy."

He should be. Long ago the shapechanger had infected her brother with a "be well" virus, then done the same to his wife when he married. It had been transmitted to their child as soon as it had been conceived.

There was much catching up to do. Everyone wanted to know

about what Alice had done and seen in Detroit. She talked a little bit about her work for Delphine but much more about the Dodges and the galas and events the immortal had gone to. There had been several.

When she walked her grandmother back home that night she talked a bit more but mostly prompted Helen to talk.

Thanksgiving Day there were a lot of visitors to the Willoughby family house of people who wanted to see Alice. She was friendly to all. After the meal she drove to Albert Moseley's house to greet him and his wife and their newborn child, a girl. She only spent an hour there, however.

She spent more time the day after with him.

His calculator and electronics store was doing well. They had expanded into the store next door and added two sales people. But his biggest success was to his online store: Bazaar.

Alice knew this since she had twice bought into it, once for ten percent of the business, then for ten percent more. Each time it had been to give him the money to expand and diversify the business. Each time his efforts had been successful. His payments to her were becoming truly hefty.

"After the New Year Julia and I are moving to Austin. We've bought a house there and I'm moving Bazaar there. Llano just doesn't have the space or the manpower to support the business."

"Llano will be sorry to see you go. Taking all that business with you."

"I thought of that. Or Julia did. She has a younger brother, Kennie, to take over the calculator store. I know him and have been giving him work. He's as smart and hardworking as she says he is; I'm not just taking her word for it.

"Also, most of Bazaar was already in Austin. I'll just turn the part of Bazaar here into the west regional distribution center. This part of Texas is expanding."

Albert was very interested in the work Alice was doing for Delphine. He wanted to know a lot of technical detail. Talking about her problems gave her several ideas about how to deal with them.

"So what's happening with Texas Aviation now that you're gone?"

"I'm in close contact via virtual meetings. Video conferencing has gotten really good with the country going to fiber optics networks. Also I can remotely access the computer network we have in place in Austin to review documents and blueprints."

She did not say so, but she could patch into the Texas Aviation network--as in all networks--and immerse herself into it as if she were an electronic ghost living inside the calculators. As ALICE, a cyborg made up of Alice+calculators, SHE thought a hundred times as fast. Further SHE could re-imagine the blueprints as functioning 3D models and set them to running and watch what happened. SHE did most of such work at night when most calculators were idle.

"We've got a new airplane in the works. I'm thinking of it as Gargantua but its official name is Condor. It's really big. The cargo version can carry automobiles and disassembled planes and even tanks. We're watching the war movement in Europe and expecting business from European militaries.

"Even if there is none, or very little, Gargantua will be useful here in the states. Airline travel is really exploding."

In fact she was expecting little military demand. If things heated up too much the immortal would intervene. She could do so in several ways, some of them subtle and some dramatic. The most of that second category would be to fly high then dive down so fast that the sonic boom she trailed behind her exploded buildings and shattered land and any armies upon them.

The next day, after many Goodbyes, the immortal left for Austin. She wanted to visit her friends there for a few days.

<>

Back in Detroit Alice tried out some of the ideas that her subconscious had come up with. One panned out: inducing magnetism in a deep and wide body of water. Being more massive the chunk of water would be slower to push down when a magnet of the same polarity was lowered over it. When it did go down surrounding water would rush in to take the chunk's place which was then magnetized in turn.

The resulting design had two long ski-like magnets that held a body above it on legs. It looked much like a sled and that's what Alice called it. Inside the bottom of the body of the sled were two magnetism-induction projectors that effectively made all the water under the sled magnetic.

From the blueprints for the sled she made a miniature test sled that would fit in her water tank. She began a series of tests. Each test began with it floating with the magnetic skis under water. This was the way real sleds would begin a trip in bodies of water. Then she applied power to the projector at a very low level. Then she increased the power till the floater sled's skis were completely above the water.

Alice had to find and fix a number of problems before she had a good enough result to show off her progress.

Easter had come and gone when Alice pulled into her parking space at the Dodge main plant. She and Delphine were still discussing an upcoming musical gala in which Anna Dodge was deeply involved with occasional help from her daughter. She turned off her motor car's engine and set its brake. They got out and went inside on a sidewalk recently swept clear of a light late-Spring snowfall.

Inside the Play Pen they hung up their overcoats and Alice steered her project sponsor to the Aquarium. Above it at head height the test sled hung on thin braided plastique ropes.

She pointed out the inch-thick four-foot long skis underneath the prototype.

"For simplicity sake I had them made up as permanent magnets not electromagnets. The tops have a north polarity so the bottom has a south polarity."

She had Delphine look down into the long open-topped wooden box which simulated the body of a boat. She pointed out two plastique-sided devices which looked like soup cans. One was in the rear of the "boat" and the other in the front.

"Those two 'cans' are the induction projectors."

Delphine said, "They're inside the boat. Does the wood of the hull absorb some of the force of the induction beams?"

Alice grinned. "Not at all. There are no beams like those of flashlights. An induction projector affects matter at a location without sending anything through the space between it and the target. That 'action at a distance' effect is giving the physicists fits. There are two, Einstein and Bohr, who are going at each other hammer and tongs about whether it even exists."

She lowered the test bed into the water till it floated. Then she dragged two wooden chairs over to a place a couple of feet from the nearest long side of the water tank made of thick glass. She picked up a fist-sized black box connected to a black cable which had been draped over the side of the Aquarium. Sitting she motioned Delphine to sit in the second chair. They could see the bottom of the boat through the glass side.

"Now I'm going to turn on the power to the projectors at their lowest setting."

She twisted a dial on the side of the black box. A click sounded as the dial reached the first position.

Immediately they could see the water in the Aquarium below the submerged skis begin to roil. The effect was very slight however, just enough to barely be seen.

"Now position two," said Alice. There was another quiet click. This time the roiling of the water was more noticeable. The watchers could also see that the skis had been pushed a bit higher above the roiling water.

Position three on the black box raised the skis just to the surface of the water. Position four raised them about two inches above it. The water surface was lowered about a half inch below the skis. Water all around the rectangular depression was flowing into the area.

"The next step is to build a test bed maybe ten to twenty times as large. I estimate that it would cruise about two feet to four feet above the water.

"At least that that is my estimate, but we won't know until we build the test bed."

Delphine said, "Any reason why we can't use an actual boat for the body of the prototype?"

"No. That would be better."

"There are plenty of old sailboats and motorboats available cheap. We could build a slip near our pier where the boat could rest near the shore. And build a boat house on shore where you could work on the prototype."

"The boat house wouldn't have to be elaborate. A tent would serve. I'll do most of the work on the skis and projectors here then add them to the full-size body inside the boat house. That last step should take a day or two."

<>

By Thanksgiving Alice had skis and projectors ready to fit to boat hulls. Delphine had arranged for the family dock on Lake St Clair to be extended and a boat house built beside it. She also bought a twenty-foot motorboat. She had won numerous boating awards, including the prestigious President's Cup, and knew the small boat markets well. She was also a careful shopper and got good prices on the hull. It was in good shape despite its deceptively decrepit looks.

Alice closed down her Play Pen engineering lab and transported all essential tools, test equipment, and supplies to the new lakeside boat house. This included several magnetic induction projectors tailored for aquatic operation and several pairs of large ski-like magnets.

She had the motorboat engine replaced with a gasoline powered electrical generator, then installed a pair of projectors inside it and skis under it.

A week after Thanksgiving Alice had the Delphine III lowered into the water alongside the dock. She and Delphine along with Horace Jr. boarded the vehicle. The shapechanger started the motor and engaged the electrical generator.

As the power came online the immortal merged with the boat, her consciousness racing all throughout the wires installed in the vehicle. This included everything connected to them: the generator, the various instruments, even the headlamps and cruising lights.

The composite being Alice+boat focused HER attention on each of HER electrical parts, then the gestalt made up of all of them, in the first few seconds of the boat's powering up. All was well.

HER consciousness flowed more slowly into the non-electrical parts including the bow, sides, and bottom of the craft. It flowed down its legs into the ski-like magnets, into the keel shortened to end at the same level as the skis, and into the rudder. SHE did not understand how SHE could merge HER consciousness with non-electrical matter but was content to let explanations wait for the future. For now SHE had tests to do.

The first was to run the generator up and down its power settings and ensure it was working properly. It was, not surprisingly. HER biological self had picked it carefully from several commercial products.

SHE flowed into the skis, sensed that the top layer had a north magnetic polarity and the working bottom layer a south polarity.

Then SHE engaged the two induction projectors at the very lowest setting, first singly, then together, synchronizing them till they worked perfectly together.

SHE found that SHE could feel the water turning magnetic, could sense that the top of the mattress-shaped chunk of water below the boat had a south polarity. This matched the bottom layer of the skis. The magnetic fields repelling each other, the water sank, the skis rose. The rise was a fraction of an inch, but it was there.

SHE pretended to examine the readouts on the dashboard in the cockpit of the cabin then spoke to her passengers.

HER consciousness was running a hundred times as fast as when SHE was purely biological. This had been a problem the first few times in which SHE had experienced it but practice had made it seem natural now. The hardest part was talking naturally to anyone, as SHE did now.

"Everything
seems
to be
working
fine.
I'm
going to
raise
her
out of
the
water
now."

ALICE increased the projector's power a click upward several times, each time carefully evaluating the floater system before increasing it power use. This happened so quickly to HER passengers that it seemed ALICE instantly went to the highest power level.

The Delphine III rose out of the water and hovered a little over two feet above the water.

When it became clear that the highest power level was stable and the setup stressed very little ALICE pushed the steering wheel steadily forward. This tilted the two projectors so that the magnetic effect on the water moved further and further beyond the read of the boat.

"Prepare
to
cast
off."

Delphine and Junior hurriedly went to stations a third of the way from the back and the front of the boat. The superbeing gave the order to cast off and HER two helpers jerked the knots on the two ropes tethering the boat to the dock. They came loose and a spring system brought each of the two ropes to coil up inside the boat.

The boat eased forward along the side of the dock. ALICE turned the steering wheel away from the dock and the boat obediently angled away from the wooden structure and out into the lake, heading eastward.

Midmorning in late November the day was chill but bright from a recently passed cold front which had brought a few inches of snow to the area. There was a brisk northwest wind which made the water choppy. This gave a jittery feel to the boat floating above those waves. The late-morning sun was ahead and above them, making the two ordinary humans squint. Twenty-plus miles ahead of them the Canadian shore line of the lake could be seen as a thin dark line.

ALICE curved the boat toward the north to spare her companions the annoyance of the looking toward the sun. SHE spent several minutes, several hours to the superbeing, testing all aspects of the boat and how it handled. SHE memorized the dozen or so changes SHE wanted to make back on land.

"Okay,
Delphine.
take
over
and
wring
her
out
a bit."

The immortal let HER sponsor swap places with HER and stood back, then plunked down on a bench seat at right angles to the cockpit. Horace Jr. was seated opposite HER, his head turned to the side to look over his sister's shoulder out of the plastique wind shield. He glanced at the superbeing and gave HER a perfunctory smile before looking out of the small cabin again.

ALICE dropped fully into HER biological part and watched idly as Delphine spent more than a half hour testing then playing with the boat and its handling. Then Delphine gave control over to her brother.

He was a good boat handler but not much interested in boats; he spent only ten or so minutes trying out his sister's new toy. Then he gave his sister back control to let her bring the boat back into dock.

<>

The trio had lunch with Anna Dodge but not Horace senior.

Though he and his brother John were retired they liked to get together at the main plant for lunch and a chat.

"How was your new toy, dear?"

Delphine swallowed from her wine glass.

"It went well. It's not very lively, though."

Alice said, "That can be improved. But floater boats without an added means of propulsion can never go very fast. Water--material of any kind--can be induced to be magnetic at any distance, maybe even miles. But the repulsion, or attraction, of any material drops off quickly the further away they are from a magnet."

This led into a discussion of how floater boats could be made fast, a discussion that Anna Dodge interrupted after a few minutes, telling Delphine and Alice to discuss it at a better venue. Junior seconded the order and the lunch discussion veered into more social topics.

<>

Horace senior was interested in the commercial possibilities of Alice's work. By the end of the evening he had approved Delphine's suggestion of starting up a marine division of Dodge. He suggested that Delphine head it up. Unlike many he had a high opinion of women's brains and initiative, or at least of his daughter's brains and initiative.

Horace junior might have been jealous of his sister being given such responsibility but he had his own interests and obsessions. He headed up a small organization within the Dodge Company devoted to auto racing. He had, when younger, driven in auto racing in the US. However he was smart enough to cede the driver's seat to professional drivers when Dodge participated in European races.

Instead he focused on the engineering side of racing. He was, for instance, supportive of his engineers' desire to add a V-16 engine to their latest racing vehicle.

Before Alice departed for Texas for Christmas holiday she pointed out, one evening after dinner, that a vehicle on a floater field did not suffer the limits on speed that one on tires did. Junior already had realized that but, focused on competitions involving conventional automobiles, had set aside any thoughts in that direction.

However, when Alice returned from her three weeks in Texas, Junior had a new interest: fast floater vehicles. He had thus ceded control over the racing division of Dodge and started up a small group devoted to fast-floater automobiles. The group had even created a design of a prototype they called Lightning. Recognizing the dangers of driving such a vehicle personally, he had hired an engineer who specialized in the new field of radio remote controls. By summer he hoped to run tests of Lightning at the Bonneville Salt Flats in Utah.

Alice followed the progress of Junior's team but she had enough to do helping the Marine Division get established to help much with the fast-floater project.

The motorboat tests had yielded useful information which Alice incorporated into tests of a larger hull: a forty-foot sailboat. She had most of the masts and other related fixtures and equipment stripped from the boat. As the sailboat was wider than the motorboat she installed four projectors inside it, two in the rear on each side of the boat and two more in the front likewise placed. As it was longer than the motorboat she installed four skis under it, two on each side fore and aft.

The basic setup was tested, problems were found and fixed and retested. Then more problems were found and fixed.

The result was still imperfect but it was good enough to go to the next stage: add a jet engine on each side of the former sailboat. In the choppy waters of the lake it was able to go about 40 knots or 45 miles per hour.

That was good enough for Alice and Delphine to declare that Alice had fulfilled her contract. They had a party with the several workers who had been added to the project and who would form the core of the soon-to-be-announced Marine Division.

The families and friends of the workers were also invited. The three dozen or so people formed a large enough crowd to get the attention of two newspapers: the Detroit American and Detroit Free Press. The American devoted the most space to the story with a full page in the Sunday edition with lots of photographs. Many of them featured Alice, who was very photogenic, and Delphine, who was not only photogenic but also a member of high society.

The next morning Alice loaded her automobile and bade a tearful farewell to the four members of the Dodge family.

An hour out of Detroit the immortal pulled her invisible force egg around her and her car and lofted high above the Earth on her way back home.

Chapter 15 - Floods

"Austin Traffic Control, this is Texas Aviation Condor Prototype 3, tail number TAX-03, pilot Alice Willoughby, copilot Joseph Carter. We are exiting Texas Aviation Hangar 7 onto taxiway."

"TAX-03, Austin Control. Acknowledged. Your flight plan?"

"Flight Plan A1301, posted this morning. We want to do ground handling tests."

"We see your plan. That ground handling plan is approved. Repeat, it is approved."

"Thank you, Austin Control. Commencing now."

"Be advised that the outgoing runway will be occupied in 33 minutes by outgoing traffic. Request you halt motion for duration of the traffic."

"Roger that, Austin Control. Will cease operations at 25 minutes and until outgoing traffic is five minutes away."

"OK, TAX-03."

The 3000-foot long outgoing runway was for planes leaving the airport and heading east. The taxiway from the several hangars allowed airplanes access to the runway, one of two. (The other was for incoming traffic.) The taxiway paralleled the runway for its first 500 feet. It was separated from the runway by 200 feet of well-mowed grass, so there was little chance of wind kicked up by the passage of aircraft on the two roadways would conflict. However, Condor was huge and caution dictated that taxiway traffic cease when an aircraft was leaving or arriving at the airport.

When the big Condor aircraft was well out of the hangar and onto the taxiway Alice turned it to face east along the taxiway. She set the brakes on the four sets of wheels and said, "Condor on taxiway and brakes set."

That was the first of over two dozen items on the test checklist that "Joey" Carter was viewing on the clipboard in his lap. This was the fourth time that he and Alice had run this series of tests as part of judging the performance of Texas Aviation's newest transport vehicle. The previous three sequences of tests had revealed a variety of problems which now had, presumably, all been fixed.

Joey checked off the first item and reported "Check."

Alice said, "Lifting onto floater field." Then she slowly increased the power to the four sets of induced magnetism projectors in the bottom of the Condor. The concrete under the plane became magnetic. This repulsed the four sets of the magnetized skis under the plane, lifting the plane slowly till it reached four feet of separation between the skis and the concrete.

"At four feet and stable," said Alice. She and Joey looked out the windows at their surroundings: the runway to their left, the hangars to their right, and the grassy terrain in front of them which reached to the horizon.

They also looked at the readouts on the cockpit dashboard.

"South wind of four miles an hour is being countered by automatic controls." The prevailing midsummer winds were southerly. The big plane would have been pushed to their left and the nearest runway if the controls of the plane didn't automatically correct for the drift.

Joey dutifully checked off this latest test.

For five minutes the two of them watched the readouts. They revealed that the southerly wind was increasing and decreasing above and below the four miles an hour earlier reported.

"Five minute mark. Plane still stable in position."

She waited while Joey scribbled a comment, then said, "Advancing downrange at ten miles an hour."

She pushed the throttle slowly forward till it clicked at the ten-miles-per-hour detent. The big plane began to move forward until it reached the two-hundred-foot mark. Alice halted it and said, "Halted at two-hundred foot mark."

At this distance they had advanced beyond the eastern edge of the hangars. Without the barriers of the hangars the wind was consequently stronger. The two test pilots observed the automatic station keeping controls for the five minutes specified in the test checklist. Then they went to the next item on the checklist.

Thus it went: the prototype Condor going forward, backward, turning, at various speeds and distances. They paused to watch the outgoing flight take off. After five minutes they proceeded with their testing, all still on the ground. Then they had to pause a half-hour later for an incoming flight. The Austin International Airport (an ambitious name) was increasingly popular with currently 53 takeoffs and landings each day.

Finally all tests were done and the two retired for lunch.

<>

In Alice's year-plus absence Joey Carter had acquitted himself well. Upon her return she requested he be named the permanent head of Development and Test. She herself wanted to be named Associate

Director of D&T and got her way. This let her be freer to do whatever the Hell she wanted to do and not be a full-time boss.

One activity she wanted to do was test the Condor. She could merge with it to become a cyborg thinking a hundred times as fast as an ordinary human. In emergencies she thus could respond unhurriedly and correctly.

Too, her normally egg-shaped invisible protective force field could be reformed enough so that she could use parts of it as very strong "hands" to help recover from problems. Its "arms" reduced to a few inches in diameter she could reach to more than fifty feet and exert enormous force.

And in the worst extremity her egg let her survive explosions and fly away from them.

Unsurprisingly, in none of the tests was there even the slightest emergency. The Texas Aviation engineers under Joey were good and hardworking. With Alice secretly inhabiting the calculator workstations when she wanted to they were damn near infallible.

By October the immortal had done the most crucial tests of the Condor. She pronounced the prototype ready for whatever further tests D&T wanted to do. However, she said, she thought D&T should instead finish the designs of the Condor passenger and cargo versions and let Texas Aviation Sales begin looking for customers.

This included customers in Europe where France and Spain were edging toward war and thus would need cargo planes for troop and supplies transportation. The Condor could land and takeoff from any flat spot with its floater undercarriage.

It was also a big plane, the largest in the world so far. It was 112 feet long, over a third of the length of a football field, and had a wingspan a few feet wider. The inside width and height of the fuselage was about a dozen feet, big enough for midsize trucks to fit into. Its rear underbelly could drop down to act as a ramp for vehicles to rapidly deplane near a battlefield. Or to take on wounded for rapid transport to hospitals.

With its two big jet engines it was also quite fast, cruising at 450 miles per hour.

<>

The cold war in Europe between France and Spain was heating up, with armies massing on both sides of their border. France's ally Germany and Spain's ally Italy also had marshaled troops opposing each other, though the numbers were much smaller. Naval forces of France and Spain jockeyed for position in the Atlantic and Mediterranean. Military aircraft flew reconnaissance over the border between the two principals and the border between the two allies.

Ostensibly the conflict was over who could fish in the Bay of Biscay off the north coast of Spain and the west coast of France. There were also national grudges.

Alice decided to do something about the real possibility of a war which might spread beyond the two countries.

<>

Paul Briand, the President of France, came slowly awake with the dawn sunlight of a Saturday morning. He turned onto his side opposite the windows and sought to return to sleep.

It eluded him because his movement did not escape the light. Sighing he sat up and wedged his dry eyelids open. What he saw jerked him fully awake and sent him scuttling back against his bed's headboard.

Beyond the foot of his bed a shining human-sized egg floated a few feet off the floor. White light flooded the room. It was as if a part of the full moon had come to visit.

Nothing happened. The egg floated serenely in the silence of a newborn day.

Except. The light began to slowly dim. The egg was becoming translucent. Inside it a human form was becoming visible.

The white light seeped out of the room. Yellow light from the window began to replace it from the slit in the velvet curtains covering the window.

The egg became nearly transparent. The figure inside it was revealed to be a slender young woman clad in a white robe which barely showed her ankles. On her feet were golden sandals. On her head was a long cascade of golden curls. Her face was fair, her big eyes were blue, her lips were full and pink.

A goddess seemed to have come to visit.

She spoke in musical French with a hint of a medieval accent.

"Good morning, President Briand."

It was rare for Paul Briand not to have a quick rejoinder to any speech but this time he had to struggle to come up with a reply.

"Who are you? Why are you here?"

"You may call me Selena. I am here to establish peace between

France and Spain. Time to get up, Paul."

"That is an impossible task."

"Yet you see the impossible before you. Get up. Take into your water closet formal yet comfortable clothing for a day of work. Do your usual toilette, dress, and return here."

Briand looked at his wife. She was still sleeping despite the conversation going on.

"What have you done to her?"

"What I've done to everyone in this building."

The Élysée Palace in Paris was the residence of the President. It was three stories high and contained many rooms for servants and their work places. It also contained offices for some to ply official business together with all the other buildings of the French bureaucracy.

"I have put her into a deep sleep. After we leave her slumber will revert to normal. I suggest you write her a note saying you've been called away by urgent business."

Briand did as bade but took his time about it in an act of passive rebellion. It went unnoticed by the being still serenely floating at the foot of the bed.

He finished all his preparations, scribbled the note to his wife, and placed it in a prominent place on his writing table.

"Come. Stand by my side."

At the command the egg, now almost invisible, descended. Its rounded bottom disappeared into the floor till the goddess-like being stood on the carpet. Moving gingerly, Briand placed himself a couple of feet to the being's right and facing the same direction as she did.

Then he lost his balance as he became weightless and the egg rose about a meter. He stubbornly feigned indifference as he wiggled to maintain the same upright posture as the being.

The egg rotated to face the doorway of the bedroom and began to move at a walking pace toward it. When it neared the doorway the door opened to let the couple pass through. Then the door closed behind them as they floated down the hall.

Near the end of the hall they entered a conference room with two tall windows letting out onto the flat roof of the second floor. One of them opened and they floated outside.

Instead of setting down the egg floated upward.

Its rate was slow at first. Briand's stomach, recovering from its constant falling sensation, settled into feeling as if he had merely jumped upward and for an instant hung suspended.

He looked all about as Paris fell away below him. The buildings and boulevards grew toylike, then into a pebbly carpet of brown and grey blocks. The curving Seine River diminished to threadlike size. The green countryside, gilded by the just-risen sun, swallowed up the city and the river and the hills below. At this early hour the shadows of the buildings below reached long toward the Atlantic Ocean, a grey line on the horizon.

The egg, facing north, rotated toward the west then rotated more so that the ocean was to their right.

They continued to rise. Puffy white clouds rushed down toward them then further down to become a carpet of cottony puffs. The horizon became indistinct and rounded, the sky darker and bluer.

They were rushing southward. Far to the left Switzerland's mountains flowed backward, northward.

Briand thought he recognized Poitiers below them and then Angeleme. If so they must be nearing the west coast. He WAS sure the city that raced below him was Bordeaux. Yes. There ran the Gironde river which connected Bordeaux to the Bay of Biscay to the west.

Then for a short distance they passed over the Atlantic just off the west coast.

Abruptly they were over land again as they flashed over the hilly east-west north coast of Spain. Briand saw Bilbao just inland of the coast.

They crossed a long valley. Then more hills. Then another valley. Then hills. Then a lowland.

Their path lowered and slowed. This was surely Madrid coming up over the horizon.

Yes.

Lower and slower still. For a few minutes they followed a river south to a big park. In the center of the park was the grey stonework of the Palace.

It was bigger than its French counterpart, five stories high, a square of stone with a square courtyard in the center. Paths crisscrossed the yard and greenery relieved the empty spaces of the yard, all in shadow.

This time they entered the palace from a service entrance on the ground floor.

"Keep quiet as we travel. I'm putting the people in our path to sleep. Don't do anything to alarm them and interrupt the process."

Briand nodded.

They floated serenely along, went up a squared spiral stairway to a second floor, floated down a hall past a huge kitchen. Inside it the French President saw people setting kitchenware down, turning off an oven, yawning, lying down on the floors, falling asleep.

He wondered if the being beside him could do the same to entire armies. He did not want to find out. Nor find out what the goddess? angel? could do if she could not peacefully vanquish an army.

They ascended another stairway up three stories then went down a long hall and ascended a final stairway. Down another hall they dead-ended in a wall centered by tall massive double doors of dark-brown wood.

The being extended a hand toward the door a few feet away. Very slowly the knobs of the doors turned and just as slowly the doors opened outward. When it was fully opened the egg slid into the room.

It grounded and vanished. Briand teetered momentarily as his weight descended upon him. He found his legs had grown slightly weak from disuse during the thirty or so minutes of the egg's flight. He shifted his weight back and forth a few times to improve his legs' blood flow.

Very quietly the immortal said, "Keep very quiet and stay behind me."

She walked to the opposite side of the room they were in. It looked like and was furnished as a sitting room, with a dark rich red carpet, brown wood-paneled walls, small paintings on all four walls, and a scattering of leather chairs clustered around small tables.

The being carefully opened a door in the wall furthest from the double-doors and went in. Briand followed, his steps quiet on the deep carpet. They were now in what was obviously a suite.

They entered yet another door, even more carefully and quietly. Briand noticed for the first time that his companion had her perfect mouth open slightly and was taking and releasing slow deep breaths. The president guessed that this was how she was putting people to sleep: breathing out some invisible agent.

His attention was caught by the sight in the darkened room of a large bed occupied by two figures under a quilt. This must be Briand's Spanish counterpart and his wife.

Embarrassment assailed him at his--their--intrusion on such an intimate and vulnerable state. He looked at his acquaintance.

She was looking back, her face dim in the near-darkness.

She pointed off to the side. Briand realized that she was indicating a corner of the room. As his eyes adjusted to the dimness he could see that they were in a bedroom not unlike his own with a sitting area in one corner. Two chairs with their backs to the walls at the corner sat at right angles to each other. At an elbow of the chairs between them was a table holding a lamp.

Briand walked to one of the chairs and sat where he could see both the bed and the being at the foot of it.

She rose in the air to a yard's height. The invisible egg turned visible with a faint white glow to its surface. The glow deepened and the figure within became increasingly invisible until it was entirely out of sight.

Nothing happened for minutes. The glowing egg continued to float serenely in place.

Brian wondered: had She done this before? To Briand? To others? To high-walled citadels and stockades protected from attack by massive armies?

But not protected against attack from above. She could simply carry a heavy stone to a great height and release it.

One of the figures in the bed stirred and turned over much as Briand had when his own bedroom had become almost as bright as day.

In his own room Briand had been coming awake and slowly realizing that the light in the room was not coming from its usual direction in the morning--

The man in the bed rolled out of the bed, reached under the table at his bed's headboard, pulled a pistol out of something, sank to his knees, and aimed the pistol toward the door to the room.

Briand froze, his eyes glued to his counterpart. If bullets started flying he was going to dive for the carpet.

The President of Spain had focused on the giant glowing egg at the foot of his bed. An egg floating two or three feet off the floor.

He watched it float, doing nothing.

Long moments later he gazed about his bedroom. He caught sight of Briand. The Frenchman could not tell if he recognized Briand.

After Briand did nothing the Spaniard lowered his gun and stood up. He looked over at his wife. She was not responding to her husband's frantic departure from their bed. The man knelt on the bed and carefully placed a hand on her neck.

He breathed out and settled back to sit cross-legged on his bed, gazing at the egg.

The immortal woman banished the egg and floated to stand on the carpet. She spoke in Spanish. Briand understood her but his command of the language wasn't good enough to tell if it had the same archaic sound that her French had.

"Interesting way to meet the day, Mr. President."

"What did you do to my wife?"

"She is unharmed. She is only sleeping very soundly. As is everyone on this floor. You may relax. Everyone is safe. Safer, in fact, than they would otherwise be if some military force attacked this building. For they would be facing me. And as you may guess, they would be in danger of being totally wiped out."

Her voice was in no way dramatic or emphatic. It was conversational.

Briand actually felt himself shiver. Only a very few times in his life had he been terrified. This was one.

"Very well. What are you doing here?"

"I am taking you and Mr. President Briand here to London where you and he, with my encouragement and help, are going to make peace between your two countries."

"That may be impossible."

Briand smiled. He himself had said almost exactly the same thing to the faery? angel? not very many minutes ago. He said as much in his awkward Spanish and, relaxing, extended his legs and leaned back in the easy chair.

Events proceeded much as they had when the being had visited Briand: toilette, dressing, packing an overnight bag, leaving a note for the wife, floating down halls to an exit, and lifting off from the roof of the palace, Briand standing/floating to the being's right, Miguel Azaña to her left.

She was silent as Madrid and then Spain dropped away. The Spanish President gazed downward, outwardly composed but Briand guessed as full of wonder and apprehension as Briand had been under the same circumstances.

Briand found himself composed. Perhaps it was the fact that he had just a short time ago risen in the air in the same way.

Then he noticed that the rise was not slowing as it had before. The trio was going straight up at a rapid pace.

The world became noticeably round. The sky turned darker blue. Then very dark blue. Then black. Stars emerged in the blackness.

When the rise stopped the Earth was a glowing sweeping curve of blue below them. To their right was the sun so they must be facing north. To their left they could see the Atlantic; most of it was in darkness still. The edge of the blackness was a crescent line separating it from the lit part of the globe.

The woman spoke.

"Have you heard," the woman said in English, "the advice for motivating a donkey? Use a carrot and a stick?" Briand noticed consciously as he had not before that it was very lovely: a medium soprano. But accompanying it was a barely heard humming sound. A lover of opera he had heard a wide range of voices, but never anything remotely like this.

She looked from one to the other as they stood/floated high above the blue planet decorated with a sweeping snowy crescent of clouds and several areas of small puffy white clouds like pastures of sheep.

The rulers said, "Si" and "Oui."

"I know both of you speak English. We shall use that from now on.

"First I will demonstrate a stick. It is only one of many types I can wield."

With that the invisible egg shape they were in tipped so that the three of them were almost head down. The blue planet below them moved up toward them as they dove.

They whipped through the crescent of cloud and Briand saw Europe to their right, the British Isles to their left, and the North Sea before them. As they neared the surface their path arced north so that they flew horizontally over the ocean. They were very low, so low that he could see waves in the water.

Then the view tilted. They were flying straight up.

Their flight stopped, instantly. They were standing/floating upright.

Their view shifted off to the side, away from the path they'd followed. Then they rotated, turning back toward the path.

A skyscraper high fence of a white fountain of water traced their path toward and beyond the horizon.

"Imagine what would have happened to ships on the water if I flew over them as I just did. Or a line of tanks and cannons and soldiers. Or a city. Or a country side, perhaps one sown with grain or orchards or corn."

The being was silent for the time it took for the white water to subside.

The immortal would not really take such public action against the militaries of the two countries. She would use subtler methods. But this threat was spectacular enough to make her threat persuasive.

"Now the carrot." As she spoke their bubble rose again and moved south. "From now on you two will share some of my health. You will be immune to sickness and feel and be strong and healthy. Should you get injured your pain will quickly subside to soreness and your wounds will heal very fast and leave only the faintest of scars behind.

"Further your health will infect those you touch. It is not a quick process; you have to touch them often. So your family and friends and useful strangers will become like you.

"But this beneficence has a price. By this Friday at 6:00 pm you must craft an agreement which will benefit your two countries equally, which also means be equally painful. If you cannot agree you two will suffer some debilitating illness, perhaps severe food poisoning. Severe enough that your task must be taken over by your deputies, whoever they may be."

Briand felt anger rise in him and fought it down. Miguel Azaña did not. He swore and named all the forces that made such an agreement impossible: his military and labor and the church and his own supporters.

The angel or demon listened patiently and Azaña eventually ran down. So did the egg that they were in: it arced down, passing over ocean onto land. Brian recognized the land: England. And coming up toward them: London with the serpentine Thames River running through it.

Nearer he made out the green rectangle of Hyde Park and a thousand feet to the east Buckingham Palace. Close to the park's southern edge was the French Embassy. Nearby were other embassies, among them Hungary, Germany, and Romania. The Spanish Embassy was a little further to the south.

None of those were their destination. It was one of the dozens of hotels in the area: The Belgravia. It was a dozen stories high, took up half of a city block.

The flat top of the edifice came up to them. It was covered in some whitish material and had a dozen squat round towers dotted about it.

They landed. The barely visible egg around them disappeared. They fell an inch or two, had to catch their balance as their shoes hit the surface, which could be seen to have a grainy appearance as if it embedded tiny stones.

Directly in front of them was a boxlike enclosure. The pale creature stepped forward and twisted a doorknob. Opening the door she descended into what Briand could see was an unlit stairwell.

He bowed to the Spanish president, motioning him to precede him. The man glared back but went ahead into the enclosure, his back stiff.

Briand descended after the others, holding on tightly to the pipe-like handhold beside the stair and stepping carefully as he traveled downwards. Even so he almost stumbled and fell when his shoe met the dim landing before the doorway into the top floor.

The Spanish president was mock-courteously holding the door open into the floor. Briand stepped onto a gold carpet and said, "Gracias."

The angel/demon was halfway down the corridor and Briand hurried a bit to catch up to her. On the way he passed a second corridor. Looking to left and right he could see that it stretched in both directions for a good distance.

The creature had stopped at a second cross corridor. The corridor they were in continued on for some distance.

"I've rented this floor for the four weeks of this month. One of you will have one half for it for your use, the other the other half. Follow me."

She turned into the cross corridor and proceeded to walk several dozen feet till she turned left into what seemed to be long narrow room. It was set up as a reception area with a desk near the wall opposite the door.

She motioned toward the corridor.

"As you can see there is another identical room opposite this one. Each of you will have these rooms as your reception areas. The phones in both these areas work. I want each of you to take possession of one half of this floor. Purely at random I've chosen this side to be French, the opposite side to be Spanish.

"You are now in command of the mission. I suggest you contact your embassies and get people over here to guard you and work for you. Get supplies, establish schedules, whatever. You are both capable administrators, and smart enough to get other administrators to handle details for you.

"Starting now you are in a race against each other, and against time. I will return Friday afternoon at 6:00 pm. If by then you do not have an agreement both of you will fall ill and replacements will take your places."

Azaña said, "I repeat now. You have given us an impossible task. Each of us has many forces we must respond to. Our military, labor, the church, the--"

"I understand that. I do not order you to do the impossible: come up with something everyone will accept. I ask only one act: come up with an agreement that serves your countries evenly. Nothing more. Just an agreement between the two of you."

Briand looked at the being intently, then turned to his opposite. Azaña was shaking his head. In acceptance, Briand thought, not in denial.

"Once that agreement is made it will be the job of others to make it work. Your job will be done. I remind you that you will feel, look, and be ten years younger. Immune to disease, resistant to hurt, and able to confer that reward on your wife and children and whoever else you value."

Briand thought of his mistress, an ambitious film actress who had reached the age of thirty and thus had begun the slow descent into (what French men thought) cronehood.

"Will my wife lose the same ten years you claim I will?"

The being might have read his mind. Or not. She said, "Everyone who comes in close contact with you for long periods of time."

Briand looked at Azaña speculatively. Then he turned and walked quickly to the reception desk bare of everything but a phone. He lifted the receiver and asked for a line to the French embassy.

While he waited he rounded the table and sat in the chair against the wall. Azaña was scurrying out of the door to his own, opposite, reception area. The faery being was gone.

<>

In Europe and elsewhere there was much happiness when the possibility of a war which might expand to engulf all Europe disappeared. And some unhappiness among those who profited from war. But not that much; there was always war and the possibility of war SOMEWHERE.

An unexpected development had happened as well. The two smart, ambitious men, perfectly healthy and enormously energetic in a second near youth, had somehow decided that they had been chosen for some great purpose. The angel had only been the immediate agent of some perhaps celestial authority.

They said nothing about her. Instead they claimed that they had long been in contact with each other and united in the understanding that the Latin countries were destined for a greater future. They had put out feelers to Portugal and Italy to join them in a borderless economic union. This New Roman Union, perhaps joined by speakers of the dozen or more other Romantic languages, would be an economic powerhouse.

Alice was amused by the way in which the two men had assuaged any feelings of victimization. She also saw that the Union might turn into some sort of expansionist entity requiring her to interfere again in European affairs.

Meanwhile Alice and many other people had something more immediate to concern them. Hurricane season had already delivered several strikes and near-strikes on the eastern seaboard. Now another hurricane was bearing down on the US. This one was approaching the Louisiana coast.

Alice was very young when Galveston, Texas, was hit by one of the worst hurricanes in American history. Thousands died, much property was destroyed. But s/he had experienced other watery disasters in her four hundred years of life. S/he began to prepare for yet another.

Even an immortal with nearly godlike powers could only do so much. One way was to prepare for the inevitable flooding of Louisiana's coastal cities and especially the largest, New Orleans.

Much of her waking time she spent designing a rescue vehicle for flooded areas. There would be many in New Orleans, as low as it was.

She named the vehicle the Skater. It was basically a big catamaran with two pairs of long floater legs which would lift it out of the water. In the disaster areas this would be important because there would be much debris in and just under the surface of the water. Ordinary boats, of which New Orleans had many, would have to sail very carefully lest the boatmen cease to be rescuers and came to need rescuing.

In this endeavor Alice was aided by Delphine Dodge's marine division of Dodge Automotive. They came up with a quick and dirty solution which could be made quickly and cheaply, billing it as a prototype to test production versions of the catamaran. It, funded by Alice with some money from Delphine, was soon being turned out in the dozens.

Or at least the parts were. They were designed to be sent by railroad to the Louisiana coast and assembled there.

It soon became clear that New Orleans would be near the center of Hurricane Hannah's arrival on the Louisiana coast. The manufacture of the parts was put on two shifts and the schedule sped up for the stockpiling of the parts in the city of Baton Rouge about 70 miles to the west and inland of New Orleans.

Alice and a crew of Dodge Marine Division workers traveled to New Orleans and began assembling Skaters. They were quickly renamed Skeeters by the locals employed to help assemble, test the vehicles, and prepare to drive them to the areas of New Orleans where they would be needed. This would be made easier because the Skeeters could float above highways and railroads and (if needed) any fairly level ground.

The process was soon well under way under the direction of Adam Boudreaux, a commander in the Louisiana Disaster Relief Agency.

Finally the day came when it became clear that the hurricane would indeed cross onto land near New Orleans. Many people abandoned their homes and moved further inland. Many did not.

Over three days the hurricane approached and crossed over onto land, pushing a flood of water ahead of it, then began to die away over land. As it receded the Louisiana Disaster Relief Agency moved into the New Orleans area. One of its resources were almost four dozen Skeeters which made the seventy mile trip to New Orleans under their own power, trailed by tankers of gasoline to fuel them and trucks carrying needed supplies such as tents and bedding and food.

In a strategic location the Skeeters landed to set up a camp. Crews of a half dozen each remained on each Skeeter. They cast off to find and rescue stranded people.

Ahead of them went Alice.

She had brought from Detroit a small disassembled catamaran. It was a single-seater vehicle though it had a cargo space which could hold a badly crowded dozen people. Its purpose was to act as a scout to find those who needed rescuing and their locations called in via short wave radio to large Skeeters to do the actual rescue.

It could travel up to a hundred and fifty miles per hour. The first time it took off from the camp it impressed everyone watching. Alice started the engine, lifted to four feet height, and shot like a rocket into the distance, wind following in her wake.

Watchers if there had been any further along her path would have been even more impressed. Out of sight of the camp the immortal expanded her egg around her and her vehicle and ascended rapidly to several miles height.

From there she could get an overall picture of the devastation. It was spread all throughout the New Orleans megaplex, which curved like a smile on the south shore of Lake Ponchartrain.

Undoubtedly the surroundings of the city were equally affected but the people in the less crowded areas would have to risk--and surely suffer--death and privation. The rescue effort, unhappily, would have to focus on rescuing the largest possible numbers.

Alice felt sorrow over that. But in four centuries of life the immortal had been forced to harden herself to tragedy.

She picked an area to the west of the center of the city and dove to find survivors in peril. It did not take long to find them.

The day wasted away as Alice and the crews aboard Skeeters swarmed the swamped and slowly draining landscape. Soon a trickle then a stream of refugees began to come into the camp. There they were treated for exposure and accident by doctors and nurses and an increasing number of volunteers, then housed in tents.

The rescuers in Skeeters worked into deep twilight till they had to cease work else they suffer disasters themselves. A few continued to work under the guidance of Alice. She seemed to be able to see in the dark. And of course could. She took her Skeeter up to ten feet, an engineering impossibility though no one knew that, and shined a powerful spotlight on people who needed help, some of them perching dangerously atop slanted roofs.

Even those few efforts had to cease nearing midnight. The big Skeeters retired to the camp. Behind them Alice worked alone. The being never tired and worked through the night, dropping supplies from her vehicle sometimes, taking aboard her small vessel small groups sometimes.

The relief agency was working to a plan. Inevitably experience revealed the shortcomings of the plan and it was adjusted then re-adjusted as needed. Part of the plan was for the rescue site to expand. It did so several times.

Alice continued to work on, every few hours stopping at the base camp to eat a huge meal, nap briefly, and then return to work.

A second base camp was set up to the east of New Orleans. Two of Texas Aviation's Condors brought Skeeters and personnel and supplies from Detroit to Louisiana to set it up. Then they traveled elsewhere to pick up supplies and people to further build up the base. Being able to land and takeoff from almost any flat surface was a big help.

As the days passed Alice rarely stopped working. She would eat then nap for a few hours then return to her Skeeter.

Stories began to circulate about her. Once when someone fell off a house into water Alice dove into the water to pull her out and then into her Skeeter. Once she parked her Skeeter in the air near a tree and jumped into the tree to rescue a cat, then jumped back into the vehicle.

Those who traveled with her at night swore that her Skeeter went higher than a few feet and flew much faster than it was seen to do during the day. This was debunked; the Skeeter had a wraparound windshield but that would not protect riders from such much faster speeds. In fact, the debunkers said, didn't the reporters claim that there was NO buffeting wind during those mythical flights?

Another even more fantastical story went around. Alice had many times proven able to heal people's hurts by laying hands on them. This was taken to be yet more of people's need for miracles in the midst of monumental tragedy.

The debunkers were ignored. People started to call Alice The Redheaded Angel. And The Angel of New Orleans. And finally just The Angel.

Alice ignored the stories and continued working. Soon she was joined by three other small Skeeters, quickly dubbed Scouts. Pilots were assigned to them and they joined Alice in finding people in need.

Three weeks after Hurricane Hannah hit New Orleans the biggest push of the rescue of the city slowed to routine. At some point, no one knew just when, Alice disappeared. She turned up a day later back in Austin. She was said to be working on a new project.

Chapter 16 - Space

The devastation wrought by Hurricane Hannah had exposed the limitations of weather observations. Alice was convinced that if the US had become aware of the oncoming hurricane and its path much earlier the country would have been much better prepared to deal with it.

Or maybe not, her friend Albert Moseley said during one of her visits to his home in Austin. She and Albert were sitting in rocking chairs on his front porch watching the clouds to the west which were displaying the gold and red of the dying of the day.

"Government officials only look to their next election. They've not interested in long-term problems. And especially not interested in spending money to deal with those problems."

Alice was distracted by Robert, Albert and Julia's son, who was sitting in her lap. He had just pulled on her hair.

"Peepee," he said, and struggled to get down from her lap. She let him climb down, one hand poised over him in case he had problems. He did not.

Julia, coming onto the porch just now, had seen what was happening. She was never very far away from Robert. She was very visibly pregnant. The baby would be a girl, Alice knew, but she'd said nothing.

"'Ats a good boy," she said. "Come to Mommy."

Robert did so but did not put up his arms to be picked up. Instead he said, very firmly, "Peepee" and set off around her to journey to the bathroom.

Julia smiled at her husband and Alice and turned to trail after her son.

"Got a mind of his own," said Alice with a smile. Then she returned to their discussion.

"I'm thinking of proposing the government establish a weather observation service that sends planes into the Caribbean during hurricane season to give us better warning of hurricanes and to track their paths."

"There's a better idea. Put a satellite in space with telescopes and cameras to observe weather patterns and send down visuals. There's a fellow named Tsiolkovsky in the Russian Federation that's written a book about that."

Alice had heard the name but could not remember when or where.

"Quite a thinker, the Russky. I've read all his books or summaries of his books. He posits a lot of the ideas that come up in science fiction. In fact, I think he may be the source of them.

"Poor fellow. He's in Paris being treated for cancer. I suspect he's not long for this world."

"Oh?"

"A great loss it will be when he passes. Would you like me to loan you his books?"

"I'd like that."

For most of the next week Alice read all the books Albert had given her, then she read more widely about the use of rockets to travel in space. She especially wanted to know who else were thinking similar thoughts.

Then one day she took to space, arced over toward France, and descended into Paris. She located the hospital where Tsiolkovsky was recovering from his latest cancer surgery and entered by way of the top floor.

She took on the appearance of a grey-haired aged nurse or nurse supervisor and found where the fresh sanitation gowns were stored. Donning one, she asked a hurrying orderly where "the Russian" was. In a hurry the man barely glanced at her.

It was about 3:00 at night when she quietly entered Tsiolkovsky's room and locked the door. She removed the gown and changed her appearance to that of a Chinese lady of middle years but who had light African black skin color. Her clothing was a light blue long sleeved high-collared tunic over pants of a matching color, an ensemble which looked vaguely like a uniform. Her grey hair faded to black and arranged itself into a bun.

She walked to one side of Tsiolkovsky's hospital bed and touched his nearest hand. Into it she injected a flood of the same shapechanger genes that gave her perfect health. Over the next half hour or so they migrated into every cell in his body then began working.

After about forty minutes the Russian's body dissolved sleep away as he became modestly healthy on his way to robust health. He began to wake up.

The first thing he saw when he opened his eyes was a stranger sitting relaxed in a chair near his bed.

"Who are you?" he said in Russian.

Alice's Russian was nearly two centuries rusty. She replied in French which she knew he knew.

"I am a doctor though one educated in a place far away. I've injected you with a cure for your cancer. I imagine you can feel it working already."

He stared at her, taking in her quasi-Oriental face and costume somewhat resembling a uniform which might be worn in a foreign country's hospital.

He spoke, having to clear his throat first.

"I feel something. It might be a deadly drug that gives a feeling of euphoria."

The alien smiled. "Yes. That's true. I guess you'll just have to wait and see what happens."

He struggled to sit up in his bed. Alice stood and helped, plumping up his pillows to give him better support. She then sat down again.

He had gotten a better look at her. He said, "You're not Chinese, are you? You have something of their look."

"I am a mixture of all the races you know and of several more that don't exist on this planet. You see, Academician Tsiolkovsky, you are right. Life does exist on other planets. I am from a place thousands of light years away."

Alice had continued over the years to have those not-dreams which seemed to be memories or fragments of them which had led to her ability to fly. By now she had pieced together a sketchy vision of the people and other life forms living elsewhere in the Galaxy. She suspected that her powers were inherited somehow from visitors to Earth by alien creatures.

He was inspecting her very closely. He tried to speak again but his voice was husky. He turned to the bedside table upon which a plastique pitcher of water sat. Alice quickly forestalled any further efforts by pouring half a glass of water and handing it to him.

He drank a swallow and said, "Thank you. It's amazing. I felt no pain, no soreness, not even weakness, when I moved. Thank you for my life."

"You were pretty far gone. Your surgeries did almost as much damage to you as your illness. But you are free of it now and it will never recur. Nor will any illness afflict you from now on."

"Why did you do this?"

"You are a mind too important to let die early."

In particular Alice wanted his future contributions to space travel but would not say that lest it interfere with that purpose.

"I'm flattered. Though..." He got a faraway look in his eyes. "I suppose I have contributed in small ways to bettering the human race."

He appeared pleased at the idea. Alice hid a smile. This was not a modest man.

"Don't get overly ambitious, Konstantin. You will be weak for many days to come. Your beard and hair will fall out and then regrow. Your skin will become more youthful. But don't think you are immortal now. You can still die from stepping off a city curb too soon. Or get stabbed to death by a jealous husband."

He snorted a laugh at that. Looking closely at her he said, "I see it's true. Miscegenation of the races does make a more attractive race eventually. And no doubt many more superior abilities than any one race alone."

Ahh! So Tsiolkovsky believed in those idiotic eugenics theories. She kept her mouth shut. It would take too much effort to reform his ideas, or even to soften them.

The door knob rattled. Someone was trying to get in.

"Goodbye, Konstantin. Live well."

"Wait--!"

But Alice had already pulled her egg about her and instructed it to hide her. As she floated toward the door her image faded. By the time she unlocked the door and stood aside to let in a nurse she was an almost invisible blur.

Then she was gone.

<>

As the immortal learned more about space travel the more she realized what a big undertaking it would be. Entire technological fields would have to be improved or even invented. Armies of people would have to be mobilized. Millions of dollars would have to be spent.

She herself could contribute a few million but more would be needed. She had to get some of those short-sighted politicians involved.

She also had to get more minds involved. One group of them was in Pasadena, California, in the California Institute of Science and Technology. A professor named von Karman and some of his associates and students were experimenting with rockets. These were fired off in the Arroyo Seco, a mostly dry stream bed near the world famous Rose Bowl stadium.

Alice designed a satellite launch vehicle. It would have two parts.

The largest would be a piloted vehicle which would go to 100,000 feet where the air pressure was one percent of air at ground level. It would then drop a rocket that would go the rest of the way into orbit.

Crucial to getting a jet able to fly that high would be the design of the jet engine. The higher a plane went there was less air resistance to its motion, a plus. But there was less air to give the jet engine thrust, a minus. Alice tried a number of approaches to improve the efficiency of jet engines at higher altitudes.

One approach produced contradictory results. That engine seemed to produce MORE thrust the higher it went rather than less. She ran several tests at higher and higher altitudes and continued getting those results. At 100,000 feet the odd engine was most efficient.

Alice puzzled over the engine's modifications and made slight modifications to it. Some lessened the effect, some amplified it.

It seemed that inside the volume of space affected by the induced magnetism projector phantom air was created. It could be pulled into the engine and pushed out of it, producing thrust. Outside the projector's field the phantom air reverted to empty space.

So far the high-altitude tests had been made on a small drone vehicle that took it far out over the ocean where it exploded and its fragments dropped into the water--hopefully not falling onto some hapless ship.

Quite aside from the ethics of such an approach each expensive drone was lost. So was any data that it could have collected.

Texas Aviation had introduced the SuperSwift, a newer model of the Swift, larger and with a longer range. It did not obsolesce the older model but sales of the older model dropped. Alice took over the oldest of them for her research. She replaced the two engines with her new experimental engines and tested the aircraft out at lower altitudes. The engines still worked as desired. Then she went higher and higher still.

At the highest altitudes the cabin pressurization began to fail. This was good in one way. In fixing those problems Texas Aviation was able to use the lessons learned on its other aircraft and advertise them as capable of higher flight.

Finally Alice took the experimental aircraft to 100,000 feet but not under its own power. The air was too rarefied to support the gasoline engine powering the electrical generator which powered the jet engines. The aircraft was just within her egg's ability to carry it. She went from 5,000 feet to 100,000 feet at several thousand miles per hour.

Cabin pressurization showed no signs of failure when Alice let her egg release the craft. Not that even total failure would be a problem for her. She could always draw her egg back around her again. But the successful pressurization of cabins was important to the future of Texas Aviation.

She checked the charge on the battery that supplied power to the jet engines and the rest of the Swift. It was nearly 95%, having been continuously charged at lower altitudes. That left her a comfortable margin.

She slowly increased her height to 110, 000 feet, then higher still. She noted several problems. With the ever thinner air the control surfaces were less effective. She also sensed that radiation normally blocked by air was increasing. Any true space vehicle would have to take those effects into account.

That was fine. Weather satellites would be unmanned. But it was something to keep in mind for when it came time for people to leave the bounds of Earth behind.

The power level was still well over 85%. She said to heck with it. She tilted the nose of the Swift upward and accelerated.

At a hundred miles the sky was black. The Earth was noticeably round and blue. White dots of clouds made tiny pastures of sheep above the blue, and white crescents of clouds revealed weather fronts. The Swift was slowly rotating in two axes, giving Alice views of both sky and Earth outside the windows.

The immortal again expanded her egg outside her skin and into the airplane. S/he became one with it, its body HER body. Its senses became HER senses.

SHE took hold of the space/time/universe and oriented HER airplane so that down was under HER craft and stayed there. SHE was floating out over the ocean off the Texas coast.

SHE looked to see just what was below HER and saw Cuba a bit to the south. SHE pivoted to face back the way SHE'd come and began to return home.

<>

At the next Monday morning Texas Aviation board meeting when the meeting took up New Business Alice plopped onto the table three copies of a report. It was titled HIGH ALTITUDE JET ENGINE STUDY. She shoved two copies toward her partners.

They glanced at the cover of the thin document. Louis Delacroix opened it and scanned the table of contents. Llwellen Porter just looked at her and waited for comments from Delacroix, the leader of the business meetings.

"So, you've finished your study. Give us a 25-word summary." He did not really mean exactly 25 words, just a brief statement.

"I made a discovery that's going to revolutionize high altitude air travel. We can now go so high that we can leave the atmosphere. Maybe even go to the Moon." Or Mars or Venus or to the asteroids, though she didn't say that.

"She-it," said Porter. "You're not joking, are you? What is this great discovery?"

"Read the report. It's Part 5. Just look at the abstract."

Both partners turned pages of the report. Delacroix just read the abstract. Porter, the engineer, read that and began to skim how she'd discovered "phantom air" and how it could be used as propulsion fluid in a jet engine.

The Frenchman, attuned to selling rather than engineering, said, "We've got to change the name. 'Phantom air' doesn't cut it. Think of some fancy term that will impress people."

Porter said, putting the report down, "Some term nobody will understand, he means."

Alice paused to think, said, "'Virtual...matter.'"

Porter gave a hand clap that turned into a two-gun finger point at Alice. Then he said, "So where does this, ah, virtual matter come from? And where does it go? Are we going to be spraying it out of the engine? That would really get us into trouble with the 'be kind to nature' folks."

"My theory is that space isn't really empty. It's actually made up of some undiscovered quantum particle. Which only shows up under the induced-magnetism field. When it leaves the field it reverts to it original state."

She paused to reconsider her statement.

"Or I think so. We really need some quantum physicists to look into that."

<>

To research virtual matter Alice first considered the colleges and universities closest to home, such as Austin University and Rice University in Houston. She soon looked further, mostly the East Coast.

She rejected the pre-eminent Harvard and Yale Universities as they hired no Jewish professors, a big consideration as many of the best minds in physics were European Jews. Princeton did hire such thinkers, such as the Relativity theorist Albert Einstein, but only in the Institute for Advanced Study. Though housed on the Princeton campus, it was a separate institution.

On the West Coast Alice considered the University of California in Berkeley and Stanford University in Stanford, California. In the Los Angeles area she considered the University of California at LA, the University of Southern California, and the California Institute of Science and Technology in Pasadena. She also considered the University of California San Diego.

CalSci interested her most. Though small it was an internationally known research university especially in physics. Its president was Robert A. Millikan, a Nobel Prize winning physicist, and it had faculty from all over the globe, including Russia, China, Nigeria, and Argentina. It certainly had no prejudice against Jews. Visiting faculty had included Einstein and several other Jews.

CalSci also interested her because of its professor Theodore von Karman. He was the director of the Guggenheim Aeronautical Laboratory. GAL-CalSci had built one of the first wind tunnels in the country and was studying rockets.

Accordingly, Alice sent letters to Robert Millikan, the President of CalSci, and von Karman, the director of GAL-CalSci. She also wrote a letter to Donald W. Douglas Sr. He was the founder and head of the Douglas Aircraft Company headquartered in Santa Monica. The campus and manufacturing facility was about two miles from the Pacific. Texas Aviation had a contract to help upgrade their famous DC-3 passenger and cargo airplane. Douglas wanted to add floater landing gear and replace its two propeller-driven engines with jet engines.

She had received replies from all three asking her to visit them at her earliest convenience. So on the week after the 4th of July in 1939 she did so.

<>

Josephine von Karman spoke to her older brother, Theodore von Karman, and pointed at a futuristic looking silver aircraft coming in to land. "That must be her. I can see why they call it a Swift."

They and a dozen others from CalSci were at the LA area's

principle airport, Glendale International Airport in Glendale, California, the city just west of Pasadena. They were to meet Alice Willoughby.

As it neared them they could see that rather than riding on wheels it was a dozen feet above the runway riding on air coming from the bottom of the two jet engines at its waist. Nearer still and lower still it began floating on an induced-magnetism field. The loud hissing of its jet engines died away.

"Todor, isn't it beautiful?"

Her brother said, "Pipo, it is. And not just outside. It is a technical marvel inside."

They watched as the aircraft left the runway for the taxiway in front of the Visitor's Center and the long stretch of hangars to the left and right of the center. It stopped near the Center for several minutes. Then the door in its side folded out and down to become stairs.

From the darkness inside the plane came a woman with long bright curly red hair. She had a slender feminine figure and wore blue jean pants with worn lighter patches at its knees, a blue-and-white checked flannel blouse, and a blue jean jacket over the blouse. On her feet (Josephine squinted to get a better look) she wore brown cowboy boots.

Jo laughed. "She's certainly dressed for comfort!"

Todo said, "She's rich. The rich can wear whatever they please." He was not being critical. Though he was formally dressed in a suit and tie, as was his entourage, he was well-known for swapping formality for comfort.

Jo nodded. She well knew the social signaling of people's clothes. She herself wore a mid-ankle dark-blue dress fashionably cut and low-heeled ankle boots. Her long blond hair hung over her shoulders in a riot of curls. She was a bit sturdier than was currently popular but few would notice that. She shared the same elegant facial features as those of a currently acclaimed Hollywood movie star born in Hungary.

The visitor directed a couple of orange-uniformed workers to remove some luggage from the airplane's cargo hold and then set off for the Visitors' Center trailed by the luggage handlers.

Just inside the glass doors of the center waited the von Karman party. One of the students in the entourage held up a big white piece of cardboard blazoned with the text DR WILLOUGHBY.

Alice Willoughby smiled and headed toward the von Karmans.

The professor stepped forward and held out a hand for his visitor to shake. She did so, letting herself be drawn closer for an air kiss near each cheek. Then Jo joined the two and the two women went through the same routine.

The von Karmans did not introduce the dozen or so people with them, intending to do that later and better when they arrived at their house. Alice would be staying there during the time she'd be on the West Coast.

Josephine "Pipo" von Karman and her brother led Alice to a late-model car and drove several blocks to enter one of the freeways for which the LA area was famous. It took some twenty minutes to reach Pasadena traveling at speeds exceeding sixty miles per hour, a speed limit every driver seemed to consider a quaint suggestion. The von Karmans said little, leaving Alice free to eye the hills rising up to their left and the valley falling away to the right and below the freeway. The immortal could also see the towers of downtown LA ten miles away.

The home was a rambling Spanish-style house in a tree-shaded neighborhood with a huge dining and living room. In it the von Karmans' mother Helen met them in the kitchen where she was cooking up a big Hungarian meal. Alice's mouth watered as she smelled cabbage seasoned with spicy red paprika and the subtler smell of goulash.

Already waiting were several other students and professors and others besides the ones who'd followed "Pipo's car" to the house. Each was eager to meet the celebrity but most were courteous enough (or shy enough) to retire from her company, leaving her with the von Karmans in the kitchen.

Pipo helped her mother with the cooking. Shortly Alice and the professor retired to the large dining room between the kitchen and the equally large living room where most of the guests sat and stood. Alice recognized scraps of speech in Hungarian, German, and French as well as English. She also heard Spanish. Pipo spoke it to the Mexican maid who apparently was a fixture at the von Karman house. She was as fluent in that language as the Hungarian she spoke with her mother.

Alice commented on that fluency.

"Oh, yes, she's a natural linguist, speaks at least a dozen languages as if born to them."

The two of them settled at the big oak dining room table. Shortly they were served with iced tea by the maid, Emilia. Alice spoke to the woman and the two exchanged rapid-fire remarks.

"I see you are also a linguist," said Todor as he had insisted she call him.

"Yes. I even speak Chinese, the Bei-Ping kind which Westerners call Mandarin."

"You said in your letter that you wanted my help with fluid vortices and quantum physics."

"I want your help in anything to do with space travel. My time helping out with hurricane relief convinced me we need weather-observation satellites badly."

"That's quite ambitious. Most of the research I know of is more earth bound, rocket assists on take off and the like. I'll be glad to contribute my time but, at the risk of sounding mercenary, I think you would also do well to contract with the company I started with a few friends."

"Aerojet. I know. I've figured it into my plans."

"Your facility with Chinese would be helpful. One of our employees is a talented young fellow who has taken my studies of vortices further than I could."

Todor turned his head. "He just arrived." He raised his voice. "Bo! Bo! In here!"

Into the room came a very young man, apparent to the shapechanger's eyes as barely out of his teenage years. He was wearing Western clothing: jeans, red tee-shirt under a blue jean jacket, and running shoes.

"Boss?"

"I keep asking you to call me Todor!"

"And I keep listening to you with great respect." He was grinning.

Sighing, Todor said, "Alice, may I present to you Liu Bo-Hai? Bo, this is Dr. Alice Willoughby."

Interestedly the Hungarian managed to get the Chinese accents of his young employee's name right and his name in the right order, family name first.

Alice stood and bowed with the inclination of an older person to a younger. Bo answered with the style of younger to an elder.

Alice said in Mandarin, "It is with great pleasure that I meet you. May your family prosper and you never grow hungry."

Bo showed no surprise though Alice saw it. That and great respect.

"I am also pleased and wish that you never grow hungry."

The man's intonations suggested that he'd grown up speaking the Hakka dialect rather than that of the Mandarin, or Bei-Ping, dialect. She resisted her impulse to switch to that dialect. It was just barely believable that a "big nose" would speak Mandarin, but not the minority Hakka dialect.

"Sit," said Todor. "We were about to talk about the reason Dr. Willoughby is here."

"First I must pay respects to your honorable mother and sister."

Von Karman waved the man toward the kitchen and he left in that direction.

Bo came back with a saucer holding a cup of hot tea and sat. Todor asked Alice to repeat the reason for her visit.

"Bo--if I may be informal--I am planning to design vehicles to put satellites into orbit using a radical new engine. That's where Dr. von Karman and you come in."

Their conversation was soon interrupted when von Karman's mother Helen announced that it was time to eat. She did so with a meaningful look at her son, who instantly ceased talking about more than everyday matters.

The big heavy table was quickly populated by other guests. Those not so quick were nevertheless served or allowed to serve themselves and retire to the living room to dine.

Much of the conversation focused on Alice. Her actions at New Orleans had been widely reported, but many of von Karman's regular guests already knew much about her work at Texas Aviation. One even recalled to the others her actions in the Mexican Border Conflict.

Alice had no modesty and no compunction about using celebrity to further her projects. Foremost among those projects right now was her weather-satellite space program.

She did support Helen von Karman's desire to eliminate work talk from dining by telling everyone that she'd refuse to answer any questions until after eating.

Even then she refused to talk about "work," for she joined all the women in cleaning up the dining table and the kitchen and washing up. She recognized that these activities were less a reinforcement of the idea of women as servants and more of a female bonding ritual.

Talk in the kitchen revolved mostly about who was making and breaking romantic attachments and about mundane matters such as shopping and homemaking. Alice had little to say until the topic turned to fashion. She was asked about how being a "Texas Girl" affected fashion, being an icon of that style in Austin and even having a fashion line named after her.

Finally she was settled in the living room on a couch beside von Karman and she was able to encourage discussions of space travel. In the next couple of hours the conversation veered into many aspects of it from technical to general.

Alice said little. She was more interested in finding out who there might be useful in furthering her weather-satellite project. There were a fair number there, among them three women students. CalSci had recently become a coed college, a radical move no other institution of higher education had taken in the US. The first female graduating class was only eleven. The number of female professors was one: Dr. Mary Adler, a mathematical genius.

The crowd shrank as those left who'd come for Helen's cooking rather than Alice's presence. Within an hour there were left only von Karman, thirteen students, and the very young professor: Adler.

Von Karman had rarely spoken up, being content to listen to others. Now he roused himself.

"You spoke earlier about getting my help with your weather satellite project. I would like to do that within the context of my new company, Aerojet. Not so much to make money--though I'm hardly averse to that--but to provide a structure and aid for my efforts. The company can provide that."

"That seems reasonable to me."

"Very well. Let's go to the dining room table. It will be much more convenient to do business there."

The heavy oak table had been cleared, well wiped down, and gleamed discreetly under the electric lights and sunlight from the midafternoon sun coming in through the windows. They all found seats, the professor at the head of the table and Alice at the other end. Josephine sat to her brother's right and the rest found other seats. They almost filled the table with one empty seat to Alice's right.

Alice began further talks by requesting everyone sign a non-disclosure agreement. She got up and retrieved the briefcase that she had left in the kitchen when she'd arrived. From it she took a folder and gave it to von Karman.

Opening it he saw a piece of typing paper. It had a heading in large letters.

NON-DISCLOSURE AGREEMENT
HIGH-ALTITUDE ENGINE AND DERIVATIVES STUDY
Abbreviations: HiD or colloquially Heidi

Below that were several paragraphs of legalese and spots to sign and date the signature. He read it over carefully and signed it. Alice then signed in the Witness area.

Josephine von Karman had been reading the document. She took it from him and finished reading it. Done, she gave the folder and NDA back to Alice.

Alice and von Karman signed and dated a second copy of the NDA. She gave it to the professor.

The professor said, "As it happens, those of us here are the people who make up Aerojet. Before we go further everyone also needs to sign non-disclosure agreements."

"I came prepared," said Alice. She took more NDAs from her briefcase and gave two to each of those in the living room. Josephine gave an explanation of her presence as she took hers.

"I'm the secretary-treasurer of the company. Eventually we'll get a professional for the treasurer office, but for now I'm it."

It took several minutes for everyone to sign and date their NDAs (one for Alice and one for themselves). Then Alice spoke.

"Originally I envisioned a vehicle to take weather satellites into orbit made of two stages. The first stage would be an aircraft powered by induced-magnetism jet engines. It would carry a second stage powered by a rocket engine for travel into the vacuum of space.

"But I made an accidental discovery as I experimented with jet engines that would work at high altitudes. One engine gave results that astounded me."

She paused.

"It worked BETTER the higher the aircraft went, the opposite of what we'd expect, given that there is less air to pull into and push out of the engine."

She looked around the room. Josephine merely looked alert. The rest were frowning, had eyes narrowed in thought, or were skeptical.

"I know. I was doubtful too. I recalculated everything. I re-checked the engines.

"I could find nothing wrong. I put the tests aside. Then came back when I'd had some mental distance from the work. Still could not find an error.

"Lastly I took a plane to 100,000 feet which was powered by the anomalous engine. Air pressure there is one percent of sea level. The plane worked perfectly. Ladies and gentlemen, I think we have an engine which will work in vacuum."

Half the table registered doubt, including Dr. Mary Adler. The other half showed amazement. This included Bo, who spoke up.

"You went that high? That is surely a record. Did you tell anybody of this feat?"

"No. By now I was fairly sure of the results. If true, this could be enormously valuable. I didn't want to complicate the process of putting the effect into use in our aircraft."

"You should patent it. Immediately."

"I already filed a patent application. We routinely do that at Texas Aviation, so we've streamlined the process."

"Good."

"Now that you are covered by NDAs I can tell you that we, Texas Aviation, have established a group we call the Texas Aviation High-Altitude Division. We plan to use this engine in passenger and cargo aircraft and retrofit it in some of our older ones.

"We have not publicized another side of the division. We plan to make spaceplanes which can function both on and off this planet."

Josephine and Todor von Karman were smiling at Alice. Von Karman said, "Now it's your turn to sign a non-disclosure agreement. Will you?"

"To keep Aerojet's secrets, certainly."

Josephine got up and returned shortly with a folder containing two non-disclosure agreements. Von Karman and Alice cosigned them, each keeping one copy.

Von Karman said, "Good. Now I can tell you that we at Aerojet have leased an area at Douglas Aircraft Company in Santa Monica so that our high-performance rockets fall into the ocean. They land by parachute and have a flotation package that lets us pick them up if we can locate them. We are usually able to do so as the radio beacon in them is fairly powerful. Only once have we had a failure to recover the high-altitude photographs taken automatically aboard the rocket.

"We planned to build rockets to launch balloons to radio back weather information. Now it looks as if we might, if Texas Aviation agrees to let us use your more capable engines, launch weather observation vehicles much higher. Possibly even into orbit."

Alice said, "I'm here at CalSci because I don't understand how these, what I call space jet, engines work. Or, for that matter, the air jet engines. I want to better understand the abilities and possible dangers of using induced magnetism in products such as the jets.

"I suspect quantum mechanical effects, a subject of which I have very little understanding."

She went on to say that, in exchange for the scientific studies she desired Aerojet to perform, the company would be allowed to use the space jet to create vehicles. That is, as long as they did not create manned vehicles. That capability Texas Aviation wanted to keep for itself.

To that limitation von Karman and crew had no objection. They had no ability or desire to create the sort of vehicles needed to support human pilots and passengers.

The next few hours were spent discussing details of very-high-altitude and orbital flight. The discussions were wide ranging.

Alice had traveled to the Moon out of curiosity about the body and encountered several types of radiation and magnetic plasma. They could not harm her in her egg but the egg did let her sense them. She presented her knowledge but referred to it as a guess.

Adler, based on topics mentioned in Tsiolkovsky's papers, had done mathematical analyses of the types of orbits satellites could follow. One type of orbit was especially interesting. The higher a satellite went the more time it took to circle the Earth. At about 22,300 miles up it took a full day. As this matched the time the Earth took to revolve, the satellite would stay over the same spot on the Earth below.

This triggered much discussion of the possible uses of such "geosynchronous" satellites. Someone pointed out that three radio transceivers positioned equally around Earth could form the basis of a global communication network.

Bo said, "It could also photograph the Earth below, save the images on temporary data storage, and send a copy of them to a ground base. That would support Alice's weather observation function. But it could support much more. We might observe color changes in crops and changes in river paths and...and lots more."

That set off a new discussion: of what kinds of equipment to pack into the satellite: cameras, data storage, communications, and more.

Such as: How to keep the satellite and so its camera pointed in the right direction and orientation.

At one point Mary Adler broke into the discussion. She was seventeen and a small blonde, yet everyone instantly shut up. She was not only a professor but had won several prestigious mathematical awards and was widely recognized as a giant intellect.

"I've found that when solving a problem one should break it up into its parts and see if we need to add a missing part. Or if we can subtract one part.

"That second possibility is the case in this discussion. We're assuming that all the parts of the system must be on the satellite. This is not so. We need no onboard memory to store images. We can simply beam the images to the ground as the camera takes them and store the images there. This way there is no delay saving them to memory on the satellite and more delay retrieving them. Nor does the satellite have to be so heavy, having no memory storage to carry into orbit."

Bo smiled and said, "That's what I get for being so persuasive. Everyone instantly assumed the system I described was the right way to accomplish the mission."

At that point Helen came into the room and said that she needed the table. She was about to start cooking dinner and wanted to set the table for dinner. She also wanted to know how many of those at the table would be staying for the meal.

Dr. von Karman said, "This sounds like a good time to end this board meeting." He called for a vote and got a unanimous one for adjournment.

All but one of the Aerojet people stayed for dinner, which seemed to be as usual. From the dinner conversation it had become clear to her that they all pretty much considered themselves family.

When the leisurely dinner was over the women, including Alice and Adler, made fast work of washing up. The process was aided by several of the men helping remove eating ware from the table to the kitchen.

Most everyone settled in the living room except a few who went outside for a smoke. Mother von Karman would not abide smoking inside the house. Several had after-dinner drinks, coffee or tea and cream and sugar supplied by the von Karmans. Some also had alcoholic drinks which Mother von Karman insisted they bring. The house alcoholic beverages were only for the family. Honored guests were an exception. Alice was offered and accepted a glass of chilled Hungarian white wine.

The first topic brought up was actually the continuation of one begun during dinner. This was the recent visit by Josephine to a Hollywood studio where Hungarian émigré Bela Lugosi was acting in a film.

Mary Adler, who seemed to be close to the older woman, teased "Jo" about being sweet on him. Josephine conceded that he was quite handsome when he wasn't made up to look like a vampire or some other monster, but that was the extent of it. What man would look at her when he was surrounded by glamorous starlets all the time?

The conversation ranged widely, not just about scientific subjects. CalSci had a football team which was edging up in its wins and several of the students were fierce and hopeful fans. Nearby Hollywood being the center of the movie industry plenty of people at CalSci had opinions about or even connections to the movie industry. The recent advent of the first color film, "The Wizard of Oz," heralded a new era in film-making according to some.

About one scientific subject Alice had something to say: life on other planets. She had continued having "dreams" which were really memories about life in the larger universe. They were short, sometimes mere fragments, but years of them had slowly built up a consistent picture.

"I've been reading everything I can get about travel into space, especially the works of the Russian Konstantin Tsiolkovsky. He recently published a book about this very subject. Has anyone here read it?"

Dr. von Karman said, "It's on my list of books to read as soon as I find time, but no."

After the Russian's surprising recovery from his cancer and the surgery to remove it he had switched from physical and mathematical studies to chemistry and biology. Alice could not guess whether it had happened because of his illness or because of his miraculous cure by a woman who claimed to be an alien from another planet. He had published a series of papers in Russian and French about the possibility of life on other planets. Recently they'd been collected into a book. Alice had the French version.

"The first part describes how life arose on Earth. He says that the right conditions were a large ocean into which all sorts of chemicals washed into them and were dissolved. There the water was struck by lightning and bathed in ultraviolet light from the sun. This made them combine chemically in various ways.

"Only some ways are possible. There are eight involving hydrogen and oxygen: HO and HOO are two. H2O and H2O2, water and hydrogen peroxide, are two more. Very rare are H2O3 through H2O5. Finally there is H3O.

"That's it. No other combinations of hydrogen and oxygen are possible. And of all those possible only a few survive for more than microseconds, mostly water and peroxide."

She looked at the dozen people surrounding her. All were used to complex scientific thinking and were very focused on her.

"The situation is the same with most other combinations of different elements. Few of them survive long. So the evolution of more complex molecules follows only a few limited paths."

Josephine stood up from her seat and gestured with a bottle of the white wine. Alice nodded and let the woman top off her wine glass.

"Carbon atoms are especially important because they are tetravalent. They thus can form long chains and circles and spirals of carbon atoms with various other elements attached at various points. These compounds are very important to living things, so much so that carbon chemistry is called 'organic' chemistry, chemistry of life.

"In other words, planets in the warm zone about stars with lots of liquid will almost inevitably 'grow' lots of organic molecules. A tiny but substantial fraction of those are likely to evolve into living things."

A young man with Italianate good looks said, "But there are very few such worlds, from what little we know about stars outside our solar system. But--"

He held up a hand as if to stave off objections, when it was only he who had brought up the subject of rarity.

"There are maybe a hundred million stars in our galaxy. And there seem to be many clusters of galaxies, maybe billions. So Yes, I agree that life must exist many times over in all that space."

"And all time," put in another student. "The universe is several billion years old."

A third put in, "In fact, life may have appeared many times and disappeared too."

The discussion of space travel and life in space became general after that. Alice stayed fairly quiet.

At about 10 pm the party broke up, helped along by Josephine who insisted that her brother and she had to get up early. Jo made sure that Alice was comfortable in the von Karmans' guest room and wished her Good night.

<>

The next morning, after a substantial breakfast made by Mother von Karman, von Karman bicycled himself to work and Josephine drove Alice to CalSci. There Josephine introduced Alice to Robert Millikan, the President of CalSci.

The two chatted for a time and then he took her a short distance to the Athenaeum, a faculty club and private social club with a restaurant and a few private suites for visiting guests. There a reception was held for Alice. It was attended by a large fraction of the faculty and professional staff.

A good many people wanted to talk to Alice, a few blatantly trolling for research grants from a very rich woman. More just treated the time as a general social event and only said Hello to Alice and, duty done, left for more interesting companions.

Professors von Karman and Mary Adler were at the reception but let others have their turn at the celebrity. When those who'd wanted to meet the immortal had done so Mary moved to speak to her. One man near Alice took a seemingly random step to block the young woman's approach. The shapechanger casually but inexorably moved him aside to greet the young woman.

"Dr. Adler I presume? I've so much wanted to meet you. How are you finding the West Coast after growing up in Florida?"

Mary ignored the byplay with the man and said, "I much appreciate the dry air and the fact that it gets cool when the sun goes down. I'm less happy about the fire and earthquake danger."

Alice laughed. "I've yet to experience either. I suppose I'll continue being a 'snowflake' until I've done so."

As the unhappily displaced man moved away Alice said in a lowered voice, "I hope I haven't gotten you in trouble with him."

"Cartwright? Not any more than usual and I've had plenty of practice handling the like."

They continued chatting until a fresh person showed up to greet Alice then Mary faded into the background again.

At the end of the reception von Karman approached and spirited Alice away to the professor's office. There they began the legal work of formalizing and finalizing their business relationship. This would eventually take more than a week until all details were nailed down and agreed upon, mostly by an Austin legal firm and a Pasadena legal firm.

Los Angeles Chronicle
All the News of the SoCal Heartland
Sunday Edition - Lifestyles Section
(Lyle Everard I COLUMNIST)

Meeting Alice Willoughby for the first time can be disconcerting. She looks like a teen cheerleader playing dress-up in her mother's fashionable outfits.

Yet she has the utter confidence of the powerful and very rich woman that she is. You soon become convinced that she is a force of nature. If she walks toward you your instinct is to step aside hoping she gives you a nod in passing.

This reporter had the privilege a few days ago of joining a group of possible investors on a flight to show off the newest airplane in the Texas Aviation stable of aircraft: the SuperSwift.

Like all of the Swift line it is a silver vehicle which can be painted in the colors and style of the owner. This is likely an airline but sometimes a powerful businessman or rich dilettante. It has swept wings and tail and looks--and is--very fast.

On this bright SoCal day we get a quick pep talk about the SuperSwift by Miss (honorary Dr.) Willoughby. We do this as we sip Champagne in a conference room in the Santa Monica headquarters of the Douglas Aircraft Company. DAC has a friendly pact with Willoughby's Texas Aviation.

Alice (she told us to call her) has a hypnotic delivery which could persuade troops to follow her to Hell. She also speaks briefly, just long enough to finish a glass of wine. Then we surrender our glasses to a waiter and follow our female Pied Piper outside across concrete to take short stairs up into the SuperSwift.

Inside there are two rows of seats separated by an aisle. There is enough headroom to stand upright. The seats are comfortably shaped and padded. You find a seat and sit in it. The door is closed behind you and you find that the plane is air conditioned. Outside the thick-glassed window you can see the busy activities of Douglas Aircraft.

You can see Alice seat herself in the cockpit and speak to the pilot. She puts on big cup-sized earphones. Moments later you hear her voice over a loudspeaker. "Good morning. This is Captain Alice Willoughby. My copilot is Jonathan Carmichael. We shall soon be away as Jonathan has cleared us with traffic control to take off. Please put on your seat belts. Sit back and enjoy."

CAPTAIN Willoughby? COPILOT Carmichael? A woman is flying this plane? You have been told that she is one of the designers of Texas Aviation's aircraft. And an expert pilot. Interesting. But that was academic. Now it's your life which is on the line.

A man in a white-shirted black-pantsed uniform walks down the aisle from the cockpit checking to be sure your seatbelt is on and tightly secured. He returns to the cockpit. That must have been Copilot Carmichael. A minute passes.

You feel the bottom of your seat push up on you as the plane rises a few feet into the air. Then your seatback pushes on your back as the plane slides forward. The plane reaches a point on the concrete runway and rotates. It is now pointing toward the one-mile-distant Pacific Ocean off Santa Monica.

Minutes pass. Then the discreet hum of the engine grows a bit louder. Your seatback pushes strongly on you as the aircraft surges forward. Faster and faster the landscape outside moves behind you. The nearby sights fall away below. The tall buildings of the city are visible outside off to one side. The deep blue of the ocean is below.

"Captain Willoughby again. We are well away and rising to 20,000 feet. As you can tell we have the usual perfect weather in Southern California. But even if we did not we'd be well above any rain and storms. Now we will give you a few sights of your southern shore line."

The plane tilts and turns to the left and levels off. Outside below the shoreline comes into view. There is Marina del Rey, El Segundo, Manhattan Beach. At Redondo Beach the plane turns right out over the ocean and U turns and we head back north. The cities, a bit further away, pass below.

Another right turn and we head back toward Douglas's Santa Monica airfield. We lower, the shore line comes closer. There is the runway. It comes up to us. There is no bump as we lower onto the floater undercarriage. Our seatbelt tightens, tightens more. We are slowing, slowing, are slow.

Then we are down. Miss Alice Willoughby has taken us on a journey and returned us safely home.

<>

The Chronicle's first news story on Alice is not the last. She is interviewed about Texas fashion with accompanying color photos in the weekend Style section of the Chronicle. She visits a movie studio, meets a movie star, parties at another star's home. Has dealings with the head of Douglas Aircraft. Helps design the first Aerojet suborbital probe which lands by parachute in Australia, the land of the kangaroos. Is caught by a photographer shopping in Beverly Hills with Helen and Josephine von Karman who managed to get a picture of the threesome smiling at the camera.

Not caught on camera is another threesome: Alice and Josephine von Karman and Mary Adler clubbing on Mary's 18th birthday.

With December the time is approaching for Alice to return to Austin. She does lots of shopping and leaves, but not before leaving lots of holiday presents for friends made during her stay on the West Coast. She vows she will return.

<>

"Did you actually see Rita Hayworth?" Julia Moseley wanted to know this as she removed items from the sacks of groceries her husband and Alice had bought during their first visit together since Alice had returned from California.

Alice was sitting at the small dining table in the kitchen to avoid intruding into another woman's domain. Albert was playing with Robert in another part of the house.

"As close as you and me."

"What did she look like?"

"Pretty much like in her movies. She was wearing a blue business suit and heels but low enough to walk in comfortably. She looked like she was going to a meeting."

"Wow. In the flesh. Imagine that."

"Here's a secret. Movie stars--"

"Robert's out like a light," said Albert. "What's a secret?"

Albert came over to his wife, touched her very pregnant belly like touching a good luck charm, and kissed his wife's cheek.

"I think Alice was going to say something silly. Likely that movie stars are just people like the rest of us."

"You know me too well. Yes, they are. I met several when I was there, went to the houses of some, spent some time doing ordinary things with them."

She recounted some of those events but left out the one where she sat by a swimming pool at night commiserating with a young famous starlet weeping about having to break up with a boyfriend. He had been secretly stealing money from her.

That night she went to bed at the Moseley home rather than her own a few blocks away. Julia was due on Christmas Eve and Alice wanted to take her and sure-to-be-frantic Albert to the hospital for the birth. Everyone agreed that she would be in the birth room and that Albert would not.

Her presence was not physically necessary. Alice had long ago insured that Julia was in perfect shape physically and would have short, safe, and painless births. But emotionally her presence was very much welcome.

When Christmas Eve came Alice judged the time was right for Julia to have her baby. She touched an arm while helping with laundry and two hours later the contractions started. Five hours later Julia's mother and Albert's mother were standing on both sides of Julia's hospital bed while the new mother nursed a baby girl.

<>

Julia was not the only one to benefit from the shapechanger's attentions. Porter's wife Angela, a petroleum baron's heiress, had a child in February. Happily married Victoria Delgado had likewise had a child a month later. In both cases the immortal was in the birth room.

Wives of Texas Aviation's staff and workers benefited as well, though not directly. Texas Aviation was now one of Austin's biggest employers. Its construction line was half a mile long and turning out several aircraft every day. It had its own emergency hospital and a busy medical staff to insure each worker and, just as importantly, worker's family had medical insurance and access to hospitalization.

Texas Aviation's influence extended to several other institutions. A big modern medical park had been established just a few miles away. It included a big hospital. Austin University had a big aeronautical engineering department. A large number of graduate students worked as interns at Texas Aviation some of whom became employees after graduation.

Texas Aviation's influence extended to the cultural scene in Austin. All three partners sat on committees for art (Delacroix), music (Porter), and dance (Alice). Naturally each of the three contributed to several cultural organizations in their areas of interest.

They had political influence as well but a carefully neutral one. They funded a big chunk of an organization called Get Out the Vote rather than support either political party.

The partners had been called The Three Musketeers in an article in the Austin American newspaper and the name was routinely used in the paper. The latest gossip column, for instance, used it when catching up the "Austin Community" on the Three. Porter and his wife were seen trundling a stroller in the city park carrying the "darling new addition to the city." Delacroix "was serious" about an Austin University professor of French language and culture. Alice was reported seen dancing with a visiting teacher of the Argentine tango and "looked to be romantically involved with the handsome gentleman."

An article in the business section reported that Texas Aviation's latest aircraft were now able to fly at 30,000 feet where air pressure was a third that at sea level. However, the article noted, the aircraft had a ceiling of 35,000 feet. Above that it would have to carry its own oxidizer for the engine such as liquid oxygen.

That ceiling was fine with Porter and Delacroix as that put them at or above par with all other aircraft makers. Alice acknowledged that but convinced them to side with her on researching oxidizers.

Rather than do the research in-house Alice established a set of prizes which could be won by anyone who could come up with an oxidizer which had practical application for aircraft. There quickly followed several using hydrogen peroxide and several other peroxides.

More slowly came oxidizers using the halogens: fluorine and chlorine and such. They received a prize but not one of the higher ones as they failed the requirement that burned fuel be safe for the environment.

As the year wore on there came more exotic solutions such as several acids and solids.

At the very end came solutions that did not use gasoline or kerosene as fuel. Instead they used methane, ethane, hydrazine, and such.

Early on Alice settled on kerosene and kerosene-gasoline mixtures as fuel and hydrogen peroxide as oxidizer. She continued offering the prizes in the hopes that eventually someone would came up with a more successful answer.

A year passed. Then two. In the third year Alice settled on a particular line of aerospace craft, named the Darter after a large water bird with a long neck. The name was quickly shortened to the Dart.

The first three prototypes were mockups of increasingly realistic detail. The next four flew but only short distances and rather low. Their purpose was to test the pilot controls, navigation subsystem, radio communication subsystem, and other features. Later prototypes focused most on engines and the air pressurization subsystem.

In each case the immortal was the first test pilot. She merged with each craft to become a godlike cyborg who always had a force-field escape available in case of disaster.

<>

"Austin Traffic Control, this is Texas Aviation Dart Prototype 17, tail number TAX-17, pilot Alice Willoughby. I am exiting Texas Aviation Hangar 23 onto taxiway."

"No copilot, Girl Musketeer? That thing still looks like a two-engine aircraft to me." The national flight rules required multiengine aircraft to have two pilots.

"Nope, Sandy. That is you, Sandy? It just has two air intakes, as we've gone over before."

"Roger that, Willoughby. Just haven't had my second cup of coffee. Yeah, we got your flight plan, still good."

The traffic controller briefly summed up the weather conditions and the local traffic, not much this early in the morning.

"Austin Control, TAX-17, got your briefing loud and clear."

"TAX-17, Control. You are good to go."

"Control, roger that. Rolling."

Sandy, one of three air traffic controllers on duty today, looked down from the control tower appreciatively at the bright white arrowhead floating serenely above the taxiway toward the outbound runway.

He looked up as the Austin University intern on duty today set down Sandy's second coffee mug. A wetback, what was the world coming to? Five years from now he'd be an engineer making twice what Sandy did. But a good kid, always remembered the mix of sugar and cream Sandy liked and always had a cup ready when Sandy needed it.

"Beautiful bird, isn't it?" the intern said.

The kid had not departed but instead was standing looking down at the aerospace craft. That was what they were calling the real high-flyers nowadays.

The vehicle was shaped very like an arrowhead if it had two fangs near its nose pointing forward. These marked the air intakes. Otherwise it was perfectly smooth and white with black lines on its surface outlining the location of various hatches.

The kid glanced to the side and left to serve another controller.

Sandy said softly to the departed intern, "Yes, it is."

He glanced out the huge windows onto the outside at the ground area below and sky above for which he was responsible, then at the radar screen before him. Mentally he reviewed the two distant aircraft approaching, then returned his attention to the arrowhead.

It reached the entrance to the outbound runway and rotated to face east. It paused.

"Austin Traffic Control, TAX-17. Departing."

Sandy replied, "TAX-17, Control, departure time 07:33. Ya'll come back now."

The arrowhead glided forward, surged forward, racing, racing into the distance. Then it tilted back and streaked into the sky. From one instant to the next it was visible as a white line. Then it was gone. Left behind was a rolling thunder which quickly faded away. Alice Willoughby was on her way to space.

<>

It had taken Alice three years and the work of over a thousand people and millions of dollars, much of it her own, to get here, at 5000 feet and climbing rapidly.

Flat-bottomed cumulus clouds appeared ahead. Her path led the Dart up into one, passing from clear brightness into dimness. Almost instantly she was through it, her shapechanger eyes instantly adapting to her emergence into brightness.

At 8000 feet she tilted to the right and altered her path from east to east of southeast, the direction of Houston, Texas. She was traveling just below the speed of sound to keep from striking the ground below with a supersonic shock wave.

At five minutes in she was 50 miles along the 150 miles to Houston and was at 20,000 feet, about four miles up. No shock wave would be heard below. She accelerated.

A 1000 miles an hour...1500, 2200. Sprawling Houston appeared on the horizon. It slid rapidly toward her and then behind her. She was at 3000 miles an hour.

The blue waters of the Gulf of Mexico were below.

She was at 50,000 feet and 5000 miles an hour. The horizon visibly rounded. The blue of the air ahead was trending toward the blackness of space above.

She passed over the tip of Florida. Miami on the east coast was just a grey spiderweb against the green of the surrounding land.

At 100,000 feet she was traveling at 10,000 miles an hour and still accelerating. The Atlantic Ocean took a half hour to cross.

The green of the west coast of Africa was suddenly sliding below. She was moving at 17,000 miles per hour at 90 miles up.

She eased her acceleration down to just enough to press her gently against her seatback. She was in orbit.

There was no effective air resistance at this height. The Earth seemed to tilt up as her left wing tilted down.

Automatically she readjusted to an upright position with faint exhalations from her attitudinal space jets.

Exhalations of what? The scientists of CalSci told her it was "virtual air." If they were to be believed empty space was not really empty. It contained "neutral-energy quanta." A properly tuned magnetic induction field turned the "virtual" matter to actual matter with magnetic properties. This matter could then be acted upon by magnetic fields inside "space jet" engines. Leaving the engine the actual matter reverted to virtual matter so space jets had no exhaust.

The immortal watched as her spacecraft passed over the

approaching edge of night blanketing Africa. Nigerian cities showed as dots, blots, and spider webs of yellow light. The black jewel of Africa was a key country in the United Kingdom, integrated so long so fully that the Blacks below spoke English with posh accents and thought of themselves as Brits. Nigeria had even twice provided the UK with prime ministers. The African empress Temilade part of her who'd lived a century before Nigeria existed had a hard time believing it.

The rapidly approaching east coast of Africa showed as a ragged line of yellow light. Then there was pure blackness below. The Dart crossed the equator and flew further south.

Alice visually checked the many readouts on the panel in front of her for the hundredth time. For this flight she was and would remain in her biological self rather than in her cyborg self. This maiden voyage of the 17th Dart was a test of the vehicle as it would be experienced by all the humans who in the future would be its crew and passengers.

All the working prototypes before had been flown by the superhuman cyborg ALICE. SHE could feel and understand HER mechanical insides at dozens and hundreds of times the speed at which ordinary humans lived. ALICE was able to quickly find and label for a fix any mechanical problems. SHE also could react to any disaster and escape from the vehicles inside HER egg. Happily, partly because of the oversight of the unhuman creature, only mild disasters had marked the progress of the Dart project.

Alice awoke from her near-dream state as she approached the bright crescent of morning on the planet below. Ahead was Australia.

Soon the continent slid below her, its central portion mostly brown, its coastal areas showing lots of green, especially the east coast.

Halfway from and to home, it was now time for the public portion of Dart-17's flight.

Alice pushed three buttons in rapid succession. On the underside of Dart-17 a hatch slid open. From it extended a mechanical arm. At its end a metallic bulb opened like a flower blooming. The parabolic antenna turned, hunted briefly, and locked onto the direction of Sydney, the largest city in Australia.

"Sydney Air Traffic Control, this is Texas Aviation aerospace craft TAX-17. I am above you at 98-mile height, pilot Alice Willoughby. I hope ya'll are having a good morning."

A couple of minutes passed. The navigation beams coming from the airport were weak at this height and distance but the digital signal was clear. Alice knew that the beam of her own down-pointed signal was clear; the Dart's radio had been well-tested.

She decided to prod the air traffic controllers below.

"Sydney Air Traffic Control, aerospace craft TAX-17. If you look west at about 35 degrees up you should see me. I will look like a bright white star visibly moving upward from your viewpoint. Do you see me?"

Another minute passed, then another.

"Unknown vehicle, we do not appreciate you bothering us. You are interfering with critical functions. Get off the air."

"Don't try to kid me, Sydney. I can see you with my binoculars. You have neither incoming nor outgoing flights. All your aircraft are still roosting in their hangars."

By now Sydney was approaching below. Dart-17 would be visibly larger at 75 degrees above the horizon. The city sprawled along the east coast of Australia, radiating outward from Botany Bay and its seaport, the biggest on the coast. It was visible mostly as a granular grey carpet.

Two more minutes passed. Dart, moving at a little over 17,000 miles per hour, was now almost directly overhead.

"We see something, unknown vehicle. How do we know it's you?"

"I'll do a somersault. You should be able see me as a tiny white arrowhead."

Alice started a roll forward. Slowly the Dart made a complete rotation till it came back to facing forward again.

"Hope you saw that, Sydney. Now my orbit is taking me away. Bye for now."

The reply was staticky and incomplete. Dart was now well out over the Pacific.

Twenty-five minutes later the west coast of the U.S. slid toward her. She keyed her microphone as the radio signals from the city became clear.

"Glendale Air Traffic Control, this is Texas Aviation aerospace craft TAX-17. I am out over the ocean at 101-mile height, pilot Alice Willoughby. I have you in sight."

Glendale ATC was much faster with their response. It was the biggest of several airports in the LA area and had the biggest and most experienced ATC staff.

"TAX-17, Glendale Control. Do you need service, TAX?"

"Glendale, TAX. Negative, just wanted to say Hello. Hope you had a great lunch."

By now the sprawling metroplex of Los Angeles was visible.

"TAX-17, Glendale Control. So kind of you. What do you look like?"

Alice repeated the somersault scenario she'd used to prove to Sydney that she was real and not a joke. She had no time for further communication with the west coast before she was out of range.

Five minutes later she was close enough to Austin for a few minutes of conversation. This was long enough for air traffic control to tell her waiting partners in Texas Aviation that she had indeed circled the globe.

That was enough proof for her partners to begin a long-planned publicity campaign. They released a statement to the Austin American and to all the other newspapers in the area about the Dart and Alice's feat.

By the time that Alice was well out over the Atlantic the news had traveled to all the major centers of the US via telephone lines. Several of the cities put out special newspaper editions to pass on the news. Hundreds of radio stations announced it as well, as did the few fledgling TV stations.

The news, passed through undersea cables, reached Europe and Africa before Alice did.

The world had turned toward the west in the 100 minutes of her flight. This meant that she crossed over the Equator near the east coast of Africa rather than the west coast.

The largest city on the east coast was Nairobi, Kenya, the center of the economic powerhouse of the East Coast African Community. It was just past sundown when she spoke to Nairobi Air Traffic Control. The news of her flight had already reached the city and she had a cordial though quick conversation with the ATC people.

Then she was again out over the Pacific.

By now the flight had become routine. She would make several more orbits before returning to Austin. During the publicity following her feat Texas Aviation would discuss several possible future aerospace craft and space missions. This included a better weather observation and prediction program, much faster cross-continental and transcontinental travel, and even more advanced programs.

The immortal was already thinking much further ahead.

Seated in her cockpit, munching a sandwich and drinking a squeeze bottle of wine, she could look down on the dark Pacific but chose not to. Instead she looked up at the blackness of space bejeweled by stars.

In her dreams-not-dreams she had "met" several humans and two humanoid aliens, one with grey skin and one with green. She had also met blue-skinned and -furred centaur-like creatures with cat-like bodies rather than horse-like ones.

With only fragments of memories Alice could only make guesses about the reality they reflected. However, the cat-like aliens had struck her as liking humans, perhaps more than the humanoids liked humans. She would love to meet them.

And she would.

www.ingramcontent.com/pod-product-compliance
Lightning Source LLC
Chambersburg PA
CBHW060630310726
48982CB00003B/726